P9-AGA-177

A Love Woven True

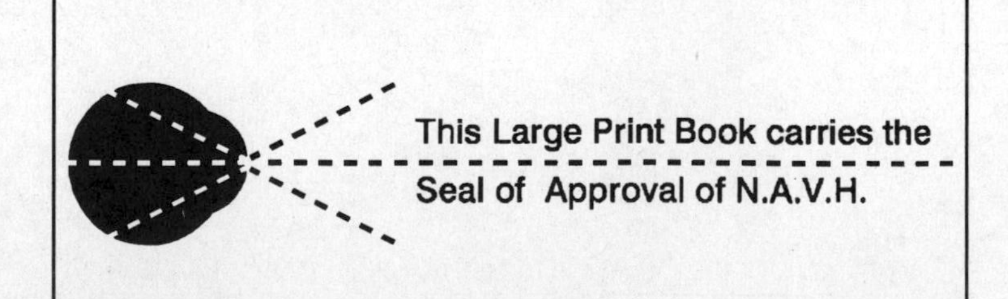
This Large Print Book carries the
Seal of Approval of N.A.V.H.

LIGHTS OF LOWELL, BOOK 2

A Love Woven True

Tracie Peterson
and Judith Miller

THORNDIKE PRESS
A part of Gale, Cengage Learning

GALE
CENGAGE Learning

Farmington Hills, Mich • San Francisco • New York • Waterville, Maine
Meriden, Conn • Mason, Ohio • Chicago

Lights of Lowell #2.
Scripture quotations are from the King James Version of the Bible.
Thorndike Press, a part of Gale, Cengage Learning.

Thorndike Press® Large Print Christian Historical Fiction.
The text of this Large Print edition is unabridged.
Other aspects of the book may vary from the original edition.
Set in 16 pt. Plantin.

LIBRARY OF CONGRESS CATALOGING-IN-PUBLICATION DATA

Names: Peterson, Tracie, author. | Miller, Judith, 1944– author.
Title: A love woven true / by Tracie Peterson and Judith Miller.
Description: Large print edition. | Waterville, Maine : Thorndike Press, 2016. | Series: Lights of Lowell ; #2 | Series: Thorndike Press large print Christian historical fiction
Identifiers: LCCN 2016030503 | ISBN 9781410494245 (hardcover) | ISBN 1410494241 (hardcover)
Subjects: LCSH: Fathers and daughters—Fiction. | Women landowners—Fiction. | Lowell (Mass.)—Fiction. | Abduction—Fiction. | Freedmen—Fiction. | Widows—Fiction. | Large type books. | GSAFD: Christian fiction. | Historical fiction.
Classification: LCC PS3566.E7717 L688 2016 | DDC 813/.54—dc22
LC record available at https://lccn.loc.gov/2016030503

Published in 2016 by arrangement with Bethany House Publishers, a division of Baker Publishing Group

Printed in the United States of America
1 2 3 4 5 6 7 20 19 18 17 16

To Gerry Perry
a woman I greatly admire

Chapter 1

October 1849, Lowell, Massachusetts

Jasmine Houston trembled uncontrollably. Surely her brother-in-law was mistaken!

"I'm to return home to The Willows immediately? Please," she said, extending her shaking hand in Nolan's direction. Her voice sounded strangely foreign to her own ears, and she cleared her throat before attempting to once again speak. "Permit me to read the missive for myself." The high-pitched quiver remained in her voice, ruining any hope of appearing unruffled by Nolan's news.

Nolan's brow furrowed into deep creases. "I'm sorry. In my haste to arrive, I failed to bring the letter with me."

She lowered herself onto the ivory brocade settee and met her brother-in-law's concerned gaze. "Does my father say why he penned the missive to you instead of corresponding directly with me? And why did

Samuel say nothing of our mother's failing health when he was in Massachusetts? Surely if Mother's health hung in the balance, Samuel would have sent word." Giving Nolan a feeble smile before continuing, she said, "Perhaps Mother is merely languishing since suffering with yellow fever this summer. What with her bouts of melancholy, she tends to be somewhat slow in healing from any illness. I suspect Father is hoping a visit from little Spencer and me will cause her to rally."

"It certainly could do no harm."

Jasmine gave an emphatic nod. "It will take time to make preparations for the journey. Traveling with a child of nearly two is not quite as simple as one might think. And, of course, I'll need to make inquiry concerning when a vessel will be sailing. Also, I must see to Grandmother Wainwright. She's been ailing this past week." She hesitated for a moment. "And you say Mammy isn't well either?" Her thoughts were jumbled, and she now realized her words had poured forth in a mishmash of confusion.

"That's what your father indicated in his letter," Nolan softly replied.

"I must admit I am exceedingly surprised to hear that piece of news. The fact that

Mammy would remain in a weakened condition after her supposed recovery several months ago is disconcerting. She's always been strong and healthy. Perhaps Father was overstating matters in order to ensure my return to The Willows for a visit."

"There is always that possibility. And your grandmother? What ails her? I thought she might give consideration to making the journey as well."

Jasmine began pacing, quickly covering the length of the parlor and returning several times. "The doctor fears she may have pneumonia. Grandmother says it's merely an attack of ague and will soon pass. However, she does have a troublesome cough, and I doubt whether she's strong enough to travel. Then again, she's a stubborn woman. Who knows what she may decide. But unless she makes a quick recovery, I believe she should remain in Lowell."

"You're likely correct on that account. The journey from Massachusetts to Mississippi could prove harrowing for her. Hearing of her condition only serves to confirm the decision I made upon receiving your father's letter," Nolan said.

Jasmine glanced over her shoulder as she continued crisscrossing the room. "And what decision would that be?"

"I plan to accompany you and Spencer to The Willows."

Her pacing came to an abrupt halt at the far end of the room. Turning toward him, Jasmine flushed at the overwhelming sense of warmth she felt for Nolan. His obvious concern touched her. "I can't ask you to do such a thing, Nolan. The commitment of time required to make the journey is unreasonable to ask of anyone — other than a family member, of course."

His gaze fell. "Am I not family?" His question was barely audible.

"Oh, what have I said? Of *course* you're family. My comment was directed toward Father's request that Spencer and I make the journey." Taking several quick steps, she came to a halt in front of him before meeting his questioning gaze. "Surely you realize that Spencer and I couldn't have survived since Bradley's death without you. Spencer has come to look upon you as his very favorite visitor. In fact, he often demonstrates his displeasure over the fact that you live in Concord rather than Lowell. He would, of course, prefer more frequent visits."

Nolan gave a slight nod, but his lips remained fixed in a taut, thin line. She feared he was weighing her response much too critically, so she hastened to explain further. "I find the fact that you would be away from Massachusetts for such a long period of time to be a matter of grave concern. I can't expect you to make yourself available every time difficulty arises in my life."

His gaze softened. "Of course you can. That is *exactly* what I want. You and Spencer are my only remaining family. How could I ever consider any request from you a burden? Besides, you *didn't* ask me — I offered to accompany you. As for my work, you may recall I can write as easily at the plantation as I can in Concord — or anyplace else, for that matter."

"Yes. In fact I remember quite well." A faint smile crossed her lips as she recollected the antislavery articles Nolan had penned after his first visit to The Willows. Words that had stirred the hearts of abolitionists and also drawn the fiery criticism of the proslavery movement. Words that had set Nolan at odds with his brother, Bradley, and provoked a seething anger from her father and other Wainwright men. And it had been Nolan's words that had convinced those same men their anger was misplaced. With carefully chosen words, he had cajoled them into admitting they supported free speech and, in turn, his right to argue against their stance on the slavery issue. Finally they had decided to call a truce. With the distinct understanding, however, that such an agreement merely served as permission for all of them to disagree in a civil — and silent — manner over their personal feelings on the topic of slavery.

"I imagine you do," he said, returning her smile. "Incidentally, I hope you won't think me intrusive, but I did take the liberty of sending word to Mr. Sheppard at Houston and Sons that you will be sailing as soon as preparations have been completed for your journey. I have little doubt there will be a ship awaiting us when we arrive in Boston."

"I'm certain your foresight will prove helpful in expediting our voyage," she replied, giving him a pensive gaze. Jasmine knew they would be traveling after the first picking, and any slowdown in cotton shipments could prove costly. "Let us hope our journey won't interfere with the crop shipments. No doubt harvest will have begun in earnest by the time we arrive, but I wouldn't want my personal travel to be the cause of any delay."

"Your father requested your presence at The Willows. I'm certain he values your visit more highly than the cotton crop. Please don't fret over any possible delay with the ship's voyage to New Orleans."

"So long as it's Wainwright cotton, I suppose you're right. However, I doubt any of the other producers would be so forgiving should their shipments be hindered. Did you happen to inquire regarding their future schedules?"

"As a matter of fact, I met with Mr. Sheppard last week to examine the books of Houston and Sons, and he gave me what he hoped would be a final plan for the upcoming month. Our travel should coincide nicely. By the way, you'll be pleased to know that all is in order with the shipping company. It continues to turn a nice profit, and the investments you're setting aside for Spencer are accumulating handsomely. Of course, the cotton shipments between New Orleans and Boston provide our greatest profit."

"Thank you, Nolan. Since Bradley's death, I've never once worried about Houston and Sons Shipping Line. I know you've performed the necessary duties to keep everything operating smoothly. And I'm pleased you retained Mr. Sheppard. I think he feared losing his position when you assumed management of the business."

He chuckled. "We both know that would

have been a disaster. I would be miserable attempting to operate any business on a daily basis. This arrangement has succeeded nicely for all of us. In fact, his work load has increased steadily as the business has grown. I'm amazed at the amount of cotton the company is now shipping. A mixed blessing, I suppose."

She nodded in agreement. "I understand what you're thinking. It's a complicated situation I find myself thrust into. With much of the cotton being grown on Wainwright plantations, I feel somewhat the hypocrite when I attend the antislavery meetings or when I state my opposition to the Southern bondage. Speaking of the Southern mindset, you still haven't told me why Father wrote his letter to *you.*"

Nolan directed her back toward the settee and then patted her hand as though she were a fragile piece of china that might fracture at any moment. "I believe your father worried you would be overly distraught receiving news of the ongoing illnesses of both your mother and Mammy. He decided his concerns might be less worrisome if delivered personally — knowing someone would be with you when you actually heard the news. As for your questions regarding your brother Samuel, you must remember his schedule is continually filled with business meetings when he is in Lowell. Besides, with all of his traveling, I doubt he has been able to spend much time at The Willows during these past months."

Jasmine wrung a lace-edged handkerchief between her fingers and frowned at Nolan. In spite of October's chilly sting, she blotted the linen square to her cheeks and forehead. "It's terribly warm in here, don't you think?"

"As a matter of fact, I thought the room rather cool and drafty. I hope you aren't taking ill. Are you feeling faint?"

"Of course not! You're beginning to sound like Father, always thinking women will faint at the first sign of bad news," she replied while continuing to dab her face. "I'm perfectly fine. Now tell me more of what Father said in his letter." Before Nolan could answer, Jasmine's gaze shifted toward the stairway. "It sounds as though Spencer has awakened from his nap. If you'll excuse me," she said while tucking her handkerchief into the pocket of her apricot merino dress.

"Please," he said, immediately jumping to his feet, "let me go and fetch him. It's been nearly two weeks since my last visit. I'm anxious to see my nephew."

She resettled herself on the settee. “As you wish.”

Nolan’s pleasure was obvious as he bounded toward the stairway. “He’s likely grown at least an inch during my absence,” he ventured, his words floating into the parlor.

“I don’t believe he’s grown quite that quickly, but there’s little doubt your presence will bring him great delight,” she called back toward the hallway.

The sound of Nolan’s footsteps grew fainter as he hastened up the stairs. Had Bradley ever hurried in such a fashion to see his own son? If he had, Jasmine could no longer remember. Of course, Spencer had been only an infant when Bradley died; her comparison was doubtless unfair. Yet that realization didn’t quiet the longing that stirred deep within her. In only moments she would hear Spencer’s unbridled cries of joy burst forth like a heralding trumpet. How she longed to have a father for her son — how she longed to have a loving husband’s arms embrace her . . . and to lovingly embrace a husband in return.

Regrettably, she harbored only unhappy recollections of her marriage to Bradley. Oh, he’d professed to love her in the beginning, but even then she’d known their marriage was no more than a profitable liaison between the Wainwrights and himself. The true desires of Bradley's heart had been power and money. The Wainwright family had provided a viable connection to the cotton Bradley needed to procure for his success — and their marriage had sealed the much-needed link to secure his lucrative future. Unfortunately, their union had been a fraud from the beginning.

When Bradley met with his untimely demise, most who knew him felt either pity or revulsion for the life he'd led. As for Jasmine, she had experienced a little of each, but her focus had remained on Spencer. He was her joy: the light of her life, the pure pleasure God had given her. Spencer had burst forth from a dismal marriage like a single rose unfolding each petal and coming into full bloom after an unforgiving drought. His tiny life had given her more pleasure than she imagined possible, and had it not been for Spencer, Jasmine would likely have harkened to her father's plea and returned to live at The Willows.

Her nerves had been taut with anxiety. How could she suitably explain her decision to remain in Massachusetts without causing her family sorrow? After all, most people would view a young widow's return to the bosom of her family quite appropriate — would even expect it. In addition to being a youthful woman set apart by her widow's weeds, she was a misplaced Southerner living amongst Yankees, both facts that her father would quickly draw to her attention. She had carefully prepared, however, her words judiciously framed as she pointed to Grandmother Wainwright's increasing dependency upon her as she grew older and her health began to fail. She'd also explained that the rigors of making such a move would likely prove an overwhelming task so soon after Spencer's birth. However, the truth had been that Jasmine didn't want her son reared in a culture that perpetuated slavery. Making such a statement to her father would have breached their relationship — perhaps permanently, a risk she was unwilling to take. Although Jasmine fervently disagreed with her family's views on slavery, she would never intentionally damage her relationship with them. She disagreed with her family, but she loved them in spite of their beliefs.

And now the news in her father's letter. She stood and began to once again pace the length of the room. It was difficult to believe both her mother and Mammy suffered from illnesses to such a degree as to summon Jasmine to their bedsides. She wanted to believe her father was merely anxious to see Spencer and have the two of them come to The Willows for a lengthy visit. Yet Malcolm Wainwright was not a man to use such methods to draw his family home. He would have been straightforward in his request. A hollow feeling edged into her consciousness, then yielded to fingering tendrils of fear that slowly crept into her thoughts and began to take root.

"What if one of them should die before I arrive?" she murmured. Her fingers spread wide as she placed an open palm against her chest and dropped onto the brocade divan. Giving voice to her fears now caused her to face the possibility that one or both of the women she loved might be dead before she arrived home. "Oh, surely not! If I'm not careful, I'll soon become as histrionic as some of Grandmother Wainwright's acquaintances," she muttered.

"Mama!" Spencer screeched from the hallway. The boy pointed a chubby finger in Jasmine's direction before turning back to hug Nolan's neck in a tight bear hug.

Jasmine gazed up at the two of them, warmed by their obvious affection for each other — a devotion that was obvious to even the casual observer. So much so that Velma

Buthorne had taken exception to Nolan's relationship with Spencer upon her first visit to Lowell, as well as on each of her two subsequent visits. It had been during her final visit six months ago that she had given Nolan an ultimatum — choose Spencer or choose her. He had quickly chosen Spencer, deciding that if Velma's security was threatened by a mere child, she was not a woman with whom he wanted to build a future. And now with the news of this imminent journey to Mississippi, Jasmine was exceedingly thankful she could accept Nolan's offer of assistance without worry of offending Velma.

Nolan sat down beside Jasmine and adjusted Spencer's wriggling body on his lap. "I shouldn't have left you alone for so long. You've obviously done nothing but fret since I went upstairs. There's not a drop of color in your cheeks. Shall we go outdoors and get a breath of fresh air?"

Nolan's suggestion elicited an immediate reaction from Spencer, who instantaneously attempted to wiggle off his uncle's lap. "Out, out!" he cried, pointing toward the doors leading into the garden.

Spencer's enthusiasm brought a faint smile to Jasmine's lips. It was difficult for unhappiness to reign while young Spencer

Houston was up and about. The child pulled at her fingers, tugging as though certain his efforts would bring his mother to her feet. "All right. We'll go outdoors, but first you'll need a coat." She grasped his plump hand in her own, and he toddled alongside while they fetched his jacket and cap.

Nolan remained at her other side, holding on to her elbow. She glanced toward him and said, "I promise I'm feeling better. You need not fear for my well-being. If you'll take Spencer's hand, I'll gather my cape."

"I will admit your color has returned, but I don't want to take any chances," he said, his features a strange fusion of apprehension and cheerfulness.

"I'm fine," she insisted, careful to speak in a firm and confident tone.

The three of them walked into the small flower garden that had recently been given over to Spencer as a play area. Jasmine no longer fretted over the trampled or picked flowers. The perennials would shoot up voluntarily again next year, and she'd be required to choose new annuals next spring anyway. In the end, Spencer would remain a toddler for only a short time, and if his wobbly feet carried him into the roses, mums, or azaleas, so be it. Truth be told, she enjoyed his occasional offering of a partially defrocked rose or daisy.

"You appeared deep in thought when I came downstairs," Nolan commented, though his gaze was still fixed upon Spencer as they sat down on one of the benches. "Were you worrying over your mother's condition?"

She followed his line of vision toward the tiny, robust child, who was examining a newly fallen leaf. "To be honest, I was thinking about Velma Buthorne — rather, I was feeling somewhat thankful that Velma is no longer a part of your life. I was selfishly grateful." She leaned down and picked a handful of golden mums that bordered the walkway.

"Were you?" he asked. His tone was almost playful. "And why is that?"

She met his gaze and then quickly looked back across the garden. "Because Velma would have objected to your offer to accompany us on the trip."

"Hmm. Only a short time ago, you told me you didn't want to impose upon me, and now you're pleased I'm making the journey?"

"I was merely being polite when I said I didn't want to impose," she said, giving him a sheepish grin. "There is no doubt that having your assistance will prove invaluable, and I know Spencer will find the journey much more to his liking with you along."

"It's my desire that my presence will make the journey more pleasant for *both* of you. And since we're discussing the voyage, have you come to any decision regarding when we might sail?"

"I can be ready by week's end. I hope that will give you sufficient time for your return to Boston to make preparations — if you still intend to accompany us," she hastened to add.

A sheepish grin tugged at his lips. "I made my preparations before leaving Boston. I had Paddy take my trunk out to the barn when I arrived."

His words brought back the reality of the situation. Surely Nolan must believe the circumstances ominous if he had already prepared to make the journey. Her thoughts were in a state of unrest — one minute calm and collected, the next fearful and apprehensive — uncertain what to expect when she arrived at The Willows. "I see. Well, then, I suppose I had best begin packing. With Kiara to assist me, I think everything should be in readiness by the day after tomorrow."

"Why don't you go inform Kiara of the

news and I'll remain out here with Spencer? I'm certain he'll be happier playing outdoors."

"And likely will sleep better tonight," she replied. "Thank you."

Nolan reached into his jacket and pulled Malcolm's letter from the inner breast pocket while he watched Spencer tug at a small purple bloom. The child appeared to be completely engrossed with the blossom, unaware of the activity that swirled about him. Nolan held the envelope between his thumb and index finger, his guilt beginning to take root as he stared at the missive. It went against his nature to tell untruths. In fact, all his life he'd prided himself upon his truthful nature.

"It was a kindness to withhold the truth," he muttered. Revealing the full contents of her father's letter would have been nothing less than cruel. After all, Malcolm had written to him instead of Jasmine in order to protect her from the truth — at least until her arrival at The Willows. And Nolan didn't intend to second-guess Malcolm Wainwright's decision. He unfolded the missive and reread the carefully scripted second paragraph.

I fear my wife's condition hangs in the

balance. The doctor has not given me hope that she will live much longer. However, knowing that Madelaine's life is in God's hands, I believe the possibility exists she may rally. Therefore, please do not convey the gravity of her mother's illness to Jasmine. It is useless for Jasmine to spend the entire voyage fretting over her mother's condition. Try to assure her that although I've summoned her home, she should remain calm. Being unduly distraught over Madelaine's condition will serve no useful purpose.

Nolan believed Mr. Wainwright's position was the correct one. However, his confidence waned as he considered how Jasmine might react once confronted with her mother's condition or possible death. Perhaps his thoughts were selfish, but he didn't want to be the object of Jasmine's anger when she discovered he'd withheld information from her. Yet he felt an obligation to honor Malcolm Wainwright's request. For now he would say nothing further and continue to pray for Madelaine Wainwright's recovery.

Spencer struggled to remain upright as he wobbled across the uneven terrain of the small garden. A winsome smile tugged at his bow-shaped mouth. Reaching Nolan's side, he extended his chubby hand to offer a large fall mum, now minus its leaves and the majority of its purple petals. "Well, thank you very much," Nolan said while taking the fading bloom from the child's hand. "Why don't we take your flower into the house and see if we can revive it with a vase of water."

"Wa-der," Spencer said in a childish attempt to mimic his uncle.

"Yes, water. I fear you may be seeing more water than you'd like in the next several weeks. But we won't worry about that for the time being. For now, we'll get your flower a drink."

Chapter 2

Jasmine extended her gloved hand. "Thank you for your assistance throughout our voyage, Captain Harmon. I know having us aboard has caused delays in your schedule that will require you and your men to make a return trip in record time. My prayers will be with you for steady winds and clear skies."

The bewhiskered captain appeared embarrassed by her gratitude but quickly recovered. "It's been an honor having you sail aboard the *Mary Benjamin* once again, ma'am. And it appears we've made a sailor out of young Spencer too," he said, tousling the boy's thatch of soft brown curls. "I hope you find your mother's health much improved, and I look forward to returning all of you to Boston whenever you're prepared to depart. I've had one of my men take your trunks to be loaded on the *River Queen*. Once you reach Rodney, the smithy should have a carriage available to take you to the plantation."

Hoisting Spencer into his left arm, Nolan extended his right hand to the captain. "Thank you, Captain Harmon. I'll send word once we've finalized the plans for our return."

Spencer soon grew restless aboard the *River Queen,* entirely weary of being restrained. "Only a little longer," Jasmine promised as the boat finally neared the dock.

"We're going to ride in a carriage for a little while and then we'll see your grandpa," Nolan added.

"Horthie," the boy excitedly yelped.

Jasmine smiled at Nolan. "At this point, even a carriage ride sounds appealing to him," she said with a laugh.

They disembarked the moment the captain gave his permission, Spencer more wobbly than usual when he finally was able to walk about on dry land. He giggled as he tottered around, attempting to remain upright.

"He looks like he's imbibed a bit too much," Nolan said with a hearty laugh. "I'll check on the carriage, and by that time they should have our trunks unloaded and we can be on our way."

When the carriage finally arrived at the plantation, Jasmine was exhausted and frightened at what news might greet her. She scanned the front of the mansion, praying there would be no black shrouds draping the expansive front porch or gallery.

She gazed at Nolan and nodded toward the house. "Either they've elected to await our arrival before shrouding the entries or death has not descended upon the household."

Nolan's eyes widened. "You expected your mother to be dead before we arrived?"

"The thought certainly entered my mind. I wondered if perhaps you and Father were attempting to protect me until my arrival. Forgive me for misjudging you."

"Of course that possibility could exist," he ventured. "It's been nearly two months since your father wrote his letter."

She adjusted her bonnet, her brow furrowing ever so slightly. "Then you *did* anticipate Mother's death?"

Nolan nervously brushed at some unseen spot on his pant leg. "With lingering illness, death is always a possibility, isn't it? However, I was praying all would be well and that both your mother and Mammy would be much better by the time we arrived."

The carriage came to a halt in the circular

driveway fronting the Wainwrights' balconied Greek Revival mansion. And although Jasmine couldn't be certain, she thought Nolan emitted a loud sigh of relief as he jumped down from the carriage. She assumed he was pleased to have their discussion come to an end. Before she could say anything further, he held out his arms for Spencer and then assisted her down.

"Look who's arrived!" her brother David bellowed as he hurried out the front door and down the steps. Her father and her younger brother, McKinley, followed close behind.

"Jasmine! How good it is to see you," her father greeted. He pulled her into an embrace, then turned his attention toward Spencer. "And how this young man has grown. He looks much like McKinley did as a child, don't you think?"

"Yes, of course. How is Mother? May I go up and see her?"

Malcolm's smile faded and his mood abruptly turned somber. "Of course you may see her, but don't expect much response. She's not spoken for days now, and although I don't claim to be a physician, she appears to shift in and out of consciousness," he said, but quickly added, "but perhaps she's merely sleeping."

"Perhaps seeing Spencer would help," Jasmine suggested.

"Why don't we wait until you've had some time alone with your mother. We can take Spencer up after he's had an opportunity to eat and play for a short time."

"I'll be happy to attend to him — unless you'd like me to accompany you upstairs," Nolan offered.

"Spencer will likely be more content if you remain with him," she said before turning her attention back toward her father. "And Mammy? How is she faring?"

"She remains the same. I told her you'd be arriving, and she's anxious to see both you and Spencer. The doctor assures me there's no possibility of contracting illness from either your mother or Mammy."

"I'll visit her once I've seen Mother," Jasmine said, quickly moving up the front steps of the house, then stopping and turning toward her brothers. "There's plenty of baggage to be unloaded if the two of you would be so kind."

"Of course," McKinley said. "You go on now."

"She's lived in the North far too long," David muttered. "I'll have Solomon fetch the trunks. My sister has apparently forgotten we have slaves."

"Quite the contrary," Nolan replied. "I don't think she forgets for a moment that the South is filled with slaves."

Jasmine stood outside her mother's bedroom door for a moment to prepare herself. Should her mother be awake and detect any sign of concern, she'd likely become overwrought. Jasmine tapped lightly on the door and then entered the room. The heavy green velvet drapes had been pulled to prevent the infiltration of daylight, and Jasmine hesitated until her eyes adjusted to the darkened room before tiptoeing to her mother's bedside.

She leaned close to her mother's ear and whispered, "Mother, it's me, Jasmine. I've come to visit with you. Can you open your eyes? Mother?"

The only response was the chirping of a bird outside the window. Jasmine pulled her mother's rocking chair close to the bed and sat down. Grasping her mother's limp hand in her own, she began quietly telling her of the journey with Nolan and Spencer, of Spencer's antics on board the ship, and of the news that he was now downstairs in the parlor being entertained by McKinley and David. "He is quite the little boy. I know you will enjoy him," Jasmine said. "When you awaken from your nap, I'll bring him up to see you if you'd like." She fought back the tears that began to form.

She didn't know how long she'd been sitting by her mother's bedside, but when she could think of nothing else to say, she leaned back in the chair, still holding her mother's hand, and began to sing the lullaby her mother had sung to her when she was a little girl. She closed her eyes and repeated the tune over and over again in her sweet, soft soprano voice. A faint tug of her fingers caused Jasmine to startle.

Although her eyes were barely open, her mother's lips curved into a feeble smile. "Jasmine," she whispered, her voice barely audible.

"Yes, Mother, it's me — Jasmine. I've come all the way from Lowell just to be with you. And I've brought Spencer too."

Her mother stared back at her with dull, lifeless eyes. "Water."

"Yes, of course." Jasmine jumped up from the chair and, propping her mother in the crook of her arm, held the engraved goblet to her lips.

When she sputtered and coughed after only a few sips, Jasmine lowered her mother back onto the pillow. "Would you like me to wash your face and perhaps brush your hair,

Mother?"

"Later. I need to rest," she whispered. Her eyes closed, and the rasp of her shallow breathing began to once again fill the room.

"Yes, of course. I'll come back and see you in a little while," Jasmine said, feeling compelled to announce her departure, yet knowing her mother did not hear.

She walked from the bedroom and closed the door softly behind her. Spencer's childish jabbers floated up the staircase, and Jasmine smiled as she peeked over the balustrade at the enchanting scene below. Young Spencer was seated in the center of the parlor floor playing with a set of carved horses that had been McKinley's favorite toys as a young boy. Nolan and her father, however, appeared to be engaged in a serious conversation.

Both men stood as she entered the room, their discussion coming to an abrupt halt. "I do hope you two haven't discussed Mother's condition without me. If so, I fear you'll need to repeat everything you've already said," Jasmine remarked, her gaze directed toward her father.

"Please join us, my dear. I'm sure you'd enjoy some refreshment. I was beginning to wonder if you were going to leave your mother's bedside," the older man said, walking to the corner of the room and pulling down on a thick gold cord.

"When did you have the bell cords installed?" Jasmine inquired.

Before her father could answer, a young light-skinned girl scurried into the room. "Yassuh?"

"Bring the tea tray," he ordered.

Jasmine smiled at the girl. "Please," she added.

"Please?" There was a note of irritation in her father's voice. "Since when do you say *please* to slaves?" He didn't await Jasmine's answer. "Dr. Borden is due at any time. He's been stopping to see your mother every afternoon. I'm certain he'll give you a full report."

"And you, Father? What is *your* report? You know Mother better than anyone else. Do you believe this is simply a reoccurrence of her chronic malaise, or has she not fully recovered from the yellow fever?"

Nolan sat down beside Jasmine. "Your father is obviously uncertain; that's why he wants you to wait and talk to Dr. Borden."

"Nonsense. My father has an opinion about everything — especially where Mother is concerned."

The older man gently tugged at his collar. "If you're going to force me to render a judgment, I'd say it's a combination of both. I don't think she ever fully recovered, but that could be due to her ongoing propensity toward melancholy."

Before Jasmine could further question her father, a knock sounded at the front door. Jasmine stared in disbelief as her father jumped up and hurried to the door.

"It's become quite obvious Father is trying to avoid me," Jasmine said quietly to Nolan. "I've *never* seen him answer the door. The servants are likely going to spend the afternoon worrying they'll receive punishment for not moving quickly enough."

Jasmine listened to the muffled voices in the vestibule for several minutes before Dr. Borden finally appeared in the parlor doorway. "Your father and I are going upstairs to see your mother. I look forward to visiting with you when I come back down. It's nice to see you, Jasmine," he added almost as an afterthought.

She knew she had been intentionally excluded. However, she would honor her father's wishes — at least for the time being. "If you don't mind watching after Spencer a little longer, Nolan, I believe I'll look in on Mammy. Father, am I correct to assume she's still in the same bedroom off the kitchen?"

"Yes, of course."

"You go and see her," Nolan said. "Spencer and I will be fine."

Jasmine offered her thanks and then hurried off to the rooms used by members of the kitchen staff. She greeted each of the slaves by name before making her way into the small room where Mammy lay upon a narrow rope-strung bed that sagged under her weight. Safra, one of the kitchen slaves, hurried into the room carrying a straight-backed wooden chair.

Jasmine offered the woman a smile and took the chair. "Thank you, Safra. The next time Mammy is out of bed, could one of you tighten the ropes on this bed? The mattress is barely off the floor."

"I's sorry, ma'am, but she don' git outta dat bed long 'nuf for no rope tightenin'. We's lucky to get clean beddin' under her."

Jasmine nodded and took Mammy's hand. It was the second time this day that she'd held the limp hand of someone she loved. "Mammy, it's Jasmine. I've come home for a visit."

The old woman's eyes remained closed, but her parched lips opened ever so slightly. "Chile, I's glad you come home. You need to be tendin' to your mama. When she's better, you come and see me."

"The doctor is with Mama right now. Has he been caring for you too?"

She gave a slight nod of her head. "Yes'm, but there ain't nothin' no doctor kin do fer me. I'm just waitin' here for da good Lord to come and take me home."

"Now, I'll hear no more of that kind of talk. I've come all this way to see you, and you tell me you're just going to lie here until you die? Why, I've even brought little Spencer along, and neither you nor Mother can hold your eyes open long enough to see him." The words sounded cruel to her ears, but Jasmine hoped to startle Mammy into fighting for her life.

Mammy's eyes opened, and her dry lips cracked as the beginnings of a smile began to form. "You is still a sassy chile. Now git upstairs and see what dat doctor got to say 'bout your mama. You can bring yo' baby in to see me after you find out what dat doctor has to say. I want a report. Ain't nobody willing to tell me nothin' about her."

Jasmine nodded her agreement before standing. "I'll be back after I've talked to Dr. Borden." Carrying the chair under one arm, she deposited it in the kitchen and headed up the back stairway to her mother's room.

■ ■ ■ ■

"You know she's dying, Malcolm. It's likely going to be only a matter of days before you'll have to bury her."

Jasmine clutched the doorframe, her fingernails digging into the hard, cold cypress wood. "What are you saying?" she nearly shouted. "My mother isn't going to die. You're a doctor — do something to make her well. My father engaged you to heal her, not to issue a death sentence." She inveighed against him as though her very words would serve to strengthen his medical prowess. "Tell him, Father." She hissed the words from between clenched teeth, her gaze riveted upon her mother's lifeless form. "Tell him to make her well."

"Come with me, Jasmine," her father said, firmly taking her by the arm. "We'll discuss this matter downstairs."

Jasmine leveled an accusatory stare in the doctor's direction. "You *will* be joining us, won't you, Dr. Borden?"

Her father tightened his hold on her elbow. "Of course he will. And you need to remember your manners."

"Manners? He's just said that Mother is dying. I'm not concerned about manners;

I'm concerned about my mother," she rebuked.

"As am I," he came back in a hushed voice. "Do you think you are the only one feeling pain and sadness? If so, you are very mistaken. The thought of living the remainder of my life without your mother is unbearably distressing. Yet I would prefer Dr. Borden's honesty to false platitudes. I've asked him to be forthright."

It was obvious these past months had taken their toll on her father. He had grown thinner, and his once taut skin now sagged, mapping creases and folds that hadn't been evident a year ago. A dull weariness had replaced the glint of joy and excitement she'd grown accustomed to seeing in his eyes.

"Of course, Father. I apologize. I've been here only one afternoon, and I'm passing judgment on everyone who has spent these many months worrying and caring for Mother. It's just — difficult." A lump rose in her throat and tears threatened to spill at any moment. She dared not say anything more or she'd fall into her father's arms weeping, and that was a burden he didn't need. What he did need was a family that would be strong and supportive.

"Difficult. Yes," he said, patting her hand.

"But with God's grace, we'll get through this. Now let's go down to the parlor."

Dr. Borden's report was exactly what she'd expected: Her condition was weaker today; nothing more to do; wait; pray; he would return tomorrow; he would check on Mammy.

His final words brought Jasmine to attention. "After you've seen Mammy, will you tell me how she is faring?"

The doctor gazed down at Spencer making a stack of wooden blocks and massaged his forehead. "Unless something unexpected has occurred since yesterday, I can tell you her condition is quite similar to that of your mother. To be honest, Mammy's illness was one of the worst cases I've seen. I didn't expect her to make it through the first weeks. However, whether it's because she was a little stronger or because she had the will to live, I'm not certain. But I do know that from time to time she speaks about the need to hang on a little longer."

"For *what*? Has she said what it is she needs?" Jasmine asked, hope beginning to kindle in her heart. Maybe she could supply whatever it was Mammy wanted and the old slave would be miraculously healed.

The doctor shook his head back and forth. "I have no idea. She hasn't confided in me, but whatever the reason, it seems to have sustained her for now. I'll look in on her and stop to see you before I take my leave."

"Thank you." Jasmine waited only a moment before turning to her father. "Mammy will tell me what it is she needs. Whatever it is, we'll see to it for her, won't we, Papa? We'll be able to help her regain her health."

"Or give her the freedom to rest easy and die."

Jasmine slumped down into the chair. "Is *that* what you think? If we help her, she will give in and die?"

"I don't know, Jasmine. I have no answers for you."

Jasmine's brothers came into the parlor and looked at the subdued group.

"If I knew how to resolve any of this," Malcolm continued, "it would already be accomplished. But I do know the doctor is correct. While your mother appears to have no will to live, Mammy has fought to survive, especially when I told her you were coming home." A tear glistened in her father's eye. "I wish it would have had the same effect upon your mother. I'm not certain she even heard me when I told her you and Spencer would be here for a visit. I've not been much use around the plantation. I've relied upon your brothers to take care of things."

"And we've been happy to do so," McKinley said. "If nothing else good has come from this, both David and I have learned a great deal about the business."

Her father gave a weary nod. "There's truth to that statement. And you've both performed admirably. And from what the Associates report, so has Samuel," he said, glancing toward Nolan.

"Other than through Jasmine's shipping business, I know little of what goes on with the Associates, Mr. Wainwright. However, if anything were amiss, I'm certain you'd receive word. I do know Samuel's schedule is very busy."

"I can attest to the fact that he's busy, for we seldom see him when he's in Lowell on business," Jasmine added.

"I'll discuss that situation with him. Business is important, but keeping strong family ties is even more essential. I fear I learned too late in life just how important my family is to me," her father said with a sad ache in his voice.

The sound of Dr. Borden's footsteps caused all of them to look toward the doorway. "She's much the same, although she remembers you are here, Mrs. Houston. She told me you'd brought your baby and come home to visit. I take that as a positive sign," he said while giving Jasmine a tentative smile. "However, please don't interpret my remarks to mean she is recovering. I'm merely saying that I'm somewhat encouraged that she spoke to me and that she remembered talking to you a short while ago."

"Of course," Jasmine replied, her lips bowing into a radiant smile. Hiding her elation would be as impossible as telling the sun not to rise in the east. If Mammy's condition worsened in the future, she'd deal with it then. But for now, she would take the doctor's words of encouragement and be thankful for this moment of joy.

By day's end, Jasmine was exhausted. She'd run back and forth between the bedsides of the two women she loved, attended to Spencer's supper and readied him for bed, eaten a late supper with her family and Nolan, and then fallen into bed consumed with guilt because she hadn't been at home to assist in her mother's care and also with fear that two of the most important women in her life would soon be gone from this world. Unbidden dreams plagued her sleep. When Spencer tugged at her hand the next morning, Jasmine could only moan in acknowledgment. The child finally resorted to crawling into her bed and prodding open her eyelids with his small fingers until she'd finally succumbed and forced herself to awaken.

The morning passed quickly, and after quieting Spencer for his afternoon nap, Jasmine sat down in the parlor with Nolan. Following last night's restless sleep, a brief period of relaxation would serve her well.

"I'm pleased to see you're going to take a few moments to yourself," Nolan said. "You need to take care of yourself or *you'll* be taking ill."

Before Jasmine could utter a response, a sharp rap sounded, followed by the incessant ringing of the servant's bell above the front door. "Who can that be, and why don't they give us an opportunity to come to the door? That bell is going to awaken Spencer," Jasmine said as she hurried from the room, unwilling to wait for one of the servants.

Yanking open the door, her look of anger and exasperation immediately wilted. "Cousin Zachary . . . I mean, President Taylor," she stammered.

"Jasmine, my dear, has your father relegated you to the position of housekeeper?" the president asked with a grin.

"No, of course not. Do come in," she said,

stepping aside. "What a pleasant and unexpected surprise."

"Why is it you're answering the door here at The Willows? I thought you were living in Massachusetts."

She took his hat and handed it to Bessie, who was now scurrying into the hallway. In a hushed whisper she told the girl, "Go tell my father that President Taylor is here." Then turning to the president, she squared her shoulders. "Quite honestly, I didn't wait for one of the servants because I feared the ringing bell would awaken my son from his afternoon nap," she replied with a grin. "And I do live in Lowell. However, Mother's failing health brings me back to The Willows."

"Yes, your mother's health. Exactly why I've come," he said, striding into the parlor with an ease that spoke volumes. "Zachary Taylor," he said, extending his hand to Nolan.

"An honor," Nolan said, standing quickly and obviously stunned by a visit from the president of the United States.

"Do sit down. I'm not royalty and I'm no longer a general — merely the president. You need not remain standing in my presence," he said with a hearty laugh. He glanced toward Jasmine. "Is your father close at hand?"

"Yes, of course. I told Bessie to fetch him. He should be here any moment. I'll ring for tea. Do promise you'll stay for supper. I know Papa will be disappointed if you refuse."

"What will disappoint me?" her father asked as he rounded the corner and entered the parlor. "Zachary! What a wonderful surprise. Tell me what brings you to Mississippi. Nothing unpleasant, I hope."

Jasmine watched as the two men clasped hands and then embraced. They were relatives by marriage, a bond that had subsequently developed into a deep friendship.

"Visiting Mississippi is always a pleasure, Malcolm. Even when I'm greeted with unpleasant circumstances," he said with a brooding look in his eyes. "There were matters that needed my attention at the plantation. I made mention of them, and my dear Peggy insisted I personally attend to them. I didn't understand her resolve until she read me a letter she had received from Madelaine saying she'd contracted yellow fever. Peggy's concerns have continued to mount as time passed with no further word from her cousin."

Her father briefly closed his eyes and nodded. "I didn't realize Madelaine had written. I know Peggy's condition is tenuous, and I didn't want to cause her undue concern, Zachary. However, I fear anything I would have written could have only served to worry Peggy further."

"My wife is an amazingly strong woman," Taylor said in a bittersweet manner. It left Jasmine wondering exactly what ailed the president's wife.

"I wish I could say the same about Madelaine."

"So she is no better?"

"Dr. Borden says her prospects are grim. She appears to have lost the will to live."

Zachary frowned. "Unfortunately, both of our wives have been plagued by melancholy throughout their lives. Since taking up residency at the White House, Peggy has retreated to her upstairs rooms. I rely upon our daughter Betty to act as my hostess at formal functions and, I must admit, she is becoming quite accomplished at the task. I'm thankful for her assistance."

"And her husband — he's a colonel now, isn't he?" Jasmine asked.

"Indeed. A fine man. Fortunately, we became fast friends from the very beginning. I heartily approved of Betty's marriage to Colonel Bliss."

"Unlike your daughter Knox. Her marriage to Jefferson Davis was a bitter pill for you to swallow, wasn't it, Zachary," Malcolm stated.

Nolan glanced toward President Taylor. "I didn't realize one of your daughters married Jefferson Davis."

"Against my wishes. She died of malaria three months after they wed. Jefferson and I finally settled our differences when we fought together in Mexico. I know it would have pleased Knox. I only wish our reconciliation had occurred before her death. However, it was important to set aside my pride, so I extended an olive branch. Jefferson accepted. I learned a difficult and valuable lesson through that ordeal: I don't let the sun go down on my anger with any member of my family. They come first in my life."

"I've certainly been much more taciturn in that regard. For far too long, I placed my business and financial concerns before anything else — even to the detriment of Jasmine's welfare."

Jasmine watched a look of despair etch itself upon her father's face. If the conversation continued down this path, he would soon be miserable. Jumping to her feet, she extended a hand toward the president. "Why don't I take you up to see Mother before Spencer awakens from his nap? Once he is up and about, I doubt there will be much peace for any of us."

"Yes, of course," he replied, accepting her hand. "Peggy will expect a full account upon my return to Washington."

Chapter 3

Later that evening, President Taylor escorted Jasmine into the dining room, followed by Nolan. The president pulled out one of the ornately carved mahogany chairs for Jasmine and greeted her brothers and father, who were already seated around the end of the table.

"Tell me about life in Massachusetts, Jasmine," the president said. "Unfortunately, I've not yet had the opportunity to visit Lowell." He sat down beside her, obviously interested in what she had to tell him.

"I hope you'll come and visit one day soon. In my estimation, the town is quite progressive and has much to offer. The textile mills are the primary industry, although locomotives are now being manufactured in Lowell, aren't they, Nolan?"

"Indeed. Both ventures have proven to be financially successful for those involved. And of course most of the other machinery and tools used directly in the mills are manufactured in Lowell as well," Nolan replied. "And it appears one of the most recent undertakings is patent medicine. From all appearances, Lowell is beginning to diversify, which is good for the economy."

The president helped himself to several pieces of crisp fried chicken and a generous portion of creamed peas before heaping a mound of roasted potatoes and a slab of corn bread onto his plate. "You live in Lowell also, Mr. Houston?"

Nolan shook his head. "No. I make my home near Boston, but I do visit Lowell frequently. I don't want my nephew growing up without knowing me," he said with a grin.

"Good for you," the president said. "You and young Spencer will both be the better for it. Time spent with children is a sound investment in their future."

"Nolan also oversees the shipping business that was owned by my late husband, who was Nolan's brother," Jasmine added. "His assistance has lifted a great burden from my shoulders."

"Ah, yes. Your late husband was responsible for pursuing the purchase of cotton from our Mississippi and Louisiana planters on behalf of the Boston Associates, wasn't he?"

"Yes, although Samuel had taken over that particular aspect of the business prior to Bradley's death."

"I understand your brother is doing an excellent job — at least where my plantation is concerned," the president remarked.

Nolan took a drink of coffee and leaned forward to meet the president's gaze. "I hope you won't think me boorish for asking, sir, but I do wonder if you would tell me how you've managed to win the *Northern* vote when you own a plantation and more than a hundred slaves."

President Taylor shrugged. "There are those who say it was my military record that appealed to the Northerners, while my slave ownership lured the Southern vote. I'm not certain if that's true, but in retrospect, I suppose each side chose to believe I was loyal to their camp. Neither gave consideration to the fact that I am my own person. I place my loyalty where I feel it best serves the nation's interests and welfare, though I know there are many around these parts who consider me a doughface in reverse."

Jasmine saw a twinkle in the president's eyes when Nolan's brow furrowed. President Taylor obviously realized Nolan was confused by his remark.

"A *Southern* man with *Northern* principles," Taylor explained. "Believe me, I heartily disagree with those who would characterize me in such a manner. I consider myself a patriot and, fundamentally, I believe in the Union."

"Please don't think me impertinent, President Taylor, but if you consider yourself a Unionist, how do you justify slave ownership?"

"Justify? Why would I feel a need to do so? Never have I attempted to hide my ownership of a cotton plantation and slaves. You must remember that I was a slave owner before I was elected president. Although there are many who abhor the thought, I shall be a slave owner when I leave the presidency. And I might add that the owners and workers of those famous textile mills in Lowell are more than a little dependent upon our Southern cotton."

"True enough, yet there is valid argument that the slaves should be given the freedom to choose whether they desire to remain on the plantations or seek a life of their own in some other place. Does it seem fair and equitable that one man has the freedom to choose while another does not?" Nolan asked while spreading apple butter onto a warm piece of corn bread.

President Taylor speared another piece of

chicken and then leaned back in his chair. "There are many things in life that are unfair, Mr. Houston, for both Negroes and whites. Surely you don't desire *or* expect the men in Washington to solve every injustice."

"No, I don't, but I *do* expect the government to resolve issues that threaten to tear apart the very fabric of this country."

"Then rest easy, my boy. I will not permit such a thing to occur," President Taylor replied easily.

Jasmine glanced toward her father as he straightened in his chair and then loudly cleared his throat. The tension in her neck began to relax as she realized her father was going to call a halt to any further political discussion at the supper table.

"Word down here is that you've forsaken us, Zachary. We hear you're urging settlers in New Mexico and California to draft their own constitutions and apply for statehood, that you've advised them to bypass the territorial stage. But don't think for a minute we're oblivious to the negative effect that piece of advice will have upon the South," her father candidly remarked.

Jasmine stared at him in disbelief. Obviously *any* topic was now considered acceptable table conversation.

McKinley nodded and smiled. "They'll come in as free states since neither of them is likely to draw a constitution permitting slavery."

Jasmine stared at McKinley, surprised at the seeming pleasure in his tone.

"Exactly! And don't think your behavior is going to sit well with Congress, Zachary," Malcolm added. "They don't like having their policy-making prerogatives usurped by anyone, not even by the president. If you continue in this manner, you're going to alienate the entire country."

"There's no way to make everybody happy over the slavery issue. Why, I daresay there's no way I could please even the few gathered in this room. Ultimately there will be those who will be unhappy, no matter what the decision," President Taylor said while glancing around the table. "Why, I'm sure they're quite unhappy to find me absent from Washington. I know the men who traveled with me were surely displeased to awaken this morning and find me gone, but I am fully capable of seeing to myself. And I won't worry overmuch about wooing them into better humors when I return. Just as I cannot concern myself with wooing each and every voter whose nose is out of joint."

"Well, I think you would at least attempt

to woo your Southern brothers who placed their faith in you," Malcolm fumed.

The president emitted a loud guffaw. "And the Northerners who voted for me think I should take a harsh stand against slavery. Should any of you young folks have a hankering for politics, you should remember your allegiance likely will be called into question on a regular basis. I constantly find myself in quite a quandary."

"I don't think I would ever aspire to a political future," McKinley commented. "There is little doubt repercussions will be forthcoming no matter what the outcome of the slavery issue. And should Congress pass a law requiring the return of fugitive slaves, I doubt that even the freed slaves up north will be safe."

"What law is this you're talking about?" Nolan inquired.

"McKinley is speaking out of turn. There have been rumors, nothing more," David retorted.

"Not so!" McKinley protested. "Matters have moved beyond rumor. I hear there are men who have already drafted legislation in the event California and New Mexico follow the president's advice to avoid becoming territories and move forward with statehood."

Nolan turned his attention to McKinley. "And what are the provisions of this possible legislation?"

President Taylor pushed his dinner plate aside. "In answer to your question, Nolan, it appears there are those who desire a law that would make it the responsibility of every person to return runaway slaves. I would tend to agree with McKinley. The possibility has moved beyond rumor for I, too, am privy to the information."

McKinley nodded vigorously as he met Nolan's gaze. "Yet it goes far beyond the mere return of slaves: this law would actually mandate the involvement of every citizen who encounters a possible runaway."

"Which is as it should be," Malcolm replied. "Think of the financial investment. The North wants abolition and the president obviously isn't going to take a stand for slavery. We must have some sort of protection for our investment. Expansion of the Underground Railroad continues with Northerners not only aiding runaways but practically encouraging slaves to leave their owners — and the antislavery do-gooders seem to be increasing their numbers daily."

Jasmine frowned and discreetly shook her head when Nolan glanced in her direction. She prayed he would heed her warning and remain silent. Continuing down this path would only cause her father to become more distressed.

"I see many problems with such a law," McKinley commented.

Startled, Jasmine tilted her head to one side and briefly contemplated her brother's behavior. His actions this evening appeared completely out of character. She'd never seen him enter into a passionate discussion on any topic other than finances. "What difficulties do you predict?" No sooner had she uttered the question than she wished she could recall the words. There was little doubt further explanation by McKinley would only serve to inflame her father.

McKinley didn't hesitate for a moment. "Such a law will make men greedy. They will accuse freed men of being escaped slaves, and they'll find disreputable Southerners willing to look the other way if they can pay a lesser price for another healthy slave. They won't take the time or energy to see if there's validity to the Negro's claim."

"Absurd!" Malcolm retorted, his cheeks flushed in anger.

Unfortunately, her father was reacting exactly as Jasmine had anticipated — he couldn't seem to hold his temper in check when it came to the issue of slavery and those who opposed it. However, McKinley's views *had* come as somewhat of a surprise to her. Granted, her youngest brother had always been kind to the household staff and, unlike Samuel, McKinley abhorred going out into the fields or to the slave quarters. Instead, he remained close to the big house, working on the accounts and honing his skills to become an astute businessman. Was he beginning to see the evils of slavery? His comments this evening seemed to indicate he was at least giving consideration to antislavery sentiments. If so, he might prove to be an excellent Southern connection for the antislavery movement in Lowell. Trusted Southerner antislavers were in demand. Jasmine touched the linen napkin to her lips and wondered if her father would later take McKinley to task for speaking his mind this evening.

David's knife clanked onto his plate with such force Jasmine thought the china would surely be chipped or cracked. "You're absolutely correct, Father. As usual, the Northerners are attempting to force their will upon the entire nation. They have always considered themselves superior to the genteel people of the South, quick in their attempts to force their choices upon all of us."

Although David had offered little to the dinner conversation this evening, Jasmine knew his loyalty would unfalteringly remain with their father and the South. She was keenly aware of his lifelong struggle to gain their father's attention. Even at an early age, Jasmine had recognized her brother's longing to be noticed by their father. Always anxious to please, David never disagreed with their father, never voiced an independent idea, and never failed to do exactly as instructed. Consequently, he remained the overlooked middle son, still attempting to gain some glimmer of recognition.

"True enough. As far as I'm concerned, they speak from both sides of their mouth. On one hand, they want our cotton, but on the other, they wish to do away with the slaves needed to raise the crop. Ridiculous!"

"No need to get into a heated political debate over supper, Malcolm — bad for the digestion," the president said calmly. He turned toward Jasmine and graced her with an affable smile. "Tell me, my dear, how is it that you chose to remain in Lowell rather than returning to Mississippi — especially since you have Mr. Houston to assist with your business interests in Boston."

Jasmine sighed with relief. The conversation was finally taking a turn for the better.

She gave the president a radiant smile. "You may recall that Grandmother Wainwright lives in Lowell?"

"Ah yes, now that you mention it, I do seem to remember the fact that Alice went north. After your father's death, wasn't it, Malcolm?"

Her father nodded.

"Having Grandmother Wainwright in Lowell was a true blessing, for a move after my husband's death would have been difficult. Spencer was a mere infant. However, since that time I have expanded my interests by purchasing a horse farm, where Spencer and I are now living."

"A horse farm? Now that's an unusual investment for a young woman with no husband. How did you happen to become involved in such a venture?"

"My husband had purchased several fine horses before his death — beautiful animals. When an unforeseen opportunity arose to purchase a farm several miles out of town, I immediately made a bid on the acreage. There was no way I could have expanded the horse business on the property I previously owned. My bid was accepted, and we moved to the farm a month later."

"I'd say your daughter has some of that same spunk you had when you expanded your cotton business, Malcolm."

Her father appeared to soften at the president's praise. "Once she had all the facts and figures, she wasn't afraid to move forward. And from what I've seen and been told, she made a wise decision."

"Thank you, Papa. We've increased our stock and have earned a good reputation. In addition, we've gained the trust of the locals, and that's always helpful."

"Perhaps I'll have to make that trip to Lowell in the very near future. I've been looking for a pair of carriage horses. I'm thinking you might have something you could recommend to me."

"Better yet, something she could *sell* to you," her father said with a loud guffaw.

Jasmine blushed at her father's assertion. "I would be honored to discuss my horses with you, President Taylor. And should Cousin Peggy's health permit, it would be my privilege to have the two of you be my guests in Lowell."

"I'll discuss that possibility with her, my dear. She hasn't been inclined to do much visiting and, as I mentioned, Betty sees to formal functions at the White House. However, I've been encouraged by the number of friends and kinfolk Peggy has welcomed to her upstairs sitting rooms. She regularly worships with the family at St. John's Episcopal Church, even though she steadfastly refuses to become involved in the Washington social functions. So there is a good possibility she might consider a visit to Lowell. Now tell me more about your horses."

"Why don't we adjourn to the sitting room, and I'll tell you about my farm," Jasmine suggested.

"We'll join you in a few moments, my dear," her father stated. "I'd like to have a glass of port and a cigar. I'm certain the other gentlemen will want to join me."

"Yes, of course. Since Nolan doesn't partake in cigars, I'm certain you'll excuse him. He promised to make a final visit to Spencer's room."

"Surely the boy is in bed by now," the older man said.

Nolan rose from his chair. "He's likely asleep, but I'll go up and make certain. I don't want to break my promise."

Malcolm nodded and gestured for the others to follow. "Whatever you think best — we'll be in my library if you want to join us once you've looked in on Spencer."

Jasmine waited only a moment before pulling Nolan aside. "I know we didn't have an opportunity to talk prior to supper, but I do wish you hadn't begun a discussion of the slavery issue with President Taylor. Surely you realized the topic would be unpredictable."

Nolan gave her a sheepish grin. "I suppose that's a correct statement. However, I wanted to see for myself where the president's loyalties are placed. I must admit he surprised me. I assumed he would hold fast to the Southern ideology. When he stated he was a Unionist, I was taken aback. I gathered from his comments that he's willing to do everything in his power to stop any talk of cessation. He's against slavery expansion, yet he supports its continuation in Southern states, all the while saying the fugitive slave laws should not be more stringent. It's obvious he doesn't intend to bow to Whig leadership in Congress."

"And it's also obvious my father disagrees with him on almost every account. Nolan, I would prefer this be a gracious visit. Mother's illness leaves Father weary and quick to temper, and I don't know when the president will be able to return for another visit. For approximately four years they spent a great deal of time on their plantation across the river in Louisiana, and we would visit several times a year. However, the Mexican War put an end to those visits. And now that they live in Washington and neither Mother nor Cousin Peggy is in good health . . ."

"I understand. I apologize for my thoughtless behavior. Of course, I could argue that McKinley added to the strife — and even you asked a few leading questions."

"You're correct, and if I could have snatched back my last question to him, I would have done so." They stopped then and stood side by side, very close. Jasmine became very aware of Nolan's presence — the scent of his cologne, the rich blueness of his eyes. Realizing she was staring, Jasmine cleared her throat and headed for the door. "We had best go up and check on Spencer."

"Yes, of course," he agreed, following her into the foyer. "I must say I was astonished to have the president appear at your front door. How is it you never mentioned being related to him?"

"Mother and Mrs. Taylor are second cousins, so I'm not actually related to President Taylor. I'm barely related to his wife," she said with a giggle. "But I always enjoyed visits with the Taylors and their daughters. I was especially fond of Sarah. The family called her Knox, but I always thought the name Sarah much prettier.

Betty and I were both withdrawn, while Sarah was full of vigor, always a leader. We were quick to follow."

The two of them stood in the entryway to the bedroom. Spencer was fast asleep, and Bessie was sitting nearby in a wooden rocking chair mending the torn pocket on her apron. "He wen right to sleep, ma'am," she whispered.

"Thank you, Bessie. Would you consider remaining with him until I come upstairs for the night?"

The older woman gave her a toothy grin. " 'Course I'se gonna stay. You go on now. I'm mo' than happy to sit here."

"I believe I'll look in on Mother while I'm up here, Nolan. Why don't you join Father and the others?"

"If you're sure you don't want me . . . to come with you?"

There was something akin to longing in his expression, but Jasmine quickly looked away. "No. I'm certain she's sleeping, but I'll feel better if I stop in and check on her. I'll come down momentarily."

Jasmine met her father's questioning gaze as she entered the parlor some time later. "She's asleep. Her breathing seemed rather shallow, but she didn't appear to be in distress."

Her father sighed, obviously relieved to hear the brief report, while the others settled back in their chairs.

"While we were enjoying our glass of port in the library, your father mentioned you have some Arabians, Jasmine. I'm interested in hearing how you came to own them. They are, after all, rather rare here in America, and quite honestly, one of the most beautiful animals in God's creation."

"I couldn't agree more, President Taylor. However, I didn't realize you would be interested in anything so . . ."

"Costly?" he asked with a wide grin.

"Well, they are expensive, but Arabians are also quite showy."

"Exactly! Sitting astride one of those beauties could make anyone appear grand and powerful. President Washington is patent confirmation of my observation. Have you viewed the paintings of him astride his Arabian? He looks absolutely magnificent — like a powerful warrior. Why, if I'd been riding one of those magnificent animals in Mexico, I would have given serious thought to prolonging the war just for the pure pleasure of riding the beast into battle!" He slapped his knee and emitted a loud guffaw.

Jasmine smiled, certain the president was joking — at least about the Mexican War. "I assumed you were looking for animals that are more unpretentious."

"I care little whether others find my choice of horses pretentious — and I *expect* to pay dearly for fine horseflesh."

"In that case, I'm certain we can accommodate you," she said, "but if you've set your mind upon Arabians, I would truly encourage you to visit us before you make your final decision, as we do have some others you might find entirely suitable."

He scooted forward on his chair and bent forward, resting his arms upon his thighs. "Tell me, how is it you happen to own Arabians? Quite frankly, I didn't realize anyone was breeding them here in America."

"Interest in the Arabian breed continues to increase and, truth be told, there have been occasions when we've been unable to meet all requests."

"How did you happen to develop an interest in Arabians?"

Jasmine glanced toward Nolan. "Actually, it was my deceased husband who first acquired the Arabians with a thought toward breeding. A relative in England assisted him in securing the animals."

"Who has taken charge of the horse business since your husband's death?" the president inquired, looking in Nolan's direction.

"Bradley didn't actually enter into the care and breeding of the horses," Jasmine explained. "He was more an admirer and entrepreneur. Frankly, we had excellent help with the farm prior to his death, and those employees have remained with me. Our stable master has trained young Paddy O'Neill. Paddy is an acquisition from Lord Palmerston, a distant relative of Bradley."

The president's eyebrows arched like two woolly caterpillars. "How so?"

"Paddy and his sister, Kiara, were both sent to our home as the result of a game the elite gentry visiting Lord Palmerston had devised. Paddy and Kiara's parents died in the potato famine, leaving them penniless and starving. The small parcel of land where the O'Neills farmed was owned by Lord Palmerston. He was in Ireland on holiday when Kiara went to his manse seeking aid. As part of that game or wager, Kiara and Paddy were sent to my deceased husband as indentured servants."

"Surely you jest!" Taylor exclaimed.

"Unfortunately, the story is true, and I fear that the two of them might have starved to death if they'd been left to their own devices in Ireland. However, I heartily disagreed with keeping indentured servants and made my distaste known to my husband. When Bradley died, I granted both Paddy and Kiara their freedom. Since Bradley's death, Kiara has married Rogan Sheehan, and they live in a small house on my acreage. Paddy remains with me, working in the stables. His ability with the horses never ceases to amaze me."

"I'm pleased to hear matters have ended well for both of them. But I am surprised your husband didn't see fit to grant them their papers when they arrived. Releasing them from their indenture would have been the more Christian thing to do."

"There are those who would say that freeing the slaves is the more Christian thing to do, also, but we know that's not what folks in Mississippi and Louisiana believe," McKinley remarked.

Jasmine frowned at her brother. Once again, he had startled her with his stance, but more importantly, she worried his reply would cause another inflammatory discussion regarding slavery if she couldn't turn the course of the conversation.

"I believe you would find a journey to Lowell time well spent," Nolan said. "Not only would it give you ample opportunity to view the horses, but you could also tour the textile mills."

"I know you would find the mills fascinating," Jasmine's father agreed.

"Absolutely!" Jasmine graced Nolan with a pleased smile, thankful he'd prevented further turmoil.

The president stood and began pacing in front of the fireplace as though formulating a plan. "I do believe I could fit Lowell into my schedule, although it might not be as soon as I would like. And you're correct, Nolan: a visit to the mills could prove advantageous in many ways. Speaking of activities in Lowell, I would surmise the gold rush west has created a changing face upon the workforce. Have you noted any consequences?"

"More than the Boston Associates care to acknowledge," Jasmine replied. "At several meetings of our Ladies' Aid Society, the women say their husbands are gravely concerned. The loss of skilled mechanics is disquieting, and there is anxiety over —"

The sound of footsteps could be heard scurrying through the upstairs hallway. Jasmine leaned forward and met Bessie's wide-eyed gaze as the servant hurried toward her.

"Miz Jasmine, you best come with me.

You, too, Massa Wainwright," she said. "Ain't lookin' none too good for the mistress." The black woman wrung an old handkerchief between her fingers as she spoke the soulful words.

Jasmine jumped to her feet and fled toward the stairway, her heart pounding wildly. "Not yet, Jesus, not yet. Please don't let her die. I'm not ready." She whispered the words over and over until she reached her mother's bedside. Leaning down, she embraced her mother's body before placing a kiss upon her ashen cheek. Backing away from the deathbed, Jasmine glared upward as though looking through a window into heaven. "Didn't you hear me? I'm not ready!" she accused, but only a deafening silence replied.

CHAPTER 4

Elinor Brighton peered into the hallway mirror, straightened the ribbon on her hat, and exited the boardinghouse. Giving an extra tug on the doorknob, she listened as the metal latch gave its familiar click. Nodding in satisfaction, she marched down the two front steps and off toward the regularly scheduled meeting of the Ladies' Aid Society. Her final determination to attend hadn't been made until after preparing and serving the noonday meal. However, neither the substance of the meeting nor anyone who might be in attendance had influenced Elinor's decision. Her choice to attend had been based solely upon whether there would be sufficient leftovers for the evening meal.

Likely the girls would protest eating repeated fare for the evening meal, but Elinor had listened to their tiresome complaints before. They grumbled if the food was too hot or too cold, if they disliked a particular vegetable or meat, if they thought their sleeping space was too small, or if another girl snored — she had heard all manner of whining since she'd become a boardinghouse keeper for girls working in the mills. While listening to each petty grievance, she always maintained her silence, although she yearned to lash out at their triviality. She loathed feeling as though she were *their* servant, at *their* beck and call and constantly required to perform on their behalf. But as much as she disliked her position as a boardinghouse keeper, she knew she would remain, for she had no choice.

The silly-minded mill girls had no idea what it was like to experience the cruel hardships of life, but their day would come. Years ago she'd thought life was good and the world was hers for the taking, back when she'd sailed from England to make her home in Lowell with Taylor and Bella Manning, her brother and his new bride. That had been a lifetime ago, or so it now seemed.

Perhaps if she had remained in England and had not married at the first opportunity, things would be different now. But her past couldn't be changed, and her future appeared bleak. While the sun consistently shone upon others, her life continually filled with heartache and failure. A gust of wind whipped at her cape and Elinor shivered, longing for the warmth of her long woolen cloak.

In the distance she could see several buggies and carriages lined in the circular driveway that fronted the Donohue home. Perched upon a small knoll, the house was surrounded by several large trees. Elinor watched a curling trail of smoke rise from the chimney and blotch the horizon with a fading charcoal stain. The reminder of a warm fireplace beckoned her onward, and she bent her head against the wind until reaching the front door. She thumped the brass knocker and pranced from foot to foot in an attempt to ward off the chill that now permeated her entire body.

The door swung open, and Daughtie greeted her with a bright smile. "Elinor! It's so good to see you. You look lovely, as usual. I feared you weren't coming when the hour grew late."

Elinor removed her cape. "I had to prepare and serve the noonday meal for my boarders, clean the kitchen, and then walk to your house. Unlike many of your members, I have daily duties that require my time and attention. And, of course, I don't have a buggy at my disposal either. I suppose you should expect that I will always be late."

"My words weren't meant as a condemnation, Elinor. I'm pleased you chose to join us. Come in. We're just beginning the meeting. Let me get you a cup of tea to warm yourself," she said, leading Elinor into the parlor.

"No. I don't want to make a spectacle of myself. I'm already late arriving. I'll wait and have tea with everyone else. Please," she said firmly.

"Very well. Ladies, I believe we can now begin our meeting. I'm excited to report that all of the donations have been put to good use. However, with the onset of winter, we will need to collect even more warm clothing and blankets. Most of the runaways have only the clothes on their backs, and they are generally of a lightweight fabric. When these winter escapes take place, the people are ill-prepared for the cold weather that greets them as they proceed north. I'd suggest we work diligently both at our meetings and in our homes to help meet the needs that will soon face us. I hoped we could choose to either set a personal goal for contributions or set a goal for our group as a whole. What do you think?"

Mrs. Harper reached into her bag and pulled out a piece of embroidery work. "I've brought along some sewing to work on while we talk. If we all would stitch while we conduct our meetings, we could accomplish more," she proudly suggested.

Elinor glanced at the handiwork and gave a disgusted groan. "She's doing fancywork for runaway slaves."

Nettie met Elinor's reproving stare. "Better to create something of beauty than contribute nothing at all." She poked her needle into her fabric.

Elinor's eyes flashed with anger. "Why, whatever do you mean, Nettie Harper?"

"I may take longer to complete my projects because I value quality over quantity, but you appear to value neither. I haven't seen you making *any* donations to the cause."

"I don't have the freedom to sit at home and perform charitable work all day while my maid completes the household duties. You seem to forget that I actually work to support myself," she bristled.

Nettie looked up from her stitching. "We're all aware of your station in life, Elinor. You've made your situation clear to all of us — again and again."

Daughtie moved to gracefully position herself between the two women. "As I was saying, I think if we could set reasonable goals, it would be helpful. I'm concerned about our lack of preparation. Most of our runaways continue onward to Canada. In the middle of winter, it's a cruel journey, especially for those not accustomed to our cold New England weather."

"It would appear best for all concerned if they waited until spring," Elinor offered.

A small gasp circulated throughout the room. "Slaves must take any opportunity available, whether it comes in the heat of summer or dead of winter," Daughtie gently replied. "If they don't run when the opportunity arises, they may never again have a chance at freedom."

Elinor tilted her head and gave a slight nod. "I cannot disagree with your argument, Daughtie. But you must remember that it's easy to offer an extra measure of charity when you're prosperous. Try doing the same when you're struggling to make ends meet. What you ask is too much."

"Daughtie contributed profoundly when she was still a mill girl," Lilly Cheever put in. "Perhaps more with her time than her money, but her dedication and hard work were worth more than any money the rest of us donated."

"Don't speak on my behalf," Hannah Peabody said while leaning forward to make eye contact with Elinor. "I'm like you, a boardinghouse keeper. Even though I don't have much money, I can still be of assistance and help to free slaves by donating my time and energy."

"I don't see how you can donate much time or energy if you're keeping a decent boardinghouse."

Daughtie sighed and patted Elinor's hand. "Why don't we talk later, Elinor?" she whispered. "I'd like to move forward with the meeting."

Elinor shrugged and glanced heavenward. "If that's what you'd prefer. It's your meeting."

Cupping a hand close to her lips, Nettie leaned toward Daughtie. "I don't think Elinor is committed to freeing the slaves. Discussing confidential issues in her presence may prove to yield disastrous results," she said in a hushed voice.

"I heard your whispered accusation, Mrs. Harper. I resent your implication that I might divulge information that would place runaways in jeopardy. When I joined this group, I signed the same pledge as you." The volume of Elinor's voice escalated as she continued arguing her defense. "I've never broken my word to any of you, and I resent the unseemly attack you've made against my morals."

"I don't think she meant her remark as an accusation," Daughtie stated in a hushed tone.

"No need to whisper. Everyone in this room heard Nettie accuse me of disloyalty. The entire group may as well enter into the discussion. Perhaps you'd like to bring the topic of my ouster before the group, Nettie?" Elinor asked, straining her neck to catch Nettie Harper's eye.

"I was merely expressing what I thought might be a valid concern," Nettie said, glancing around the room.

Elinor clenched her hands into tightly coiled fists and momentarily wished she were a man. She would poke Nettie Harper right in her pompous nose. "I have a right to express my views without my loyalty being accused. Although I do not contribute as much as some, I will not break my word."

"I believe we should move along to the real reasons why we've gathered," Daughtie interjected. "Since I'm in charge of the meeting, I'm requesting that you both hold your tongues."

Nettie squared her shoulders and pursed her lips into a tight knot while several other women arched their brows or nodded their heads in obvious approval.

"Fine with me," Elinor muttered.

Daughtie looked in her direction and gave a slight shake of her head before continuing. "As I mentioned earlier, we're expecting a number of runaways throughout the winter. Liam and I have reason to believe our farm is being watched. We're not certain, but we've seen enough indication that we must be careful — especially in light of the difficulty with the group that came through earlier this month."

Elinor turned and was met by Nettie's accusatory gaze. "Did *you* know when the last group of runaways was coming through?" she hissed.

"As a matter of fact, I did," Elinor muttered.

"Ladies, *please*! You are trying my patience," Daughtie admonished.

"I didn't know there was any problem. Why wasn't I told?" Hilda Schultz complained.

Daughtie briefly massaged her temples. "There was no need, Hilda. We've all agreed that the less discussion regarding particulars, the better. Suffice it to say there were a number of us who were nearly discovered while moving runaways to the next station. Now that I've explained our problem, I hope there will be a few of you willing to open your homes and become stations for the runaways, at least on a temporary basis. Once we're certain our house is no longer under surveillance, Liam and I will renew our efforts."

Hilda clasped a hand to her chest. "After hearing what you've related about difficulties with the last group as well as your concerns that you're being watched, I don't think I could possibly offer my house. Especially since I'm a widow. Why, I'd have no one to protect me if something went amiss," she said, dabbing a handkerchief to her eye.

Elinor gazed at Hilda, wondering if the older woman had any notion of her good fortune. Widow or not, Hilda possessed a home and sufficient finances to care for herself. The old woman had never wanted for anything since her husband's death; she'd never been required to seek employment or consider taking refuge with relatives. Harvey Schultz had been dead for more than ten years, yet Hilda spoke of her widowhood as though her husband had died only a few months earlier. Besides, Hilda should expect widowhood — she was probably every bit of forty and five years. The woman's behavior stuck in Elinor's craw like an ill-placed hatpin.

While Hilda sat in her fine home stitching fancywork, Elinor scrubbed floors and prepared meals for a household of ungrateful girls who were nearly as unappreciative of their good fortune as Hilda Schultz. Elinor watched as the mill girls freely spent their pay on fancy ribbons, fabric, earbobs, and other whims. They attended lyceums and weekly French and music lessons and, of course, there were the gentlemen callers. The girls would descend the stairs with their new hair ribbons and fine dresses to sit in the parlor and bat their eyelashes at one of the mechanics or salesmen who came calling, while Elinor remained in the kitchen washing their dirty dishes and setting bread to rise. And when she was done, she would fall into bed, only to awaken the next morning and begin again. If she were Hilda's age, perhaps it wouldn't seem so dreadful. But at twenty and five, her future loomed before her like a long, dark shadow, her youth and beauty fading and then dying a little each day.

"It's settled, then!" Daughtie said, startling Elinor back to the present.

"Mary and Jacob Robbins' home will be the new station until Liam is certain our house is safe. You're certain Jacob is in agreement? I can wait to tell Liam until you've had an opportunity to talk with him."

Mary's lips turned up in a gentle smile. "Jacob told me that should the need ever arise, I had his permission to offer our home. In fact, we've even created a hiding space and have some extra provisions," she announced.

"Wonderful!" Daughtie exclaimed. "There's little doubt God's hand is at work in this, Mary. Give our thanks to Jacob. And now I'm certain everyone is ready for a cup of tea."

Elinor checked the time on the walnut mantel clock and jumped to her feet. "If you'll excuse me, Daughtie, it's late and I have the evening meal to prepare for the girls. By the time I get home —"

"Please stay. I'm certain there's someone here who would be happy to take you in her buggy. And if all else fails, Liam will be home in sufficient time to take you home."

"No, I'd best take my leave. I believe the remainder of your afternoon will be more pleasant if I'm gone. If you'll get my cape," Elinor insisted while moving toward the foyer.

She donned her cape and hat while Daughtie enumerated a myriad of reasons why she should remain. "You know your early departure will merely serve to set tongues wagging."

Elinor secured her hat and turned to face Daughtie. "Of course! We both realize there must be some exciting topic of conversation at each of these meetings. Today it will be my insufferable behavior and bad manners. I imagine my departure will give Nettie sufficient bravery to actually suggest my expulsion."

"Then remain and defend yourself," Daughtie urged.

"I haven't the time nor energy. If the group feels I'm untrustworthy or my contribution is insufficient, then I'll quietly withdraw. I care little what most of them think. However, I want to assure *you* that I would never do anything to compromise the runaways or anyone who is lending aid on their behalf. However, I realize my comments are sometimes harsh."

"I hope I'm not overstepping my boundaries, Elinor, but I fear you're permitting your past difficulties to ruin your future happiness. You are so filled with anger and resentment that you seem to alienate anyone attempting to befriend you. Yet I'm certain that's *not* your intent," she said softly.

Elinor tugged at her kid gloves, carefully adjusting each finger before meeting Daughtie's concerned gaze. "Perhaps it's not my intent, but I have little time for friends, so I see no need to tiptoe around a group of women who have already judged me unworthy of their confidence."

"Nettie means well. Unfortunately, she's a bit high-strung and tends to fret overmuch. Both Nettie and Hilda are good women who, like the rest of us, want to help the runaways."

"Thank you for your kindness, Daughtie, but I must be on my way. I've supper to prepare and serve and a multitude of other duties awaiting me."

"I understand, but please promise you'll come to the next meeting."

"We'll see," she said. "Please go take care of your guests. I can see myself out the door."

With a smile and brief hug, Daughtie hurried back toward the parlor, and Elinor exited the Donohue home, glad to be back in the fresh air and away from the unpleasant atmosphere. "They likely think *I'm* the one with the biting tongue," she chuckled aloud, certain the women had already determined that her quick exit was due to a guilty conscience rather than their own unpleasant attitudes.

Red and yellow leaves swirled along the path as Elinor trudged toward home with

Daughtie's parting remarks churning about in her head. Obviously Daughtie believed Hilda and Nettie to be kind Christian women with only goodness in their hearts. If so, she was an extremely poor judge of character and much more naïve than Elinor would have thought.

"I suppose we can't all have the ability to see others clearly," she muttered. The wind stung her cheeks, and she burrowed her head closer to her chest, concentrating on the final leg of her journey.

When she finally turned the corner and headed down Jackson Street, her face and fingers were nearly numb. "I should have set aside my pride and accepted Daughtie's offer of a buggy ride," she chastised herself aloud as she neared the front door of the boardinghouse.

"Excuse me?"

Elinor gasped and jumped back a step. "Who are you, and *why* are you on my doorstep?"

"Oliver Maxwell. My apologies," he said, bowing and sweeping his hat in front of him in an exaggerated gesture. "I didn't mean to startle you, good lady."

It took only a moment for Elinor to notice his case. "You're a peddler, I see. Obviously you know the girls haven't returned from work yet. No guests and no salesmen until after supper — house rules."

He stroked his narrow blond mustache. "I'm a shoe salesman," he replied, clearly not bothered by the sharp, cold wind. "Frequently the girls keep me busy when I come calling in the evening, and I don't have an opportunity to visit the boardinghouse keepers. Consequently, I decided to make some early calls while I'm in Lowell for that very purpose. A good pair of shoes is a necessity in cold weather, and winter will soon be here."

"It feels as though winter has already arrived. I really must go indoors. If you want to return at eight o'clock, there should be any number of girls anxious to purchase a new pair of shoes."

"And *you,* dear lady? Could I not interest you in a pair of shoes? I'd be delighted to take your measurements before the girls return home, and then I'll be on my way."

He was charming with his blond hair, wool frock coat, and proper manners, but Elinor really couldn't afford a pair of new shoes. She couldn't afford even a new ribbon. "It's the mill girls who have money to spend on themselves, not the keepers," she replied.

He nodded and smiled, radiating a kindness she'd not seen for far too long. "If you're truly in need of a pair of shoes, I'm certain I could find something within your budget. And although I require the girls to pay in full when they place their orders, in your case, I would be willing to arrange for payments."

"Why don't you come inside," she said after a moment of silence. "It's much too cold outdoors."

"Well, if you're absolutely certain. I don't want to keep you from your chores," he said, his voice as smooth as cream.

"Not at all. Come in," Elinor said while turning her key in the lock. She took his hat and coat and hung them beside her own on the wooden pegs inside the front door. The sight of a man's coat next to her own appeared strange and yet achingly familiar. "Why don't you sit down in the parlor while I make a pot of tea. A cup of hot tea would help ward off the chill, don't you agree?"

He rubbed his hands together in quick, exaggerated motions. "Indeed. Something warm would be most satisfying."

Mr. Maxwell had opened his case and was removing the contents when Elinor returned with a tea tray. She settled herself on the couch and poured him a cup of tea while glancing at his samples. "You have some lovely shoes," she said, offering him the cup.

"I'm pleased you think so. I pride myself on the quality and variety of shoes I sell. Have you decided to take me up on my offer and order a pair?"

"I believe I will," Elinor replied, pointing toward a soft kid boot.

He graced her with a charming smile as she extended her foot. "An excellent choice. Now I need only measure your foot." Mr. Maxwell wrapped his fingers around Elinor's ankle as he carefully removed her shoe. His fingers trailed the length of her foot before he placed it atop the measuring paper. Her eyes widened as an unbidden tremble coursed through her body.

Chapter 5

Jasmine sat staring at the distant horizon in a trancelike stupor, feeling as though someone else had inhabited her body and rendered her immobile. She should be getting dressed, yet her limbs were heavy, weighed down by an intense aching sorrow — a sorrow she hadn't anticipated. The entire family had expected her mother's death, known it was coming, and in the end, waited upon it. Yet when death finally had its way and sucked the last remnant of breath from her mother's body, an unexpected pain had seared Jasmine's heart, for she knew that her life would never again be the same.

The bright, sunny morning seemed strangely out of place — not the type of day one envisioned for a funeral. Nolan had taken Spencer downstairs several hours earlier, likely thinking she would immediately don her mourning clothes and join the rest of the family. But she had no desire to enter the parlor, where her mother's body lay awaiting the undertaker's hearse. Better to let the coffin be closed without once again staring down at her mother's lifeless face — a picture that had already etched itself into her memory. She had listened and watched as their friends and neighbors attempted to impart comfort, yet there was nothing they could say or do that would assuage her grief. Most of them knew little of her mother. Visitors had not been encouraged in later years, at least not by the mistress of The Willows. However, now they needed no invitation to call; now they came because it was proper.

Somewhere in the distance she heard her name but pressed her face closer to the window, wishing it were springtime and the magnolias were in bloom. Her mother had loved magnolias. Instead, it was November and her father was as concerned over the cotton harvest as his wife's death — or so it appeared. She had listened while he'd discussed his disappointment over the prices with Uncle Franklin yesterday. Instead of lamenting his wife's death, they had talked of cotton and the prices they had hoped to receive with this crop. Never once did she hear either of them mention their remorse over her mother's death. She'd not yet seen her father shed a tear — and each time someone grew near and offered condolences, he would cover his face in a mask of grief, only to be replaced by his normal appearance once they turned away.

"Jasmine! Have you not heard me calling?" Her father's voice was followed by several loud raps. "Are you ill?"

"Come in," she said, still unable to force herself away from the window.

"I was concerned . . ." He hesitated, staring at her. "You're not dressed for the funeral. People have begun arriving. Thankfully, Samuel has finally arrived. You can't wear that dress. Change into your black gown and come downstairs. I've given Spencer over to Bessie's care for the remainder of the day. You need to gather your wits about you and behave like a grown woman, Jasmine. I need you to act as my hostess."

"Hostess? This isn't a party, Father. You don't need a hostess at Mother's funeral." She choked out the words and flung herself toward him. "She's *dead*! Don't you care?" Hot tears rolled down her cheeks as she pounded his chest.

He wrapped his arms tightly about her, holding her until the sobbing subsided and she relaxed in his arms. "Of course I care. She was my wife and I adored her, but I can't bring her back. And no matter how deep my grief, there is a funeral about to take place. I would greatly appreciate it if you would get dressed and join us in the parlor." He released his grasp and looked deep into her swollen brown eyes. "I apologize for my choice of words. You're right. I don't need a hostess. However, I do want my daughter to join me — I need to be surrounded by my family."

She saw the glisten of tears in her father's eyes and, for the first time since her mother's death, realized his pain was fresh and raw — hidden from view, yet as absolute and deep as her own. "I'm sorry, Papa." She drew him into a brief embrace and then leaned back to meet his gaze. "I thought because you and Uncle Franklin have been consumed by business discussions since Mother's death, you weren't feeling any loss."

"We all grieve in different ways, my dear. I prefer to remain composed in front of others, and the only way I can accomplish that feat is to talk of the crops or weather or some other mundane topic that won't remind me of your mother and the fact that now she is gone. At night I remind myself that one day we'll be together again. But for today, we must give your mother a proper burial, and I would very much like you by my side."

Jasmine nodded. "I'll join you as soon as I've changed clothes."

Her father leaned forward and placed a kiss on Jasmine's forehead. "Thank you, my dear."

When the last of the visitors finally departed, Jasmine turned to Nolan. "I must look in on Mammy. I promised to share the details of Mother's funeral with her, and I've not yet been to see her today."

"Shall I go with you?"

Jasmine's shoulders sagged a bit, and she forced a weary smile. "It's probably best that I go alone, but thank you for your kind offer."

"Promise that if Mammy's asleep, you'll return and get some rest yourself. I'm worried about you, Jasmine. You're going to become ill if you don't take care of yourself."

"You have my word."

Jasmine inhaled deeply as she walked down the hallway and neared the small room off the rear of the kitchen. Unfortunately, it didn't help. She honestly doubted there was anything that would calm the roiling tumult of fear that had taken up residence deep within.

She tiptoed into the room and sat down on the marred wooden chair beside Mammy's bed. There was no sign of life in the old woman. However, before she would permit panic to clench a final hold over her, she held her hand above Mammy's face. A faint rush of warm air tickled her palm.

"What you doin', chile? Plannin' to smother me?" Mammy asked with a hint of a smile on her cracked lips.

"I couldn't see you breathing, and I was frightened," Jasmine admitted. A tear trickled down her cheek as she leaned against the wood slats that backed the chair.

"Ain't no need to be cryin'," Mammy said, reaching for Jasmine's hand. "Now tell me 'bout your mama's buryin'. Did the preacher say fine words over her?"

Jasmine nodded and squeezed Mammy's hand, unable to push any sound around the large lump that had risen in her throat.

"She's in a better place, Miz Jasmine. You got to remember dat."

"I know, but with Mama gone and you so ill, I feel as though my whole world has turned upside down. I don't think I could bear it if you died. Promise me you'll get well," she begged.

"Umm, um, chile, you know I can't be

promisin' such a thin' as dat 'cause the good Lord, He be callin' me home. But you listen to your ole mammy and you listen good. You need to be lookin' to the Lord to fill dat place inside o' you. He's the only one dat'll pull you through the hard times, the only one dat's always there when you need Him, the only one who never changes — He's faithful and true and won' never leave you, chile. So it's *Him* you need to keep fixed on — not your ole mammy. You understan' what I'm telling you?"

Jasmine folded her arms around herself and rocked back and forth on the hard wooden chair. The slats jarred her spine and caused a pain as real as the ache in her heart. "I know what you say is true, Mammy, but my prayers seem like vapor. I wonder if God even hears them. I pray and pray, but I don't feel His presence. I don't think I can bear any more loss."

"The Lord is always with you, chile, even when you don' feel Him. Been lots a times in my life when I thought I couldn't bear no more pain, but da hurt came and the Lord saw me through, just like He will now. You keep yo' faith in God. Ain't nothin' more important in dis life. I want you to remember dat when I'm gone. Will you do dis for me?"

"I'll try," Jasmine whispered.

"Good. Now, why don't you get your ole mammy a drink of water. I gots somethin' I needs to be askin' you, and I'm thirstin' mighty bad right now."

Jasmine jumped up and fetched the old woman a drink from the bedside table. "I'm so sorry. I should have gotten you some water as soon as I arrived," she said while cradling Mammy's head in the crook of her arm.

"Umm, dat sure tastes good," she said, running her thick tongue along her parched lips. "Now sit back and listen to your ole mammy 'cause I'm fixin' to ask you somethin' important. Way back when you was jest a baby, your pappy bought me and brung me here to De Willows."

"Yes, I know. Mother told me how Father looked everywhere to find a wet nurse for me because she was sick after I was born and couldn't nurse me. She said he had a hard time finding someone."

Mammy nodded. " 'Cause your pappy weren't willing to separate families."

"Mother said your baby died and your husband had been sold to another plantation, so Papa bought you to be my wet nurse."

"Dat's right, only dat was a lie I been livin'

with all these years."

Jasmine bent close to hear her words.

"My baby *weren't* dead. He was a big strong boy 'bout half a year older than you. He had a smile bright as all outdoors."

"But why didn't you tell Father? He wouldn't have bought you, Mammy."

"Ole Massa tol' me he'd kill my baby iffen I didn't go or iffen he found out I tol' I had a chile. He said I better *never* tell 'bout my Obadiah."

"That's your baby's name, Obadiah?"

"Um hum. Dat name come straight outta da Bible. 'Course I don' know if the massa let him keep dat name or not, but he promised me he'd keep da boy safe on his plantation so long as I didn't tell. Miss Jasmine, I wants you to find my Obadiah and see if you can set him free. I don't want to die knowin' I never did nothin' to help my boy outta da shackles of slavery."

Questions flooded Jasmine's mind. "How have you been able to remain silent all these years, Mammy? How could you bear knowing you had a child you'd never see again and not ask for help before now?"

"Dat's what I been tryin' to tell you, chile. You can bear da pain if you got Jesus holdin' yo hand. And dat's what you gotta do from now on: reach out and take hold of Jesus with all yo might. Weren't hard to keep my mouth shut 'cause I knew if your pappy went back to try and buy Obadiah, ole Massa woulda killed him right in front of your pappy and all the other slaves jest to make sure they all understood what would happen to dem if they disobeyed. Couldn't take that chance with my baby's life. Better he be raised without me than to have him die."

"Couldn't Papa have bought you both?"

"No," she whispered. "Ole Massa never turned loose of big, healthy boy babies. He raise dem up like prime stock. He didn't care none 'bout losing me. I 'most bled to death birthin' Obadiah, and he knew my days fo' having babies was past. 'Sides, he had other young slaves to wet-nurse my boy, and your pappy was willin' to pay a high price fo' your ole mammy."

Jasmine's stomach wrenched in pain. "It's because of *me* that you were forced to leave Obadiah."

"Now don't you be dwellin' on dat. I only tol' you bout Obadiah so's maybe you could help set him free. Would you try and help him for your ole mammy?"

"You know I will. Do you remember anything about where you were or any names that will help us?"

"I's hoping he's still with Massa Harshaw. Dat's where I was — at Harwood Plantation, but I can't tell you how to get there. Don't seem like it took us terrible long to get to Da Willows, but I was so sad, I don't 'member much about da journey from one place to da other."

"But you're certain it was Harwood Plantation and the owner was Mr. Harshaw?"

"Dey used to call it Harshaw Plantation, but when ole Massa married, he changed de name to Harwood to make the new mistress happy," she explained.

"I'll do everything in my power to find Obadiah, and when I do, you can be certain I'll buy his freedom. Now I want you to get some rest. I'll be back to see you in the morning."

The old woman's lips formed a faint smile and she closed her eyes. "I'm gonna do jes' dat, chile. I'm gonna rest in the arms of Jesus."

Jasmine brushed a soft kiss onto Mammy's fleshy cheek before leaving the room. The hour was late and her body ached with an overpowering weariness, yet she felt a determined purpose as she ascended the rear stairway to her bedroom. She would find Obadiah and bring him to meet his mother. Seeing her son would surely cause

Mammy's health to rally. The thought made Jasmine smile, and when she finally slipped into bed a short time later, she thanked Jesus for this opportunity to help Mammy. She fell asleep with renewed optimism and enthusiasm for the task with which she'd been entrusted.

Jasmine caught sight of Nolan talking quietly with her brothers and father in the parlor as she descended the stairway the next morning. The group stood shoulder to shoulder in a tight half circle surrounding the hearth like a decorative fire screen.

She entered the room and met their somber gazes with a gentle spring in her step and a gleam in her eyes. "I slept well last night, although it appears the five of you could use more sleep," she commented. "Shall we go in to breakfast?"

"Sit down, my dear," her father requested while gently leading her to the divan.

"This sounds ominous," she said. The others lingered in front of the fireplace, staring at her. With their arms locked behind their backs, they reminded Jasmine of toy soldiers set in place to guard an imaginary fort. The spectacle unsettled her, and little by little, she could feel her joy slipping away.

Her father reached out and took her hand,

and she noticed his hands were shaking. "I don't want you to become unduly upset, but I fear it is left to me to give you more sad news. Mammy died during the night."

Jasmine stared at him, unable to speak. She heard the slaves talking in the kitchen, their voices muffled and distant, echoing as though they were calling to her from a deep cavern.

"Jasmine! Open your eyes. It's Nolan."

He was dabbing her face with a cool cloth. She willed her eyes to open. Nolan was kneeling beside her, peering directly into her eyes. "What happened? Please tell me I didn't faint. I abhor fainting women," she said, pushing herself up on one elbow.

Nolan laughed. "I fear that's exactly what you did. Fortunately, you were on the sofa and didn't hurt yourself."

But now she remembered the reason for her disquietude. Her father's words came rushing back and invaded her mind. "Mammy . . . she's —"

"Yes," Nolan whispered. "Bessie said she went peacefully during the night."

"I should have known. We talked last night, and when I bid her good-night, she said she was going to rest in the arms of Jesus. She was telling me she knew her time on earth was over, but I was too foolish to understand. I should have remained with her through the night."

Her father tenderly embraced her. "Don't be so hard on yourself, Jasmine. Mammy wouldn't have wanted you sitting in that room all night long. We both know that."

"Sitting up one night is the least I could have done. Think of the many nights she remained awake caring for me when I was a child. She was always there when I needed her. She even came to Lowell when I married Bradley, even though she didn't want to leave Mississippi. I want her to have a proper burial, Papa."

Her father's eyes widened as he pulled away from her. "When have I ever *not* given my slaves a proper burial? I'm not akin to those who would hearken to any less."

"I know, Papa. I'm sorry if my words hurt you."

"I'll take care of the funeral arrangements, and everything will be very special, if you'll promise to come in and eat some breakfast. You can go upstairs and rest as soon as you have something to eat."

Jasmine sat in the carriage beside Nolan. The funeral had been the finest ever held for any slave at The Willows — likely for any slave in all the South. But a fine funeral wouldn't fill the void of Mammy leaving this world.

"Time will heal the loss of your mother and of Mammy. I hope you find comfort in the fact that you were able to spend some time with each of them."

She nodded and gave him a faint smile. "I need to discuss something with you, Nolan. Something Mammy asked of me, a deathbed request that I promised to fulfill. I'm hoping you'll agree to help me."

"Of course. Anything. Surely you're aware you need only ask. What is it she requested?"

Nolan listened intently as Jasmine explained Mammy's heartrending tale of being separated from her son when he was a mere babe. "And she asked you to find this son and purchase his freedom?"

"Exactly! But I've never heard of Harwood Plantation. Of course, I'm certain there are many plantations in Louisiana and Mississippi that I've never heard of, but I'm not certain how to locate the place without arousing interest. I don't want to answer a multitude of questions, especially from my father. Mammy didn't want him to ever find out about what had occurred. She said it would serve no purpose at this late date. I suppose she's correct. Papa would be either angry that Mr. Harshaw had lied to him or distressed that he'd separated a family."

"Or both," Nolan remarked.

"True," she agreed. "Can you think of any way we might easily be able to secure the information? I don't want to alert anyone in the family of our plan."

He rubbed his jaw. "Let me take care of it. I'll think of something," he said as he drew back on the reins and the carriage came to a halt in front of the house. "Now let's go inside. I believe your father expects all of us to have dinner together."

"I want to check on Spencer; then I'll join you in the parlor," Jasmine said as she passed through the foyer.

After assuring herself the boy had eaten and was taking his nap, Jasmine once again entrusted him to Bessie's care and hurried back downstairs. "I hope I didn't delay dinner," she said, glancing toward the dining room, where the servants were busy placing food on the oversized serving buffet.

"No, we were just preparing to go in. I trust you found everything satisfactory at the service?" her father inquired.

"Yes. In fact, I wanted to tell you that several of the slaves expressed their gratitude for your kindness in seeing that they always receive proper burials."

The comment appeared to please her father. Jasmine's preference was to have all of the slaves freed, but she knew it would do no good to speak of that matter.

"I trust you're still enjoying your work for the Associates, Samuel?" Nolan inquired.

"Absolutely. I regret the fact that it keeps me away from The Willows so much, but it seems I'm traveling most of the time."

"You certainly haven't had much time to spend visiting with me or Grandmother in Lowell," Jasmine said.

Samuel grimaced at his sister's remark. "I apologize. However, most of my business is in Boston. I venture into Lowell only on rare occasions upon the specific request of the Associates, and I've attempted to see you on each of those visits."

"Lowell is not so very far from Boston, Samuel, and Grandmother isn't getting any younger," Jasmine said. "I'm certain she would have appreciated a visit during her recent bout with pneumonia. Stopping for a cup of tea from time to time wouldn't take long."

"Duly noted, sister. I shall consider myself thoroughly educated on proper etiquette," he said with a grin.

Jasmine set her glass down with a force that caused the contents to slosh over the rim and onto the linen tablecloth. "I'm not speaking of etiquette, Samuel. She's your *grandmother* and soon she's going to die too. You should spend more time with her while you have the opportunity," she said, her voice laced with emotion.

"I'm sorry. I didn't mean to make light of your request. I'll make an effort to visit more often," Samuel replied with his gaze focused upon his dinner plate.

"Have you been able to expand any of your markets here in Mississippi?" Nolan inquired, giving Jasmine a sidelong glance. He was obviously intent upon defusing the attack upon her brother.

Samuel sighed and directed a visibly appreciative smile toward Nolan. "As a matter of fact, I was telling Father only yesterday that I signed on two new growers three months ago: one in Mississippi and one in Louisiana. Both of them have large plantations that yield as much cotton as The Willows. I plan to leave The Willows tomorrow morning and call at a number of plantations before I leave. I've been negotiating with the owners and hope to have at least one of them sign a contract before I board ship for Boston next month. My discussions with all of them appear promising."

"Sounds as though you've been very successful. Have you heard mention of Harwood Plantation? I seem to remember someone saying they were known for huge cotton crops years ago."

Samuel nodded enthusiastically. "Not only years ago. Jacob Harshaw currently operates one of the most prosperous plantations in Louisiana. In fact, I successfully negotiated a contract with him only this year. Although we weren't able to agree upon a price for this year's crop, we will be purchasing his entire crop next year."

"Well, that *is* quite an accomplishment. I'm certain the Associates were elated over your ability to win over Mr. — did you say Harshaw?"

"Yes, Harshaw. His plantation is located across the river in Louisiana and about thirty miles south, not too far from the river — good fertile land. He's well known among the southern Louisiana growers. You've met him, haven't you, Father?" Samuel asked.

Jasmine glanced toward her father, who had placed a finger alongside his cheek as though attempting to recall the name before he answered.

"Yes, as a matter of fact, I have. I've talked with him on several occasions at the docks in New Orleans. Not a man I'm particularly fond to know on a social level — rather crass and uncouth, although I'll give the devil his due. His crops are exceptional."

"Have you ever seen his plantation?" Jasmine ventured.

Deep ridges creased her father's brow. "Yes, I have." He hesitated a moment and rubbed his forehead. "Seems strange discussing Jacob Harshaw today, of all days. You see, Harwood Plantation is where I purchased Mammy."

"Really? Peculiar how a topic will arise at the most unexpected moment," Samuel said. "From what I observed at Harwood, I'd say Mammy was very fortunate you purchased her. Unlike The Willows, the whip is used freely by Jacob Harshaw on all of his slaves."

Jasmine gave an involuntary shudder. She wondered how many lashes Obadiah may have taken from Master Harshaw's whip.

CHAPTER 6

December

The time for departure had arrived. Jasmine could no longer delay leaving her father and brothers. The trunks sat in readiness beside the front door, and the family was waiting downstairs. Picking up her reticule, she checked her appearance in the mirror and glanced about the room one last time, as though she must commit each item to memory. She detested good-byes, especially now. Farewells seemed much too final. What if her father took ill before she saw him again — or one of her brothers? Suddenly life seemed very fragile.

Spencer was tugging at McKinley's pant leg and begging for a horsey ride when Jasmine entered the parlor. She smiled and shook her head. "You've spoiled him with those rides around the house, McKinley. I'll never be able to handle him once I get home," she said, giving her brother a wide smile.

"Then I suppose I'll have to come to Lowell and entertain him for you."

"Oh, *would* you? Come for a visit, I mean? I would truly love that, and it would give us something to plan and look forward to," she said, feeling a renewed enthusiasm. "You'll come too, won't you, Father? And you, David! *All* of you."

Her father laughed and wagged his head back and forth. "And who will tend to this place if we all go traipsing off to Lowell?"

"Uncle Franklin and the slaves," she replied. "Please say you'll come."

"I won't promise we'll all come at the same time, but we'll all come for a visit. How's that? Besides, if we spread out our visits, it will continually give you something to anticipate."

"Either way, I won't argue. Just so you come," she said while accepting his embrace.

Her father took hold of her arm. "I'd like to have a few words alone with you before you depart, Jasmine. I'm certain your brothers and Nolan can look after Spencer."

"What is it, Papa?" she asked as they walked into her father's library.

"I know we haven't always seen eye to eye on things, and I still regret forcing you into a marriage with Bradley, but . . ."

"That's all in the past, Papa. You apologized long ago, and I forgave you. Besides, had I not married Bradley, I wouldn't have Spencer now, and he's the joy of my life. You know that. Please don't worry yourself with regrets over my marriage any longer."

"It's not just the marriage. I feel as though I failed you — both you *and* your mother. Perhaps if I had left this place long ago, things would have been different. I fear I was so busy becoming prosperous, I didn't give your mother the attention she deserved."

"Papa, that's all behind us. There's no way to change the past. If you regret where you've placed your values in the past, you have the rest of your life to make changes. I know your life is going to be very different without Mama. However, you'll have ample opportunity to evaluate how best to live your remaining years — and you can begin by coming to visit Grandmother, as well as Spencer and me."

"You're right," he said. "Perhaps I'll even journey to the capital and stop for a visit with Zachary and Peggy. What do you think of that?"

"I think a visit to Washington would be a splendid beginning."

He pulled her into an embrace and placed a kiss upon her forehead. "Always remember I love you, Jasmine. While I don't have high expectations, please remember that I would look favorably upon having you and Spencer move back to The Willows."

Jasmine stood on tiptoe and kissed his cheek. "I think it's wise of you to keep expectations of me returning to The Willows *very* low."

"I know, I know, but you can't fault me for trying," he said. "I suppose we had best get your trunks onto the carriage if you're going to get on the road before nightfall."

After all the good-byes were finally said and the carriage pulled away from the plantation, Jasmine leaned back against the leather-upholstered seat and sighed. Spencer wriggled onto her lap and, wrapping his chubby arms tightly around her neck, placed a wet kiss upon her cheek. "Thank you, sweetheart," she said, ruffling his curls. "A kiss is exactly what I needed."

"Had I known, I would have come to your rescue long ago," Nolan said with a roguish grin.

A blush colored Jasmine's cheeks. "Nolan Houston!" she said with a giggle. Her heart began a rapid beat that suggested more than girlish amusement.

Spencer quickly moved to take his place between them on the cushioned seat, and Nolan momentarily gazed out the window before turning back to face Jasmine. "About Obadiah," he began.

"I think we should attempt to find him before our voyage home. Do you think we have sufficient time?"

"It's not far out of our way; I was planning exactly the same thing. We can go down river the thirty miles and then hire a conveyance to the Harwood Plantation. If we're fortunate, we'll easily locate someone who knows Jacob Harshaw. If his reputation is what Samuel has indicated, we should have no difficulty."

"Let's pray all goes well. From the little Mammy told me, I doubt we'll have an easy time convincing Mr. Harshaw to sell Obadiah."

"*If* Obadiah is still there. However, there's no need to worry yet," he said. "As you said a moment ago, perhaps a word of prayer is what we need."

The smell of dead fish and wet moss filled Jasmine's nostrils as the carriage neared the river at Rodney. When the horses came to a stop near the dock, Nolan jumped down and quickly assisted Jasmine and Spencer while the driver unloaded their trunks.

"Thank you for your help, Louis," Nolan said. "You can return to The Willows and tell Master Wainwright you saw us safely to the docks at Rodney."

"Yessuh," the black man replied. "Been good seein' you, Miz Jasmine. You have you a safe trip back home, ya hear?"

"I will, Louis, and you take care of yourself — and Bessie," she added.

"I be doin' dat fo' sure," he said with a toothy grin. He clucked at the horses and turned the carriage. Jasmine watched as he waved and headed back down the road.

"I'll go to purchase tickets and see if anyone knows where we should go ashore if we're planning to visit the Harwood Plantation."

"I believe I'll take Spencer for a short walk near the river. He'll be intrigued with the water, and I'm hoping the walk will tire him. Hopefully he'll take a nap once we depart," she said, giving way to the two-year-old's insistent tugging at her hand. "We'll meet you on the dock or in front of the general store if it doesn't take long to purchase the tickets."

"Is that quite safe? I mean . . . to go unescorted."

Jasmine smiled. "I'll be fine. This is the land of my birth — I know it well. Besides, a lady needn't worry about being accosted — at least not in the same manner that she might in the North. Southern manners and etiquette generally keep the rogues at bay. Still, you won't be that far away should the need arise to rescue me."

Nolan nodded his agreement and strode away while Jasmine turned Spencer by the shoulders in the direction of the dock. "Come along, Spencer. Let's go see the water."

The child needed no further encouragement, and Jasmine was immediately thankful she had placed a tight grasp around the boy's tiny hand before making the suggestion. Spencer was delighted to splatter his hands in the murky river water and watch as the twigs he dropped made a tiny splash and floated off.

Jasmine thought of the long trip home. She longed for Lowell and the farm, yet she knew a certain sadness in leaving the South. It was a bittersweet hurt. Her mother would say she was waxing nostalgic, but Jasmine couldn't help it. So much had happened on her visit. Her mother and Mammy had both departed, leaving her regretful for all the time and distance that had separated them. What if she returned to Lowell to find her grandmother gone as well? What if her father were to die before he could journey north to visit her again?

Spencer laughed with glee as he dropped a rock into the water. His revelry forced Jasmine to leave off with her sorrowful ponderings. Life was fragile. It was but vapor — a mist, as the Bible suggested. Here and then gone. Smiling at her son, Jasmine knew that the past could not hold her captive. Not when Spencer was her future.

Jasmine turned at the sound of approaching footsteps. "You certainly weren't long," she said, gracing Nolan with a pleasant smile.

"I paid for our passage and was able to gain information without any difficulty. It didn't take long to locate someone who was familiar with Jacob Harshaw and his plantation. But I must admit the comments weren't particularly flattering. Seems Mr. Harshaw is a bit abrasive, and when he's in his cups, I'm told he's an odious man."

"Then we'd best pray he's sober when we arrive. I'm going to remain optimistic."

Nolan lifted Spencer into his arms and pointed toward the water. The boy watched and then giggled as Nolan skipped a pebble across the water. "If Obadiah is at Harwood, we'll find him. And there's little doubt in my mind you'll somehow convince Mr. Harshaw he should sell Obadiah to you."

"Are you saying I'm somewhat overbearing?" she asked with a grin.

Nolan chuckled. "Oh, not at all. However, I would say you have strong powers of persuasion." He glanced toward a group assembling on the dock. "It appears as though the captain has begun gathering the passengers to board."

"Then we best not keep him waiting. Were you able to gain specifics on how far we'll be required to travel after disembarking?"

"Indeed. It won't be long at all compared to our journey upriver, and then we'll travel another hour or two by carriage — perhaps longer if the roads are muddy and difficult to traverse."

"Let's hope it's less. I wouldn't want to spend the night as Mr. Harshaw's guest. Do you know if there will be another boat coming to the landing before nightfall?"

"Only one, and I have my doubts we'll be able to return by then. We'll see how things progress at Harwood Plantation. If we're required to find accommodations elsewhere, we'll do so. However, it was my understanding you were intent upon finding Obadiah. . . ."

"You're right. I shouldn't be creating a problem before one exists. Forgive me. I can certainly push aside any ill feelings I might have toward Mr. Harshaw if it means we'll be able to find Obadiah and secure his freedom."

The instructions Nolan received were accurate. The boat reached Pappan's Landing early in the afternoon. By the time they arranged for a carriage and entered the driveway to Harwood Plantation, it was approaching three o'clock. Two large dogs loped alongside the carriage and remained on either side until their coach stopped in front of the main house. A large man carrying a coiled whip called the dogs to heel. A deep, jagged scar lined the man's cheek, and his clothing bore evidence of more than several days' dirt and grime.

"Do you think that's Mr. Harshaw?" Jasmine whispered.

"I have no idea. Let us hope not." Nolan quietly replied before leaning forward and waving to the man. "Is it safe to alight from the carriage, or will your dogs consider me their supper should I step down?"

The man emitted a deep belly laugh before spitting a stream of tobacco juice from between his brown-stained teeth. "You're safe so long as I'm nearby. Get on down," he commanded, his smile widening as he met Jasmine's wary gaze.

"Got ya a good-lookin' woman. Too bad I didn't see her afore ya, or I'd have fought ya for her hand," he said, his gaze going up and down the full length of Jasmine's form.

"Don't tell him I'm a widow," Jasmine whispered when Nolan came alongside her. "I don't want him making unseemly advances toward me."

"I was jest getting ready to ride off when you got here. What can I do fer ya?"

"Quite the host," Jasmine murmured.

Nolan grinned at her disdainful rejoinder. "Be careful," he whispered while bending down and scooping Spencer into the crook of his arm. "He may hear you, and we need to remain on good terms if we're to find Obadiah."

The man wiped one hand on his dirty pant leg before reaching to shake Nolan's hand. "Jacob Harshaw. I'm the owner of Harwood," he said, waving his arm in an expansive motion.

"Nolan Houston," he said. "And this young man is Spencer Houston, along with his mother, Mrs. Houston."

"Pleased ta make yer acquaintance." His leering gaze came to rest upon Jasmine's bodice. "What brings ya to Harwood?"

"Slaves," Nolan said.

"Well, I got me plenty of them, but ain't

particularly set on sellin' any," he said while massaging his ample belly. The front door opened and a dour-looking woman with a tightly wound knot atop her head strode forward to take her place beside Mr. Harshaw.

"Appears we got company. How come ya didn't let me know?" the woman asked with a modicum of irritation lacing the question. Before her husband could reply, the woman turned her attention toward Jasmine and Nolan. "I'm Rosemary Harshaw, mistress of Harwood." Her seeming annoyance turned to obvious pride as she made the announcement.

"Pleased to make your acquaintance," Jasmine and Nolan replied in unison and then grinned at each other.

"You want to bring the boy inside?"

Jasmine glanced toward Nolan, hoping he would give her an indication of what he considered most helpful.

"We were telling your husband we're wanting to purchase some slaves and heard that Harwood had some fine specimens. I'm particularly interested in a good buck or two. We'd like to look at any you think might meet our needs."

Harshaw narrowed his eyes and ejected another stream of spittle. "Don't know as

I'd be willing to turn loose any of my best breedin' stock, but I can have my overseer bring them for you to inspect. Never know — we might be able to come to some sort of agreement."

Mrs. Harshaw hissed an inaudible remark to her husband and then turned toward Jasmine and Nolan. "I can offer ya a cup of tea while we wait. It'll take the mister some time to get the slaves up here. You can best review 'em from the upstairs portico. That's where we go to watch when he whips the runaways."

"You watch when they're punished?" Jasmine gave the other woman an incredulous look.

" 'Course! Outside of going to town once in a while, it's the only entertainment around this place," she stated harshly. "Besides, we gotta keep our darkies under control. We're not like you folks that buy only a few slaves to help operate your small farms. We own nearly a hundred, and they gotta know who's in charge. Otherwise, they'll run at the first opportunity. Can't let that happen. We got too much money tied up in our slaves."

"Perhaps kindness would cause them to stay of their own volition," Jasmine commented.

Mrs. Harshaw cast a disdainful look in Jasmine's direction. "It's obvious you haven't had many dealings with slaves. Come along. We'll go up and have us a look from upstairs while your husband examines 'em close up. I'll educate you on how to deal with slaves, and you'll have little trouble after that . . . if you follow my ways."

Jasmine followed along behind the woman, hoping she wouldn't be quizzed any further about why they were in the area. She certainly didn't want to divulge the fact that Malcolm Wainwright was her father. Jacob Harshaw might not remember selling Mammy some twenty-one years ago, but there was always the possibility he would recollect past events if he realized she was a Wainwright.

A stoop-shouldered black woman appeared in the hallway as they entered the front door. "You can serve us tea on the upstairs portico, Hessie. And be quick about it." Mrs. Harshaw turned to Jasmine. "You want the boy to come with us or you want Hessie to look after him?"

Jasmine tightened her hold on Spencer's hand. "He had best stay with me. I'm certain Hessie already has more than enough chores to keep her busy, and Spencer is quite a handful."

"Got him spoilt, have ya? Slaves and children — they both need to be treated with a strong hand." Her stern glare caused Spencer to immediately tuck himself behind Jasmine's skirts.

Had circumstances been different, Jasmine would have told Rosemary Harshaw exactly what she thought of her malevolent advice. Instead, she remained silent and lifted Spencer up into her arms and followed the older woman. Mrs. Harshaw escorted Jasmine upstairs and then to the outer gallery, where she took a seat in one of the willow chairs along the east end of the gallery. Spencer sat near her side until the old slave emerged a short time later, bearing a sizeable silver tea tray. Obviously the sight of flaky pastries, fruit-topped cakes, and berry tarts was enough to fortify her son's bravery. Spencer rushed forward the moment Hessie placed the tray on a small table near Mrs. Harshaw, with his chubby fingers aimed toward one of the tasty-appearing delicacies.

"Don't touch!" Mrs. Harshaw barked. Her eyes had suddenly narrowed to mere slits, and she leveled a formidable gaze that sent the child scurrying back to his mother.

Jasmine pulled her son into a protective embrace before she removed a lace-edged handkerchief from her dress pocket and wiped away his tears. "He is but a young child unaccustomed to such harsh words, Mrs. Harshaw."

"Youth is no excuse for ill manners."

Jasmine bit her lower lip for several seconds before responding. "I believe we likely disagree about what constitutes proper behavior. However, if my child has offended your sensibilities, please accept my apology."

Mrs. Harshaw's shoulders squared as she drew herself up straighter in the chair and looked down her bulbous nose at Spencer. "Apology accepted," she said and then placed one of the tarts on a napkin and offered it to the boy.

Instead of accepting the treat, Spencer buried his face in Jasmine's bodice. "Perhaps later," Jasmine said on the boy's behalf.

"Here they come," Mrs. Harshaw announced, pointing a finger toward the dirt road leading up to the mansion. "Finest-looking bucks you'll find this side of the Mississippi."

Jasmine watched as the overseer herded fifteen sturdy male slaves into two lines at the east end of the house. The overseer cracked his whip, and the first slave stepped forward as Mr. Harshaw called out a name and methodically recited the man's pedigree to Nolan. The procedure followed for each of the men in the front line before continuing to the second row.

"Obadiah," Mr. Harshaw called out as the first man in the second group stepped forward. "This here boy is a strong one, and I can vouch for his bloodline. A good, strong buck from over at the Elmhouse Plantation sired him. I paid a hefty fee to have this one sired, and I'd be willing to let him go at a fair price."

They went through the entire line like this. Harshaw calling out names, suggesting each man's strong points, even commenting on the scars, pointing out that each man had been given very few beatings and hence was well behaved.

Jasmine watched as Nolan pretended to take each man under great scrutiny. The minutes seemed to tick by like hours until he and Mr. Harshaw were once again standing in front of the man called Obadiah. Nolan appeared to be saying something, although Jasmine couldn't hear the words.

Mr. Harshaw poked and prodded at Obadiah as though he were pointing out the attributes of a prized bull. Jasmine leaned forward and peered over the railing a little more closely. Mr. Harshaw said something indistinguishable, and Nolan appeared to nod in agreement. "Go fetch the woman and boy," Mr. Harshaw called out to the overseer.

"You strike a bargain on Obadiah?" Mrs. Harshaw called down to her husband.

"Quit your hollering, woman. I'll talk to ya later."

"You'll talk to me now!" she said, jumping up from her chair.

Jasmine stared after the woman as she stomped into the house and appeared downstairs beside her husband a few moments later. Mr. Harshaw pulled her aside, and the two of them moved away from Nolan and engaged in what appeared to be a less than amicable conversation.

Nolan glanced up to the gallery and motioned for Jasmine to join him. When she and Spencer came alongside Nolan, Mr. and Mrs. Harshaw were still occupied with their private conversation. "Has he agreed to sell Obadiah?"

"Yes, but he insists we purchase Obadiah's wife, Naomi, and their child."

"Seems a strange request from a man such as Mr. Harshaw. While my father would never separate slave families, I have difficulty believing the Harshaws are concerned about preserving the sanctity of a slave's family."

"I don't think this has anything to do with pleasing the slaves. Mr. Harshaw is anxious to be rid of Obadiah's wife, Naomi. Seems Mrs. Harshaw has an intense dislike for the female slave. Harshaw says it has to do with his wife's persistent and unfounded jealousy."

Jasmine cupped her hand across her mouth and suppressed a giggle. "I'm sorry, but I can't imagine Mrs. Harshaw as a woman concerned about losing her husband's attentions."

Nolan smiled. "Nor can I, but let's not question our good fortune. I doubt whether Obadiah will consider us his benefactors if he's forced to leave his wife and child with the Harshaws. I'll strike a bargain for the three of them, and unless you're inclined to accept the hospitality of the Harshaws, I suggest we go back to town and stay at the hotel. I'll ask Harshaw to have one of his men deliver Obadiah and his family to us in the morning."

Jasmine focused on the perimeter of the grounds and watched as a young woman carrying a child approached. "If Mr. Harshaw is giving special attention to Obadiah's wife, I can now understand Mrs. Harshaw's jealous reaction," Jasmine whispered as the woman drew nearer. "She is a beautiful woman."

The stark contrast of color among the small family was disquieting. While Obadiah bore the rich chocolate brown skin and onyx eyes of his mother, Naomi's complexion was a soft, tawny shade and her eyes a golden brown. And the child — Jasmine couldn't withhold her stare. The child's limbs were skeletal and pasty — so pale, in fact, that had Jasmine not known better, she would have believed the boy to be white.

The next morning Jasmine and Spencer joined Nolan in the small restaurant adjacent to their hotel. Once they had completed their breakfast, Spencer began fidgeting, obviously anxious to leave the table. "If you want to stroll around outdoors with Spencer, I'll go to the loading dock and ascertain our departure time. Since we were detained an extra day, I'm hopeful your family's cotton has been loaded and we can soon be on our way. Mr. Harshaw or his overseer should deliver Obadiah at any moment."

"I'll watch for their arrival," Jasmine said as they exited the small restaurant.

Spencer toddled after a small frog he spied hopping in the roadway, giggling each time the creature would croak and jump. Enjoying the sight, Jasmine followed along behind him until she saw Mr. Harshaw jump down from his wagon in front of the hotel. She lifted Spencer into her arms and hurried forward, waving to gain his attention.

"Mr. Houston has gone to the docks, but you may leave the slaves in my care," she said as they approached.

Giving her a look of disdain, Mr. Harshaw shook his head. "No chance you can control Obadiah if he decides to run. You gonna buy the shackles?"

Jasmine looked into the rear of the wagon. Iron hinges lined both sides of the wagon bed, with Obadiah secured to one of the hinges by a shackle encircling his leg. His other leg was shackled to Naomi. Jasmine recoiled at the sight. "Remove the irons. We're not concerned that either of them will run. After all, exactly where would they go?" She leaned forward a few inches, as though preparing to include the man in some dark conspiracy. "To be completely honest, Mr. Harshaw, we don't believe human beings should be restrained in any manner."

Mr. Harshaw spit a long stream of tobacco juice and tugged at the unraveling hem of his silk vest. "Human beings? These here darkies are *property* — same as livestock, but I s'pose you can call 'em whatever you want — they're yours. Mark my words, though, you're gonna be sorry. First opportunity that comes along, they'll run. Just don't come back to me expecting your money back. You been warned," he growled while unlocking the heavy irons that secured Obadiah and Naomi.

"Thank you for enlightening me," Jasmine replied.

Two perpendicular creases formed between Mr. Harshaw's eyebrows. "If I didn't know you were a lady with proper manners, I'd think you were mocking me."

"Why, Mr. Harshaw, why on earth would anyone consider scoffing at you — a man of obvious worth and distinction," she said, her voice taking on a heavy Southern drawl.

Loosening the final leg iron, Harshaw motioned the three slaves out of the wagon and then leveled a heated gaze at Jasmine. "Your husband needs to gain control over you, Mrs. Houston."

"My husband is deceased, Mr. Harshaw. Nolan Houston is my late husband's brother, *not* my husband."

"With your lack of respect, it's unlikely you'll ever attract another," he crossly rebutted. "I believe our dealings are complete." He hoisted himself onto the seat of the wagon.

Jasmine graced him with a demure smile. "Good day, Mr. Harshaw."

Several passersby had stopped to listen to the exchange and now stared at the strange-looking group. Obadiah's strong arm now embraced Naomi, who held the emaciated child close to her breast, the two of them staring wide-eyed at Jasmine. Meanwhile, Spencer was tugging at Naomi's tattered dress, obviously hoping to gain a better view of her child.

"We need to talk," she said to the slaves. "Let's go over to those trees and sit down."

She strode away, unsure whether they would follow, yet hoping her act would exhibit a level of trust. There was no indication they had moved along behind her, so she sat down, carefully arranging Spencer beside her before turning her gaze toward the street. They stood transfixed where she had left them. Jasmine smiled, motioned them forward, and then patted the grass beside her, hopeful they would take her cue.

When Obadiah took Naomi's hand and began walking toward her, Jasmine's smile widened. "Please, sit down," she encouraged as they grew nearer. "There are many things I want to share with you before we board the ship."

Naomi's lower lip trembled. "Where you

takin' us?"

"That's what we need to discuss. Won't you sit down?" Jasmine waited until they had arranged themselves beside her on the grassy mound. Immediately, Spencer got up and began tottering across the uneven terrain, obviously intent upon reaching Naomi and the child she held in her arms. "Spencer, come back and sit down."

"I don' mind. He's jes curious," she said, reaching out to take Spencer's hand in her own when the boy stumbled. "You wanna see my little Moses, don' ya?" she asked, her gaze fixed on Spencer.

"Moses? That's your little boy's name?"

"Yessum," Obadiah replied. "We's all three got names from the Bible. When dis here youngun was borned, I tol' Naomi he should be like his mammy and pappy — have a name from da Good Book." His eyes shone with pride while taking in the sight of his wife and child.

"That's an inspired decision. Choosing a name from the Bible would have pleased your mother."

"Don' know nothin' 'bout what would have pleased my mammy — never knowed her, but I do know Moses was a man used by God. If my boy lives, I'd like for him to be a man of God too. Maybe help free our people."

Jasmine nodded. "I know that idea would have pleased your mother also. You see, Obadiah, your mother was my mammy from the time I was an infant. My father purchased her from Mr. Harshaw when you were only a year old. My mother was ill and my father was looking for a wet nurse, but he didn't believe in dividing families. Had he known you were alive, he would have insisted on purchasing you, but Mr. Harshaw told him Mammy's child had died only days earlier and he was willing to sell her."

Obadiah's gaze filled with suspicion. "If dat be the truth, how come she didn't tell your pappy once they left Harwood Plantation? And how come you know all dis now, but nobody knowed nothin' afore?"

"Mammy never told anyone because Mr. Harshaw threatened to kill you. Even though she knew she couldn't see you again, there was comfort in knowing you weren't going to die. Your mother didn't divulge your existence until just before she died. It was her final request that I find you and purchase your freedom."

"*Dat's* what dis is all about? So now we's yours. Where you takin' us dat we gotta get on a ship?"

Jasmine brushed a leaf from her blue plaid wool dress. "You aren't required to go with us. Mr. Houston has your papers, and we plan to sign them, showing you've been freed. However, the last thing I want is to give you your freedom without helping you plan for a future. Otherwise, you'll not survive. Remaining in the South would be far too risky. You'd be picked up and, papers or not, you'd be sold back into slavery. You know that's true, don't you?"

He lowered his gaze. "Yessum. So what you plannin' for us?"

"Although I grew up in Mississippi and my family still owns cotton plantations, I no longer live here. When I married, I moved to Massachusetts."

"Dat up north?" Obadiah asked, his eyes shifting to Naomi.

"Yes. And although there are few Negroes living near my home, there are many people who are committed to aiding runaways and who are anxious to see slavery abolished. I thought perhaps you would want to come and live at my farm and work for me. It's a horse farm, not a plantation, although I do have a vegetable garden," she said with a smile. "There's a small stone outbuilding where the three of you could live. If you decide to remain, we could build something more suitable."

His brow furrowed. "Where else you think I might be wantin' to go?"

"Most of the runaways we help don't remain in the United States. They go farther north to Canada."

"Um hum, I heard tell o' dat place. Been three or four of Massa Harshaw's slaves run off tryin' to get north to dat place." He wagged his head back and forth. "Dey never made it. Massa brung 'em back and whipped 'em till dey was near dead." He massaged his forehead as though he could somehow erase the memory.

"If you like, you could work for me until you decide. You would always be free to leave, Obadiah. There will be no shackles, no restrictions on your coming and going — you are all free to make a choice about where you will live and how you will earn a living."

"Don' think I'd be much use to ya, Missus. I don' know much 'bout horses," he said soulfully. "Massa was 'fraid we'd steal a horse and run off, so we didn't do no tendin' of the horses."

"You can learn, Obadiah," she said before turning her attention to Naomi. "If you'd like to earn money of your own, Naomi, I can always use help in the house and with

Spencer. I'm hopeful Spencer and Moses will become good friends."

"Moses be a sickly kind o' chile. He don' play much."

"He does appear very thin. We'll have the doctor see to him once we arrive home." She took in the child's sad eyes. "Does he eat well?"

"Massa force all the younguns to stay in the nursery, and dat fat ole woman he got watchin' after dem chillens don' care if dey eat or not. She lick their plates clean afore dey get much chance to eat. I tried complainin' to Massa, but den dat ole woman in the nursery begun to hittin' on Moses, so I was afeared to say no mo'."

Jasmine gave her an encouraging smile. "We're going to fatten him up in no time. Why, I'm certain he'll be as big as Spencer within a few months."

Naomi's eyes sparkled and she leaned toward Jasmine. "Fo' sure? You think dat's possible?"

"I certainly do. Ah, here comes Mr. Houston," she said, motioning toward Nolan as he walked toward them. "I'll go visit with him while the two of you decide what you'd like to do."

"No need, Missus. We's gonna come with you. We ain't willin' to take our chances in dis here part of the country."

Jasmine smiled. "I'm glad, Obadiah. Why don't we go and join Mr. Houston? Once we're on board ship, I want to spend some time telling you about your mother. She was a wonderful woman. I only wish she could have lived long enough to be reunited with you. I know she would be proud of you and pleased to know you are now a free man."

"Dat would be nice," Obadiah said.

"Your mother came to Massachusetts and lived with me for a while," Jasmine said as they approached Nolan.

"Did she like it dere?"

Jasmine laughed. "She said the winters were too cold for her old bones. When we returned to Mississippi, she was ready to remain in the warmer climate. I was sorry to leave her behind when I returned home, but I saw her on each of my visits to The Willows. She was a wonderful woman who taught me many things. She loved to talk about Jesus. I was home when she died." Jasmine looked up into the onyx-colored eyes that reminded her of Mammy. "I had returned to Mississippi due to my mother's illness. It seems both of our mothers contracted yellow fever and never fully recovered. They died within only a few days of each other, and I know my life will never be the same without them. I'm so very thankful we were able to find you and I could do at least this much for your mother. I loved her very much."

Obadiah hesitated, shuffling back and forth for a moment. "If you loved her so much, Missus, den how come you never did set *her* free?"

CHAPTER 7

Late February 1850

Spencer took Jasmine's hand, and together they walked the newly formed path between the main house and the brick and stone outbuilding now occupied by Obadiah and his family. Jasmine smiled down at her son. His sturdy legs appeared to lag behind his body, unable to keep pace and deliver him to his desired destination. He had struggled from Jasmine's arms, determined to make the trek under his own power. Jasmine pulled her cloak more tightly around her body and shivered as a gust of wind stung her face. Spencer's cheeks were a ruddy red by the time she knocked on the heavy wooden door.

Naomi pulled open the door with Moses by her side. Both boys squealed in delight at the sight of each other and rushed forward as though they'd been separated for weeks. "You don' need to never knock on the door, Missus. Jes' come on in."

"This is *your* home, Naomi. I would never consider entering without knocking, but thank you for your kind offer."

"Here, let me hang up dat coat and get you warm by da fire."

Jasmine handed Naomi her cloak and showed her a length of fabric she'd been carrying beneath it. "I brought you some material I had at the house. I thought you might want to use this for a dress, and this piece would make some fine new curtains."

Naomi pressed her hand back and forth across the cloth, the flecks of gold in her brown eyes glistening. "Oh, Missus, I can't afford to be buyin' all this. Obadiah says we got to be careful with our money till we figure how to spend it proper."

"This is a gift, Naomi. Please tell Obadiah I insisted you accept it. Or I'll tell him, if you prefer."

Once again, Naomi gently touched the fabric, stroking it as though it were the finest silk. "I can tell him, but iffen he says I gotta return it, I hope you won' be gettin' angry with me. He already thinks you done too much for us. He says it ain't natural for white folk to be so kind."

"I wish I could argue that point, but I fear what Obadiah says is true. However, there are many white people who are working very hard with the Underground Railroad and are adamantly opposed to slavery in any form."

Naomi glanced at the two boys as they sat playing side by side. "I don' know nothin' 'bout that, but I do know you been merciful to us. Jes' look at Moses and how he's growed since we come here to live."

Jasmine turned her attention to the children, who were busily stacking small pieces of wood Obadiah had carved into various shapes and sizes. So light-skinned was Moses that when the boys' hands were intermingled, it was difficult to tell them apart. "He's grown nearly as big as Spencer. Why, by this summer, they'll likely be the exact same size. I can't tell you how much Spencer looks forward to his playtime with Moses."

"Yessum. They sho' do play good together. Obadiah says it was God's plan for us to come here. He tol' me 'bout how you wanted to free his mammy but you couldn't 'cause o' your husband."

"It's true that Bradley forced Mammy's return to The Willows, but she was never my slave; I didn't own her so I was unable to free her. She belonged to my father, who has never freed a slave. Even if I could have gained Mammy's freedom, Bradley was insistent she return to Mississippi. To free her and leave her in the South with no means of support would have . . ."

Naomi nodded her head up and down. "Jes' like me and Obadiah. Somebody's hounds woulda chased her down and put her in shackles. But she free now, ain't she, Missus? Up there in glory, reapin' her reward."

"Precisely. You know, even as she lay dying, she was thinking of others — wanting to assure Obadiah could live as a free man."

"Don' surprise me none. Ain't no way I could ever forget Moses. Can't be forgettin' a chile after carryin' him in your belly and birthin' him, now can ya? It's like they's a part of you forever. I don' know what I'd do if somebody took my chile. I don' think I could go on livin' if that happened."

"But if she hadn't gone on living, Obadiah wouldn't be a freed man today," Jasmine whispered.

Naomi's eyes widened and her lips curved into a faint smile. "I reckon dat's the truth. Ain't no way to know what God's got in mind for us, is dere?"

"I don't think so," Jasmine replied, mirroring Naomi's smile. "I'm going to have to return to the house and complete some tasks. You tell Obadiah I want him to give you permission to accept the fabric."

"I'll tell 'im, but can't make no promises on what he'll do."

Jasmine took her cloak from a wooden peg near the door. "Come along, Spencer. It's time to go home."

Both boys began howling the moment Jasmine gave the command, and Naomi shook her head back and forth. "Listen to dat wailin'. You'd think somebody took a hickory switch to 'em. It's fine wib me if Spencer stays here. I'll have Obadiah bring him home once he gets done in da barn."

"If you're certain he won't be —"

Naomi bent her elbows and placed a hand on each hip, her arms fanned open like two chicken wings. "He won' be no trouble. He'll keep Moses busy. You go on now and leave him to me."

The boys' tearful protests ceased once they realized their separation had been postponed — at least for the present. "Come give me a kiss," Jasmine said, opening her arms. Both boys hurried to her, each placing a wet kiss on her cheek before returning to their play. "You're certain bringing Spencer home won't be a burden?"

" 'Course not — you don't need to be worryin' at all 'bout such a thing as that youngun bein' a burden."

Careful to fasten her cloak before opening the door, Jasmine gave Naomi a warm smile and then directed her attention to Spencer. "You be a good boy," she cautioned before hurrying out into the bitter cold.

The shortened winter day had already faded into nightfall when Obadiah came to the door with her sleeping child in his arms. "He's tuckered out from playin' all day. Moses be sleepin' too. Naomi fed 'em supper, and afore she knowed it, they was fast asleep. You want me to carry 'im up to his bed?"

"Yes, thank you," Jasmine replied while leading the way. She stepped aside when they neared Spencer's room and watched as Obadiah tenderly placed her son on his bed.

"Naomi says jes' leave him wrapped in dat blanket so's he don' wake up," he whispered as he stepped back and looked down on Spencer's sleeping form.

"You can tell her I'll return the quilt tomorrow," Jasmine said softly. "I was having a cup of tea when you came in. I'd like to visit with you for a few moments; would you join me?"

Obadiah's eyes opened wide, and his eyebrows raised high on his forehead. "You want *me* to have tea — wib you?" He moved back several steps and stared down at her before emitting a loud guffaw. "Can you jes' 'magine what ole Massa Harshaw woulda thunk of me sittin' down to tea with a lady like yo'self?"

Jasmine joined him in his laughter and then pointed to the dining room chair. "Please. Sit down, Obadiah. I truly do want to talk to you."

He gingerly lowered himself onto the chair and sat poised at an angle as though ready to jump and run at a moment's notice. "Don' want no tea, Missus. I ain't never took a likin' to it."

"Very well. Now that you and Naomi have had time to settle into your new home, I was wondering how you like working with the horses. I know you had fears about adapting to the animals, but Paddy and Mr. Fisher indicate you've done very well."

"I's likin' dem pretty good — some better den others. Dat Paddy, he's good with *all* dem horses. He sure do love 'em, and he's been showin' me how to handle 'em. Paddy says horses is like people, takes 'em a while to get used to ya," Obadiah said with a wide, toothy grin.

His smile was a duplicate of the giant beams of approval Mammy had bestowed upon her as a child, unleashing a torrent of memories. Jasmine steadied her hand before pouring a cup of steaming tea. "I'm pleased you're beginning to feel more at ease with the animals and that Paddy is helping you. I'm hopeful you and Naomi are beginning to make plans to remain on the farm. Once spring arrives, I'd like to begin construction of a more acceptable home for your family."

Obadiah sat back in the chair and began shaking his head from side to side. "Oh, no, Missus, we be jes' fine in the place we're livin'. Naomi got it fixed up good, and she's set herself to makin' curtains out of dat cloth you gave her. And I'm thankin' ya for that — I was gonna say somethin' when I first got here and den fergot."

"You're quite welcome. Aside from the fact that the place you are living in is no more than an outbuilding for storage, I *want* to construct a more suitable home for your family, Obadiah. Building a home for your family would give me great pleasure."

"Don' know how to put dis into proper words, Missus, but all you's doin' for us, well, it's hard to understan'. I keeps thinkin' I'm in a dream and gonna wake up to Massa's whip any minute."

Jasmine's stomach lurched at the mention of a whip. "This is no dream, Obadiah. You have the papers showing all of you are free, and it would give me much joy to have you agree to remain here on the farm. However, if you think your family would be more content elsewhere, I'll not attempt to force you to remain in Massachusetts."

"Don' see how there could be anyplace we'd be treated better, Missus. This here has been a blessin' straight from God. When we was livin' with Massa, I spent mos' all my time worryin' 'bout Naomi and Moses. Didn' matter none if he beat me, but I didn't want him hurting Naomi."

Deep ridges creased Jasmine's forehead. "Why on earth would anyone whip Naomi? I can't imagine her ever causing a problem. She's so gentle and sweet-spirited."

Obadiah paused a moment before speaking, his voice almost a whisper. "Ol' Massa didn't whip her. He used her body for his own pleasure. Knowin' what he did to her, dere was times when I wanted to kill dat man with my bare hands. 'Specially what with her bein' his own flesh and blood and all. You'd think that woulda stopped him. But weren't nothin' got in Massa Harshaw's way when he was drinkin' and wantin' him a woman."

Jasmine sought to hide her incredulity, but her jaw had gone slack at the revelation and she couldn't seem to regain her senses. "Naomi is Mr. Harshaw's *daughter*?" she asked in a hoarse whisper.

Obadiah gazed down at the patterned wool carpet and nodded his head. "Never made her life no easier, neither. The missus hated Naomi from the day she was born. When Naomi got older and the massa begun having his way wib her, there was no help for Naomi. She was abused at night by the massa, and the next day his missus would be taking a whip to her, acting like it was Naomi's fault."

"He didn't *bother* her after you became her husband, did he?"

Obadiah released a deep growl. "Only reason he let us get married in a slave ceremony was to make his missus think dere was nothin' more goin' on with Naomi. When he'd come to our cabin at night, he said Naomi weren't my wife 'cause slaves ain' got no right to get married. First time he come, I tried to stop him, and he went and got the overseer. Overseer near beat me to death while ol' Massa stayed in da cabin with Naomi. After dat, Naomi said she was gonna leave me if I didn't let the massa have his way with her. Naomi said he'd kill me nex' time, and she wasn't going to be responsible if dat happened." Obadiah buried his face in his large callused hands. "I didn' want her to leave me."

"You ought not feel ashamed. You did the only thing you could — you gave her comfort and loved her."

"Sometimes dat ain't enough," he lamented. "Tell you the truth, we don' know *who* be Moses' father. I knows one thing fer sure. Miz Harshaw thought Moses was sired by da massa. She did everythin' she could to get da massa to kill the boy. I don' know why, but he didn' give in to her."

Jasmine could hear the pain in Obadiah's voice as he recounted their past. "Probably because he feared killing Moses would be an admission to his wife that he had been continuing in his reprehensible behavior with Naomi after she was married to you."

"I never thought 'bout dat. You's prob'ly right. But dat ole mistress forced Naomi back to the fields and made her leave Moses in da nursery. Naomi even begged to carry da baby with her to the fields. We knew dat ole slave in the nursery was gettin' extra rations fer treatin' Moses poorly and not feedin' him, but there wasn't nothin' we could do. For sho' Moses would be dead if you hadn't come and saved us from dat place. I tol' Naomi it was da hand of God dat worked through you and saved us."

Jasmine stared at him, taken aback by his pronouncement. "I was merely doing what your mother asked of me, Obadiah."

"Well, we all is God's instruments, if we jes' listen and do what He asks. I'm sho' glad you took it upon yo'self to be obedient." Obadiah got to his feet. " 'Less der's somethin' else you need to talk 'bout, I bes' be gettin' back home. Naomi's gonna be wonderin' if I got myself lost between here and dere." He chuckled loudly at his own humor.

"No, nothing else. I merely wanted to tell you about my hope that you and your family would remain here on the farm and my desire to build a house for the three of you come spring."

"Like I said, dat place we got now is plenty fine, Missus. We ain't plannin' on goin' nowhere."

"I'm pleased to hear that," she said while escorting Obadiah to the door. "Tell Naomi thank-you for looking after Spencer this afternoon," she called after him. She could see the outline of his muscular arm as he waved.

"Glad to have him." His deep voice resonated though the cold night air like a vibrating tuning fork.

Long after she closed the door, Jasmine

weighed the revelations spoken this night. She believed every word of what she'd been told. There was little doubt Naomi's bloodline was mixed, but Jasmine had never considered the possibility that Jacob Harshaw might be her father. The thought sickened her. Yet that same repulsive man had likely fathered sweet little Moses. Moses with his pale, buttery skin. Moses, more white than Negro. Moses, sired by his own grandfather! A chill ran through her being. Obscene!

Jasmine stood inside the front door of her home and welcomed each member of the Ladies' Aid Society. This marked the first time she would be acting as hostess since her return to Lowell, and she was pleased to see the group was continuing to increase in numbers. Thankfully Kiara had helped with preparations and would assist with serving while Naomi maintained a mindful watch over Spencer for the afternoon.

"Don't stray too far," she whispered to Daughtie Donohue. "I'm not certain I remember the names of some of the ladies."

"I'll be right by your side as soon as I hang my cloak," Daughtie replied.

"Never ya mind. I'll be takin' that for ya," Kiara said, grasping the cloak before

Daughtie could object.

"Kiara insisted there was nothing that needed to be done in the kitchen until later, and she might as well impress the ladies with her ability to act as my maid," Jasmine said. "She is a dear friend."

"She isn't still working for you, is she? I'm certain Rogan's wages are sufficient, although I know there are days when Liam hasn't enough work to keep him busy."

"On those days when Liam can't keep Rogan busy, I do. He helps out with the horses at every opportunity. Paddy and Mr. Fisher do a fine job, but there's always plenty of work around here. Now that I'm certain Obadiah is planning to stay, I may buy some additional land and increase our stock."

Daughtie raised her eyebrows. "So he's decided to remain in Massachusetts? I thought they might feel safer if they went on to Canada."

"They're safe right here. He has his papers showing he's free, and he lives on my property."

"We both know that even papers are sometimes not enough to keep a freed man out of shackles. For their sake, don't ever involve them in helping the runaways, Jasmine. There's little doubt that their house is the first place where bounty hunters are going to look. Eventually, they'll come to realize that they're not involved, but you should prepare Obadiah for his house being searched and possible ill treatment."

Jasmine arched and straightened her shoulders until she looked like a soldier standing at attention. "Not while he lives on my property!"

Daughtie motioned toward a group of women entering the house and then whispered to Jasmine, "Anyone in this group you don't know?"

"No. I remember all of them," Jasmine whispered in return before turning her attention to the clustered visitors. "Welcome, ladies. Kiara will take your wraps, and then you may go into the parlor."

After all the expected members had arrived, Jasmine welcomed the group before requesting Daughtie come forward to direct the meeting.

Appearing younger than her thirty and five years in a golden taupe silk dress, Daughtie gracefully moved forward to face the assembled group. "I'm pleased to see so many in attendance and want to first tell you that your good works have helped many on their journey to freedom. However, we cannot rest upon our past good deeds. There is much work that remains before us, and I hope each of you will prove equal to the task. We've received word that arrangements are being made for the movement of another large group of runaways. They will assemble together for their journey northward."

"How many and exactly when are they arriving?" Nettie Harper inquired.

"I can only tell you early spring, Nettie. Quite frankly, the less information we have, the better it is. A slip of the tongue can prove dangerous," she said with a pleasant smile.

"I merely wondered how much time we would have to acquire goods for them. There isn't much left on hand."

"Exactly," Daughtie said. "We are in dire need of replenishing supplies, and that is why I asked Jasmine to hostess this meeting. None of us realized there would be so many provisions required for the last large group that passed through. And, of course, there have been several smaller groups since then. At this particular point, we couldn't be of substantial assistance to even a small number of runaways."

"Except to hide them and escort them onward. I'd say that's substantial," Elinor stated.

"Well, of course, Elinor," Daughtie agreed. "Our highest priority is to provide safe haven, but my prayer is that we will concentrate our efforts and do much more than that."

Elinor moved to the edge of her chair and leaned forward to gaze upon the assembled women. "I suppose you are all aware that the South is not going to continue tolerating Northern assistance to runaways. Is there some plan how the Society is going to handle that matter?"

Jasmine glanced back and forth between Daughtie and Elinor. "Having recently been in the South, I don't think we have major concerns at this point. Let's not borrow trouble."

"My thought also. You're always expecting the worst instead of celebrating our successes," Nettie Harper snapped.

Elinor glared at the older woman. "Perhaps life has taught me to proceed with caution, Nettie. Unlike you, I've encountered more tragedy than success in my years."

"If we could get back to the reason why we've gathered," Daughtie interjected, "I'd like to focus our energies upon collecting necessities. I've given thought to having each of you take charge of one specific type of goods."

Nettie waved her handkerchief in Daughtie's direction. "I'd like to be in charge of quilts and blankets."

"I've assigned quilts and blankets to Hannah," Daughtie replied. "With your exceptional needlework, I hoped you would agree to take charge of clothing for babies and children."

"Well, 'tis true my stitching is finer than most," she said, pursing her lips into a tight knot. "I suppose I *am* better suited for something more difficult than blankets and quilts."

"Might be good for you to check the Scriptures addressing the issue of pride," Elinor muttered.

"Speak up, Elinor. You're mumbling," Nettie snapped.

Jasmine noted the flash of anger in Elinor's eyes and interrupted before an argument could ensue. "What about *other* articles of clothing, Daughtie? Have those been assigned?"

Daughtie glanced at the list she was now holding in her hand. "Elinor, I wondered if you would take charge of shoes. Is that acceptable?"

Elinor looked around the room, obviously expecting someone to challenge her assignment. When there was no objection, she nodded her head. "I'm certain many of the mill girls can be persuaded to donate their old shoes. We need only tell them we're collecting for the needy. I'll ask the other keepers to spread the word."

"That's a wonderful idea," Jasmine commented. Finally, Elinor was exhibiting some enthusiasm!

Elinor gave her a modest smile. "Do you think so?"

"Absolutely," Jasmine replied.

Nettie tapped on the walnut table beside her chair until she gained the group's attention. "That may well work for ladies and even the older children, but how do you propose getting shoes for the men? Now there's a task you'll not resolve quite so easily."

"Rest assured I'll find a solution," Elinor curtly assured.

Chapter 8

June

Elinor brushed a damp curl from her cheek and absently tucked the strand of loose hair behind one ear. Momentarily gazing into the cloudless sky, she continued walking. The scorching sun had slipped beneath the horizon, yet the penetrating afternoon heat lingered. Days of abnormally high temperatures had passed without any sign of intruding rain, and now strained tempers and harsh words had begun to gain a stronghold among members of the community. Elinor had not been immune to the scourge. Standing over a hot stove and cooking three meals a day while performing the myriad of other chores required of her to keep her boardinghouse had taken its toll.

The stir of a faint breeze cooled the beads of perspiration forming along her upper lip and forehead and provided a momentary respite from the heat. Clouds of dust billowed from the roadway as horse-drawn wagons and carriages passed by. Elinor angrily brushed the mounting layers of grimy film from within the folds of her foam green gown.

"I should have remained at the boarding-house. I'll have to beat the dust out of this dress before I can wear it again," she muttered.

"Talking to yourself?"

Elinor whirled around and was met by a smiling Oliver Maxwell. "Mr. Maxwell! I didn't realize you were walking behind me."

"Actually, I was running. For such a little lady, you have quite a stride. Might I ask why you find it necessary to maintain such a rapid pace — if you don't think me overly bold for inquiring," he hastily added.

"I'm on my way to the antislavery meeting at the Baptist church, and if I stand here much longer, I'm going to be late. There won't be a seat remaining. Do forgive me for hurrying off, but I'm already weary and I don't want to stand throughout the meeting."

"Well, isn't *this* a fortunate coincidence? I'm on my way to the very same meeting. I would be most pleased to accompany you," he offered while brandishing his black hat in a grand sweeping motion and bowing from the waist.

The wind whipped at Elinor's skirts, twisting the chambray fabric around her legs. She gave a tug to her skirt and then pushed her teetering hat back into place. Her lips formed a diminutive frown. "Strange, but in all the visits you've made to the boardinghouse, I don't believe I've ever heard you make mention of being involved in the antislavery movement," she said as she placed a firm hold on her chapeau.

"During my travels I've learned to keep my personal feelings and beliefs to myself." His gaze shifted and he glanced over his shoulder. "One never knows who can be trusted. As I'm certain you're aware, even the various residents of a boardinghouse may have differing opinions when it comes to the slavery issue."

" 'Tis true there are a few girls in my own boardinghouse who disagree with the antislavery movement. However, those girls have no ulterior motive. They are merely self-involved youth with seemingly little compassion for anyone. I wonder, however, if you fear that your shoe sales will be affected should you divulge your opposition to slavery?"

Oliver tilted his head to one side and scrunched his eyebrows. "My intentions are sincere — I remain silent only to protect those connected with the cause. I consider myself much like you: I simply want to help where needed."

Elinor's cheeks flamed with embarrassment. "I apologize, Mr. Maxwell. I'm certain you think me rather suspicious, but it seems I come in contact with many who have ulterior motives. While I believe there are those who need help as much as the slaves, I do not think it appropriate to become attached to a cause merely to benefit oneself. Wouldn't you agree?" she asked as they continued onward toward the meeting.

"Certainly I concur with your opinion. The country would be in far better condition if we would all place others before ourselves. Those poor slaves are suffering beyond what any of us can imagine."

Elinor merely nodded her agreement. However, she wanted to tell him that she, too, had suffered beyond what anyone could imagine — not at the hands of a cruel plantation owner, but her suffering was every bit as painful. She had buried two husbands and been left in poverty — forced to support herself by keeping house for unappreciative mill girls. Yet, she remained silent. Voicing the afflictions she had been forced to tolerate would make her seem trivial and self-indulgent — the very traits for which she had berated others only moments earlier before being reminded by a nagging, clawing guilt that she had attended her first antislavery meeting simply because she feared isolation. She then joined the small group aiding the Underground Railroad, for she knew the meetings would provide her with much-needed social contact — not because she genuinely believed in the cause. She continued attending more from a need to escape the boardinghouse than a genuine desire to free the slaves from their bondage. However, being a part of the effort had begun to alter her beliefs. She now took pleasure in reaching the goals assigned by the small group. The days of believing life intolerable were fewer, and she even indulged herself with a small glimmer of hope from time to time. She also enjoyed the larger gatherings, where they heard orators proclaiming the good being accomplished by Northern activists.

"We'd best take these seats. Doesn't appear there's anything closer," Oliver remarked.

Elinor agreed with his advice and, after gathering her skirts, edged past several couples already seated in the row. "This will be fine. I don't think we'll have any difficulty hearing the speakers," she said as Oliver situated himself beside her.

"I see several of the keepers are in attendance," he said, nodding toward Mrs. Ebert and Mrs. Wynn.

"Yes, they generally attend," Elinor absently remarked. "Oh, it appears they're ready to begin. We got here none too early."

In a show of unity for the cause, ministers from several churches were seated on the dais, and each took a moment at the lectern to expound upon the good deeds accomplished by their individual congregations on behalf of the antislavery movement. After listening to the preachers ramble on for nearly an hour, the sound of shuffling feet and agitated murmurs began to permeate the room.

The minister of the Freewill Baptist Church finally stepped forward. "I'm sorry to announce that our speaker for the evening has not yet arrived." The balding pastor glanced over his shoulder toward the preachers seated behind him and then turned back toward the gathered crowd. "We had hoped that Mr. Alderson might appear during our introductory remarks. However, it's obvious he's been detained, and it now seems quite doubtful he will arrive in time to present his scheduled lecture. Since the evening is warm — especially in this overfilled room, I think it best if we dismiss — unless you absolutely insist upon staying to hear about the good deeds of *my* congregation."

A smattering of laughter could be heard as the crowd rose to its feet and began inching their way out of the room. Silently chastising herself for having left home without a fan, Elinor flapped her limp handkerchief back and forth, hoping to create a breeze. Turning sideways, Elinor continued moving forward, irritated at those who blocked the passageway as they stopped to visit with one another.

"Finally! I thought we would never get through that group."

Oliver smiled down at her, revealing a small dimple in his right cheek. "Just appeared as though folks wanted to stop and exchange pleasantries for a few minutes," he remarked.

"Boorish behavior," Elinor snapped. "Those who wish to visit should step out of the aisle. It's much too warm to be held captive in that narrow passageway by a swarm of people. For a moment I thought I might faint."

"Rest assured I would have caught you

before you neared the floor," Oliver nobly stated.

Elinor fanned her hanky a bit more rapidly. "Why, thank you, Mr. Maxwell. I take comfort knowing you were looking after my welfare."

"I am hoping you'll grant me the opportunity to look after your welfare a bit longer. If you don't object, I'd be honored to escort you home," he said as he offered his arm.

"I suppose that would be acceptable." Elinor surveyed the crowd before taking his arm.

"Afraid someone might see us together?" he inquired, his grin returning.

"No. Well, yes, I suppose I am," she admitted. "The girls who board with me take pleasure in gossiping. I'm certain they would find great delight in discussing the fact that I am in your company."

"Is *that* all? Well, let them talk! They can whisper and giggle and make up any story they so desire. If they derive pleasure from seeing us together, let them have their enjoyment."

"They don't enjoy *observing* us, Mr. Maxwell. They enjoy *gossiping.* If one of them sees us, she'll spread the word. By week's end, everyone at the Appleton Mill will have us betrothed."

He tipped his hat at a passerby and then turned back to Elinor. "They could say much worse. In fact, I'd be flattered if folks believed a lady as lovely as you would consider marrying an itinerant shoe peddler."

She gave him a demure smile. "You flatter me, Mr. Maxwell."

"Not so, Mrs. Brighton. I speak the truth," he said as they continued down the street. "I admire a lady who has proven she can not only support herself, but also keep her beauty and charm intact while doing so."

"Thank you for your kind words. Now tell me, where do you call home, Mr. Maxwell?"

"Wherever I put my head down for the night," he cheerfully replied.

"Surely you have someplace you consider your home," she pressed.

"Baltimore is where I was born and reared and where my mother and sister continue to reside. However, I much prefer New England. My shoe business has flourished in this area. Of course, the cold weather means folks need good warm shoes and boots."

"From the number of shoes you sell in my boardinghouse alone, it would appear you could permanently remain in Lowell. Seems the girls always have money to spend on themselves. Why, I believe some of them have at least three pairs of shoes — and the money they spend on jewelry and fabric . . . why, it's almost sinful. They could put their money and energies to better use, if you ask me. While girls in the other boardinghouses show a genuine interest in helping with the antislavery cause and expanding their minds at the lyceums or writing for the *Lowell Offering,* none of the girls in my house appears interested in anything other than spending money on herself and finding a husband."

"They're young and will likely expand their horizons in a year or two. However, I do understand your exasperation with their behavior. Especially when more help is always needed for good causes such as the antislavery movement and the Underground Railroad."

Elinor stopped and turned toward him. "You know of the Underground Railroad movement in Lowell?"

"Of course. I likely shouldn't tell you this, but I know you can be trusted. There are hundreds of runaways who have benefited from the simple maps I've drawn for their use. With my constant travels throughout New England, I'm aware of new roads and houses — you know, changes taking place along the route into Canada. I update the maps as needed. I like to think I'm providing a useful service to those operating the Underground Railroad as well as the runaways."

Elinor's brows furrowed and creases lined her forehead. "I didn't realize." She hesitated and stared up into his cobalt blue eyes. "I've never heard anyone speak of your connection with the Underground."

"I'm pleased to know my involvement astonished you. That alone verifies the fact that my participation in the Underground hasn't been widely exposed."

She nodded her agreement. After all, anonymity was vital to the cause. There were likely hundreds involved whose identities were unknown to her. "How long have you been helping?" she ventured as they walked down Merrimack Street.

"Many years. I find the work gratifying, don't you?"

"Oh, yes. However, there are times I worry about difficulties that might arise. I certainly can't afford to lose my position with the Corporation."

"Oh, I don't think you need worry in that regard," he said. "I'm certain they have much more important matters worrying them than a few employees aiding the Underground Railroad. Besides, it's my understanding that the mill owners are publicly supportive of the abolitionist movement."

"You're probably correct on that account, but one can never be too careful." They reached the front door of the boardinghouse. "Would you care to come in for a glass of lemonade?"

"Something cool to drink would be most welcome," he replied.

Elinor entered the hallway and carefully removed her hat. "Why don't you have a seat in the parlor and I'll fetch our lemonade."

She hurried off to the kitchen, pleased to see none of her boarders were in the parlor. Had any of the girls known Mr. Maxwell would make an appearance this evening, they would surely have been present. All of the girls made it a point to be at home when Mr. Maxwell came to sell his shoes. He was, after all, a handsome bachelor who had a way with words. Elinor poured the lemonade into two tall glasses and placed them on a wooden tray, along with a plate of sugar cookies she'd baked early that morning.

"Here we are," Elinor announced as she

returned to the room. She centered the tray on a small table in front of the sofa and then offered Oliver one of the glasses of cool lemonade. His hand, warm and firm, wrapped around her fingers. The liquid sloshed toward the lip of the glass as she hastily tugged away from his grasp. "*Whatever* are you *doing?*" Her fingers splayed and she placed one hand to her chest. Perhaps the pressure of her clammy palm would still the erratic pounding of her heart.

Oliver's eyes widened as she retreated to the other side of the room. "I'm sorry. I didn't mean to offend you. Please accept my apology. I thought . . ."

Retrieving her handkerchief from the pocket of her gown, she delicately wiped her brow. "I know *exactly* what you thought, Mr. Maxwell. You believe I'm quite like the fawning mill girls who scurry to the parlor and vie for your attention the moment you enter the boardinghouse. You've decided I am a lonely widow in need of companionship who will compromise her behavior and morals. Well, I am *not*! I offered you a glass of lemonade, nothing more."

"Dear lady, please forgive me. You extended your hospitality and friendship, and I behaved boorishly. I meant no harm. I find your conversation refreshing after endless hours of listening to the prattle of mill girls who insist upon having me call on them two or three times before placing an order for their shoes."

"Is that what they do? There is no doubt such behavior would soon become incommodious."

Oliver nodded and took a sip of his lemonade. "I don't want to strain our friendship further. If you prefer I leave immediately, I will abide by your decision. However, it is my fervent desire to remain in your company and become better acquainted."

Elinor loosened her grip on the wadded handkerchief in her hand. "I suppose it would be acceptable since we now understand each other."

"Thank you for your kindness. Now, won't you please sit down? I know you must be weary."

Pleased by the obvious concern in his voice, Elinor sat down opposite him and picked up her glass of lemonade. "Do tell me more of your association with the antislavery movement. How did you become involved?"

Oliver rubbed his forehead. "I hope you won't be offended, but I'm not at liberty to discuss any further details of my involvement. I've likely already told you too much.

What with my travels, I've become acquainted with many people like yourself who are helping with the cause. I've made it a practice never to divulge names or relate facts that might jeopardize those who are a part of the movement. I would never want it said that Oliver Maxwell was the cause of a failed escape."

"An admirable quality, Mr. Maxwell. How could I possibly be offended? I realize the need for secrecy. Even our small group of women who help with the Underground Railroad must remain cautious. We've learned that attendance at antislavery meetings doesn't necessarily mean one favors the cause."

"Exactly my point," he agreed. "Of course, there is no doubt in my mind that you are trustworthy, or I wouldn't have even told you about my work preparing maps. On second thought, I don't believe it would be imprudent for me to share more of my background with you."

"No, no — I wouldn't consider encouraging you to do such a thing," she replied hastily.

"Then if it wouldn't pain you to discuss your past, I would be honored if you would tell me more about yourself."

Elinor hesitated. Revealing private information with someone who was practically a stranger was foreign to her. Aside from her brother, she lived in a town filled with strangers. How could she expect to form friendships if she remained unwilling to disclose even a part of herself?

"My childhood was quite pleasant. I came to America when I was nine years of age. My brother, Taylor Manning, and my uncle, John Farnsworth, had come to America to work for the Corporation. Taylor had recently married, and he and his new bride, Bella, came to England on their wedding trip. I returned with them and have been in America since that time."

"Your parents?"

"Deceased. Taylor and Bella were good to me, and living in their home made me desire the pleasure of a good marriage such as theirs. When I was seventeen I met Wilbur Stewart, and we were married when I was eighteen. He was a kind young man and I loved him very much," she said, pausing momentarily.

"I trust you were happy in your marriage to Mr. Stewart."

Her eyes clouded briefly. "He drowned only weeks after our marriage. I thought I would never love another and yet, two years later I met and married Daniel Brighton.

We moved to Philadelphia, where Daniel worked for the newspaper. He contracted yellow fever and was dead six months after our wedding day."

Oliver hunched forward, his hands folded together as he met her gaze. "My dear, dear Mrs. Brighton. How you have suffered. Having buried two husbands, I understand your fear of ever again giving your heart to another. Yet I would be honored if you would count me among your friends."

Elinor tugged at the lace edging of her handkerchief before glancing up at Oliver and sending him the ghost of a smile. She wondered at her own willingness to share such private information with this stranger. Yet he seemed to sense her fragile condition. "Thank you, Mr. Maxwell," she whispered. "Your kindness has touched my heart."

Chapter 9

Jasmine hurried down the stairway at the sound of her grandmother's voice. "Grandmother, what a pleasant surprise!"

"I was anxious for a visit with my great-grandson. I suppose you're going to tell me he's napping or some other nonsense," Alice Wainwright said while offering her cheek for a perfunctory kiss.

Jasmine bent and kissed her grandmother's rouged cheek. "Of course not. However, he is with Naomi and Moses. They can't seem to escape the house without him. Naomi comes over to help with chores or ask a question, and Spencer insists upon returning home with them."

"I hope you're not giving in to the boy's every whim, Jasmine. You don't want him to grow up thinking he can always have his way. Discipline! That's the key to excellent child rearing."

Jasmine looped arms with her grandmother and led her into the parlor. "He doesn't always get his way, Grandmother, but I do encourage Moses and Spencer to play together. The boys learn from each other — each of them needs a sibling. They fill a void for each other, and I've grown to love Moses. He's a sweet child."

"I agree that Moses is a fine little boy, but Spencer needs a brother or sister of his own. You need to cease this foolishness of being a contented widow and agree to marry Nolan. And I don't mean a year or two from now. As far as I'm concerned, you should be planning your marriage to Nolan at this very moment."

"I'm not certain Nolan would agree, Grandmother."

"I don't know why not. Men never want to be included in making wedding arrangements. And if you're concerned a large wedding is inappropriate for a widow, plan something simple — yet elegant, of course."

Jasmine sat down beside her grandmother. "Since Nolan has not asked me to be his wife, I think he would be somewhat surprised to hear I'm planning the details of our wedding."

"What?" Alice's pale lips formed a large oval, and she clasped a hand to her chest.

Stifling a giggle, Jasmine grasped her

grandmother's hand. "I know you believe the rumor that Nolan had asked for my hand shortly after Bradley's death, but it isn't so, Grandmother. You seem to forget that even though Bradley was not a loving brother —"

"Or husband," Alice interjected.

Jasmine nodded. "Or husband — there is still a need for honor and respect. Nolan has been a true friend and I care deeply for him. . . ."

"Oh, pshaw! The two of you need to stop this nonsense. It's obvious you love each other. Why hasn't he declared himself? Must I travel to Boston, grab him by the ear, and personally escort him to Lowell in order to force his proposal?"

"Grandmother! I can't believe you would even entertain such a notion. If and when Nolan asks me to become his wife, I want it to be his idea — *not* yours. Please promise me you will not interfere."

"When he finally asks, you'll agree to marry him? You do love him, don't you?"

Jasmine lowered her eyes. "Yes, I love him, and I would be pleased to marry him."

"Well, then, that's settled. Now, when do I get to see my great-grandson?"

"If you like we could walk over and you could see the progress being made on the new house for Naomi and Obadiah."

"That sounds like an excellent idea. I know you feel an obligation to Obadiah, but I want you to remember the concern that arose when Mammy was here in Lowell — folks upset that a slave was living under your roof. Since you have Obadiah's family living on your property, there are those who will assume they are slaves."

"There is a vast difference between the two situations. After all, Mammy *was* a slave. That fact aside, if there were concerns, I think I would have heard some rumors by now, don't you?"

"It's difficult to know. The mills give rise to a more transient populace, and there's always the chance someone will arrive in town, pleased to cast aspersions."

"Both Obadiah and Naomi carry their papers showing they are free, and all of the local merchants know them as freed. Should any question arise, I think there are many who would vouch that they came here as freed slaves and live on my property by their own choice. They come and go at their own pleasure and are paid a wage the same as the others who work for me. If they were white, no one would question the arrangement."

"You need not defend yourself to me, Jasmine. *I* realize they are free. I merely ask that you remain alert. Ah, I see my great-grandson is not afraid of becoming dirty," she said, pointing toward the boys.

"They seem to think that mound of dirt is their personal playground. It takes quite a dousing to get Spencer clean after he's been hard at play."

"From all appearances, I can only imagine," Alice agreed. "It looks like Obadiah has made good progress on the new house. Have you hired any additional help, or is he doing all the work himself?"

"I've hired several men to assist with the labor. I've recently purchased additional horses — breeding stock. Paddy and Mr. Fisher need Obadiah's assistance in the barns. I don't expect Obadiah to spend his days working with the horses and helping with farm chores and then build a house by himself."

"You're much too defensive, Jasmine. I was merely inquiring, not preparing to condemn you. It's of no concern to me if you have the entire house constructed for him."

"I'm sorry, Grandmother. After your earlier comments regarding the slavery issue, I suppose I felt a need to defend all of my decisions regarding Obadiah." Jasmine turned her attention back toward the two little boys. “Spencer! Look who’s come to see you,” she called.

The boys glanced toward the two women, and both came running on wobbly legs. Naomi stood in the doorway of the house, wiping her hands on a frayed calico apron. “Moses! You stay here. That ain’t your granny.”

Moses stopped momentarily, his gaze shifting between his mother and his little friend, who continued running toward the women.

“It’s all right,” Jasmine called to Naomi. “I’ll look after him.”

“But I gotta take food over to da Marlows. You want me to tell Obadiah to come fetch Moses when he be done working in da barn?”

“That will be fine. You go ahead,” Jasmine said.

“Naomi is cooking for another family?” Alice asked as Spencer bounded into her skirts, his chubby fingers clinging to the deep folds of fabric.

“Yes. Nancy Marlow has been ill for several weeks. Henry asked Naomi if she would prepare meals for them. He has no family nearby, and with three strapping young boys, he needed help. I told Naomi she didn't need to feel obligated to take on the additional work, but she said she wanted to earn the extra coins. I think she's hoping to earn enough to purchase some new items for the house," Jasmine explained. "I fear your gown will need a cleaning," Jasmine continued while pointing to the smudges of dirt on Alice's rose and paisley print skirt.

"Seeing this happy little fellow is worth the trouble." Alice grasped Spencer by the hand. "Come along, young man. Let's go back to the house and have some cookies, shall we?"

"Tookie," Moses mimicked.

"Yes, Moses. We'll get you a cookie," Jasmine replied, taking him by the hand. "If you'd like to fix a plate of cookies and some lemonade for the boys, I'll see if I can wipe some of this grime from their faces and hands."

Once the boys were settled with their cookies, Alice gave Jasmine a thoughtful look. "I believe Spencer is getting old enough to come home with me from time to time. What do you think?"

"I don't think he'd be happy to make an overnight visit without me."

"No, of course not. But he could spend the afternoon occasionally, don't you agree?"

"Yes, but you must remember that he's become accustomed to having Moses nearby. I doubt you could handle both of them for an afternoon. They can become quite rowdy."

Alice chuckled and nodded in agreement. "Yes, I can well remember having three boys of my own years ago. Your father was always antagonizing one of his brothers."

"And I'm certain Uncle Franklin and Uncle Harry caused their share of problems also."

"Indeed, the three of them were quite a handful. I do miss those days. Don't let this time slip away from you, Jasmine. I wish I had spent more time with my children when they were young. Back then I thought it more important to attend social functions than be with my children. Now I have all the time in the world to attend teas and parties, but what I desire is having family near me."

Jasmine noted the tears clouding her grandmother's hazel eyes. "If it's that important to you, Grandmother, we can decide upon an afternoon and I'll bring Spencer each week. Would you like that?"

"Yes," she said, the gleam returning to her gaze. "What about Wednesdays?"

Jasmine nodded. "We'll begin next week

and see how both you and Spencer make it through the afternoon."

"Good. I'll go home and begin making plans for our first afternoon together. You need not see me to the door. You stay here with the boys," Alice said before kissing Spencer's cheek and hugging Moses goodbye.

Alice called out a final farewell as she departed the front door. "We'll see you on Wednesday," Jasmine called in return.

Moments later, Jasmine spun around at the sound of the front door closing, which was immediately followed by footsteps and chattering. "Look who was arriving as I was leaving the house," Alice chortled, pulling Kiara forward. "I couldn't leave. I wanted to see your face when she tells you her news."

Kiara was beaming, her cheeks flush and her dark brown eyes shining. "I'm goin' to have a baby," she said. "I was goin' to wait to tell, but Rogan is announcin' the news to every stranger he meets," she said. "He can't seem to keep the matter to 'imself."

"I'm so happy for you, Kiara. I know how much this means to you and Rogan. When do you expect the baby?"

"Not until the end of January. That's why I told Rogan 'twas foolish to be spreadin' the word so soon."

"I don't blame him. He's happy and proud, and I'm happy for both of you," Jasmine said, embracing Kiara. "And what does young Paddy think of all this? Is he anxious to become an uncle?"

"Aye. Between Rogan and Paddy, there seems to be nothin' else to talk about. I told them by the time the baby finally arrives, they'll be weary of the idea."

"I don't think so," Alice said. "They'll have him out riding horses before he turns a year old!"

Kiara tilted her head to the side and laughed. "I told Rogan and Paddy I'd have their hide if they told ya before I had the chance, Jasmine. They said if I didn't come over and tell ya soon, they'd not be held responsible. I wish I had time to stay for a visit, but I must get back and fix supper."

"Promise you'll come back tomorrow when you have more time."

"I promise I'll come if ya do na mind me workin' on my lace while we visit. I've orders I can na keep up with."

"Bring your lace and whatever else you must, but please come and visit with me."

"It's agreed, then. If ya're leavin', Mrs. Wainwright, I'll walk out with ya," Kiara said.

Jasmine followed along behind the two women, with Moses and Spencer each clasping one of her hands. The three of them watched from the wraparound front porch as their guests departed and then remained outdoors, with the boys playing on the porch while Jasmine sat embroidering an intricate pattern on a pair of silk stockings.

"This is certainly our day for unexpected company," Jasmine said to the boys as a horse-drawn wagon turned into the driveway and came to a stop in front of the house.

"Good day, ma'am. Oliver Maxwell's the name," the man said while jumping down from the wagon and removing his hat with a flair.

"Good day."

"I'm a shoe peddler well acquainted with the residents of Lowell but decided I would begin including some of the surrounding community when I come to call upon the boardinghouses and other residents in town. Would you be interested in the purchase of a pair of new kid slippers for yourself or perhaps some new riding boots for your husband?" Oliver glanced toward the two boys. "Or some fine new shoes for your sons?"

"Shoes," Spencer said, pointing toward his feet.

Moses giggled and pulled at his shoe. "Shoes."

"Yes, you both have shoes," Jasmine said with a smile. "But they are certainly worn, and you could both use a new pair. In fact, I imagine everyone in the household would benefit from some new shoes. Why don't you measure the boys' feet, and then we'll go out to the barn. I have several men working for me, and you can measure them also."

Jasmine watched as the salesman removed Spencer's shoes and carefully made drawings of her son's feet. The peddler had a way with the children, making them laugh as he traced around their small bare feet.

"What names should I place on the drawings?" he asked.

"Spencer on the larger size and Moses on the smaller," she replied.

"There's a size difference in the boys' shoes, but your sons appear to be about the same age. Are they twins?" Mr. Maxwell asked.

Jasmine smiled at the question. "No, they're close friends. But you're correct about their ages. They were born within nine weeks of each other."

He gave a triumphant nod. "Are you

certain they're not related — cousins, maybe? They sure favor one another with that dark wavy hair and those big brown eyes."

It was difficult for Jasmine to keep from laughing aloud. She'd often thought the same thing when the boys were toddling about the house or playing in the yard together. Grandmother Wainwright called their resemblance uncanny, and Jasmine agreed. No one, including Mr. Maxwell, would ever guess one of the boys was a Negro. Jasmine waited while the salesman returned his tools to the buggy and then mounted the box of his small wagon. "If you'll follow the driveway to the back, it will lead you to the barn. I'll meet you there."

"Thank you, ma'am," he said, once again tipping his hat and giving her a broad smile.

By the time Jasmine had corralled the two boys back through the house and out to the barn, Mr. Maxwell, Paddy, Obadiah, and her old groomsman, Richard Fisher, were all gathered together.

"Papa!" Moses cried as he scurried with outstretched arms toward Obadiah.

Mr. Maxwell looked in all directions and then watched with widened eyes as Moses buried his tiny cherub face in Obadiah's pant legs. The peddler's fingers tightened around the leather reins until his knuckles were void of color. His mouth was compressed into a thin, hard line. She should have told him, for he was obviously embarrassed by his earlier remarks.

"Why don't you measure Paddy first, and then he can water your horse, if you like," Jasmine suggested.

Mr. Maxwell jumped down from the wagon seat and turned toward Padraig. "I'm sure the horse would appreciate it, and I know I'd be pleased," he said to the boy. "I've quite a ways to travel yet today."

Paddy rubbed one hand down the horse's withers and gave the strawberry roan a firm pat before leaning down to pull off his boots. "Sure and that's a fine-lookin' mare ya got. I'll be pleased ta water her for ya," he said, pushing a tousled mass of black curls off his forehead.

"I'm certain she doesn't compare to the horseflesh you're accustomed to taking care of around here, but she serves me well," Mr. Maxwell said, placing a piece of paper atop a wooden board.

Paddy placed his foot on the paper and watched as Mr. Maxwell carefully traced around it. "I'm learnin' horses are a lot like people. Can't be judgin' 'em only by appearance or ya'll be disappointed. Sometimes the ugly ones turn out to be much better than the beauties. Kinda like they need to be provin' themselves because they do na have their beauty to depend upon."

"You're wise for your years, young man. Beauty is only skin deep, but there are those of us that will never completely learn that lesson. We like a woman that is easy on the eyes," Mr. Maxwell commented as he finished the drawings.

Paddy pulled on his boots. "I'll na be denying a pretty lass is hard to overlook, but it's the plain ones that cook up a tasty stew and keep yar house in order."

"Well, I think there are many exceptions to that observation," Jasmine said with a grin. "Your sister, Kiara, being the first one that comes to mind."

"Aye, and for sure ya're right about Kiara as well as yarself, ma'am," he hastily added. "But most times the pretty lasses depend upon their looks rather than their skills ta carry them through life. Do ya na think that's so?"

Mr. Maxwell gave Paddy a hearty laugh. "Sometimes it's best to cease defending yourself. I believe this may be one of those instances. Why don't you go ahead and care for my horse," he said, giving the boy a quick wink.

Paddy left the others and approached the horse. "Top of the day to ya," Paddy said as he reached up to stroke the animal's mane. "For sure ya're a lovely one. I don't suppose yar owner would be havin' time for me to unhitch ya and treat ya proper, but we'll be doin' our best."

Paddy walked back to the wagon, released the brake, and then came alongside the mare once again. "We'll just be headin' over yonder for somethin' to drink." The animal seemed completely at ease with him. Kiara often told him he had a gift from God. A sort of ability to know what the horses were thinking, and because of this the animals would work for him in ways they would not for other people. Paddy didn't know if that was exactly the truth, but he knew he loved the beasts.

As the horse drank her fill, Paddy studied the pattern of her coat. He hadn't seen but one other strawberry roan in all his life. The mottling color was a wonder, to be sure. The undercoat was basically that of a chestnut, but the body was covered with white hair, giving it a pinkish tint against the reddish brown. Paddy thought it quite lovely.

He ran his hand down the muscular shoulder and forearm, immediately noticing the clubbed right foot. The inward turn wasn't overstated, but it was enough of one that a trained eye could easily spot the trouble.

"Ya're a fine one," Paddy said, running his hand up the mare's leg. "For sure ya don't let your infirmities stop ya."

The mare turned her head ever so slightly and bobbed it up and down as if agreeing. Paddy gave a hearty laugh. "Ya'll do just fine, I'm thinkin'. I wouldn't mind havin' ya meself." He walked the mare back to the barn and resecured the brake. "I'll be findin' yar master and lettin' him know ya're ready to go." Paddy glanced over his shoulder conspiratorially and added, "But first a wee treat." He pulled out a piece of dried apple and offered it to the mare. She gobbled the treat quickly, then nuzzled his hand for more.

"Now don't be greedy, lass. Come back and see me again, and thar'll be more of that."

Paddy walked away whistling a tune. He loved his life here in America. He sometimes remembered the bad days in Ireland. The pain of losing his da and ma had been like nothing he'd ever known, but Kiara had always been good to him — always watching out for him. Even when there'd been no food, his sister had found ways to see that he ate — even when she went hungry. The memories sometimes turned him to great anger and sorrow, but then like a fog lifting from those emerald shores, he'd remember those days were gone and could no longer hurt him.

"Like Kiara says, they can only be hurtin' me if I let them."

"Who you talkin' to?" Obadiah asked as Paddy entered the barn.

"Meself. I'm the only one who'll be listenin' to such foolery," Paddy replied with a grin.

Obadiah laughed. "And what you be tellin' yo'self?"

"That the bad things of the past can't be hurtin' me unless I let them." Paddy's serious tone had a sobering effect on the broad-shouldered man.

Obadiah nodded slowly. "Dat be da truth — no foolery there. I think that most of da time. Bad times come to mind, but they be in da past and need to stay dere."

"Aye, 'tis true," Paddy answered, knowing that the black man had much more to fear from his past than did Paddy. " 'Tis true."

■ ■ ■ ■

Elinor hurried to the front door as the persistent knocking grew louder with each passing moment. She pulled on the doorknob and looked down into the watery blue eyes of a young boy dressed in a ragged shirt and breeches. Elinor stared at the child's crusty fingers surrounding the soft, supple beauty of a small bouquet of roses, momentarily taken aback by the contrast.

"Mrs. Brighton?"

His voice brought her back to the present. "Yes. Are these for one of my boarders?" she inquired.

"No, ma'am. I was told they're for you." The child thrust the bouquet toward her hand.

Elinor reached to take the offering. "Who sent you?"

"Don't know. There's a note in the flowers," he said before racing back down the street.

She held the mixture of greenery and pink roses to her face, inhaling a fragrant whiff and permitting herself to be transported back to another time, happier days when she was married to Daniel and life was filled with joy and excitement. Removing her cut-glass vase from the uppermost shelf of the china closet, Elinor remembered how she would scold Daniel for picking the neighbors' flowers as he came home from work on a summer's evening and how his deep laughter would fill the room while he placed the flowers in water.

"Stop this reminiscing or you'll soon be weeping," she chided herself while discarding the damp paper surrounding the bouquet. The boy had been correct. There was a note tucked deep among the flowers. The words were written in a strong masculine script:

> Dear Mrs. Brighton,
>
> I realize my behavior earlier this week was far too bold. Please accept my apology. It is my fervent desire you will accept my offer of friendship. I ask nothing more.
>
> Your humble servant,
> Oliver Maxwell

"Oliver! I never expected such gallantry," she murmured.

The sound of the front door closing echoed through the house and was soon followed by the chattering girls returning home for supper. Elinor automatically checked the clock sitting on the mantel. It appeared she was on schedule and the meal would be ready on time.

"Are those flowers for Jane?" Nancy Engle inquired while walking into the parlor.

Elinor glanced over her shoulder. "No, they're for me."

"For you?" Nancy turned toward the other girls, who were now entering the room behind her. "Why would *you* receive flowers?"

"Yes, do tell us," Jane concurred. "I'm especially interested since we have no way of knowing if the flowers were actually sent to you or meant for one of us."

Elinor's jaw tightened. "Have I ever lied to any of you? These flowers were sent to me, but if you believe otherwise, please take them," she said, yanking the flowers from the vase. She thrust the dripping bouquet at Jane, who was staring at her in open-mouthed surprise. "If they're so important to you, by all means take them," she commanded through clenched teeth.

Jane stepped back, her gaze fixed on the dripping stems. "You're getting water on the rug." She pointed toward the floor while taking another step away from Elinor.

"I don't care about the water or the carpet. If you girls think these flowers belong to one of you, please take them." Her words were low and measured as she once again propelled the flowers toward the group. "I am *not* a liar or a thief, and I *certainly* am not so anxious for a bouquet that I would claim flowers sent for one of you."

Jane nudged Nancy's arm. "I didn't mean to imply you were lying," Nancy said. "It was an honest mistake. Harry Lorimer said he was going to send Jane flowers. Didn't he, Jane?" Nancy turned a pleading gaze toward the girl.

"He did say he was going to send flowers, but we believe what you've told us, Mrs. Brighton," Jane said. "Please don't be angry. We meant no harm."

Elinor turned on her heel and placed the flowers back in the water-filled vase. "Instead of boarders who are intent upon educating themselves and doing good works, the Corporation sends me the ill-mannered, unpleasant workers. All of the fine, upstanding girls are sent to board with the other keepers. I have yet to have one girl who thinks about anyone except herself," she muttered as she returned to the kitchen.

An abnormal silence pervaded the supper table that evening. The girls filled their plates without the usual chatter, occasionally glancing toward Elinor with uncertainty. There was no diatribe about disliking the food she had prepared, nor was any comment made when the evening meal was served a half hour late. In fact, Elinor decided afterward, the evening had been the epitome of civility.

CHAPTER 10

Malcolm gave his youngest son a sidelong glance. The little boy had disappeared and was now a man of twenty and four years. McKinley's youth had evaporated as quickly as fog rising off the bayou, and the realization caused a twinge of sadness to seep into Malcolm's heart. Too late, he had acknowledged a lack of involvement with his children during their youth. Back in the days of their childhood he had eased his conscience by telling himself rearing children was a mother's responsibility. After all, he had the plantation to run and little time for anything else. It wasn't until after Madelaine's death that he'd given serious consideration to the fact that his wife might have fared better with her bouts of melancholy had he helped more with the children — or at least had given *her* more attention. But it was impossible to change the past — one could only hope to do better in the future.

McKinley brushed aside a golden-brown wave of hair that was creeping downward onto his forehead. "You're particularly quiet this morning, Father. Are you reconsidering our visit to President Taylor?"

Malcolm jerked out of his reverie and met McKinley's puzzled gaze. "No, of course not. In fact, Zachary would be irate if he discovered we were in Washington but failed to call upon him. That fact aside, I'm anxious to hear how he has been doing since we saw him last fall. After reading newspaper accounts for the past several months, I'd like to hear Zachary's version of what's been happening in Congress. I'm certain we'll receive a colorful recitation."

McKinley drank a final sip of coffee and placed his cup on the matching white china saucer. "Did you send word we'd be visiting? There's always the possibility he's away from the city. As I understand it, folks in these parts often escape the heat and dangers of the city. I believe they have trouble with fever, just as we do in the South."

"I sent a letter back in May telling him we planned to visit in late June or early July. I did pen a note after our arrival last night and left it with the hotel clerk. He promised to have it immediately delivered to the president. Besides, I doubt Zachary would depart the capital with Fourth of July activities in the offing. Have you finished your breakfast?" Malcolm asked while surveying McKinley's empty plate.

McKinley nodded and patted his flat stomach. "I've gorged myself as much as I dare. If I eat any more, I'll need to have my buttons set over at least an inch."

"Then we'd best leave — I don't want to be party to such a calamity," Malcolm said with a wide grin on his face as he pushed away from the table.

McKinley touched his father's arm and nodded toward the front desk of the hotel. "The clerk is signaling for you, Father."

Malcolm's gaze shifted to the portly clerk, who was waving a folded missive above his head. Malcolm advanced with quick strides, arriving at the desk in record time. "May I assume that message is for me?"

Thick fleshy folds settled over the clerk's collar as he lowered his head and thrust the letter toward Malcolm. "From the White House," he proudly announced while glancing about the lobby.

As Malcolm began to unfold the envelope's contents, he noted the clerk's beefy torso extended across the counter. "I'm certain you're not attempting to read my personal mail," he said as he met the man's inquisitive eyes.

The clerk jumped away from the counter. "Oh no, sir," he said, shaking his head like a wet dog attempting to dry itself.

Malcolm scanned the contents of the letter and told his son, "Zachary will be expecting us for the noonday meal. We have ample time to do a bit of exploring about the city before then. Why don't you hail a carriage, McKinley?"

The clerk was once again leaning across the counter. Eager anticipation filled his face. "You're joining the *president* for dinner?"

"You appear to have a penchant for prying into the business of the hotel guests, don't you?"

"I apologize, sir. It's just that I've never met anyone personally acquainted with the president."

The excitement in the man's voice lessened Malcolm's irritation. "Truly? Well, Zachary Taylor is a mere mortal made of flesh and bone. No different from the rest of us."

"My children will be agog when they hear I've met someone who dined with the president."

Malcolm's looked deep into the clerk's eyes and was taken aback by the awe reflected in the man's gaze. "Here — take this to your children." Malcolm handed him the missive emblazoned with Taylor's strong signature and strode off toward the front door.

Zachary entered the room, his twinkling eyes and wide smile momentarily erasing the worry lines from his craggy face. "Malcolm — and McKinley! I can't tell you what pleasure it brings having the two of you come for a visit. Peggy has made me promise we'll dine upstairs in her sitting room. She's anxious for news about you and the children. And she needs to see for herself that you've been taking care of yourself since Madelaine's death."

Malcolm clasped the president's outstretched hand. "If you're certain she's feeling up to our visit."

"I think it will improve her spirits greatly," Zachary replied. "But first, would you care for a little tour of these rooms?"

"I most certainly would. I cannot imagine coming all this way and not seeing the people's house."

"The people's house is right," Zachary said. "The people are here morning, noon, and night. That's one of the reasons my poor Peggy seeks the confines of her room.

There is never a moment when this place isn't overrun. You've come at a good time, however. Some of my staff have taken a large assembly of do-gooders and congressmen to one of the local eating establishments. They should be gone long enough to give us some liberty." He motioned them to follow.

The house was as grand and glorious as Malcolm had often heard said. He was impressed with the variety of furnishings, some which went back to the original orders of James Monroe.

"This is a lovely room," Malcolm stated as he followed his friend.

"We call it the blue room. Van Buren painted it in such a manner and it's seemed a natural color to maintain. I like its oval nature."

"As do I. It seems an entertaining room. Very unusual," Malcolm mused.

McKinley joined in pointing out the chandelier. "I believe this style would suit us well in our dining room back home. I know you've talked often of replacing the one there now."

Malcolm studied the wood and cut glass encircled with acanthus leaves. "Yes. Yes. I believe you're right."

"I can put you in touch with a workman

who might be able to replicate this piece," Taylor told them.

They continued touring, enjoying many fine parlors and receiving rooms, and even a grand dining room. Malcolm was notably impressed with all of it. "I'm glad for this opportunity, Zachary. I truly would have hated to pass from this life without seeing this wondrous house."

"I agree," McKinley added. "I shall cherish this memory."

"Now, are you quite certain Peggy will be up to this visit? I certainly wouldn't want to overstay our welcome or overtax her."

"To be honest, I think Peggy's overall health improved once Betty accepted the official role as my hostess. Peggy never did enjoy public life. She prefers the company of close friends and family. And I believe the two of you fit into both categories. But we dare not remain down here discussing anything of a personal nature or Peggy will force us to repeat our entire conversation. She made me promise to bring you directly upstairs."

"Then we had best do as instructed. Lead the way and we'll follow along," McKinley said.

Malcolm gave a hearty chuckle as they walked up the stairway. "You know, Zachary, the clerk at our hotel would be incredulous if I were to tell him you do your wife's bidding."

Zachary looked over his shoulder, his smile returning. "How so? Isn't that the first rule we husbands are taught?"

"I suppose you're right, but the hotel clerk was quite impressed that I know you. In fact, I believe I've made a lifelong friend. I took a few moments to tell him you're quite common — even told him he might see you walking about the city unobserved from time to time."

"It's one of the few things that helps me maintain my sanity while attempting to deal with those bullies who call themselves representatives of the people. There's nothing I enjoy more than making my way about this town without anyone taking notice. Amazing the things you can see and hear when folks have no idea you're the president," he said with a grin.

"I'm certain that's true," Malcolm said.

An insistent tapping could be heard as they approached an open door. "Is that Malcolm Wainwright's voice I hear in the hallway?"

"Indeed it is, my dear," the president replied as the three men walked into Peggy's sitting room.

Zachary's words were true. Peggy sat in a dark blue brocade chair, with her feet clad in silk slippers that were propped on a matching footstool. At first glance, the ornate ivory cane she held in her hand gave the appearance of a royal scepter. Attired in a dress of peach fabric with her thick white hair perfectly coifed in the latest fashion, Peggy appeared healthier than Malcolm had seen her in years. There was now a pink tinge to her cheeks, and her piercing blue eyes held a spark of vitality. Only when she stood to take Zachary's arm and walk to the dining table did her frail health become evident. She leaned heavily upon her carved cane with one hand and held tightly to her husband's arm with the other, the tap of her cane slow and labored, unlike the insistent knocking he'd earlier heard.

Malcolm watched as Peggy slowly settled herself at the table and then turned her gaze toward him. "I want to hear how your family is managing, Malcolm. I can see that McKinley has turned into a handsome young fellow. I can't imagine how you've managed to escape all those Southern belles, young man."

McKinley grinned at the older woman. "I've not yet met the young lady to whom I'm ready to commit the rest of my life. And who knows — I may decide to leave the comfort of The Willows one day, and most Southern women prefer to remain among their families."

Peggy nodded her affirmation. "I'd say you've a sound head on your shoulders, McKinley. Marriage is not a commitment to be taken lightly. The vows you make are not only to the one you love, but also to God. You'll know when the time is right. And how is Jasmine? Has she decided to return home to Mississippi and care for the Wainwright men?"

Malcolm's gaze remained fixed on McKinley, for he was still not completely certain he'd understood his youngest son's reply. McKinley had never before indicated a desire to leave Mississippi.

Peggy gave an insistent tap of her cane. "I was asking about Jasmine's returning home, Malcolm."

Malcolm rubbed his jaw as though he were suddenly plagued by an aching tooth. "No, I don't believe any of us gave that idea much consideration — including Jasmine. She is quite happy living in the North, and I doubt she could be convinced to leave. In fact, we're on our way north on business and will be staying for a visit with Jasmine and my mother."

"I'm certain it would ease your loss if she would return to The Willows," Peggy said.

"I wouldn't consider asking her to do so. She would be eternally unhappy. In addition, I fear my mother has turned Jasmine into a Northern sympathizer."

Peggy leaned forward, her fork in midair. "How so?"

"I believe she's become an antislavery activist and forgotten her true Southern heritage."

McKinley shifted and edged forward on his chair. "Just because Jasmine opposes slavery doesn't mean she's forgotten her heritage."

There was a spark of anger in McKinley's gaze, and Malcolm knew he'd offended his son. He no longer knew with certainty what McKinley was thinking, but he didn't want his comment to escalate into a family argument. "No, of course not. Tell me, Zachary, how are you progressing with issues before the Congress?"

With a hand on either side of his plate, Zachary used the table for leverage and leaned back against the chair's hard wood. "I suppose you've already heard about my stormy conference with the Southern leadership back in February — I managed to anger most of them."

Malcolm smoothed the fringe of hair that circled his bald head. "I think it could be more appropriately stated that you angered *all* of them, Zachary. I wonder if that whole ordeal couldn't have been handled more diplomatically."

"They're hardheaded when it comes to the issue of slavery, Malcolm. You know that better than most. There's no reasoning with them. They all believed I would bow to their whims because I own slaves. You know as well as the next man that I respect slave-holders' rights in the fifteen states where the institution is legal. I adamantly oppose the extension of slavery. I am not going to jeopardize the Union because of the extension issue. My position was clear, but I sat quietly and permitted them the courtesy of expressing their views. Yet, after they saw that I would not be swayed, they began talking of secession. It was at that point I told them that if they rose up against the laws of this land and the Union, I would personally lead the army against them."

"If memory serves me, you also told your Southern brothers you wouldn't hesitate to hang them just as you had done to deserters and spies during the Mexican War," Malcolm added.

"More than that, I told them that if they

were taken in rebellion against the Union, I would hang them with *less* reluctance than I'd shown toward the traitors in Mexico — and I meant every word I uttered."

Malcolm stared at Zachary, unwilling to believe the words his friend and kinsman had spoken. "Surely you don't fault the men who are willing to fight in order to protect their very livelihood."

"I'm doing nothing to change how they live and support themselves; I'm not proposing an end to slavery in any of the states where it presently exists. I'm merely standing in opposition to extension. You would think they'd be willing to accept the fact that their lives will not change a jot if they'll simply leave well enough alone. I had hoped to assuage their concerns by purchasing a sugar plantation and another sixty slaves several months ago. Wouldn't you think my actions should have made a strong statement to the Southern elite?"

"But you're sending mixed messages to the entire nation. The North thinks they'll sway you into their antislavery camp while the South hopes you'll return to where your true allegiance should rest. Your loyalties are divided."

"They are *not* divided, Malcolm. My loyalty is with the Union," Zachary refuted between clenched teeth.

"Enough of this talk, gentlemen," Peggy said. "You can discuss the state of the nation once you've departed the dinner table. For now, I'd like to hear about the rest of your family, Malcolm. How is David? Any prospects for marriage?"

"As a matter of fact, I believe David will soon wed. He's been keeping company with a fine young lady for over a year now, and I think he's soon going to declare himself. I know the girl's father is anxious for the union — he owns several cotton plantations in Mississippi and I think he sees the marriage of his daughter as a way to expand his own holdings."

Zachary emitted a loud guffaw. "Then her father doesn't know you very well, does he?"

"She is a good match for David, and I believe they may elect to live at The Willows," Malcolm replied.

Peggy clapped her hands together. "What an excellent arrangement! Now that's the type of news I enjoy hearing. Tell me more about this young lady. Do we know the family?"

"The Burnhams — father's name is Winstead Burnham. He inherited the plantation from a great-uncle and they've been in Mississippi for only the last two years. Prior to that, they lived in Georgia. Winstead was happy to receive the inheritance — he's the second son, and the family holdings in Georgia were destined for his brother."

Peggy appeared to be deep in thought. "Would his current holdings be the Twin Oaks Plantation owned by John Hepple?"

"Indeed, that's the one. Winstead's made a number of improvements to the home, and I think he had a fair crop this year, but I don't believe he has the financial means needed to get the place back in top-notch condition. John's health was bad for many years, and his overseer did a poor job of keeping the place running properly."

"Be certain to tell David that we will expect an invitation to the wedding. I don't know if my health will permit the journey, but if Zachary is able, he'll attend. Won't you, dear?"

"I'd count it a pleasure," the president assured. "I do have some meetings this afternoon, Malcolm, but I insist the two of you join me for some sightseeing tomorrow. Perhaps I can sneak about town unrecognized before we return back here to the White House. Peggy and Betty have been planning some special festivities for the family's Independence Day celebration. We're hoping you can join us."

The loud thwack of Peggy's cane against the marble overlay surrounding the fireplace brought all three men to attention. "Of course they'll be here. A hearty yes is the only answer I'll accept," she stated in her sweetest voice.

Malcolm's lips turned up to form a broad grin. "Having observed your ability to wield your cane with such absolute power, we dare not refuse."

The president stepped out of the black horse-drawn carriage, pushed his stovepipe hat onto his head, and instructed the driver to wait for their return. Striding into the hotel, the president paused. "Is that him?" he asked Malcolm as he nodded in the direction of the hotel's front desk.

"It is. And he's likely to be rendered speechless when he realizes who you are."

Zachary's eyes danced with mischief. "That's what makes this such fun. People don't expect the president to walk up and introduce himself."

Malcolm and McKinley stood back and watched the scene unfold. Zachary approached the clerk as though he were any guest seeking accommodations for a night or two in the nation's capital. Although the Wainwright men could not hear the conversation, the clerk laughed as Zachary obviously entertained the man with some tall tale. Moments later Zachary appeared to introduce himself and then reached to shake the clerk's hand. The middle-aged clerk pushed away from the counter with his gaze fixed on the president in a trancelike stare.

With a spirited grin, Zachary turned and waved Malcolm and McKinley forward. "You'd best confirm what I've told the clerk, or I don't believe he's going to regain his power of speech."

Malcolm approached the clerk. "Sir, when I met with the president yesterday, I mentioned your admiration of him both as our president and as a formidable adversary during his military service in Mexico. President Taylor insisted upon meeting you."

"Then this is — this is — truly the — the — president?" he stammered.

"Indeed. And he came here specifically to meet you," Malcolm reiterated.

The clerk reached across the desk and grasped Zachary's hand, propelling the president's arm up and down with the enthusiasm of a dehydrated man priming a pump for a taste of water. "Oh, thank you, sir, thank you," the clerk said, his words synchronized with each pump of Zachary's arm.

Malcolm covered his mouth with one hand lest he laugh aloud. The clerk had captured Zachary's hand in a stranglehold and continued to maintain his grasp while the president wiggled his fingers in an obvious attempt to extricate himself.

McKinley finally moved forward and stood beside Zachary. "We really must be going, don't you think, President Taylor?"

Zachary wrested his arm free and gave McKinley an appreciative smile. "Yes, absolutely. I told the driver we would be only a few minutes." He turned back to the clerk, now careful to keep his hands clasped behind his back. "Pleased to meet you. And my regards to your family."

"I see what you mean about deriving pleasure from going about the city, Zachary. That little meeting was extremely entertaining," Malcolm said as they exited the hotel.

"Poor man appeared as besotted as a lovesick debutante. And you, Malcolm, could have at least attempted to hide your enjoyment of my predicament. I had begun to wonder if I would ever disentangle myself from the good fellow's hand."

"What we needed was Peggy's cane," Malcolm said, emitting a boisterous guffaw.

"On a more serious note, don't you believe your behavior somewhat dangerous?" McKinley inquired.

"I don't normally introduce myself, McKinley, and I have yet to have one person step forward and ask if I am the president. I'll notice an occasional congressman assessing me, but he doesn't approach. Of course, I never give them any sign of recognition. I think they fear being made the fool should they be incorrect. Those pompous men fail to remember they continually make ninnies of themselves in Congress."

"No one who truly knows you would deny the fact that you are a man of simplicity, Zachary. A quality I richly admire, I might add."

Zachary swiped the perspiration from his forehead. "Thank you, Malcolm. This heat is overbearing, is it not? Let's make our way over to the Washington Monument. I'm expected there for special festivities, and I want you and McKinley at my side."

Malcolm's eyebrows arched high on his forehead. "Seems an odd place to host a celebration. From what I've seen, they don't even have a good start on the monument."

"True, but ever since the Masonic ceremonies and huge celebration when the cornerstone was laid two years ago, folks seem to think it's the place to host the celebration. However, once the official ceremonies are completed, we'll join the family for our personal Independence Day celebration. We can hope the weather will become more bearable once the sun goes down."

The captain's chest swelled like a bloated fish as he announced to the passengers they would arrive in Boston the next afternoon — virtually a full day ahead of schedule.

"He acts as though he played some large part in our early arrival. The fair weather is the only reason we've made good time on this journey," Malcolm muttered.

"The man is an excellent seafarer," McKinley replied.

"It's the weather, not his seafaring ability he's got to thank for our early arrival. He's portentous and immodest — acting as though he's accomplished some great feat through his own proficiency."

"Why are you angry, Father? The captain was merely informing us we'd be arriving early. You've been irritable since we departed Washington. Did you and President Taylor argue?"

"No, of course not. I know where Zachary stands. I don't agree with him, but I know he'll not change his mind. Frankly, it's your behavior that has occupied my thoughts since our departure."

McKinley started at the retort. "*Me?* Whatever for?"

With his chin thrust forward and hands tightly clasped behind his back, Malcolm stood against the ship's railing as though prepared to do battle. "I was taken aback by your agreement with Zachary on the slavery issues. Every time the topic arose, you either sided with Zachary or argued beyond what either of us believes. To be honest, you sounded more like Grandmother Wainwright's protégé than my son."

"And do my oppositional views make me any less your son?" McKinley's words burned with the same defiance that filled his angry eyes.

Malcolm rubbed his jaw and stared at McKinley. When had he lost his son to these irrational beliefs? First Jasmine and now McKinley! Yet it seemed impossible to believe McKinley had been swayed. He wasn't around people who could influence him with absurd antislavery sentiment — or was he?

"You've obviously been consorting with those who hold views that are in direct opposition to everything our family believes.

May I inquire whom you've been meeting with?"

"I can't imagine why you find it difficult to comprehend that my beliefs are independent of yours. We have little in common, Father. You're eager to take charge of the physical operation of the plantation while my involvement has remained in the accounting and finances."

A stiff breeze crossed the deck and Malcolm bent his head against the wind, his nostrils filling with the odor of fish and salt water. "I've maintained close supervision on the accounts throughout the years, and had you shown any interest in anything else —"

"Anything so long as it lent itself to raising cotton. If you'll think back to the time when I was ready to choose a vocation, I talked to you about my desire to become a doctor."

"Oh yes — something about becoming a physician so you could provide the slaves with improved medical care."

"Exactly. As I recall, you laughed and told me you needed someone to manage your finances and you would continue to look after the medical care for the slaves."

Malcolm turned his gaze toward the ocean. "Surely you weren't serious about such a pursuit. We're a family of cotton growers. I need my sons actively involved in the business of raising cotton, especially now that Samuel is acting as an agent for the Southern growers. Moving Samuel into Bradley Houston's old position with the Corporation in Lowell was excellent for this entire area of the South — The Willows included. However, it left me without his talent and physical presence. Hence my need to move David into his position and rely more heavily upon you to ensure the accounts and business matters are in proper order."

"The fact remains that each of us is required to perform the work *you* designate advantageous, whether we agree or not."

"I don't recall your ever being unwilling to accept your wages or other benefits derived from your occupation. However, since you find your life at The Willows repugnant, perhaps you should support yourself in someone else's employ." Malcolm enunciated each word with a clarity that bit the air like glassy shards.

"I'll give that further thought, Father," McKinley replied tersely as he strode away from the railing.

"Further thought? What does he mean, 'further thought'?" Malcolm muttered, balling his hand into a tight fist and pounding against the ship's balustrade.

Slowly the realization that his son was already weighing the possibility of moving away from The Willows began to seep into Malcolm's consciousness, and a fierce anger began to build from deep within.

Malcolm turned and faced directly into the wind, with the damp air stinging his face. "I'll *not* lose another child to the North," he vowed.

Chapter 11

Alice Wainwright beckoned to her grandson, who was descending the stairway. “Good morning, McKinley. Why don’t you escort me out into the garden? I’ve taken the liberty of asking Martha to serve us breakfast outdoors. I hope you can tolerate the foolish whims of an old woman. I enjoy spending a few hours in the garden before the heat of the day sets in, when the world still seems fresh and untouched.”

McKinley’s gaze turned toward the door leading to the garden, where Martha was giving the table her final touch. McKinley smiled at the sight of Martha wearing a wide-brimmed bonnet while arranging the garden breakfast table. Obviously, his grandmother’s hired servant was intent upon protecting her fair complexion even at this early morning hour. “I would be pleased to accompany you, Grandmother. The heat of the day up here seems mild compared to home. Even Washington seemed more stifling. Is Father planning to join us?"

"No. He had an early meeting with Matthew Cheever and some other gentlemen. He said he would return midmorning. However, he asked me to tell you that the family has been invited to dine with the Cheever family this evening and he expects you to attend and be on your best behavior. I'm not certain what that last remark meant. I told your father I'd never seen you anywhere that you weren't on your best behavior."

Alice took McKinley's ar m and walked alongside as he escorted her to the small table Martha had prepared with a linen cloth and china. "I doubt Father would agree with your evaluation of my conduct," McKinley replied as he assisted his grandmother into her chair and then seated himself across the table.

"It's obvious something is amiss between you and your father. But when I inquired, he quickly changed the topic. Tell me, McKinley, what has occurred to cause this breach? Is this something related to your mother's death?" Alice clasped a hand to her chest. "Has Malcolm been courting someone? He's come here to tell me he plans to remarry, hasn't he?"

"No, of course not, Grandmother. I doubt Father will ever marry again." He leaned back and allowed Martha to set a plate heaped with scrambled eggs, sausage, and fluffy biscuits in front of him.

Alice sipped her tea and studied her grandson. "Then what is the problem causing the two of you to scarcely acknowledge one another?"

"As you know, we spent time with President and Mrs. Taylor in Washington."

"Yes, of course. Your father went into detail regarding your activities. Of course, I was primarily interested in hearing about Peggy, but I listened to his lengthy report with as much concentration as I could muster," she said with a sheepish grin.

"Did he mention our conversations with President Taylor regarding slavery?"

A guarded smile crossed Alice's lips. "Your father and I ceased discussing the topic of slavery a number of years ago. What began as a conversation would soon develop into an argument; therefore, we decided if we were going to maintain family civility, the issue would not be discussed. I do know Zachary's position has angered your father — along with most of the Southern plantation owners, but what has that to do with the two of you?"

"I sided with the president. Actually, I went beyond siding with him and told Father I oppose slavery."

Lifting her napkin, Alice dabbed her lips. She didn't want McKinley to suspect the alarm elicited by his statement. "Sometimes there is wisdom in weighing our beliefs against timing and consequences, McKinley. Don't misinterpret what I'm saying: I believe we must have the courage to take a stand for our principles. However, it's wise to evaluate when to take such a stand. Exactly what did you say?"

Alice listened as McKinley related the conversations that had taken place, both in Washington and on board the ship. When McKinley completed the recitation, she remained silent for several minutes, staring at her roses and praying God would give her the perfect solution, some ideal method to heal the discord. "You know your father is prone to speak in anger and then regret his words, don't you?"

"I realize we all speak out of turn from time to time, Grandmother. However, Father said what is truly in his heart. If I return to The Willows, he will expect me to embrace his beliefs, but I can't do that. From the time I was very young, I couldn't understand why we owned other human beings — and nobody ever gave me a proper explanation. Consequently, I've tolerated plantation life but have not had the courage to speak my mind until now. I don't take any pleasure in causing Father pain, but I cannot continue acting as though I find slavery acceptable. I'm hoping you will agree to take me on as a temporary houseguest."

Alice clutched at her chest. "Oh, dear! It would be a treat to have you remain in Lowell. And having you live with me would prove a genuine delight. However, I'm not certain your father would ever forgive me. He already holds me accountable for influencing Jasmine in her stand against slavery."

"He can't blame you for my beliefs, Grandmother. And as I said, he's told me that if I disagree with slavery, perhaps I should find some other way to support myself."

She began fanning herself with her limp cloth napkin. "I do believe the temperature has dramatically risen since we first came outdoors."

"I've made you uncomfortable. I'm sorry, Grandmother. Forget we had this conversation. Let's return indoors." McKinley stood and then assisted Alice from her chair.

Grasping McKinley's arm, Alice met his gaze with an encouraging smile. "Don't give up on me so soon, my boy. I need only a bit of time to think this matter through. I don't want to see the family thrown into chaos, nor do I want to see you unhappy. I need some time for preparation so that we may present a firm plan to your father. Our actions will merely serve to provoke him if we have no definitive plan."

"Then you *will* help?"

"Yes, of course. How could I turn down such a request? However, you must remember we do not want to cause your father undue pain. For the present, put aside your differences and attempt to reconcile with him. Do you think you can do that?"

"I promise to make every attempt, but I don't believe Father will do the same."

"You do your part and leave the rest to me," she said as they walked into the house.

The trio sat in silence as their carriage moved through the streets of Lowell. Finally Alice turned her focus to her son. "You've not told me how your meetings progressed today, Malcolm. I trust all went well?"

"Everything went well, Mother."

"Can you say no more than those few words? Surely you have more to report —

you were gone all day."

Malcolm shifted his weight and turned toward Alice. "I doubt my business meetings are of interest to either of you. Suffice it to say our discussions were fruitful, and I'm certain the agreements we reach will prove beneficial to all concerned."

McKinley's eyebrows arched. "I thought Samuel was overseeing all contractual negotiations for the Southern cotton growers."

Malcolm directed an icy look at McKinley. "Your brother negotiates the contracts regarding prices and quantities for the growers. These meetings deal with issues more intricate and far-reaching than next year's prices — matters I don't believe we should discuss."

Alice grasped her son's arm with a gloved hand. "Forgive me, Malcolm. I shouldn't have been prying into business matters. 7Especially after a difficult day of meetings when I'm certain you're looking forward to relaxing and forgetting your worries. McKinley and I were simply interested in your day. We'll save our idle chatter for the Cheevers' dining table."

Thankfully McKinley took her cue and nodded his agreement. "Are you a regular visitor at the Cheever home, Grandmother?"

"I visit Lilly on occasion, and she frequently acts as hostess for some of the groups to which I belong. She's a fine lady. In fact, she worked in one of the mills before marrying Matthew Cheever. And this is their home," Alice said as their carriage slowly came to a halt.

McKinley looked out the window and then back at his grandmother, his brows furrowed. "I expected something more . . ."

"Pretentious?" she inquired.

"At least more spacious."

"You grew up on a plantation and equate real estate with power and wealth," Malcolm told his son. "Make no mistake: Matthew Cheever wields plenty of power, and he could live much more splendidly if he so desired. Shall we go in?"

"He takes umbrage at everything I say," McKinley whispered to his grandmother.

"Trust me — your father will soften as the evening wears on and he's around other people."

Lilly Cheever awaited them at the front door, poised in a pale blue dress edged with fine ivory lace, while Matthew stood on the front porch engrossed in conversation with several other men.

"Come join us, Malcolm," Matthew called. "We decided the parlor was much too warm."

Malcolm cast a glance toward the men. "If you'll excuse me, Mother, I believe I will accept Matthew's invitation."

"By all means — I have McKinley to escort me," she replied with a warm smile before turning her attention to Lilly. "Lilly, I'd like to introduce my grandson, McKinley Wainwright."

"A pleasure," Lilly greeted warmly. "And this is our daughter, Violet, and son, Michael. Violet, perhaps you would like to accompany Mr. Wainwright and introduce him to some of the other younger guests."

The flounces of Violet's white organdy dress gave a gentle swish as she stepped forward and clasped McKinley's arm. "I would be delighted."

"Thank you for your kindness, Miss Cheever. Grandmother?"

Alice remained beside Lilly Cheever and waved the young couple forward. "You two go along. I can manage on my own."

"Your grandson is a handsome young man. Is this his first visit to Lowell?" Lilly inquired.

"Yes, it is, and I know he'll have a much better time this evening now that he's with Violet. I don't think he'd enjoy hearing the Lowell matrons discuss their flower gardens or latest ailments."

Lilly's soft laughter filled the warm evening breeze. " 'Tis true young people have little patience when it comes to flower gardens or illness. How long will your family be visiting?"

"I'm uncertain. As you know, Malcolm has been involved in business meetings with your husband and other members of the Boston Associates. It's my understanding he'll book passage once they've concluded their meetings."

"Then we'll have to hope they are slow in concluding their business. Your grandson would make a nice addition to the few eligible men in Lowell. Ah, and here is your granddaughter."

Jasmine leaned down and gave her grandmother a warm embrace. "What's this I hear about eligible young men coming to Lowell?"

Alice pointed a finger in Jasmine's direction, her face crinkling as she smiled at Jasmine. "Now you see? That's how gossip gets started. Folks hear part of a conversation and the next thing you know, a false rumor has begun."

"I *know* I heard talk of eligible men," Jasmine insisted.

"I was telling your grandmother that your

brother would make a fine addition to the few eligible men we have in Lowell. He's a handsome young man."

"Speaking of eligible men, where is Nolan? I thought he was going to accompany you this evening," Alice interjected.

"He sent word he would meet me here. Perhaps we should go inside and permit Mrs. Cheever the opportunity to greet her guests," Jasmine suggested, gently guiding her grandmother through the front door. "And where is McKinley? I noticed Father when I arrived, but McKinley wasn't with him."

Alice glanced about and then took Jasmine's hand. "McKinley is with Violet Cheever. Let's sit in the alcove near the stairway, where we can talk without our conversation being overheard. I have much to tell you. Your father and McKinley are at odds with each other."

Malcolm wiped his brow and continued pacing back and forth across the burgundy and gold wool carpet that adorned the floor of his mother's parlor. Life as he knew it continued to change, and he didn't like it one bit. "I can't believe it!" Malcolm exclaimed, his face ashen and drawn.

Alice motioned toward the settee. "Do sit

down, Malcolm. The fact is, whether you choose to believe it or not, the president is dead."

Malcolm ceased his pacing and wheeled around. "Zachary was more than the president; he was my friend. Even though we weren't related by blood, I considered him kin."

"I understand, Malcolm. However, there is nothing you can do to change things. It's a shock to all of us. I cared for Zachary also. And dear Peggy. We must pray she'll find the fortitude to withstand Zachary's death."

Malcolm dropped onto the settee and once again began rubbing his forehead. "To think we were with Zachary when he was eating cherries and milk on the Fourth of July. In fact, I joined him and ate some of the same. The doctors conclude that's what caused his death. Seems strange that would be the source of his ailment since I was completely unaffected, don't you think?"

"The newspaper said something about the heat also. I'm surmising that as the day wore on, he became extremely overheated. I do recall you mentioned the extreme heat during the time you visited Peggy and Zachary."

"True. It was unbearably hot in Washington, particularly on the Fourth. However, I find it difficult to believe it was cherries and milk that killed the president — more likely his heart. I can't believe Peggy is willing to accept such an outlandish explanation. Are you?"

Alice tucked a wisp of white hair behind one ear. "The shock has likely caused Peggy to take to her bed, and I doubt she's intent upon discovering the cause of Zachary's death. After all, knowing the cause is not going to bring him back to her. Are you thinking you should go to Washington?"

"Matters here in Lowell will not permit me to leave at the moment. And by the time I would arrive, I doubt there would be a member of the Taylor family remaining in Washington. There's little doubt Peggy will at least be pleased to be out of the political turmoil that surrounded the family."

The sight of McKinley descending the staircase caused a faint smile to appear upon Alice's lips. "Are you leaving the house?"

Twirling his straw hat on one finger, McKinley stepped into the doorway of the parlor. "I'm calling on Violet Cheever. She's agreed to give me a complete tour of Lowell and the surrounding countryside." Her grandson's wide grin was infectious.

"Splendid! And will you be returning for the noonday meal?"

"No. Miss Cheever suggested a picnic. Fortunately the weather has cooperated and there's not a sign of rain."

"What fun!" Alice exclaimed, giving a resounding clap of her hands. "Picnics always remind me of your grandfather. He loved finding a grassy place beneath the trees, close to a river or stream, where he could relax and watch the water. He said the water had a calming effect upon him."

"Some of us must work in order to earn our keep. Instead of lazing about some grassy meadow, I'll be attending meetings this afternoon. You may want to give some thought to the difficulties of earning a living while you're staring out into the Merrimack River," Malcolm asserted.

Malcolm didn't wait for his son's reply before exiting through the parlor doors leading out into his mother's small flower garden. With a determined stride, he walked across the slate steppingstones that curved away from the garden until he reached an old elm. The giant branches provided a leafy canopy over a weatherworn wrought-iron bench. He dropped onto the cool metal and rested his arms across his thighs, staring at the ground as a crushing weariness permeated his bones.

"Zachary, Zachary — what is your death

going to mean to this country? I fear none of us can even fathom what lies in wait for us," he muttered.

"Has life become so difficult that you've begun talking to yourself, Father?"

Malcolm started and quickly turned toward the sound of Jasmine's voice. "I didn't know you were paying a visit today. Had I known, I wouldn't have scheduled a meeting for this afternoon."

Jasmine smiled and sat down, the flounces of her yellow morning dress spreading across the bench in waves of fabric and ribbon. "I needed to make some purchases at the mercantile. It is my practice to stop and visit with Grandmother whenever I'm in Lowell. I'm sorry you have a meeting, but we can share this time together, and Grandmother has invited me to remain for supper also. I won't return home until evening. You appear troubled. Are you regretting your visit to Lowell?"

"In some respects, I suppose I am. I thought this journey would be good for both McKinley and me — help us grow closer. Instead, it's had the opposite result. I believe he intends to remain here in Lowell. And now with Zachary's death, the country is bound to be in an upheaval, and I don't know what to expect from Millard Fillmore.

Of course, he may be more of an asset to the South than Zachary was. It's difficult to know what a man will do once he's in a powerful position."

"Your words are filled with sadness and disappointment, Father. I know you worry about The Willows, but you must try to remember that your life will not be measured solely by what is accomplished on that cotton plantation."

"You think like a woman, Jasmine. Men know from an early age that they are measured by their ability to gain wealth and power. Yet, at this moment in my life, I realize I've lost my children to those endeavors."

She reached for her father's hand. "Whatever do you mean? You haven't lost any of us. I know I can safely say that all of your children love you."

He brushed the back of her hand with a fleeting kiss. "Love? Perhaps. But do any of my children like me or desire to live in the home I created for them? I think not."

"David is going to remain at The Willows. I'm certain he intends to live there once he marries. And Samuel will return eventually, Father. Remember it was your suggestion for Samuel to replace Bradley. You knew his work would require him to spend a great deal of time away from The Willows, and McKinley . . ."

"Yes, McKinley. I've lost him to the North, just as I lost you. Did your grandmother tell you he hopes to remain in Lowell?"

"Grandmother said the two of you had a disagreement regarding the antislavery movement and you told McKinley he should seek other employment if he was unhappy with your beliefs."

"He condemns my way of life, yet he has never refused the benefits. My words were spoken in anger — my feeble attempt to bring him to his senses."

"Instead of anger, perhaps he needs your affirmation," Alice said as she neared the bench.

"Please sit down, Grandmother. I must go inside and check on Spencer — I'm certain he's a handful for Martha."

Malcolm watched as Jasmine made her way toward the house before he turned to meet his mother's gaze. "So you think my son needs affirmation? Of what? His belief in the antislavery movement? I'm sorry, Mother, but you know I will never side with you and your Northern allies on this subject, nor will I give McKinley my blessing to embrace such principles. I don't want him to remain in Lowell. He needs to return to The Willows with me. Once he's back in Mississippi, he will see things more clearly."

"Surely you don't think his beliefs suddenly materialized on your voyage to Boston. It's obvious to me that McKinley has harbored antislavery sentiments all of his life. Can't you see that he has feared losing his relationship with you if he truly declared his views? He's a grown man, Malcolm. Permit him the privilege of making his own decisions."

"You argue on his behalf because he has embraced your views. Have you swayed Samuel to your side also?"

Alice jerked away. "I've not attempted to influence my grandchildren. I have always answered their questions truthfully, nothing more. And as for Samuel, I see him rarely and have no idea whether his views regarding slavery have changed since he's been working closely with the Associates. However, I seriously doubt you'll lose his alliance. Samuel has always been pro-slavery. Had you taken note as the children were growing into adulthood, I think you would have seen evidence that neither Jasmine nor McKinley ever held to your sentiments."

"And David?"

"You won't lose David — he hopes to

permanently win Samuel's former position at The Willows. From the time he was a little boy, David was insecure in his rank as the second son. With Samuel's departure, David views himself as your rightful heir. You can be certain he will remain firmly aligned with any opinion you adopt. And now that he is considering marriage, his sights will be firmly set upon The Willows."

Malcolm sat up and looked deep into his mother's eyes. "You judge David harshly."

"I don't judge him at all. David holds values and opinions that differ from those of McKinley and Jasmine. You and I have differing views, but that fact doesn't change my love for you, and I hope your love for Jasmine and McKinley won't change. I know you have made great strides toward healing your rclationship with Jasmine after forcing an abominable marriage upon her. I do not see that she holds that against you any longer. So I have to believe that the love between you has also given you the power to heal the hurts. It's my prayer you'll continue down that path with McKinley. Your harsh words have caused him great pain."

"And what of *his* remarks? They were harsh as well."

Alice held his eyes with a slight smile tugging at her lips.

"Oh, I know I should be the one to make the first gesture toward forgiveness, but it seems all I hold sacred is slipping away. First Jasmine, then Madelaine, and now McKinley. I'll apologize to McKinley, but I'll let him know I expect him to return home with me."

His mother's face was filled with a profound sadness he hadn't seen since the day they'd buried his father. "Have you heard *nothing* I've said to you?"

"Yes, Mother, but —"

"Malcolm, I've not forced my beliefs upon any member of this family, and perhaps you should consider doing the same. Your children are now adults, quite capable of forming their own opinions, and you should permit them to do so. You and Madelaine gave your children a solid foundation; now permit them to put their training to use. They can, and *should,* make their own decisions."

"They still need my guidance and influence."

"That may be true, but the final decision is theirs, and you should honor their right to choose. Free choice, Malcolm — let them apply it in their daily lives and trust you've taught them well. Of course, continued prayer is helpful also," she concluded with a sweet smile.

He managed a sheepish smile. "I don't believe I'm as confident they'll make the choices I'd prefer."

Alice's laughter rose upward and mingled with the soft afternoon breeze. "Your decisions didn't always concur with my preferences, but it didn't change my love for you. We can dislike choices that are made, but our love must always remain constant — wouldn't you agree?"

Malcolm rose from the bench and helped Alice to her feet. "It's impossible to disagree with anything you've said, but that doesn't change the fact that I'll still be doing everything in my power to influence McKinley to return to The Willows."

"You seem rather sad today," Violet Cheever said as McKinley smoothed out their picnic blanket.

"Perhaps introspective is a better word," he said as he picked up the picnic basket. "Where do want this?"

She sank gracefully to the blanket and patted the center. "Right here. This shall give us easy access to all of Cook's culinary delights."

McKinley smiled, but his heart wasn't in

it. Joining Violet on the blanket, he let out a heavy sigh.

"Perhaps such heavy introspection would be more easily borne if shared with a friend?"

"Perhaps, but I would hate to burden such a new and generous friend as you."

"Pshaw, as Mother would say." She laughed, and the sound caused McKinley to relax.

"Grandmother would agree," he said, smiling.

Violet began pulling food from the basket. She never looked up but asked in a very serious tone, "Does this have something to do with your father?"

He startled. "Why do you ask that?"

"I recognized some tension between the two of you last night. Forgive me, but I asked Jasmine if something was amiss. She, of course, refused to betray any details but said I should pray for you. So I did."

McKinley eased back on one elbow and stretched his legs out across the blanket. "Father and I have grown distant — perhaps we were never all that close to begin with. We don't share the same ideals."

Violet worked to fix a plate of food for each of them. "Regarding your future? Most fathers seem quite set upon the path their sons should take, while it's been my experience that most sons have entirely different ideas."

He laughed. "Your experience, eh? You are all of what, sixteen?"

Violet looked up in absolute astonishment. "I beg your pardon!"

McKinley shot to his feet and took several paces back. He waved his hands in protest. "I was only joking. I know you're much older."

"You think I'm old?" she said, her voice changing from astonishment to irritation.

McKinley suddenly realized this wasn't at all going the way he wanted it to. "I do not think you're old. You are just the right age."

Violet lowered her face for a moment, then lifted it to reveal her huge smile. "The right age for what?"

McKinley suddenly realized she wasn't at all upset with him, she'd merely been giving him back some of his own medicine.

He dropped back down by her side and grabbed a cookie from one of the plates before she could stop him. He took a bite and grinned. "Why, the right age for a picnic by the river. What else could I mean?"

"Hmm, I cannot imagine, Mr. Wainwright, but I shall endeavor to thoroughly explore the possibilities." She gave him a most alluring simper before turning back to the food.

"Why, Miss Cheever," he said, trying not to sound too surprised, when in truth he was quite taken aback. "I do believe you're flirting with me."

Violet handed him a plate. "I believe you are correct, Mr. Wainwright. How very astute."

Chapter 12

Late August

Rogan Sheehan and Liam Donohue propped themselves against the log-hewn railing that surrounded Jasmine Houston's neatly manicured lawn and separated it from the remainder of her acreage. Rogan lifted the cap from his head and waved it high in the air until Obadiah noticed him and waved in return.

"Can ya spare us a minute of yar time?" Rogan called out before tucking his black curls back beneath the flat, billed cap.

Rogan watched as Obadiah hesitated just long enough to wipe the sweat from his walnut brown face before heading in their direction. Taking giant strides, he made crossing the distance appear nearly effortless. "Fine-lookin' vegetable garden ya've got for yarself," Rogan said. "I admire a man that can make the land produce."

"Dirt, rain, and sunshine is all provided

by the good Lord. I jes' add da toil. We had us some fine eatin' outta dat garden, and what we couldn't eat, Naomi got stored for da winter. I was jes' hoeing down some weeds. What can I do fer ya?"

"We're needin' yar help, if ya're willin'. Rogan got word there's a movement of slaves headed our way, and we're gonna need to take three wagons to get 'em back to the farm."

Obadiah's lips tightened and deep creases formed along his jaw. "Three full loads comin' at one time? Hard to believe a group dat size could make it dis far north wibout being spotted. You sho' you ain' got some bad information? Sounds to me like maybe dis could be a trap. You don' think someone's gotten wind of what's goin' on and dey's baitin' us, do you?"

"Well, now, anything is possible, but Rogan misspoke a wee bit," Liam said. "Fer sure we need to be usin' three wagons, but they'll be loaded with stone ta make it appear like it's a normal day of work fer me. I'm thinkin' we can get far fewer in each wagon, but doin' it this way will permit us to work in the daylight, which is somethin' no one will be expectin'. The only dangerous time will be loadin' 'em in and out of the wagons. With three of us to keep watch,

I'm thinkin' we'll 'ave no problem. Can we count on ya to help us?"

"I done tol' you I'd help any time you needed me. When you thinkin' dis is gonna take place?"

"In the mornin'," Liam replied.

"Tomorrow mornin'? That sho' ain' much time to be makin' my excuses for being gone."

Liam dug the toe of his boot into the dirt. "Wiser to keep people in the dark until there's a reason for passin' on the information. Less chance of word slippin' out to the wrong ears. Might be best to just tell the mistress ya're helpin' us with the runaways. She's always been willin' to aid in the cause."

"It ain't the mistress I got a problem with — I know Miz Jasmine wouldn't hesitate for a minute. It's my wife, Naomi. She's afeared somethin' bad's gonna happen to me. That woman do worry all da time. She says she don' want me helpin' no more. I tol' her dat ain' right, but she's scared."

"I find thar's times it's better to remain silent about what I might be doin'. Kiara can na worry about what she does na know."

"Naomi asks lots of questions. If I start ta sidesteppin', she's gonna know for sho' I'm hidin' somepin'."

"If ya're sure ya want to help, I'll go to Mrs. Houston and tell her I need yar help with the runaways. I do na think she'll turn me down. I'll tell her ya do na want your wife ta worry and ask that she na say anything. Ya can tell yar wife ya're going to help me haul rock and, best of all, ya'll na be telling a lie. Do ya think that would solve the problem ya're havin'?"

"If it be alright with Miz Jasmine, I think we got us a plan," Obadiah said, shaking hands with Liam.

"I'll be goin' to talk to the missus right now, and unless thar's a problem, one of us will come by to fetch ya in the mornin'. Are ya comin' with me, Rogan, or are ya planning to grow old leanin' on that fence railin'?" Liam asked with a glint in his eye.

Rogan gave a hearty laugh and pushed away from the railing. "Just catchin' me rest where I can."

"Then let's be on our way. It's gettin' dark, and I do na want to be late for supper," Liam said.

Giving Liam a hearty slap on the back, Rogan called back to Obadiah, "Ya can see that his woman has 'im well in hand also!"

" 'Tis na me woman that worries me but me stomach," Liam corrected in a loud voice as they walked toward the Houston home.

Rogan waited until he was certain Obadiah could no longer hear their voices. "Do ya think he'll have a change of heart afore mornin'?"

"He's a good man — a man of his word. If he was na goin' ta help, he would have told us. Obadiah would na want to take a chance on havin' runaways captured on his account."

"Ya're right. I hope he's able to keep his senses about him this evenin'. Otherwise his wife will get the idea somethin' is wrong and keep at 'im until he tells her. If that happens, ya can be sure we'll be needin' someone else to help us come mornin'."

"Ya worry too much, Rogan. Do ya want to be the one to talk to the missus, or do ya want me ta speak ta her?"

"I'll talk to her, but if she begins askin' a lot of details, ya'll have to fill her in," Rogan said as he rapped on the front door.

Moments later the front door swung open, and the two Irishmen were rendered temporarily speechless.

"May I help you?" McKinley Wainwright inquired.

Rogan strained on tiptoe, hoping to see Jasmine Houston approaching. "We was hopin' to have a word with Missus Houston."

McKinley's eyes narrowed. "Was she expecting you?"

"We're na the type to be makin' appointments nor havin' callin' cards, but the lady of the house knows us," Rogan replied. "If ya'd tell her Rogan Sheehan and Liam Donohue would like a word with her, I think ya'll find she's willin' to see us. We'll wait here on the porch while ya fetch her."

McKinley nodded and closed the door.

"I'm hopin' that means he's gone to fetch her," Rogan said. "Do ya know who he is?"

"I've never seen him before in me life," Liam said. "And here I been thinkin' the missus was goin' to marry Mr. Houston's brother. Looks as though she's found herself another suitor."

"I do na think he's a suitor. Fer sure I'm thinkin' she's goin' to marry Nolan Houston. Kiara has told me as much, but I do na think they've set a date."

"Kiara might be assumin' too much. Maybe he hasn't even proposed and the lass has grown weary of waitin' on him and found her someone else."

Before Rogan could reply, the door reopened, and Rogan quickly pulled the flat cap from his head. Jasmine Houston stood in the doorway with the gentleman at her side. "Rogan! Liam! Do come in," she said, stepping aside to permit them entry. "I'd like you both to meet my brother, McKinley Wainwright," she continued as they walked into the foyer.

Rogan grinned. "Yar brother, is he? Liam here was thinkin' perhaps you'd found a new suitor."

A hint of crimson darkened Jasmine's pale cheeks. "And you corrected his ill-conceived notion?"

"Aye — quick as a wink I told him ya had yar cap set fer Mr. Houston's brother."

McKinley burst into laughter. "Now will you believe me when I tell you that you wear your feelings on your sleeve, dear sister?"

"Oh, shush! Come sit down and tell me what's on your mind."

Thc men followed Jasmine into the library that also served as her business office.

"It's a private matter we need to be discussin' with ya," Rogan said, his gaze shifting toward her brother.

"If you would excuse us, McKinley? I'm certain we won't be long." There was a ring of authority in her voice that would not be denied.

McKinley nodded. "Nice to have made your acquaintance."

"Please close the door," Jasmine requested

as McKinley made his exit. The moment the latch clicked, she turned her attention to Rogan. "Runaways?" she asked, keeping her voice low.

"Aye. And we need yar help."

She listened carefully to his request. "If Obadiah has given his consent to help you, then I have no objection. Paddy and Mr. Fisher can handle the horses without him for one morning. Is there nothing more I can do to help?"

"Ya can keep this information to yarself," Rogan told her.

She jumped up from her chair, her back rigid. "What do you mean? If it's my brother that concerns you, he's sympathetic to the cause. In fact, McKinley stood against my father and has remained in Massachusetts because of his opposition to slavery. He was willing to alienate himself from our father and lose any chance of an inheritance for his beliefs. He can be trusted. And I sincerely hope you do not question my loyalty."

"Sorry I am to have offended ya, ma'am," Rogan said. "I did na mean ya could na be trusted, but we do na want Obadiah's wife ta know he'll be helpin' with the runaways. He said she does na want him puttin' himself in danger, and he does na want to tell her a lie. He'll be tellin' her nothin' but that he's helping haul rock. So if ya could find it in yar heart to tell her nothin' more, we'd be obliged."

Jasmine's face softened, and she lowered herself onto the settee. "You may be certain I'll divulge nothing to Naomi — or anyone else. I only wish there were more I could do."

"We know we can always be dependin' on ya fer aid, ma'am," Rogan said. " 'Tis thankful we are, knowin' that when there's a need ya're always willin' to help."

Before the sun had ascended the next day, Jasmine hurried down the back stairway into the kitchen. She tightened her silk robe and strained to peek out the window for any sign of Liam's wagon. For nearly half an hour she raised herself on tiptoe and braced her body against the coarse wood shelving beneath the window. Her legs trembled from the strain until she thought the ache in her legs would become unbearable. Moving to adjust her position, a barbed splinter broke loose from the wood shelving and penetrated the slick, silky fabric of her nightclothes. With a jerk, she pulled away from the window and paced the room until the plodding of horses' hooves and rumble of the wagons could be heard in the distance. Pulling the door closed behind her, Jasmine crept outside into the diffused shadows of daybreak and watched as Obadiah clambered up into one of the wagons.

Long after the wagons were out of sight, she continued her vigil, wishing she could join the men. Instead, she returned to her bedroom and prepared for the day. Nolan would be arriving this morning, and there was much to accomplish before his visit. She had promised Spencer they would have a picnic, and she didn't want to burden Naomi with the preparations. Perhaps she should ask Naomi and Moses to join them. Peeking into Spencer's adjoining bedroom, she stared at the boy with his rosy cheeks and bow-shaped smile.

Leaning down, she placed a kiss upon her son's warm cheek. He wriggled and his eyelids fluttered before finally opening to reveal his deep brown eyes. "Mama," he said sleepily, extending his arms for a hug.

Jasmine lifted him into her arms and kissed him soundly. "Are you ready to begin a new day?"

Spencer giggled and squirmed until she placed him on the woven rug beside his bed. "I wanna play now!" he commanded.

"First you must get dressed and eat your breakfast. Then we'll talk about playing," she said as she unbuttoned his nightshirt and tugged it over his head. "Such a big boy," she cooed. He was growing up so fast. Almost overnight his speech had taken on a decided improvement toward clarity. "I can't believe you have grown so much in just the last few months."

In a blink, he was running toward the door, off to discover the pleasures of a new day. "Not without your clothes," Jasmine admonished, quickly grasping his arm and shaking her reflective thoughts away. With Spencer around, there were only rare occasions that could be given to introspection.

When she had finally cajoled him into a shirt and tiny breeches, she took his hand and led him to the stairs, carrying his shoes and stockings in her hand. She would struggle through that battle while her son ate his breakfast. Spencer hurried through his breakfast and was wriggling from his chair when a knock sounded at the front door.

"Hurry, Spencer. Let's see who has come to visit," she said, following her son as he ran down the hallway.

He stretched until one chubby hand was on the doorknob before looking up to his mother. "Open, Mama."

Heeding his request, Jasmine turned the

knob and pulled back. "Look who has come to visit," she said while gazing into Nolan Houston's sparkling blue eyes.

"Good morning to my two favorite people," he greeted them.

"Unca Nolan," Spencer screeched, throwing himself into Nolan's legs.

"Now there's a welcome that makes a man happy to be alive," Nolan said while scooping Spencer into his arms. "And what of you, Jasmine? Are you as happy to see me as my nephew?"

Above Spencer's brown curls, their eyes locked. "I believe that would be a true statement," she said. "Why don't you join us in the parlor?"

After only a short time of being contained in the parlor, Spencer began tugging at his uncle's hand. "Play with me," he said, pointing toward the door.

"You want to go outside? I agree. It's much too beautiful to remain indoors. Why don't we all go outdoors?"

"If you're willing to oversee him for a short time, I'll go into the kitchen and begin preparations for our picnic."

Nolan took Spencer by the hand. "I think I should be able to handle him for a while. Any objections if he should want to play with Moses?"

"Of course not. In fact, I'm certain your job will be much more manageable with Moses to keep him company. The two boys have become accustomed to spending most of their waking hours together," Jasmine said as the three of them walked down the hallway and into the kitchen.

Jasmine watched Spencer and Nolan as they laughed and ran across the yard, Nolan pretending he was unable to keep pace with the small boy. The sight caused a smile to cross her lips, and she watched until the two of them crossed through the gated fence and stood in front of the small cottage that had been constructed for Obadiah and Naomi. Seeing Naomi's thin form as she walked into the yard with Moses in tow caused Jasmine's thoughts to quickly change direction. Were Obadiah, Rogan, and Liam encountering any difficulty on this day?

"Keep them safe, Father God, both those who lend their help and the runaways who need them," she whispered. Danger remained at the forefront of her mind as Jasmine absently retrieved a basket from the pantry and lined it with a white linen cloth.

Moving about the kitchen with her thoughts focused upon the three men and their mission, she started at the sound of Naomi's voice. "Mister Nolan said you was busy fixing a picnic. Why don' you let me finish up in here? Seems if a man come all dis way to visit, you should be spendin' some time wib him. I know he likes da chile, but it's you he's wantin' to see. 'Sides, I don' know when Obadiah gonna be home. He tol' me not to be plannin' on him for noonday meal 'cause he was helpin' cut stone — said you tol' him it was alright. How come you havin' him help with dat work, Missus? Ain't as though dere's nothing needin' done 'round this place."

Jasmine tightened her hold on the silverware she was placing in the basket and hesitated briefly as she met Naomi's questioning gaze. "Mr. Donohue and Mr. Sheehan came to the house last night and asked if they could hire Obadiah to help them for the day. Obadiah is strong and can handle the heavy rock more easily than either of them."

"Seems odd they ain' never needed no help from Obadiah afore. They say who been movin' dat heavy rock in da past?"

"No, I didn't inquire," Jasmine said, moving around Naomi. "I believe I will take you up on your offer and join Mr. Houston — if you're certain it won't be an imposition."

" 'Course not. You go on out there, and if dem boys start to givin' you trouble, tell

’em you’ll make ’em come in da kitchen with me if they don’ behave.”

Jasmine gathered her skirts in one hand as she crossed the threshold. “Please pack enough for you and Moses too. I want you to join us.”

“Yessum.”

The sound of Naomi’s soulful tune followed Jasmine through the open door, the words muted as the early afternoon breeze lifted them off toward heaven. Jasmine slowed her pace and listened, hoping she would hear the returning rumble of Liam Donohue’s wagons. Yet she knew it was much too early to expect the men. After all, Obadiah had told his wife he wouldn’t be home for the noonday meal. But if the runaways had already arrived and had been waiting, they could already be loaded and on their way.

“Enough!” she muttered while continuing across the lawn, knowing she must cease her incessant worrying. After all, weren’t they all entrusted into God’s tender care? Would He not protect them?

“Mama!” Spencer shouted as he came running toward her and buried his face in her skirts.

Jasmine ruffled his dark brown curls with her fingers. “Are you having fun?” she asked, taking his small hand in her own and walking back to where Moses sat on the grass playing with some wooden figures Obadiah had carved for him. "You boys play nicely," she said before sitting down on the woolen blanket Nolan had spread under one of the leafy oak trees.

"Where's Naomi?" Nolan inquired.

"She insisted I come and spend time with you while she completed the lunch preparations on her own," Jasmine explained.

"She's a thoughtful woman. Do remind me to thank her," he said with a grin.

Jasmine smiled in return while she arranged her skirt. "Have the boys been behaving?"

"Absolutely. In fact, I find it amazing how well they get on together," Nolan commented, glancing toward Spencer and Moses. "There were so many years between Bradley and me, we both grew up as though we were only children. You likely experienced the same feelings having been the only girl in your family."

"Not exactly. I don't recall experiencing feelings of loneliness, but then, I was always privileged to have a tutor who filled her time by either teaching or entertaining me."

Nolan smiled and nodded before continuing to regale her with tales of his childhood.

Jasmine endeavored to listen, but her mind soon wandered back to the runaways and the three men who were attempting to provide them with food and safe haven before directing them farther north into Canada. She longed to know if the runaways had arrived, how many there were, and if the trackers had followed them into Massachusetts or given up the chase farther south. She hoped for the sake of the poor runaways the pursuers had given up long ago.

"Jasmine! Will you not answer me?"

"What? Oh yes, whatever you think will be fine with me," she absently replied.

Nolan's face filled with amusement. "That is likely the most offhanded reply to a marriage proposal in the annals of history."

"What?" Jasmine cried, now giving Nolan her undivided attention.

"Now I understand how this works. Once you've actually heard the word *marriage,* you're interested," he said with a wide grin. "Several minutes ago, I poured out my heart — telling you of my love and adoration. I don't want to take the chance of once again losing you to your own reflections, so I will merely repeat that I would consider myself the most fortunate man alive if you would consent to become my wife. Will you marry me, Jasmine?"

"Oh, Nolan," she whispered, her body melting into his embrace while she momentarily enjoyed the warmth of his strong arms. Finally, she was able to experience the complete love she had never had with Bradley. "Of course I'll marry you. I was beginning to think you would never ask," she said with a soft laugh.

"I didn't want to give anyone a reason to question the propriety of our union. I had intended to wait until three years after Bradley's death, but I now know I can wait no longer to take you as my wife," he said, lowering his head and covering her lips with a gentle kiss that slowly grew more urgent. "Tell me we can soon wed," he whispered, his gaze filled with passion.

"I am in complete agreement. However, Grandmother Wainwright may not be so easily convinced."

"She'll object to our marriage?" A note of panic laced his words.

Jasmine laughed and shook her head. "No, not to the marriage itself. In fact, she was so anxious for you to propose she'd begun harassing *me.* She thought I should help you along and said perhaps you were too shy to propose. However, knowing Grandmother, she'll want to have parties and plan a large wedding."

"And is that what you desire?"

"I had all of those things when I married Bradley. I have no desire for a long engagement, but Grandmother can be unrelenting."

"We'll remain steadfast. I believe six weeks is more than enough time, and October would be a lovely time of year for a wedding, don't you think?"

"Absolutely," Jasmine replied, tilting her head to accept another kiss.

The fresh air and hearty picnic lunch caused Spencer to finally succumb. He crawled onto Nolan's lap and was asleep within minutes of nestling himself into his uncle's strong arms. Jasmine watched the two of them for a moment, obviously enjoying the picture of serenity they created.

"Shall I carry him inside?" Nolan asked.

She gave him a grateful smile. "Please. Once he's down for his nap, perhaps we can discuss our wedding plans."

"I'd like that very much."

Nolan felt an overwhelming rush of pride. She had said yes to his proposal. Not that he had truly been worried that she would refuse him. Well, perhaps there had been some concern. He chuckled as he carried his nephew to bed. Truth be told, he had done a great deal of fretting, practicing his lines over and over the night before . . . wanting to ask in just the right way.

"And then she didn't even hear me."

Spender stirred in his arms. Nolan bent to place a kiss on the boy's forehead. "Soon you'll be my son — as I've always felt you should be."

The early evening sun had begun its descent, and Nolan was enjoying a final cup of coffee when Jasmine stood and began pacing in front of the fireplace. Spencer had long since risen from his nap and was happily playing at Nolan's feet. Yet Jasmine couldn't contain her growing concern about the runaways.

"Why don't we return to the back lawn for a little longer?" she suggested.

Nolan swallowed a final sip of coffee and returned the cup to its matching gold-rimmed saucer. "Why so restless, my dear? Have you not had enough fresh air for one day?"

Warmed by his playful grin and sparkling eyes, Jasmine stood and grasped his hand. "If we are very fortunate, there may be a few fireflies on the prowl that we can capture for Spencer."

He laughed and pushed his chair away from the table with his free hand. "I think it's a little early in the evening to see any fireflies, much less capture them!"

"Play! Outside!" Spencer chimed. "I go now, Mama," he said, tugging at Jasmine's fingers.

"You're outnumbered," she said, giggling.

Much to Spencer's amusement, Nolan paraded about the yard, pretending to seek out fireflies. The young boy followed his every move while Jasmine delightedly enjoyed their antics. Bradley would never have considered such playfulness appropriate; perhaps that fact alone made their liveliness today all the more precious.

"How is your brother faring since your father's departure? I'm certain McKinley would have preferred staying with you rather than your grandmother," Nolan said as he inspected the leaves of a rosebush for possible fireflies.

"Such would have been my preference also. However, Father was quite serious about their agreement. He will expect McKinley to honor his word and return to The Willows if he doesn't find a suitable position, and that task will be more easily accomplished if McKinley is living in Lowell rather than out here on the farm."

Nolan continued to examine the thorny rosebush. "Once he begins his search in earnest, McKinley will have no problem. With the variety of businesses in Lowell and the number of men leaving for California in search of gold, there are a multitude of opportunities."

"Still, he must avail himself of such opportunities, and he can't do that if he's busy escorting Grandmother around town. He tells me she expects him to act as her escort to all of her social functions. And you know what a full calendar she keeps!"

Nolan laughed and turned in her direction. "You, my dear, are not your brother's keeper. I'm certain McKinley can hold his own with your grandmother. If he has an appointment, I know that he'll ask her to make other arrangements for an escort to her soirees," he said before cupping one hand to shade his eyes and peering into the distance. "Wonder who that could be?"

Jasmine moved to where he stood, though the sun blinded her vision. "Is it wagons?" she asked, still unable to identify anything nearing the farm.

Nolan moved to the left. "Yes. In fact, there appear to be three," he said while squinting and drawing nearer to the fence line. "Looks like Obadiah is driving one, but I can't make out the other two men."

"Liam and Rogan?"

He lowered his hand and looked at her suspiciously. "I believe you're correct. How did you know?"

"Liam and Rogan asked if Obadiah could accompany them today and help quarry stone."

"Truly? Why would they suddenly need Obadiah's assistance?"

"They said they would need to use three wagons, and since there are only the two of them available to drive the wagons . . ."

Her voice trailed off as she watched the billowing clouds of dust rising from beneath the wagon wheels.

"Odd they'd ask for Obadiah's help. You'd think they'd hire one of the Irishmen from down in the Acre. There are always Irish laborers hoping to find work."

Was Nolan looking askance at her explanation, or was it her own guilt that caused her to think he didn't entirely believe her weak explanation? Certainly Nolan could be trusted with such information — he'd supported the antislavery movement long before she had. Yet she had given Liam and Rogan her word she'd say nothing. She didn't want to break her promise, so she walked away and stood by the fence.

Obadiah waved as the wagons drew closer. “Evenin’, suh, Miz Jasmine.”

“Good evenin’ to ya,” Rogan called, waving his hat at the welcoming committee before pulling back on the reins. “Good it is ta be seein’ ya, Mr. Houston.”

Nolan approached Jasmine and stood beside her. “It’s good to see you also. I trust you had a profitable day?”

“Aye. Sure and it was more of a success than even we could ’ave imagined,” Liam replied. “Without Obadiah’s fine help, we might have lost some of the runaways. Some of ’em shied away, thinkin’ we might be bounty hunters until Obadiah put their minds to rest and told ’em we could be trusted.”

“I promised I wouldn’t tell anyone,” Jasmine said to Nolan’s unspoken question.

“You didn’t think you could trust *me*?”

“Now, don’ be blamin’ the lass,” Liam said. “I was pretty hard on her last night, and I’m the one that caused her to keep her lips sealed. ’Course, I was na thinkin’ she’d be afraid to take someone such as yarself into her confidence. Mostly we did na want Obadiah’s wife findin’ out he was helpin’.”

“I’ll explain later. Naomi doesn’t want Obadiah helping with the runaways,” Jasmine whispered. “We’re pleased all went well, but you'd better get Obadiah home or Naomi will soon be joining us. She's likely heard the wagons and will be expecting him."

"Right ya are, ma'am. It's off we are," he said, giving a slap of the reins.

CHAPTER 13

Alice Wainwright fluttered into the kitchen, where Kiara and Naomi were assisting Alice's housekeeper, Martha. Leaning over, Alice inspected the trays of petit fours and raspberry tarts. "I presume the cakes are frosted with lemon icing."

"For sure some are. Others have a wondrous rosehips glaze that Naomi taught us to make. Here, why don't ya be tryin' one?" Kiara offered Alice one of the cakes. She smiled and took the treat.

"I don't believe Martha and I would have been prepared for this engagement party if you two hadn't offered your assistance," Alice said. "Isn't that right, Martha?"

"Yes, ma'am. We're both getting much too old for these large gatherings."

Alice pursed her lips. "Tut, tut. Being around lots of people makes one feel vibrant and alive. Besides, Martha, you're only as old as you feel."

Martha sighed and looked at the two younger women. "Then I must be at least a hundred. And I think my poor feet are even older."

Alice took a bite of the cake. "Oh, but that is a delightful flavor. You'll have to leave Martha the recipe. I would very much like to serve this again."

"I'd be pleased to, ma'am," Naomi said, her gaze never quite reaching Mrs. Wainwright's.

"I do hope we'll have enough food," Alice said, gazing around the room at the trays of prepared delicacies. "It would never do to run out."

"I'm na one to be judgin' what ya're doin', Mrs. Wainwright, but I was thinkin' Miss Jasmine said she was wantin' just a small gatherin' of folks fer this engagement party ya're hostin'."

"Exactly!" Martha agreed enthusiastically.

"Jasmine is insistent her *wedding* be understated. I completely disagree with her thinking. However, I know I did *not* agree to a small engagement party. She may have assumed I would adhere to her wedding guidelines, but that would be purely supposition on her part."

"Um hum. She should know better than to think you'd do things her way," Martha retorted.

"No need to take that sassy tone with me, Martha. You've known me long enough to know it will serve no purpose."

"True enough — besides, it's too late to change things now. People will soon arrive. Let's just hope the guests of honor appear before there are too many carriages lining the street. Otherwise, they may turn and go home without even stopping," Martha said with a chuckle.

"That's not funny, Martha. I'm going to make certain Martin is at the front door. You may need to come and assist."

"Martin can announce the guests without my assistance. Besides, I'm needed here in the kitchen. Especially if it starts to look as though we'll run out of food," Martha said with a wink at Kiara and Naomi.

" 'Tis true, Mrs. Wainwright. There's more to get done than me and Naomi can handle on our own. Me mind is willin' but me body will na cooperate — the babe seems ta sap me energy," Kiara said, patting her enlarged belly.

"Fine, fine," Alice said absently. In truth, she hadn't even heard Kiara's response. Her mind was too cluttered with the many details requiring her immediate attention. "But make certain the food is promptly served. And Naomi, if you'll see to keeping the punch bowl filled?" she added.

"Yessum, I'll make certain it's full to da brim — most of da time anyway."

Alice retreated from the kitchen, uncertain whether any of the three women understood the finer nuances of handling a large party. "This entire evening may turn into a disaster," she muttered while walking down the hallway. She paused long enough to check her appearance in the gilded mirror. The blue and silver brocade gown was one of her favorites. And although it was a heavy material and the weather had been sufficiently warm, Alice still felt a bit of a chill. *I've grown very old.* She sighed and gave her upswept hair a reassuring pat. "But not too old to enjoy seeing my Jasmine happily married." She smiled and noticed that it took years off her appearance. It gave her hope that she might yet live out many long years to enjoy her grandchildren and even great-grandchildren.

Martin was standing guard over the door like a sentry guarding the king's castle. Alice warmed at the sight. At least someone was handling their responsibility in a serious manner. A knock sounded at the door, and with great bravado, Martin opened the door and permitted Nolan and Jasmine entrance. He turned toward Alice and with grand enthusiasm announced, "Mrs. Bradley Houston and Mr. Nolan Houston."

"Oh, forevermore, Martin! I know who *they* are."

Martin's face was filled with puzzlement. "But you know everyone attending the party, ma'am. I thought you said I was to announce *all* of the guests."

"Jasmine and Nolan are the guests of honor, Martin. There is no need to announce my own granddaughter."

"I see. Well, am I to announce Master McKinley or Master Samuel?"

"If the other guests have begun arriving, then you need to announce them."

"But if Master McKinley comes downstairs before they arrive, it's not necessary — even though Miss Jasmine and her betrothed are here?"

Alice sighed and gave the older man a look of exasperation. "Never mind. Just announce *everyone,* Martin."

"That's exactly what I was trying to do when you said I wasn't doing things proper," he muttered.

Nolan chuckled but tried hard to mask his amusement when Martin looked his way.

Jasmine patted Martin's arm. "This shouldn't be such a problem, Martin. There won't be very many guests."

"That's what *you* think, ma'am," he whispered.

Jasmine followed her grandmother into the parlor. The rooms were festooned with fall foliage, candles were glowing in every corner, and chairs were arranged to accommodate guests throughout the rooms and spreading out into the garden.

"How many guests have you invited, Grandmother?"

"My, don't you look pretty," Alice said, pretending to fawn over Jasmine's dark burgundy creation. "Did you have this made in town? I don't remember seeing it before, so it must be new."

Jasmine raised a dark brow. "You know very well I ordered this dress from Boston. We discussed it on more than one occasion. Now answer me. How many guests have you invited?"

With a coy smile, Alice walked toward the garden. "Come see how I've arranged the garden, my dear. I think you'll find it quite ingenious." If she could stall long enough, the guests would arrive and eliminate — for the time — further questions from her granddaughter.

"Grandmother, you are playing a game of cat and mouse," Jasmine declared.

"Mr. and Mrs. Matthew Cheever, Miss Violet Cheever, and Master Michael Cheever," Martin announced vociferously.

Jasmine looked very seriously at her grandmother, but Alice only smiled. "I suppose," Jasmine began, "you should have made this a surprise party, for I'm sure to be very surprised as the night goes on."

"We had best go inside, for our guests are arriving." Alice scurried through the door, pleased she'd been able to avoid further inquisition.

A brief time later, the rooms overflowed with laughter and conversation while the many guests circulated throughout the house.

"Come along, McKinley. I have several people I'd like you to meet," Alice said, grasping McKinley's arm and maneuvering through the crowd until she reached the garden. She stopped beside Elinor Brighton only long enough for introductions and brief conversation before moving along toward several other guests.

Alice finally came to a halt beside the Cheever family. "Matthew and Lilly, you've already met my grandson, McKinley. I don't know if McKinley has told you — or perhaps Violet — that he has aspirations of utilizing his education and skills for one of the many industrial enterprises here in Lowell. Isn't that correct, McKinley?"

McKinley grinned at his grandmother before turning his attention back to Matthew Cheever. "I certainly am interested in locating employment. Father has given me an ultimatum — if I don't find a suitable position within three months, I must return to The Willows," he replied.

"Violet did mention your father departed and agreed you could remain in Lowell," Matthew said. "However, she didn't say you were seeking employment. I assumed you were merely remaining for an extended visit with your family. What type of work are you seeking?"

"So your grandmother has outfoxed you again," Nolan said as he stole a moment alone with his intended.

"It would seem so," Jasmine replied. "Although I have to admit, I'm having a wonderful time. These guests are mostly dear friends. I suppose I cannot be cross about celebrating the happiest moment of my life with them."

Nolan smiled down at her and Jasmine felt her heart skip a beat. "I hope you know how happy you've made me," he said, his voice husky.

"If it's only a portion of the happiness you've given me, then you must be a contented man indeed."

Nolan scanned the room. They'd slipped into a smaller parlor, one Grandmother seldom used. "Dare I steal a kiss?"

"Absolutely not," Jasmine said with a smile. "For I shall willingly give you all that you desire. There's no need to steal."

With that, he pulled her into his arms and with a tantalizingly leisurely pace, kissed her long and passionately. Jasmine felt her knees grow weak. How marvelous the way this man affected her. It was all that she had wished for in her marriage to Bradley — wished for, but never knew.

"I suppose," Nolan said, pulling back, "we should rejoin the others."

She nodded, unable to speak.

He grinned. "Or we could just elope."

Again Jasmine nodded, only to have Nolan laugh uproariously at her. Jasmine could only relish the moment. He pulled her back to the party, and she clung to his arm as they circulated around the room.

"I'll procure us each a glass of punch," Nolan said, maneuvering Jasmine to a nearby chair.

She watched him as he strode through the well-wishers. The fact that he would soon be hers was still a marvel Jasmine could not quite grasp.

"You look so happy," Violet Cheever said as she joined Jasmine. "I just know your wedding will be very beautiful." She sighed. "I can only hope to have such things for myself one day."

Jasmine laughed. "And of course you will, for you are quite lovely, and rumor has it that many a young man has been intrigued by your beauty."

"Most of them are dowdy bores," Violet said, surprising Jasmine.

"I hope you do not consider my brother to be among their numbers."

Violet shook her head, and her expression almost took on a frightened look. "McKinley is certainly not in their number. McKinley is . . . well . . . he's in a place all by himself."

"Not dowdy or boring?" Jasmine grinned, enjoying Violet's comments. It was very evident the young woman was more than a little interested in McKinley. And Jasmine knew from her brother's continual questions regarding the Cheevers, particularly Violet, that he, too, was interested.

"Your brother could never be boring. I find everything he says to be quite fascinating."

"I'm sure he feels the same about you," Jasmine said, leaning closer to the young woman. "In fact, I've noticed that he hasn't taken his gaze from you all evening."

"I worry that he'll think me too forward. I'm just not myself when I'm around him. I become so extroverted and . . . well . . . I'm even given to flirting."

Jasmine laughed heartily at this as Nolan rejoined them.

"And whatever is so funny?" he asked as he handed Jasmine a glass of punch.

Violet turned red and lowered her face immediately, while Jasmine simply shook her head. "You wouldn't understand — the talk of young women, you see."

"Ah." He took a sip of his punch before adding, "Which of course always involves young men."

The next morning Jasmine hastened to the front door with Spencer in tow. "McKinley — and Violet! Do come in. What a pleasant surprise. I wasn't expecting to see you again so soon. To what do I owe the pleasure of this visit?" she asked as she led the couple into the parlor.

A broad smile spread across McKinley's face. "I wanted to share my good news with you first." Jasmine put her hand to her throat. Had McKinley proposed? Surely not. She looked to Violet as if for some sign or proof of the topic, but Violet simply smiled. "There's nothing I love more than good news. Do tell me," she said as Spencer climbed onto McKinley's lap.

"I am now an employee of the Boston Associates — hired to work as Mr. Cheever's assistant."

Jasmine gaped at her brother, astonished he had so quickly secured the impressive position. At the same time, she was very glad she hadn't blurted out some comment about a betrothal. "I'm astonished — not that I don't believe you're capable. But I'd think there would have been someone already working for the mills with more experience, someone they would have promoted into such an opportunity."

"That's what I thought when Mr. Cheever told me about the job. However, he explained he preferred someone who would come into the position without any preconceived ideas — someone who would bring a fresh perspective to the business aspects of the mills — just as he had when Mr. Boott took him on. With my knowledge of the cotton business and education in accounting, Mr. Cheever thought me the perfect choice. Needless to say, Grandmother was elated with the news."

"No doubt," Jasmine said. "She's likely penning a letter to Father as we speak. When do you assume your new duties?"

"Monday morning. I mentioned I would immediately begin my search for another place to live."

Jasmine laughed and waved her hand. "Let me guess! Grandmother became indignant that you would even consider living anywhere else."

"Exactly!" he said. "I thought she would prefer to return to the peaceful existence of living alone. Instead, she acted as though I had intentionally insulted her."

"I wouldn't consider broaching that subject again — leastwise not until you're planning to wed and purchasing a home of your own." Jasmine glanced toward Violet as she completed her comment. Violet blushed, but McKinley ignored the reference.

"I doubt Father will be nearly as pleased with the news as you and Grandmother," McKinley said. "I honestly believe he thought me incapable. A complete buffoon, unable to make my way in the world without benefit of my father's assistance."

Jasmine could see the concern in McKinley's expression and knew he didn't want to remain at odds with their father. Yet he was correct: Malcolm Wainwright would not be pleased with the news.

Violet edged closer to McKinley. "I heard my father say to Mother that he thought hiring you would be pleasing to the Wainwright family."

"What else did he say, Violet?" Jasmine inquired.

"Just that Mr. Wainwright had been anxious to have your brother Samuel working to secure cotton for the mills and that hiring McKinley would surely reinforce the Southern cotton growers' relationship with the Lowell mills." She hesitated a moment and frowned, her forehead creased into deep wrinkles. "I'm not certain I heard all he was saying. I truly don't listen very well when Father begins talking about business matters."

McKinley patted her hand. "Don't concern yourself, Violet. At this juncture, the comments would be of little consequence. Isn't that correct, Jasmine?"

Obviously McKinley wanted her to assist in easing Violet's noticeable anxiety. "McKinley is correct — the conversation changes nothing. However, I find Mr. Cheever's reasoning quite interesting," she replied.

■ ■ ■ ■

Oliver Maxwell stepped off the train and entered the bustling Baltimore depot, pleased his journey was over. He detested traveling — which was somewhat of a troublesome matter for a man employed as a traveling salesman. However, he'd never enjoyed sharing space and being forced into conversation with total strangers, especially those who believed they had a right to pry into his personal affairs. And there had been a number of them on this journey: women making coy remarks and proud men boasting about themselves as they attempted to delve into his personal life. The remembrance caused an involuntary shiver to course through him.

Tightly gripping his satchel, Oliver made his way through the station. Stretching his stiff, tired muscles, he walked with long strides toward his mother's boardinghouse, thankful the old house was nearby and he'd not be required to ride in another coach. He pulled out his pocket watch and clicked open the case. There wouldn't be time to linger at his mother's residence. He'd drop off his satchel with a promise to return for supper.

Taking the front steps two at a time, Oliver opened the front door of the house. A small brass bell over the door jingled to announce his entry.

"Read the sign. I got no openings," his mother said as she bustled from the rear of the house.

"Well, that's good news," Oliver replied. "I'm pleased to hear you've a full house and can easily make the mortgage payments."

Edna Maxwell wagged her head back and forth. "When I heard the bell, I said there were no vacancies, but I do have empty rooms."

Oliver's eyebrows arched. "Why would you lie, Mother?"

"It's not a lie. I've filled as many rooms as I can handle at one time. I'm an old woman, Oliver. I grow weary of cleaning rooms and cooking meals for ungrateful boarders who have nothing but complaints to give me in return. Look at these hands," she said, shoving them forward to ensure they were in his direct line of vision. "They're gnarled and crippled from age and years of hard work."

Oliver dropped his satchel and walked to the open ledger lying on the desk. Using his finger as a guide, he traced the entries for the last two months. He was incredulous as he shot a look at his mother and then back to the pages, flipping through them in rapid succession. "You're renting only three rooms? I'm sending you money to meet the mortgage when you've intentionally permitted rooms to stand empty?" He clenched his jaw in an attempt to keep his temper in check.

"I told you it's all I can do," she defended.

"And what of Gertrude? She may be lame, but surely she can help with some of the chores. Gertrude! Come to the parlor!" he yelled.

He fell onto the frayed settee, his anger mounting while he waited. "Gertrude! I haven't all day to wait on you."

His sister's uneven steps could be heard as she neared the parlor. With as much grace as her crippled body would permit, Gertrude entered the room. "Oliver, what a wonderful surprise. I'm sorry to keep you waiting. I was peeling potatoes — it takes me longer than it should," she apologized.

Truth be told, he didn't know how she could even peel a potato with her crippled arm and clawlike hand. The entire left side of her body, save her face, was disfigured. A freak of nature, their father said; punishment for their father's drunkenness, her mother said. But as far as Oliver was concerned, it was the plague of being poor and unable to have a doctor at his sister's birthing. The reason no longer mattered. He was left with the unwanted responsibility of a mother who no longer wanted to work and a sister who was physically unable to be of much assistance.

"Your limp appears to be growing worse," he commented as his sister neared his side.

She leaned down and placed a fleeting kiss upon his cheek. "It's no worse than when you last visited. The left side of my body grows weary quite rapidly, and when I'm overly tired, the limp appears more pronounced. Do not worry yourself, brother. I'm quite healthy otherwise."

He couldn't remain angry with Gertrude. Through all her years of pain and the added torment of enduring cruel remarks by family and strangers alike, her sweet nature prevailed. "I'm concerned over the fact that only three rooms in the house are being rented out."

"I try to help all I can," Gertrude said, "but Mother ails and is unable to do much anymore. She says it's all we can handle. Isn't that right, Mother?"

Edna shifted in her chair. "I could possibly take on one more."

"I've been taking in laundry and doing a bit of sewing to earn extra money," Gertrude said while giving her brother a sweet smile. "The money helps with groceries."

Oliver's gaze settled on his sister's lame hand. "How can you do laundry and sewing with that hand?"

"I manage. It takes me longer, but my customers seem pleased with my work."

Oliver cradled his sister's face in his palm. She was the only woman in whom he'd ever discovered virtue — the rest always wanted something from him, including his mother. "You're a fine girl, Gertrude, and I'm sorry I hollered at you earlier. I was weary from traveling and overwrought when I discovered how the rentals were being handled. It's not your fault. Please forgive me."

"Of course, Oliver. Mother and I are very thankful for all you do. I know how difficult it must be traveling about the country selling shoes. I know you'd likely prefer to remain in one place."

Edna narrowed her eyes. Oliver could feel her studying him. "I know that look. What is it you want to say, Mother?"

"We can talk later, when we're alone. You can put your satchel in room eight."

He returned his mother's steely glare. "I've a business meeting I must attend, but I'll return this evening. I won't take supper with you, as I'm certain you weren't planning on another mouth to feed," he said in an acerbic tone.

"And what business is it that needs the immediate attention of a shoe peddler?" his mother rebutted.

"I'll not always be a shoe peddler, Mother. In the meantime, I haven't noticed you hesitating to line your purse with the coins I earn selling shoes."

"You're always ready with a bit of sass and disrespect."

"And you're always quick to find fault with me, so I'd say you're reaping what you've sown, old woman. The fact that you've a kindhearted daughter who can bear living with you day after day is nothing short of unbelievable. I'll take my satchel upstairs when I return."

He strode out of the house, unwilling to be detained by her outbursts, before their argument could escalate any further. Gertrude's faint good-bye echoed in his ears as he hurried down the street. If all went well over the next year, he would buy a small house for Gertrude and send her a monthly stipend. Let his mother fight to meet the monthly bank note on her own. Maybe then she'd realize how much she relied upon him and come groveling for his help. Oliver reveled in the thought of finally forcing his mother to acknowledge her dependency on him. She withheld her love like a miser clinging to golden coins, never willing to share affection with others.

"Likely why Father found warmth in the arms of other women," he muttered as he entered a small tavern not far from the train depot.

Oliver edged his way through the tavern, skimming the sea of faces in an effort to find his new business partners. Spotting Enoch Garon near the rear of the room, he worked his way toward the tall, muscular man. Enoch wasn't bright, but he followed instructions and his brute strength was an asset.

"Enoch! You're looking well," Oliver greeted while pulling a chair away from the table and sitting down. "Where's Joseph?" He scanned the place for the third member of his business association.

"He'll be here. Told me yesterday he might be a little late." Enoch turned toward the front of the tavern. "Here he comes now."

The men greeted each other, ordered their ale, and waited until it had been served before commencing their discussion in earnest. "I take it you both have been hearing about the Fugitive Slave Act being signed by President Fillmore," Oliver said after taking a swig of his ale.

" 'Course we heard. Probably long afore you folks up in Massachusetts," Enoch replied. "Wondered if you was ever gonna get down here and get things going. There's been lots of opportunities, but me and Joseph wanted to keep our word to you. The time is now to begin hunting down them slaves that's running north. With this new policy, we're gonna be able to make some fine money."

Joseph nodded his head. "Especially since the authorities are required to help us round up any runaways if we ask. Can't ask for nothin' better than that."

"Problem is there's more and more men seeing this as a golden opportunity. The competition is going to increase, and I'm guessing more of the slaves are going to be afraid to run off, knowing they won't have safe sanctuary up north anymore. That means fewer runaways and more people out there trying to find 'em."

"Hadn't thought of that," Enoch said. "So we're really not much better off, are we?"

"Only if you're using your head to develop a plan beyond the obvious. And that's exactly what I've done," Oliver said.

The two men leaned in further, anxious to hear what Oliver had to say. "Tell us what you've been planning. You know you can trust the two of us," Enoch urged.

"I keep my eyes and ears open while I'm traveling about the countryside, and I'm certain I'll be able to pry loose information from time to time about runaways. But we need to do more if we're to make a dependable income from this new law. I'm thinking we should consider capturing some of the freed Negroes that have moved north. We can take them back down south and sell them at auction. Lots easier than actually hunting for runaways."

Enoch rubbed his hands together. "Or we can take 'em to most any plantation. Those owners won't care where they come from or if they claim to be free. You got you one good idea, Oliver. And I'll wager you know where there's some fine specimens up north that we can get our hands on."

"Around Lowell, I think I can find a number of fine-looking freed Negroes. More than either one of you can imagine," he said while beginning to formulate a list in his mind. Obadiah, the strong buck over at the Houston horse farm, made the top of his list.

Chapter 14

Alice fanned herself with a vengeance. "I did *not* agree to a small, intimate wedding, Jasmine. You took my silence as agreement, just as you did with your engagement party. If you won't consider your old grandmother and the pleasure a lovely wedding would bring to me, then think of your friends and other relatives. Give them the enjoyment of such festivities."

"A grand weddin' would be enjoyable," Kiara agreed as she sat down beside Jasmine while holding a piece of lace in one hand.

Alice gave Kiara an engaging smile. "You see? Your friends want to attend a nice affair as much as I do."

"Grandmother! Will you stop at nothing to have your way in this matter? I do not want a large wedding, nor does Nolan. We've decided upon a small garden wedding in October. I think you should be ashamed of yourself for attempting to manipulate me with your emotion-filled statements."

"To tell ya the truth, I could use some extra time to complete the lace I'm makin' fer yar weddin' veil. It's ta be my weddin' gift to ya," Kiara said.

Jasmine sighed and gave her friend a feeble smile. "You don't need to go to all that trouble, Kiara. I had a large wedding when I married Bradley. Nolan and I truly do not desire a large affair. Besides, you need to spend this time making special clothing for your baby."

Kiara's eyes clouded as she dropped the lace onto her swollen belly. "Ya do na want me ta make yar weddin' lace?"

"That's not what I meant, Kiara. The lace is beautiful and I truly appreciate your kindness, but I wasn't planning to wear a veil. Couldn't we use the lace on my dress?"

"If that's what ya're wantin'," she replied, though her dejection was obvious.

Alice poured a glass of lemonade from a cut glass pitcher and took a sip of the sweetened drink before speaking. "Now you see what you've done? You've hurt Kiara's feelings, and you're attempting to shame me for wanting something as simple as an appropriate wedding for you. I'm an old woman, and I'll likely die before I have an opportunity to see another of my grandchildren wed. I would think that instead of considering only yourselves, you and Nolan would think of bringing others pleasure also. And before you mention David's possible wedding, let me say that I doubt my health will permit me to ever travel to The Willows again. We both know David will not come to Massachusetts to wed his Southern wife, and there's no possibility McKinley will wed in the near future."

Jasmine clasped a hand to her breast and could feel her heartbeat begin to accelerate beneath her fingers. "What health problems would prohibit your travel? Is there something regarding your well-being you've kept secret from me?"

Alice took another sip of her lemonade. "Would such information change your mind?"

"No, I don't believe it would. However, if you're ill, you should confide in me so that we can find proper medical treatment. Besides, if you're truly ailing, I do not want to subject you to the rigors of planning a large wedding."

A frown pinched Alice's fine features. "I'm certain my health would improve if I could occupy my thoughts with something exciting — such as a wedding. I've been told you can trick the mind into thinking you're well if you concentrate on other matters and don't dwell on your illness."

Kiara moved to Alice's side and gave the older woman's hand a gentle pat. "I did na know ya was ailing, and ya can always look ta me to help ya, ma'am. Good I am at takin' care of those that are sick. Just ask Paddy — I could always nurse 'im back ta health."

"How sweet you are, Kiara. And I'm sure *you* wouldn't deprive *your* grandmother of something so simple as a wedding, would you?"

Kiara wagged her head back and forth. "Oh, no — I'm only wishin' me ma could 'ave been here when I married Rogan. What a blessin' that would 'ave been. And even more 'appy I'd be ta 'ave me mother see this wee babe when it's born."

Jasmine closely watched the exchange between Kiara and her grandmother. "I believe you're as fit as the day I arrived in Lowell and this whole discussion is nothing more than a charade so that I'll give in to your whims."

"Such accusations!" Alice retorted. "Do you desire a written statement from the doctor?"

Hesitating momentarily, Jasmine watched her grandmother shift uncomfortably in her chair. "Yes. I believe that would be acceptable."

Alice wilted at the challenge, yet remained unrelenting. "If you loved me, you wouldn't require proof of what I say."

Neither woman noticed Nolan enter the room. "What's going on in here? I could hear the ruckus before I entered the house. I believe I've heard fewer angry voices in the local tavern."

Jasmine's cheeks flushed. She should never have engaged in such uncomely behavior — especially with her grandmother. She grasped Alice's hand. "I apologize for my argumentative conduct."

Alice sighed contentedly. "Apology accepted, my dear. Now, shall we begin planning the wedding? I've a list of things we must accomplish before week's end, and Kiara must return to working on the lace for your wedding veil."

Nolan cleared his throat. "Ladies! The wedding plans have already been settled. The ceremony will be small and take place on the twelfth of October. We will be married in the garden, weather permitting, and a reception will follow indoors. There will be *no* changes to our plans and absolutely *no* delays."

Jasmine and the two other women stared at him, all three rendered momentarily speechless by his unyielding declaration.

Completely composed, he walked to the divan and sat down beside Jasmine. "Now that we've settled the wedding issue, I believe I would enjoy a glass of that lemonade."

Elinor Brighton sat in the last row of chairs, ready to hear a lecture on South American butterflies. She wasn't sure why she'd even come. Butterflies were of no interest to her, and her free time was so scarce that it seemed quite wasteful. Still, here she was — picking lint from her coarse brown skirt and wondering where life was taking her.

Sometimes the memories of Daniel and Wilbur were so painful that they threatened to steal away her will to live. Other times, like now, they were bittersweet, almost reassuring reminders that at one point — at one time — she had been loved.

Why were they gone? Why had they died so young? Her best memories of her life with Daniel were their times together before they'd even married. Oh, it wasn't that their intimacy as husband and wife hadn't been joyous, wondrous . . . but rather it was the time spent in conversation, walks in the park, or simple moments in each other's company that touched her most deeply.

How she missed the conversation of a man. She longed for something more than inane chatter of the mill girls. Their idea of exciting discourse ran along the lines of what new dress so-and-so had bought, and which young gentleman they were seeing at the time. They were silly and young . . . much younger than Elinor could ever remember being.

I'm only twenty-six, she thought. Not so very old. But much too old for conversations centering on hairstyles and parties. The loss of her youth to widowhood often made Elinor angry, but this time it just made her feel defeated. The reassurance of being loved faded in light of the loss.

The lecturer took his place and began to speak of his studies and eventual trips to South America. He spoke with a great booming voice that promised much authority on the matter. Elinor sighed. Jasmine Houston was remarrying in a few days. She was one of the only other young widows Elinor had ever known. Jasmine was very much in love — of that Elinor was certain, so it only seemed right that she should marry.

But I was in love too, and look where that took me.

The lecturer held up a specimen of some type of butterfly, the name of which escaped Elinor. Instead of pretending to listen any longer, she quietly got up and excused herself from the row of rapt listeners. Perhaps butterflies were meant to be a part of their world, but they certainly had no place in hers.

The streetlights shone a path for Elinor to follow home. All along the way she watched other people . . . couples . . . families. Everyone had someone. The lights that shone from the houses promised happy homes where people gathered in love. Through one of the massive widows trimmed in gauzy lace curtains, Elinor caught a glimpse of a young man lifting a small child in the air. She turned away quickly, the pain encircling her heart like a band, threatening to stop its beating.

"I wish it would stop," she murmured, picking up her pace. "I wish I could just cease to be — to hurt."

Jasmine drew her grandmother into a warm embrace. "You'll have to admit that our wedding was a nice affair, even if it didn't meet your original expectations," Jasmine whispered.

"I would agree that the wedding was nice," Alice answered. "It certainly was neither elegant nor the social event of the year, but it was a nice little gathering."

Jasmine laughed and tightened her embrace. "Nolan and I are truly pleased your illness did not keep you from attending."

"All right, young lady, you got your way. No need to harass me about my earlier tactics. Truth be told, my health isn't that good, nor will it remain stable forever. I am an old woman."

"Grandmother, are you trying to worry me?"

Alice's features softened. "No. I'm simply remembering how devastated you were to lose your mother. I won't live forever, Jasmine, and you must be prepared. Perhaps I did play at exaggerating it when trying to convince you to change your wedding plans, but you must see the truth. Each winter I grow a little weaker."

Jasmine hugged her grandmother close. "I couldn't bear to lose you."

Grandmother stroked Jasmine's hair. "But we will see each other again — in heaven. You must never fear my passing. Death is a part of life and shouldn't be feared. God has said He will never leave us nor forsake us. Never . . . not even in death."

Jasmine pulled away and looked into her grandmother's eyes. "I love you, Grandmother. So very much. I know we'll have all eternity, but I'd like a little longer here on earth."

Alice Wainwright smiled. "I'll do what I can to ensure that, but don't fret over it if God has other plans." Jasmine nodded soberly and Alice added, "You had best go upstairs and change into your traveling gown. I daresay Nolan is not going to be detained at this reception much longer."

"Do come help me, won't you?" Jasmine asked as she grasped her grandmother's hand.

"*Now* you want my help," she said with a chuckle as she happily followed Jasmine to her room.

Alice unfastened Jasmine's fawn gown that had been elegantly embellished around the neckline with Kiara's ivory handmade lace. "I do think you should have agreed to something longer than a few days in Boston for your wedding trip. I'm sure Nolan isn't pleased with your decision."

"Nolan is fine with my decision. Neither of us wanted to leave Spencer for any longer. Besides, we're imposing upon Kiara and Naomi to care for him. I wouldn't expect them to tend to him any longer than a few days — especially with Kiara's baby due in only a few months."

"I told you I would come and stay here at the farm and look after him."

"Really, Grandmother — an hour or two tending a young boy is one thing, but any longer and you would have to take to your bed. And we've just talked about your health and keeping you around for a while. I've told both Kiara and Naomi to call upon you if they need your help," she added.

A rumble of thunder sounded overhead as Alice helped Jasmine into her traveling dress of periwinkle blue silk. "As usual, you look lovely, my dear. Permit an old woman to tell you that I am very happy you and Nolan found each other. You deserve the joy of a good marriage, and I know Nolan is going to make you very happy."

"Thank you, Grandmother. I'm certain he will also." She placed a kiss on the older woman's cheek.

Alice glanced out the bedroom window. "Those clouds appear ominous. We had best get you downstairs to your groom so that you may leave before the rain begins."

Oliver Maxwell hunkered beside a large oak tree, securing what shelter could be found while permitting him a partial view of the small cottage occupied by the three Negroes. Oliver's horse was tethered in a nearby clump of trees to remain hidden from view until he was prepared to make his move. He shivered as the cool fall air pressed his damp garments against his body. The sound of an approaching wagon caused him to shrink out of sight.

"Are ya ready ta get ta work on those fences, Obadiah?" one of the men called out from the wagon with a strong Irish brogue.

Oliver edged out from behind the tree and watched in dismay as the wagon came to a halt near the cottage. Obadiah exited the house and climbed into the wagon. Leaning against the tree, Oliver slid down into a squat and tilted his head against the tree's rough bark. He'd suffered through this rain and cold for naught! Making a tight fist, Oliver slammed it into the open palm of his other hand. He had counted upon making some quick money and assured Enoch and Joseph his plan for kidnapping and selling freed slaves would prove effective.

Oliver didn't know how long he'd been sitting at the base of the tree when he heard the voices of a woman and small child coming from the opened door of the cottage.

Obadiah's wife and child! If he captured them, he could use them as bait to lure Obadiah into his clutches. Naomi walked out of the door carrying a basket of clothing and moved toward the cauldron of water hanging over an open fire. The child remained close to her side. Moving quietly, Oliver made his way to the clump of bushes and then untied and mounted his horse. With two quick jabs, he dug his heels into the horse's shanks and sped off toward the woman and child. Moving with lightning speed, he entered the yard and dismounted.

"Nooo!" Naomi screamed as he grabbed her around the waist.

Slapping his hand across the struggling woman's mouth, Oliver wrestled her to the ground. With a knee wedged into her back, he moved to quickly gag her with a dirty handkerchief before securing both hands behind her with a piece of rope. He lifted her feather-light body onto the horse and then grabbed the screaming child under his arm. With greater ease than he could have hoped for, Oliver hoisted himself up and slapped the reins.

Balancing a basket of dirty clothes under one arm and holding Moses with her other hand, Kiara ambled toward Obadiah and

Naomi's nearby cottage. "Come on with ya, Moses. Let's go and see yar little friend Spencer. The two of ya can play while yar mama and me do our washin'," she said, suddenly distracted by the sight of a horse speeding away from the cottage.

She stopped and squinted into the sun. "Stop! Stop!" she screamed, dropping the basket and scooping Moses into her arms. Running as fast as her burgeoning body would permit, she finally came to a halt and dropped to her knees, gasping for breath. The horse was now out of sight.

Clutching Moses close to her side, Kiara was uncertain what to do. Her mind raced.

"Wet go," Moses said, wiggling against her arms.

Hands trembling, Kiara loosened her hold on the child. "Don't be runnin' off — we must go find your papa."

But Liam, Rogan, and Obadiah were mending fences, and Paddy and Mr. Fisher had taken one of the horses to the farrier in Lowell. There was no one close at hand to help, no one to go after Naomi and Spencer.

"Settle yarself, Kiara. We can na understand a word ya're sayin'," Rogan admonished as he pulled her close.

Moses toddled toward Obadiah. "Papa!"

"What you doin' here, chile?" Obadiah lifted the boy into his arms and in several long strides was beside Rogan and Kiara. "What's goin' on? How come you got Moses out here?"

"She's been tryin' to tell me," Rogan said. "Take a deep breath, lass, and try ta talk."

Kiara swallowed hard, knowing she must relay the information. "Naomi came over to visit with me after the three of ya left this morning. Moses fell asleep, and I told her ta be leavin' him with me and I'd join her after he woke up. We was gonna do our washin' together. Naomi took Spencer home with her. When Moses woke up from his nap, I gathered my washin' and headed out to the cottage. The sun was blindin' me, but I heard a scream and then I saw a man ridin' off with Naomi and Spencer."

Obadiah was shaking his head forcefully. "No! Dat can't be true."

" 'Tis true. I ran as fast as I could, but I was carryin' Moses and with me in my condition, I could na run fast enough. They was down the road and out of sight before I could even make it ta the cottage."

"Come on! We gotta go get her!" Obadiah hollered.

"Settle yarself, Obadiah," Liam admonished. "If we're gonna find yar wife and little

Spencer, we've gotta be thinkin'. Ain' nobody gonna listen to a couple Irishmen and a Negro. We need ta get us some help. I'm thinkin' maybe Mr. Cheever could lend a hand. I'll take the horse Kiara rode out here and go and tell him what's happened. The rest of ya go back to the farm and wait for me there. See if ya can be findin' anything that's gonna give us some idea of what happened. Look far any clue the culprit may've left behind. We're gonna need all the help we can get if we're gonna find them."

Kiara began to sob as Rogan helped her into the wagon. "We've got ta find them, Rogan. Miss Jasmine's gonna be home in a few days. She'll never fargive us for lettin' this happen ta little Spencer — and poor Naomi, what's gonna happen ta her?"

"We'll find dem — ain' gonna rest until we find both of dem," Obadiah said, his back rigid and jaw clenched tight.

A short time later, Rogan pulled back on the reins, and the horses came to a halt in front of the barn. Obadiah jumped down with Moses in his arms while Rogan lifted Kiara to the ground. "Ya're still tremblin', lass. Ya need to keep yar faith. We're gonna find them, and I'm thinkin' the best way to help is go back over to the house and see what's in the area. Looks like the fire's still goin'," he said as they grew closer.

The woven basket was overturned near the fire, and dirty clothes and linens lay scattered on the ground. Kiara grabbed the basket and began picking up the garments. "We were goin' ta wash together," she said, glancing toward Obadiah. "I already told ya that, didn't I?"

Obadiah nodded. "Try to remember everything from da time you left da house with Moses," he encouraged.

Kiara looked at her husband, who gave her an encouraging smile. "Naomi brought both of the boys ta the house, and we had a cup of tea and visited. She said she thought Moses might be takin' a cold and that he hadn't been sleepin' well the last couple nights."

"Tha's true. He been mighty hard to please da last few days."

"For sure he was fussin', and I began rockin' him on me lap. He fell asleep, and I told Naomi to just leave him until he woke up. She said she'd be takin' Spencer back to the cottage so he wouldn't wake up Moses. We agreed to do the washin' when Moses woke up."

Rogan patted her shoulder. "Ya're doin' fine, lass. What happened next?"

"Moses woke up, I picked up my basket of dirty clothes, and we left the house. All of a sudden, I heard a scream and looked toward the cottage. The sun was shinin' bright, and I moved enough to block the sun from me eyes so I could be seein'. By that time, all I saw was the back of a man. He had Naomi sprawled across the horse and Spencer tucked under 'is arm. The boy was kickin' and cryin' as they rode away."

"And what kind of horse was he ridin', lass? Can ya be tellin' us about the horse?"

Kiara looked at the road, trying to visualize it. "The horse was na unusual — nothin' like the Arabians. It was just a horse."

"What color?" Obadiah insisted.

"A light sorrel. I'm sorry, but the sun was in me eyes," she said with a tremble in her voice. "I'm thinking it might be a mottled red."

Rogan drew her close and wrapped her in his arms. "Stop yar tears, lass. If ya're to help, ya must remain calm. Think of the boy," he whispered. "Ya'll have him upset all over again."

Kiara turned and took in Moses' tear-stained face puckered into an image of gloom. "Come here, Moses. Come sit with me." She sat on the step of the cabin and spread her arms to welcome him.

He rushed to Kiara and wiggled onto the bit of lap remaining unoccupied by the child growing inside her. Kiara began to rock back and forth as the child shoved his thumb into his mouth and rested his curly head on her breast while Rogan and Obadiah continued to search for some sign of the man.

"We's wastin' time. While we's standin' 'round doin' nothin', he's gettin' farther on down da road with Naomi and Spencer. We should take a couple of dem fine horses and go after dem — ain' nothin' to be gained standin' here. We done seen all dere is to see — which turns out to be nothin'."

"Liam said to wait, and I ain't one ta be goin' against Liam Donohue. Besides, if anyone saw us on those Arabians, they'd far sure hang us high. Sure and I can see it now — an Irishman and a Negro tryin' to explain how they happen ta be ridin' a couple of expensive Arabian steeds."

The sound of approaching horses caused both men to cease their arguing and turn their attention toward the road.

"Looks like Liam found Mr. Cheever," Rogan said as he waved at the men. They all rushed to the horses — even Kiara, still holding Moses.

Liam pulled back hard on the reins as he

and Matthew neared the cottage. “Have ya anything more ta tell us?”

Rogan shook his head. “There’s na a scrap of a clue ta be found around the place.”

“Can you think of any reason someone would kidnap Naomi and Spencer?” Matthew asked as he dismounted. “Have you had any threats against you, Obadiah?”

“No, suh, ain’ had nothin’ like dat. Ain’ nobody woulda even knowed Spencer was at da house and ain’ no reason for no one ta be takin’ Naomi. She ain’ never done nothin’ to nobody.”

Matthew removed his straw hat and wiped the beads of perspiration from his forehead. “What about your former owner, Obadiah? I know Mrs. Houston purchased your freedom, but I wonder if he might have something to do with this.”

“No, suh, I don’ think so. Miss Jasmine paid him what he was askin’ fer us. Fact is, she paid Massa Harshaw more than what anyone else woulda paid. Mean as dat man was, I don’ think he’d be tryin’ such a thing as kidnappin’ Naomi. Don’ make no sense.”

“I’m merely trying to think of any reason there might be for someone to specifically take Naomi and Spencer,” Matthew said. “I asked my wife to go and speak to Alice Wainwright. I thought she should know

Spencer is missing."

Kiara pointed down the road, where an approaching horse and rider could be seen in the distance. "Here comes Paddy."

The group stood watching the young man as he approached on one of the beautiful Arabians, the horse prancing toward them with the elegant beauty of a trained dancer.

"I was na expectin' such a welcome," Paddy said, a bright smile curling his lips. Kiara watched as her brother scanned their faces and then turned his attention to her. "What's the matter? Ya all look as though someone has died."

"Naomi and Spencer 'ave been kidnapped," Kiara told him. "I saw a man ride off with the two of them as I was leavin' the house with Moses."

"Surely ya're jokin'. Why would anyone want to be kidnappin' Naomi and Spencer?" Paddy asked. "When did they disappear?"

Once again Kiara recounted the activity leading up to the kidnapping, and though the details were few, she attempted to recall every one for her brother.

"I think we should take one more look outside the house; then Liam and I will see if we can follow their trail," Matthew said. "Obadiah, I think it's best if you remain here with Moses."

"Ya're not gonna find nothin' by lookin' again," Rogan remarked. "Me and Obadiah already done that two times."

"Then it shouldn't take long. We'll give the area a fresh look. You and Obadiah can stay with the horses, Rogan," Matthew said as he led the others closer to the cottage.

Paddy stooped down and settled on his haunches, scanning the damp ground before glancing up at his sister. "Did the kidnappin' happen before or after Mr. Maxwell came to the cottage?"

"Mr. Maxwell did na come today, Paddy," she said.

"Look at those muddy prints." He pointed to the ground as Matthew and Liam returned. "Mr. Maxwell's horse has a clubfoot. I noticed it when I watered the animal, but I do na see any wagon marks. He must 'ave been riding the horse. Did ya na say the horse was red, Kiara? Do ya think it might've been a strawberry roan?"

"May 'ave been. The sun was in me eyes, Paddy, but I thought there was a reddish color to the animal. They disappeared afore I could see very good."

"Seems we need to talk to Mr. Maxwell. Any idea where he stays when he's in Lowell?" Matthew asked, glancing around at the others.

"I heard him tell Miss Jasmine he'd be deliverin' our shoes in a month, or she could check at the Merrimack House if she was in town." Paddy replied, his chest puffing as he shared the information. "He said he'd made arrangements with the owner of the Merrimack since he always took a room there when he was in town."

Matthew patted him on the back. "You've got a sharp eye and good listening skills as well, my boy. Let's go see what Mr. Maxwell has to say about where he's been today."

"If you'll excuse me for a moment, I'll answer the door," Elinor said. "No doubt it's someone calling on one of my boarders, but none of them seems able to answer the door."

Oliver nodded and smiled before relaxing his posture and watching Elinor leave the parlor. He enjoyed the gentle sway of her hips and imagined her brown tresses loosed from the tight knot and swinging softly around her shoulders. Perhaps one day she would remove the hairpins and grant him the pleasure of such a sight. Yes, Elinor had some fine characteristics, though he could barely tolerate her when she began her wearisome complaints about the mill girls or droned on about her sad lot in life.

"We want to see him *now*!"

The sound of angry voices and clattering shoes drawing closer caused Oliver to stiffen and turn his attention to the hallway. A sundry group filled the doorway, and their anger was evident.

"Gentlemen," he greeted, standing and moving to shake hands with Matthew Cheever. "What can I do for you?"

Matthew didn't extend his hand to accept Oliver's greeting. Instead, he met the shoe peddler's smile with a steely glare. "I didn't notice a horse outside the house. Did you walk here from the Merrimack House, Mr. Maxwell?"

"As a matter of fact, I did. I've been making deliveries in Lowell all day, and when I don't have far to travel, I prefer to walk. Encourage my customers to do the same — wears out the shoes more rapidly," he said with a false bravado.

Liam edged through the doorway. "And where might we be findin' yar horse, Mr. Maxwell, 'cause it ain't at the livery stable."

"You must be mistaken. I left the animal there last night after making deliveries. What's this about, anyway?" he asked.

"We'll tell you once we've located your horse," Matthew replied.

"I'll be more than pleased to accompany you to the livery and prove there's been a mistake."

"Excellent suggestion. Why don't you lead the way," Matthew said, moving out of the doorway.

Elinor hastened to Oliver's side and directed a glare at Mr. Cheever. "You need to tell Mr. Maxwell why you're detaining him."

"We're not detaining him, Mrs. Brighton. We're asking for his cooperation. He's freely agreed to assist us, so if you'll step aside, we'll be on our way."

"I'll visit with you tomorrow, Elinor," Oliver said as he departed the house.

The group traversed the streets of Lowell, garnering the attention of both storekeepers and shoppers until the men finally reached the livery, all of them squinting as they entered the dim stall-lined structure.

"Right over here," he said, leading them toward a stall near the end of the row. His eyes widened, and he hoped he appeared surprised when he encountered the empty stall. "I don't know where she is. Maybe she's been moved to another stall," he said. "Did you happen to ask Mr. Kittredge when you were here earlier?"

"There was na anyone here — still isn't.

Are ya sayin' you do na know where yar own horse is?" Liam asked.

"I told you that I left the horse here last night and I've not been back since then. I have no idea where the animal might be — I fear it may have been stolen. I've a mother and sister to support, and I don't know how I can afford to replace my horse. Needless to say, I want to locate the animal as much as you do," Oliver said. "Are you now going to tell me what has happened?"

"I think he's lyin'," Rogan whispered to Liam while glowering at Oliver.

Matthew nodded. "Obadiah's wife, Naomi, has been taken, as well as young Spencer Houston. Whisked off on horseback earlier today."

The blood drained from Oliver's face, and his legs grew weak. "Did you say Spencer Houston?"

"Da boy was at my place when it happened. You measured him and my boy, Moses, for shoes a while back," Obadiah reminded him.

Oliver's hands were shaking as he walked from the stable, the group of men following close behind. "I'll talk to Mr. Kittredge and ask if anyone was around the livery today."

"No need. We'll talk to him ourselves," Matthew said.

Oliver leaned against the rough-hewn door, watching the group depart. Fortunately the screaming woman had alerted him he'd been seen leaving the cottage, and he'd had the foresight to hide the strawberry roan. Better still was the fact that no one had seen him leave the stables with the horse, as he'd left before first light.

Surely they'd been mistaken about Spencer Houston. He was certain he'd taken Obadiah's boy. The city marshal and constabulary force would no doubt be drawn into the disappearance of a white child — especially the white child of a wealthy family. Matters had quickly taken an unfortunate turn. He needed time to think!

Chapter 15

Kiara held Moses snugly on her lap, rocking back and forth as the child sucked his thumb. The young boy had wandered about Obadiah's cottage and yard crying for his mother until he'd grown exhausted. After using all of her feminine skills, Kiara had finally convinced him to go home with her and eat supper. With his belly full, he'd grown weary and his eyelids now fluttered, heavy with sleep.

Rogan sat opposite her, his gaze fixed upon the child. "I'm wonderin' how anyone's gonna be able to explain little Spencer's disappearance to Miss Jasmine and Mr. Nolan when they return."

"I still think it was a mistake na sending word to them. I'm thankin' the good Lord I was na the one charged with that decision. I do na think Miss Jasmine's gonna look kindly upon Mr. Cheever for his decision."

"Aye, yet I'm hopin' she'll see his aim was

to keep her from sufferin'. He truly thought we'd 'ave the child back afore they returned home."

Kiara carried Moses to bed and then returned to her rocking chair. Pulling her thread from a basket near the chair, Kiara began creating a new piece of lace. "I'll tell ya, Rogan, this whole matter is another reminder of how quickly life can be changin'. One moment everything is fine as can be and the next, yar whole life is turned upside down."

"Ya're right about that, lass," Rogan said as a long shadow fell across the floor.

Kiara turned and saw Obadiah standing in the doorway. "Come in, Obadiah. Moses fell asleep and I put 'im in bed. Sit yarself down and I'll dish ya up some stew."

Obadiah rubbed his stomach and sat down. "Thank you, but I don' think I can eat. My belly's been hurtin' all day. I been thinkin' Miz Jasmine's gonna be comin' home tomorrow and dere's still no sign of Naomi or little Spencer." He leaned his elbows on his knees, resting his forehead against his open palms. "She ain' gonna be able to bear it."

Kiara rocked her chair more fervently, her heart aching for the pain he must bear. She longed to offer him help, yet there was nothing anyone could say to ease his pain.

"Don' know what I'll do iffen anything's happened to Naomi. I can't live wibout dat woman," he said without lifting his head.

"It's times like this, when we're feelin' alone and helpless, we need ta remember God's with us," Kiara said. "And He's with Naomi and Spencer too. We need ta all be prayin' instead of thinkin' there's nothin' remainin' ta be done."

"Ya're right about that, lass," Rogan said. "I'm always figurin' I can handle things, and then when they don't work out, I get down on me knees. Ya'd think I'd learn it should always be the other way around."

"Me an' da boy been doin' our share of prayin', but I ain' so sure da Lord's hearing us. Iffen He is, He sure ain' let me know. It sho' do shake a man's faith when somethin' like dis happens. I been tryin' hard to hang on, telling the youngun da Lord's gonna bring his mama home, but as da hours keeps a passin' by and nothin' happens, I ain' so sure no more."

"I know what ya're sayin' is true enough," Kiara said. " 'Tis hard to be maintainin' faith in times of trouble, but ya must na give up hope, Obadiah. Sure as I'm sittin' here, God's gonna see ya through this."

■ ■ ■ ■

Jasmine clung to Nolan's arm, feeling strangely giddy as their carriage approached the driveway. "I can barely contain my excitement. I know it's been only a few days, yet I feel as though I haven't seen Spencer for weeks. Do you think he'll be angry with us for leaving him?"

"His anger will quickly subside when he sees all the gifts you've bought him. I'd even venture to say he'll likely encourage us to leave again," Nolan said with a hearty laugh.

The carriage had barely come to a halt when Jasmine attempted to exit. Laughing at her excitement, Nolan took her hand and then helped her down. "Hurry! The baggage can wait," she said, rushing up the front steps.

Nolan followed close behind as she rushed into the foyer, but he was forced to an abrupt halt when his wife stopped short in the doorway of the parlor. Alice sat facing them with her hands folded and back straightened into a rigid posture that seemed to emanate a foreboding message.

"What is it, Grandmother? Something has happened, hasn't it? Something dreadful. Tell me!"

"Now, now, my dear. Sit down and we'll talk," Alice said in a soothing voice.

"I prefer to stand and I want to know. Father hasn't taken ill, has he?"

"No, your father is fine." She paused, her expression betraying her discomfort. "It's Spencer, dear."

"Oh no. Is he sick? Where is he? Did he take the measles? I heard measles were going around." Jasmine started toward the stairs.

"He's not sick. At least not that I know." Alice drew a deep breath. "This will be difficult to comprehend, but Jasmine . . . he's been kidnapped."

The room began to spin and Jasmine felt her knees buckle. She attempted to move toward the divan. For some reason, her feet would not move, yet she could feel her body sinking deeper and deeper into a swirling eddy from which there was no escape. Nolan's name was on her lips, but no sound would emerge. Spencer's smiling face flitted through her memory as she slipped into the deep abyss.

"Miss Jasmine! Can ya hear me?"

Kiara was leaning over her, their noses nearly touching.

Fogginess blurred Jasmine's thoughts as she stared back into Kiara's chocolate brown eyes. She blinked and tried to recall why she was lying on the divan in the middle of the day.

"Do na worry yarself. The lad is gonna be found. I can feel it here," Kiara said, patting her palm on her chest.

Spencer! That's why she was lying on the settee. She had fainted. Her son was gone. A lump settled in her throat, squelching the scream she desired to release into the noticeably hushed room. An overwhelming grief settled upon her like the mantle of sorrow she'd experienced when her mother had died.

"Noooo," she moaned, shaking her head from side to side. This couldn't be happening. Who would take her son? Why would they take him? Money? She'd gladly give them whatever they asked for. She merely needed to know what they were after.

"Has there been any note — any letter to explain why they've taken him?"

Kiara shook her head. "None. They've taken Naomi too. We can't imagine why unless the man was afraid she'd be able to identify him."

Jasmine sat up with a jerk and immediately felt the blood rush from her head. "We must develop a plan," she insisted.

"Lay yar head back and rest. We're doin'

all that's possible ta find them."

Nolan moved to her side and knelt down. "Liam has filled me in on the details of the search, Jasmine. There's little doubt they've done everything possible to find Naomi and Spencer. The constables as well as many residents of Lowell and the surrounding countryside have been searching in earnest. I believe the best thing we can do is remain calm and pray."

"Oh, Nolan, this is more than I can bear. It hurts so much to think of him scared and alone. And all the while, I was making merry in Boston."

"We didn't know what had happened, Jasmine. We were making merry because God brought us together in love. We aren't being punished for something, so stop fretting. You've done nothing to cause this."

She let Nolan cradle her in his arms, feeling the warmth, knowing the love. "He's just a little boy, so undeserving of this. What manner of man performs such cruelties?"

"An evil one ta be sure," Kiara said, standing over Nolan. "But evil can na be standin' against our Lord. Ya must be havin' faith that God will care for Spencer and see 'im home safely."

Jasmine nodded, but her heart was so heavy. "If it be His will," she murmured.

But of course she wasn't all that convinced. After all, it should have been well within God's will that a small boy be protected from kidnapping.

Oliver stroked the dapple gray Mr. Kittredge offered. "Are you certain you won't need the horse today? I don't want to inconvenience you."

"It's the least I can do," he said. "I feel responsible that your horse was stolen. After all, if the door had been locked or I'd had the stable boy looking after things while I was gone, maybe you'd still have that strawberry roan. I keep thinking someone will find it. Too uncommon a horse to go unnoticed."

Oliver reveled in the comment, pleased his deceit had been received as truth. He waited until Kittredge was out of sight before hanging a bag of oats across the horse's back. After loading his saddlebags with additional supplies, he quickly made his way out of town.

He traveled at a steady pace, keeping to the road for several miles before veering off to the east. Moving across the hilly farmland that spread before them, he remembered the first time he'd crossed this terrain — when he'd discovered the abandoned farmhouse. It had been on one of those tiresome journeys when he'd grown weary of travelling the same route. Thinking to save time and break the monotony of his journey, he'd grown bold, never thinking of the ramifications of a broken wheel or injured horse at a remote location. But fortune had been with him, and the only thing that had occurred was a treacherous thunderstorm.

It was then, in his search for shelter, he'd located the deserted farmhouse and outbuildings. Weeds had overgrown what had once been a family garden, and the house was ravaged by years of neglect and offered little sanctuary. But he'd found the root cellar and there, beneath the ground, he'd found safety from the storm and a secret place where he could occasionally stop and lose himself in dreams of a better life. A perverse smile crossed his lips, knowing he'd outsmarted the locals. None of those men had searched anywhere near the secluded farm.

"Fools!" he muttered as he dismounted and tied the horse to a nearby tree. With the sack of grain over his shoulder, he made his way to the stall, deciding to exercise the strawberry roan after checking on the woman and child.

Oliver stopped to catch his breath after

removing the pile of branches and rocks he'd placed over the entry to the root cellar. He was certain the drugs he'd forced into the woman and child had kept them sedated, yet he'd blocked the door as an added precaution. He didn't want the woman escaping before he returned. Although he hadn't planned to revisit the site until tomorrow, he now knew he must positively establish the identity of the child he'd placed in the dank hole in the ground. His heart pounded as he pulled back the heavy door.

The woman and child were exactly as he left them, sleeping soundly on the blankets he'd placed on the ground. After all, he didn't want them getting ill. The price of a sickly Negro decreased considerably — especially for a small-framed woman and child. Pulling the drawing of Moses' foot from his pocket, he placed it against the sole of the boy's foot and then rocked back on his heels. This boy's foot was much larger than the drawing. Angrily, he thrust the drawing to the dirt floor and rubbed his forehead. He'd taken Spencer Houston. Not a black child, but a wealthy white woman's son.

"I need a plan," Oliver said between clenched teeth. He walked back up the steps, deciding a short ride on his horse would give the animal some needed exercise and would also permit him time to think. He saddled the horse and rode for nearly an hour before stopping near a stream. Sitting under a tree and watching as the horse drank deeply from the flowing water, Oliver formulated his strategy.

By the time he had returned to the barn, he knew the woman must die. He could bury her in the root cellar and then pretend to find Spencer Houston. He'd be a hero and certainly entitled to a reward. Yet the thought gave him little consolation. He doubted the Houstons would give him anywhere near what he had expected to receive when he sold the woman and child into slavery. And the thought of actually killing a woman gave him pause — he'd have to think on the matter tonight. The two of them should sleep until morning. He'd return and do what was required. He had no choice.

Naomi felt the cold in her bones before even fully awakening to the darkness around her. She had dreamed of working in the fields, only these fields weren't in the South, they were cold and unyielding. Pushing the dream away, she struggled to sit up. Her head ached something fierce, and a dizziness overcame her that seemed to settle only when she put her head back down.

After a few minutes she tried again to sit up. This time it wasn't quite as bad. She felt around her, trying to figure out her location. It seemed to be some sort of cellar. The floor was dirt, hardpacked and cold. She had a blanket but nothing else.

Reaching her hand out timidly, she was startled to feel the warm flesh of a human arm. A very small arm. Spencer! The memories of their kidnapping came flooding back. It was the shoe peddler. She couldn't even remember his name. But why had he taken them?

"Spencer?" She whispered the boy's name in case their assailant should be close enough to hear. The boy stirred but didn't awaken. Naomi pulled him into her arms and cradled him to keep him warm.

"Po' boy. Your mama's gonna be worried sumptin' fierce."

Outside there was a noise as if someone or something was digging at the door. Unable to see in the dark, Naomi could only rely on sound. But it didn't sound good. The noise continued until the unmistakable sound of a door being opened gave her mixed hope and trepidation. Either someone had found them . . . or their kidnapper was returning.

Lantern light blinded Naomi as she clutched more tightly to Spencer. "Who's dere?"

"So you're awake." The shoe peddler came down the wooden stairs, and Naomi struggled to fix her gaze on the man. What she saw, however, terrified her. The man carried a shovel and there was a revolver in his waistband, barely visible as the man's coat pulled away when he set the lantern on one of the steps.

"I've come to take care of business."

"What be yo' business with me and da boy?" Naomi asked, her voice quivering.

"Well," the man said, leaning on the shovel, "I thought I knew well enough what that was, but I was mistaken. I'm afraid I've come to put an end to your miserable life and to take the boy back to his grieving mother."

Naomi felt her breath quicken. The man was going to kill her. But why? Most of the white folks in the North had been kind to her. Why would this one want to end her life? "Why ya wanna kill a Negro woman like me?"

The man laughed, chilling Naomi to the bone. Spencer stirred but still did not awaken as the man replied, "I took you because you were a Negro woman. There's good money down south for the likes of you. But I didn't intend to take the boy. I thought he was your boy. Thought I'd entice his pappy to follow after us if I took his family. But that's not going to be the case. I took a white woman's child, and while society would most likely not lift a finger to search for a black baby, they'll move heaven and earth to locate a wealthy man's son."

Naomi knew her life depended on coming up with some reason for him to keep her alive. "I'm beggin' you, suh," she began. "Think 'bout what you're fixin' ta do. If you keep me alive, I'll take care of the chile for you. The longer he goes missin', the more thankful his mama's gonna be. I promise I won' give you no trouble. I'm thinkin' you could tell 'em you found da both of us, and I'll tell Miz Jasmine she should pay you a handsome sum of money. Ya need ta remember dis here boy is smart. He's gonna tell his mama you's da one what took us away. I can tell her he's mistaken. Ya should spend some more time thinkin' 'bout what you's gonna do."

The peddler stared at Naomi, looking confused about what he should do with her. "Surely the child isn't old enough to tell his mother much."

"Suh, he be a smart boy. Smarter'n most his age."

The man growled, then tossed the shovel to the side. "Nothing in my life is ever simple. Nothing."

Naomi gently stroked Spencer's head, more for the comfort it offered her than for any it might allow him. She would just remain silent and pray. Pray for God to see her and Spencer and to have mercy on them . . . pray for the peddler to have mercy on them too.

Chapter 16

Elinor placed a heaping bowl of green beans seasoned with bacon drippings and minced onions in front of one of the girls and then surveyed the table.

"The bread-and-butter pickles," she muttered before hurrying back to the kitchen. Without fail, Lucinda Pritchett would remind her if she didn't immediately see pickles on the table.

Placing the crock directly in front of Lucinda with a firm thud, Elinor said, "You may ask God's blessing on our supper, Lucinda."

"It's Mary's turn," Lucinda replied while opening the pickles.

Elinor sighed and looked heavenward. "Mary, would you please pray for us?"

Mary uttered a quick, unintelligible prayer, followed by a loud amen. The clatter of metal utensils against china dishes began in earnest.

"Cecilia Broadhurst told me this afternoon they think the little Houston boy that was kidnapped is dead," Sarah Warren remarked while heaping a mountain of creamed potatoes onto her plate.

"I don't know how you have time to talk to Cecilia without causing yourself injury on the machines," Lucinda said tersely. "At the speed they've got the machinery operating, it's a wonder we aren't all maimed."

"You do have a way of adding charm to dinner conversations," Sarah said with a giggle.

"I'm not the one who mentioned the dead boy." A loud clank sounded as Lucinda dropped her fork onto the china plate. "Speeding up the machinery is *not* a laughing matter. Do you realize how many mill workers have been injured this year alone? I think what they've done is sinful. It's no wonder they're permitting the Irish to work alongside us. If it weren't from pure necessity, I'd quit working for those cruel taskmasters tomorrow."

"Now you've done it," Mary whispered to Sarah. "You've gone and got her started on a tirade."

Fire burned in Lucinda's cheeks. "I heard you whispering, Mary. When it's *your* hair or fingers that're caught in one of those evil machines, you'll be singing a different song."

There were several gasps, and Lucinda's lips curled in a smug grin before loading a forkful of potatoes into her mouth.

"I believe that's enough talk about accidents and injuries," Elinor said. "Perhaps we can find another topic to discuss."

"Do you think it's true about that little boy?" Mary asked while glancing around the table at her dinner partners.

"I think Cecilia's right," Sarah replied. "I truly doubt he could live this long without his mama to care for him."

Lucinda pointed her fork in Sarah's direction. "Exactly where did Cecilia get her information? Likely her remarks are pure supposition, the same as anyone else's."

"Don't point your fork, Lucinda — I expect proper etiquette from you girls," Elinor corrected.

Lucinda directed a look of irritation toward Elinor before lowering her fork and spearing several green beans. "Well, what do you think, Mrs. Brighton? Surely you don't think a simple girl working in the mills knows what's happened to the Houston boy, do you?"

"I have no idea. The only thing I truly know is that what happened is a tragedy, and I pray both the boy and woman have survived and will soon reappear."

Lucinda wagged her head back and forth. "That's about as likely to happen as the mill owners deciding to slow down the machinery or give us a raise in pay."

Sarah glared at Lucinda. "Do you *never* tire of your negative outlook?"

"And why should I? I've never had any reason to do so. Unlike you, Sarah, my life has been filled with responsibilities and disappointment — even here in Lowell. Am I assigned to one of the floors with a kind supervisor like you? Of course not. Do the girls in my room afford me quiet time to read or meditate? Of course not. Am I able to spend my pay on fabric and jewelry like most of you? Of course not. When my life more closely resembles yours, perhaps I'll have reason to become less negative, Sarah."

"Someone from the Tremont Mill told me they found that black woman by the mill pond," Janet Wilson remarked.

"Another rumor," Lucinda said.

"She's probably correct," Mary commented. "If they'd found either of them, I believe word would rapidly spread around town."

While the girls continued their spirited discussion, Elinor thought of Oliver and the pain he'd endured knowing his horse had been used in the kidnapping. He'd suffered through the questioning by Matthew Cheever as well as the city marshal while enduring the gossip of the locals until the marshal concluded he'd not been involved. She'd personally witnessed the toll the entire incident had taken upon him, making him anxious and in ill humor, which was exactly the reason she'd taken time to bake a special apple cobbler. He'd be delivering shoes to the house this evening, and perhaps her baked goods would cheer him when everything else failed.

"Don't forget Mr. Maxwell will be distributing shoes this evening," Elinor said as she began clearing plates from the table.

Janet frowned and pushed away from the table, her chair scraping on the wood floor. "That means we'll have to wait to go shopping."

"Instead of worrying about going to the mercantile and spending more of your wages on frivolities, you should be pleased you had sufficient funds to purchase new shoes," Lucinda retorted.

Janet scowled at Lucinda before turning her attention to Elinor. "I'll be upstairs if Mr. Maxwell should arrive early."

Elinor nodded and continued into the

kitchen. By the time she'd emerged from the kitchen after washing the dishes and making final preparations for the morning meal, Oliver had arrived and unpacked the last shoe.

Shadows of concern seemed to surround Oliver as he closed his case. He moved the container to one side and then met Elinor's gaze. "I believe I've finally finished for the night. I had planned only on making my deliveries but after seeing Janet's new slippers, two of the other girls wanted to be measured."

"I hope you're pleased to have the additional business," she said.

"Yes, of course. However, I had hoped to have time to visit with you, and now it's getting late."

"It's only nine o'clock. I can't lock the door and retire until ten, so we have at least an hour," she said sweetly. "I've made an apple cobbler if you'd like a piece."

He smiled broadly. "You're too kind," he said. "May I help?"

"Why don't you have a seat in the dining room," she suggested.

Moments later they sat opposite each other, Oliver devouring his cobbler while Elinor sipped a cup of tea.

"Your cobbler is quite tasty. You do have a

knack for baking," he complimented as he picked up a napkin and wiped his mouth.

"Thank you, Oliver. I've been concerned about you. How have you been faring?"

"As well as can be expected under the circumstances. I feel as though a cloak of suspicion surrounds me, and my thoughts constantly return to that poor boy's mother and stepfather. This must be a terrible burden for them to bear — the ongoing worry about the child's welfare, not knowing whether he's alive or dead."

Elinor nodded her agreement. "It must be equally hard on the Negro woman's husband and child. I understand she has a small child about the same age as Spencer Houston. They must be suffering terribly also."

Oliver ignored her remarks regarding Obadiah and Moses. "I think the search might be more successful if Mrs. Houston offered a reward. There's nothing that makes people become more involved than the possibility of a reward. You might mention that fact to her or one of her many friends who attend the Ladies' Aid meetings."

Elinor's brow puckered into deep creases. "Several of the girls mentioned at supper tonight that there have been rumors the boy is dead. And another girl mentioned the Negro woman was found by the mill pond. Have you heard anything further regarding their whereabouts?"

"No. Although I'm certain they haven't been found. Otherwise, there would be more than a few idle rumors. The marshal and his constables would make certain everyone in town knew if they'd been successful locating the Houston boy. I still believe a reward would help. Will you be visiting with Mrs. Houston anytime soon?"

"Under the circumstances, I don't imagine she'll be at the next Ladies' Aid meeting. If you think a reward would be helpful, perhaps you should mention it to the marshal. I would feel quite uncomfortable broaching the topic with Mrs. Houston if I should see her."

"And I would feel equally uncomfortable approaching the marshal. I've given them enough of my time. I wonder what punishment will be levied against the kidnapper. Likely there would be little, if any, retribution if only the Negro had been taken, but having that Houston boy changes things, don't you agree?"

Elinor gave him a puzzled gaze. "The woman is as important as the boy, Oliver."

"Maybe in your eyes," he said, but then

met her eyes. "Of course, the woman is important, but the boy, the boy is, I mean his parents are . . ."

"Wealthy? White? Does that make their loss greater than that of the Negro woman's husband? It's that attitude that makes me even more committed to helping the runaways. People must begin to realize that the color of a person's skin does not increase or decrease one's value."

"No, of course not," he muttered. "So you're continuing to assist with runaways and enjoying your Ladies' Aid meetings?"

"Indeed. I've finally found something in which I find value, and I enjoy the thought that I'm helping others begin a new life," she said, surprised at her own anger. "I can't imagine how terrible it must be to live in some of the conditions I've heard the slavcs tell about. Helping them gives me a sense of hope," she said, giving him a wistful smile.

"I do admire your willingness to aid those who are seeking to find a better life. We are, after all, commissioned to tell others of Christ and to do good works in His name."

Elinor leaned forward and rested her forearms on the table, for the first time feeling that Oliver actually understood her conviction. "I didn't realize you were so strong in your beliefs."

"Ah, dear lady, you underestimate me. I was reared by a mother who made certain I knew the Bible. If nothing else, she wanted her children to know how to read and how to write, and to believe what she believed. I memorized my Bible verses or was beaten until I did."

"While I don't agree with your mother's methods, I do wish I'd memorized more verses during my formative years. I've just recently found that the recollection of Scriptures can be a genuine blessing in times of difficulty," Elinor said.

"That may be true for many, but I find reliance upon my own inner strength a greater asset."

"Do you? I think that's one of the many differences between men and women. Men want to rely upon themselves, while women tend to find it more comforting to rely upon others. I've wondered if that's why fewer men are able to completely give themselves over to God's authority. Girls are taught at an early age they are to be subject to the authority of their fathers and husbands. On the other hand, boys are taught they are to grow into roles of authority."

Oliver stroked his narrow mustache as though the act somehow helped him recall his memories. “My mother assumed authority without any difficulty whatsoever. I believe she enjoys control — which is likely what drove my father to drinking and an early death.”

“Life tends to take unexpected twists that we’ll never understand in this world. However, I’m beginning to learn I can use those experiences, whether good or bad, to assist me with my current dilemmas.”

Oliver squared his shoulders and gave her a confident smile. “And what dilemmas would you be facing? Perhaps I can be of some assistance.”

For a brief moment Elinor faltered, but when Oliver leaned forward and earnestly gazed into her eyes, she returned his smile. Deep within, she believed he could be trusted. “The Ladies’ Aid group has entrusted me with the task of securing shoes for the runaways. During the summer months, shoes are not nearly so important, but winter will soon be approaching, and although I’ve had success in securing footwear for women and even children, it has been difficult finding shoes for men and older boys. I’ve met with limited success by placing containers at the churches and boardinghouses asking people to leave their old shoes for the needy. However, there have been very few donations of men's shoes."

"You're correct in thinking that sturdy shoes will be a necessity. Even now, though the weather is warm, shoes would aid the runaways as they traverse the rough terrain." He tapped his fingernails on the table. "I think I can be of assistance to you."

Elinor's eyes sparkled with anticipation. "You can? Oh, Oliver, now I wish I'd spoken to you sooner. When I think of the number of runaways who could have benefited from a pair of shoes had I only taken you into my confidence."

He patted her hand. "What's done is done. We can't change the past. However, we have the future. Starting tomorrow, I'll ask my customers to donate their old shoes for the needy and will deliver them to you each time I'm in Lowell. In addition, I'm certain that I can aid you with some new shoes and boots from time to time. Occasionally someone will order a pair of shoes but fail to have the funds when I deliver, and I can also talk to the cobblers who make my shoes. They may be willing to help."

Elinor savored the taste of victory, the sweet aroma of success tingling her senses. At the next Ladies' Aid meeting, she would give an excellent report. "What a kind man you are. I look forward to your assistance. I only wish it could come sooner."

"Do you have an immediate need?"

"Yes. In fact, there's a group heading toward Lowell as we speak. I've agreed to help, yet I have only four pairs of shoes."

Oliver moved to the edge of his chair. "Truly? If you would care to confide more particulars, I will do all in my power to secure additional shoes before their arrival."

"You are much too kind, Oliver."

He stroked his mustache and smiled. "It's my pleasure to help the cause."

Chapter 17

Before Nolan reached the top of the stairs, he heard Jasmine's sobs. This had become an all too familiar sound since their return from Boston. He tapped lightly on the bedroom door before entering, without expecting an answer. When Jasmine took to her bed in these bouts of tears, she heard nothing but her own outpouring of sorrow.

"My dear," he said gently, perching on the edge of the bed and rubbing her back. "Is there nothing I can do to console you?"

"Find Spencer and Naomi."

Her reply was always the same. "We're doing all we can, Jasmine. If it were some simple matter, they would already be home. I know your concern is great — as is my own. However, you do no one any good when you become incapacitated by your fears."

"I can't help myself," she sobbed. "Have you talked to Matthew Cheever? Is there any word at all?"

"I assumed he would send word if there were anything to report, but I will go and talk to him if it will make you feel better."

"Please," she whispered, wiping her swollen eyes with a corner of the bedsheet.

"If you're certain you'll be all right, I'll leave immediately."

"I'll be fine," she whispered, her fingers wrapped tightly around the cotton lace that edged the white sheets.

Despite the early afternoon warmth, Nolan left her ensconced in layers of bed linens and blankets. He knew she would fight any attempt he made to remove them, just as he knew she would remain silent when he bid her good-bye.

The Cheevers would likely be enjoying their Sunday dinner when he arrived, yet he felt no remorse about interrupting them. Too frequently of late he found himself recalling Madelaine Wainwright's bouts with melancholy. And although Jasmine's grief over Spencer was well founded, he didn't want to see her following in Madelaine's footsteps under any circumstances. He wanted to see her rise up and fight rather than give way to defeat.

He knocked on the Cheevers' door. His mind overflowed with thoughts of the kidnapping, and he wondered when all of this would possibly cease. Would they ever find Naomi and Spencer? Were they still alive? Surely if they were still in the area they would have been found by now.

"Nolan! What a pleasant surprise," Matthew greeted. "Come join us. We're just getting ready to enjoy dinner."

"Thank you, but I can't stay. I promised Jasmine I would come by the house and see if there had been any word about Spencer and Naomi. I assured her you would have sent word, but she has taken to her bed and isn't easily consoled."

"Jasmine is ill?" McKinley asked as he approached the other two men.

"Sick of being without her child. I fear she's permitting her distress to control her life. I can't get her to leave the confines of her bedroom for even a few hours," Nolan explained.

"Visions of our mother," McKinley said quietly.

"My thoughts exactly. Yet I can't seem to find any way to shake her from her despair. I hoped you might give me some word of encouragement that I can take to her."

"I wish that I could," Matthew said. "However, we've found nothing — not a sign. In my heart I still believe that shoe peddler is involved, yet there's no further evidence of his complicity. Outside of continuing the search, I can think of nothing further to do."

"I'm giving consideration to offering a reward. What do you think of such an idea?" Nolan asked.

Matthew glanced at the floor and stroked his chin before turning his gaze back to Nolan. "I'd like to think that if anyone has information, he'd come forward without the offer of money. What makes you think a reward will help?"

"Elinor Brighton came by to pay Jasmine a visit the other day, and although Jasmine wasn't up to receiving her, Elinor left a note. I read her short missive just this morning. She made the suggestion that a reward might prove beneficial. Seems that an itinerant salesman had posed the possibility that money sometimes loosens tongues, and she wanted to pass along the idea."

"Interesting. It's true there are any number of transients passing through Lowell who might have a piece of information and yet feel no moral obligation to come forward," Matthew said.

"And a few gold coins may be all the incentive that is needed," McKinley enthusiastically agreed. "You could place an ad in the newspaper, where it will gain enough attention that the reward will soon be discussed all over town."

Violet came forward and stood beside McKinley. "Why don't you stay for dinner, Mr. Houston? We can discuss this further; and then McKinley and I can return home with you. Perhaps if we can enthusiastically present your plan to Mrs. Houston, she'll regain hope."

"How kind of you," Nolan replied. "I think you've an excellent idea."

Oliver greeted Enoch and Joseph with energetic handshakes before sitting down. He'd given them directions to a small inn located ten miles south of Lowell, where he'd not be recognized by any locals. "It's good to see both of you. I trust you had no difficulty getting here?"

"Only a lack of funds that caused us to sleep outdoors on our way up from Baltimore," Enoch replied.

Oliver ignored the remark but ordered food for all of them, hoping they'd be willing to remain compliant on a full stomach. "I've brought you here in order to help line your pockets with gold," he said. "You should be thankful, for I could have found any number of good men willing to help with my plan for much less than what I've offered the two of you."

"We are thankful," Enoch said, wiping his mouth across his sleeve. "We never doubted you was going to be loyal to us."

With a decisive nod of his head, Oliver carefully explained that a large group of runaways was expected. "With the Fugitive Slave Act in place, the marshal is required to help anyone attempting to return runaways. Once I've confirmed the information, you two go and talk to the marshal — repeat exactly what I tell you. He'll have no choice but to help with the capture and then turn the slaves over to you."

"What about you, Oliver? Ain't you gonna help?" Joseph asked.

Oliver shook his head and gazed heavenward. "You're as dumb as a fencepost, Joseph. If the law finds out I'm involved, I'll never be able to gain further information about runaways. Don't you remember how this is supposed to work? I find out when and where the runaways come through, while you and Enoch help with the capture and return them down South."

"I remember," Joseph said. "It just seems as though you're getting the easy part of the deal."

With a quick jab, Enoch poked Joseph in

the ribs. "Shut up, Joseph. There wouldn't be no slaves for us to take back and sell if Oliver didn't get the information and pass it along to us."

"If you want out, I can find others who'd be more than happy to take your share of the money," Oliver threatened.

With an embarrassed grin, Joseph said, "Naw, I was just sporting with ya."

"I'll be meeting tonight to make certain the runaways are still coming through as planned. Unless you hear from me, go to the marshal tomorrow afternoon and tell them you've word of runaways coming through the next night. I won't be there helping you, but rest assured I'll be watching from nearby," he said before slapping several coins on the table. "Sleep here tonight. I want you where I can easily find you if there's a change in plans."

The two days passed slowly. Now, waiting in a clump of bushes only a short distance from Enoch, Joseph, and several constables, Oliver clenched his jaw and listened for the sound of the runaways approaching. Elinor had confirmed they would be taking this path tonight and, for the moment, he had nothing to do but wait, hidden from both the runaways and their hopeful captors.

Suddenly he heard the hushed whispers. He held his breath, hoping the others had heard the sounds. Slowly and quietly, he exhaled. The sounds were growing closer, nearing the place where Enoch and Joseph were hidden with their weapons. He watched as several runaways made their way past the men and then signaled for the others to move forward. As the group reconnected, Enoch and the other men made their move. Completely off guard and unable to respond to the threat, most of the group immediately capitulated to the men.

Only one of the large bucks attempted to run away, and he was quickly stopped when Joseph held out a branch and tripped him. The runaway tumbled forward, striking his head on an adjacent tree, rendering the man unconscious. Had he not witnessed the event, Oliver would have disbelieved the ease with which the slaves were detained. They were unarmed and offered little resistance, and none could produce papers proving they had been freed — so all were subject to the Fugitive Slave Act.

Oliver longed to applaud the efforts of his partners but forced himself to remain quiet. Their plans would quickly unravel should the marshal learn of his connection to Enoch and Joseph. Once the group had departed, he mounted his horse and headed back to his room at the Merrimack House.

"At least something went right," he murmured. He was still wrestling with thoughts of what to do about the Houston boy and the Negro woman. The woman had convinced him that leaving her alive, at least for the moment, was the better plan. He would only need to go back to the abandoned farm on rare occasion with Naomi caring for the child. He simply would drop off supplies and resecure the prison he'd formed for them.

"I'll know if you've so much as climbed the stairs," he'd told Naomi after sprinkling flour on each step. He'd promised to kill her swiftly if she attempted any type of escape — even hunt her down should she somehow be successful. The woman seemed amply convinced by his threats, and so far he'd not noticed any attempt on her part to flee her confinement. Of course, putting laudanum in the soup and tea he brought had only helped his effort.

"Still, I must do something soon. The weather is sure to turn any day." Oliver was still muttering to himself when the lights of Lowell welcomed him back. And then, as if the lights stimulated his mind's own brilliance, a plan began to form in his mind. A plan that just might work.

The following afternoon, after delivering additional food and assuring himself Naomi and Spencer remained secure, Oliver knocked on the door of Elinor's boarding-house and waited several minutes until the door swung open.

"Oliver! I wasn't expecting you."

"I had deliveries nearby and thought perhaps you might be ready to relax a moment and have a cup of tea," he said. "You appear distressed. Is something amiss?"

Elinor tucked a straggling piece of hair behind one ear and gave him a bewildered look. "The runaways were due at their safe house last night. But they never arrived. I'm fearful they've been captured. Oh, where are my manners? I've left you standing in the doorway. Do come in and have a cup of tea."

Oliver followed her through the house and into the kitchen and watched as she deftly prepared a pot of tea and then poured two steaming cups. "Shall we remain here in the kitchen, or would you prefer to sit in the parlor?" he asked.

"The parlor. I spend far too much of my time in the kitchen."

"Let me carry those," he said, placing the

cups on a nearby tray.

Elinor wearily settled on the divan and took a sip of tea. "I am terribly worried about those poor runaways. I haven't been able to keep my thoughts straight all day. Have you heard any word in your travels this morning?"

"Truthfully, that's why I stopped to see you. However, I didn't believe it prudent to discuss the matter on your doorstep. I wanted to assure myself we could talk in private."

Elinor placed her cup on the tray and focused her undivided attention upon him. "Please tell me what you've heard."

"The constables were called in to assist with capturing the runaways under the provisions of the Fugitive Slave Act. I believe all of the runaways were detained and are possibly being returned to their owners as we speak. It grieves me to bring such devastating news, but the moment I heard, my primary concern was for you. I knew if you'd received word of the capture, you would be distraught. I wanted to lend my comfort and assure you of my willingness to help in any way possible."

"You are so very kind to put aside your own business interests to come and offer your assistance. Do you believe your information is reliable?"

"Unfortunately, I believe it is. I'm certain word will soon begin to spread about town once the constables begin discussing the incident. They'll likely find the matter a topic of interest since I believe this is the first time they've been called into service under the Fugitive Slave Act," he added.

"A terrible law! However, for those of us committed to seeing slavery come to an end, it only heightens our resolve. Don't you agree?"

"Absolutely. And I'm pleased to see this entire debacle is only one setback. I'm certain our successes in gaining freedom for the runaways will far outnumber instances such as this one."

The clock in the hallway chimed, and Elinor jumped to her feet as though the house were afire. "I must begin supper or the girls will return to an empty table."

"Already? It's but four o'clock. The girls will be working until seven, will they not?"

"You men have absolutely no idea how long it takes to prepare a decent meal. And believe me, these girls eat as much as any farmhand while expecting the food to far surpass the fare they had at home."

Oliver reluctantly followed her to the door. He had hoped to engage her in further conversation, yet he dared not push. He'd return in a few days when she had more information to share.

Elinor waited until she was certain Oliver had departed the vicinity before tying her bonnet into place and leaving the house. With a purposeful step, she quickly walked to town and marched onward until she reached the city hall.

"I'd like to speak to the city marshal. It's very important," she told the clerk who was sitting at an oversized wooden desk.

The man nodded and rose, walking into a room off to the left. He soon returned with a tall man whom Elinor immediately recognized from a number of antislavery meetings. She walked toward him.

"I am Elinor Brighton. May I speak with you privately?"

"Of course. Why don't you come into my office," Emil Baxter replied.

Elinor followed him until they reached his office, where he offered her a chair and then sat down at his desk. "Now, how may I be of assistance to you?"

"I've been told you are an active participant in the Underground Railroad. I know I've seen you at antislavery meetings in the past, but of course there are many who attend those meetings yet do not assist with the Underground," she said, her words tumbling out like bubbling water in a brook.

"And if I am?" he inquired evenly.

"There was a group of runaways due through Lowell last night. They've not appeared at their station. I've been told by a reliable source that you were involved in their capture under the requirements of the Fugitive Slave Act. Is that information correct?"

Mr. Baxter stood and placed his palms on the desk, leaning forward across the wooden expanse until they were nearly nose to nose. His face had turned a deep shade of red. "Did your informant say where he received such information?"

"No. Why does it concern you where the information came from?"

"Because no one was told of the incident; the runaways were apprehended and left immediately with their civilian captors. Those of us who were required to assist vowed to remain silent regarding the entire matter. Consequently, I'm wondering how your friend acquired the information — unless he was somehow involved."

Elinor's mouth dropped open, dumbfounded by the announcement.

Chapter 18

Once again borrowing Mr. Kittredge's horse, Oliver loaded his wagon and headed eagerly toward the outskirts of Lowell. He kept to the road until he was well out of town. Maintaining a watchful eye, he made certain no one was in sight when he turned off the dirt road and headed toward the abandoned farmhouse. His excitement continued to build as he neared the dilapidated barn. He jumped down and led the horse and wagon into the structure.

Enoch stepped out of the shadows, the shuffling sound of his feet causing Oliver to hesitate. "It's me, Oliver. I thought you was never gonna get here. Do you know how hard it's been keeping all these runaways quiet?"

"You won't be complaining when you get all that money we're going to make off of them. Just be thankful I told you to bring along shackles, or the two of you wouldn't have gotten any sleep last night. I've brought some supplies, and I have one more runaway for you to take along," he said. "I'll go and get her while you transfer the supplies to your wagon."

A short time later, Oliver returned. He held Naomi firmly by the arm as they neared Enoch. "You need to get her in shackles right away. She'll run if given any opportunity," he warned.

"She's sure enough a beauty, but she don't look like she could run ten feet. She sickly?" Enoch asked.

"Once the laudanum fully wears off, you'll have your hands full. I've been keeping her drugged until I could get her back down South. She fought me every step here, so be warned. She's easy to look at but full of lies, so don't believe a word she says and don't trust her for a second."

"This one will be worth the trouble," Joseph said. "She'll fetch a handsome price."

Naomi glared at Oliver. "What you gonna do with da boy? His mama'll have ya strung up fo' what you done." She spat at his feet. "You ain' nothin' but trash."

Oliver raised his hand, but Enoch swiftly grabbed his wrist, halting the blow he had intended for the rebellious woman. "Don't mark her!" Enoch hollered.

Wresting his arm from Enoch's hold, Oliver stormed to the wagon. "Get this wagon loaded and get moving. The sooner you're out of here, the better!" he shouted in return.

"What ya gonna do with da boy?" Naomi screamed over and over again as the wagon rolled out of the barn.

"Gag her!" Oliver called out to Joseph and then relaxed when he could no longer hear Naomi's haunting voice.

He turned the horse back toward town, knowing the boy would sleep. He'd given him a dose of laudanum, but he must soon find a way to return young Spencer Houston. No telling what ill effects the ongoing medicine might be having on the boy.

Oliver slapped the reins, forcing his horse into a trot while straining forward in an attempt to see the group gathered outside the livery.

"What's going on?" he inquired as he jumped down from the wagon.

"We're organizing another search party. Some of the men have already departed. They'll be searching north and west of town. This group will divide and head south and east."

"I'd like to assist. Which group is heading

south?" he asked.

The man nodded toward a group at the rear of the livery. Oliver made his way through the crowd and approached a constable standing with the group. "I'd like to help," he said.

"That group could use an extra hand," the constable said, pointing toward a smaller cluster of men.

Oliver hesitated, glancing toward the group. "I'm a shoe peddler and know more of the area to the south. I think I could be of greater assistance if I remain with this group."

The constable shrugged. "Whatever you want. Prager, why don't you go with that other group? Let's get going. We're wasting daylight."

Oliver silently rejoiced at his good fortune. These men had solved his problem. He couldn't have planned a more opportune solution to his dilemma. The men rode off toward the south, as Oliver followed behind with the wagon, obeying the constable's orders when he directed them to dismount and search one area and then the next.

When they finally neared the area where the abandoned farm was located, Oliver called out to the constable.

"What is it?" the constable asked as he

rode back to the wagon.

"Long ago when I first came to Lowell, I got off the road hoping to travel cross-country and save some time. Instead, I managed to get lost. I remember coming upon an old abandoned farmhouse somewhere off in this area. I'm wondering if anyone has searched that old place."

The constable removed his hat and scratched his head. "I don't know, but it's worth looking at. Think you can find it again?"

"I'm not certain, but surely one of these men may recall the place," he replied evasively.

Using his stirrups for leverage, the chief constable lifted himself up off his saddle and surveyed the group. "Anyone remember seeing an old vacant farmhouse around these parts?"

Oliver listened to the murmurs among the men. Surely one of these men knew of it. He didn't want to be the one to direct the group to the farmstead.

"I think the old Ross place is about three miles off the road and maybe another two miles west," one of the men called out.

The lawman directed the group to fan out in the direction of the old farm. Oliver aligned himself with several other men who were moving in a direct line toward the house. He hoped they would have enough sense to check the root cellar without prompting. Although he wanted to assure himself the child was found, he didn't want to be overly involved in the rescue, lest he arouse suspicion.

When the group dismounted, Oliver remained in close proximity as the search began in earnest. He followed along, encouraging his group to begin at the house rather than the barn since the other men were nearing the outbuildings.

"You two go upstairs and check things out," the constable directed. "You two look around down here, and I'll go with Martin and see if there's a cellar anywhere nearby." The man pointed at Oliver. "If you get done down here before we do, check for a well or a springhouse. No telling how many places there might be to hide a child around here."

They'd barely begun their cursory search of the downstairs rooms when they heard a loud whoop. "We found him! We found him!" a male voice hollered before firing a shot into the air.

Oliver remained in the distance, permitting the others to gather around the child. "He looks dead. You sure he's still breathing?" one of the men asked.

"He's breathing, but it's shallow," Martin Simmons replied. "Best we get him to the doctor right away. Don't appear to be no broken bones. I ain't never seen the boy afore, so I don't know if he looks okay or not, but to my mind, I'd say he's mighty pale."

"Take him to his home. Someone with a fast horse ride for the doctor and have him meet us at the Houston place," the constable ordered. "The boy will do better with his mother close at hand."

Jasmine heard the commotion outside and jumped from the bed. Her heart raced as she went to the sill and threw open the window. "What's happened?" she called down.

The collection of men, which her husband was now joining, stopped in midsentence and looked up at her. She watched with wide eyes as one of the man placed a child in Nolan's arms. What she couldn't see was whether the child was still alive.

Without waiting for their reply, she pulled on her shawl and ran for the stairs. She reached the bottom step just as Nolan entered the room. "He's alive, but . . ."

"But what?" Jasmine cried, coming to the

limp form of her child. "What's wrong with him?"

"He's been drugged. I can't rouse him."

"Oh, dear Lord, help us," she moaned, pushing back Spencer's hair. The child was filthy, but his shallow breathing reassured her. "Has someone sent for the doctor?"

Nolan nodded, meeting her eyes. "He should be here any time now."

"Let's get him cleaned up. The doctor might have a better time of caring for him."

"I'll take him to the kitchen," Nolan suggested. "We'll have plenty of hot water and such." He paused and leaned down to Jasmine. "It might be wise to see to yourself first. I can begin to clean Spencer, but I'd much rather my wife be gowned properly before all of Lowell ends up in our house."

Jasmine looked down at the nightgown and shawl she'd worn for several days. She was reluctant to leave Spencer's side. "But what if something —"

"He's home now, sweetheart. He's home."

Jasmine drank in Nolan's loving gaze. "Yes," she murmured. "He is home."

Hours later, Jasmine rocked a less lethargic Spencer in her arms, still unable to believe her son had been delivered safely to her care. Dr. Hartzfeld had quickly determined the boy had been drugged with laudanum or some other similar tonic in order to keep him asleep. He prescribed rest, nourishment, and fresh air, but with the steady stream of visitors during the first hours after his return, rest had been impossible. Realizing the celebration was taking too great a toll on the boy, Jasmine had taken him upstairs and remained secluded, permitting only Moses in the room. Their delightful reunion had brought tears to her eyes. She took pleasure in seeing their joy, yet the pain of knowing Naomi remained missing made their happiness a bittersweet sight.

Once most of the visitors had departed, Jasmine returned downstairs, with Moses on one side and Spencer on the other. She could hear Nolan's and Obadiah's voices and walked down the hallway toward the kitchen.

"Papa, Papa," Moses chanted. "See Spencie," he said, pointing toward his friend. "Spencie come home."

Jasmine could see the tears forming in Obadiah's eyes. "I'm so sorry, Obadiah," she said. "I was certain they would be found together."

He nodded. "Yessum. You know I's happy as can be dey found Spencer. Jes' hard," he said, his voice fading.

"You go rest. Moses is fine here with us. The boys don't want to be separated right now, anyway," she said.

"Thank you, ma'am. You be a good boy, Moses. I'll be back ta fetch ya after a bit," he said while walking out the back door.

Jasmine glanced at her husband. "I feel terrible. I wish there were something more we could do. The search party promised to go back again tomorrow and search for further clues, but the constable indicated there was nothing more to be found."

"All we can do is offer our encouragement. The marshal said no one is entitled to the reward we offered since the authorities were involved in finding Spencer. But I've told Obadiah I'm going to continue the offer in the hope that someone will come forward with information regarding Naomi." He pulled her close and kissed her forehead. "I believe Violet and McKinley are waiting to see you in the parlor, if you feel up to more visitors."

"I'm always happy to see my brother and Violet. Come along, boys. Uncle McKinley is here."

The boys walked down the hallway, their small feet clattering on the hardwood floors. "Unca Mac!" Spencer hollered, flinging himself into McKinley's arms. Moses followed, and the two boys soon were clamoring for McKinley's undivided attention.

Violet grinned and shook her head. "McKinley, why don't you and the boys go to the other room so Jasmine, Nolan, and I can visit for a few minutes."

"Better yet, why don't we go upstairs to your playroom? Uncle McKinley wants to find a special toy to play with," McKinley said, hoisting Moses under one arm and Spencer under the other.

Jasmine watched as the giggling boys ascended the steps, tucked under her brother's arms like two sacks of flour. "McKinley is so good with children," she said, returning her attention to Violet.

"He does have a way with them," Violet agreed. "I know how relieved you must be to have Spencer home with you again. You've been forced to bear a terrible burden. I'd wager you're ready to celebrate."

"No," she said with a faint smile, "I'd hardly say I want to celebrate. Don't misunderstand — I'm forever grateful for Spencer's return. Yet my heart breaks that we've not yet found Naomi. I never suspected that when we found Spencer we'd not find Naomi too. Poor Obadiah is grief-stricken. And Naomi was much like the sister I never had. We'd become very close since they came to live here. And with the boys being so near the same age, we had much in common."

Violet gasped, her eyes wide. "Jasmine Houston! How can you even think such things, much less say them aloud? Referring to Naomi as a sister — Naomi is a *Negro.* You best not talk like this around anyone else. People won't accept or understand such remarks. Working to free the slaves is one thing, but you must remember that even here, Negroes have their place."

"And what place is that, Violet? Naomi, Obadiah, and Moses are like family to me. I see them more often than I see most members of my family. Naomi has been a faithful friend to me and to Spencer. I owe her family more than anyone can imagine. Obadiah's mother cared for me all of my life — our roots are deep. I'll not compromise my love and concern for their family merely because it may offend someone else."

Violet stiffened slightly and cleared her throat. "Well, of course. I understand you are upset. You've been through trying circumstances," she said. "I'll go upstairs and see if McKinley is ready to return to Lowell. We're expected at my parents' home for supper."

■ ■ ■ ■

"It was good to see my sister so happy," McKinley said as he climbed into the buggy and joined Violet.

"Beware she has some peculiar ideas."

McKinley put the horse in motion. "Such as?"

"She told me Naomi was like a sister to her. That the entire family had become quite important to her — that their roots ran deep."

McKinley frowned. "I'm not sure I understand."

"It seems odd that she would attach herself so completely to a Negro family. As I told her, it's one thing to free the slaves but an entirely different matter to embrace them into our society. They certainly won't be accepted there."

"No, I suppose not. I'm sure you misunderstood her intent, however. Jasmine's nurse was Obadiah's mother. I'm sure it causes Jasmine to hold special feelings for his family. That's probably all it is."

"But why?"

"Well, you must understand the role Mammy played in her life. In mine. We were raised by her — she provided for our every need. We seldom saw our parents during the day, except for meals when we were old enough to join the adults in the dining room."

"Truly?" Violet seemed completely amazed.

"We were raised in the nursery until we were old enough for school. Even then, it was Mammy who continued our care. Jasmine was even more sheltered and nurtured. Father sent us boys away to school for a time. Jasmine remained home and was tutored. Mammy couldn't read or write, but she would spend hours telling Jasmine stories from the Bible and talking about the life Jasmine would have when she grew up."

"How is it you know so much about what Jasmine discussed?"

McKinley smiled. "She told me. I guess I was one of the only ones who was still around to listen. We're only two years apart. David is five years older than Jasmine, and Samuel is eight. That's a long span of time when you're children. Jasmine and I have always listened to one another."

"Then perhaps you should arrange to have a talk with her about her attachment to the former slaves. The Northern states are sympathetic to the Negro plight, but the people of Lowell and Boston will hardly allow for them to intersperse themselves in our social circles."

"Unless, of course, they're holding a tray of refreshments," McKinley said under his breath.

"What was that?" Violet questioned.

He shook his head. It wasn't an easy topic no matter how they looked at it. "Nothing. Nothing of import." Abolitionists would press to see the slaves freed, but he wondered seriously how faithful they would be to concern themselves with housing, jobs, churches, and social interaction. Freeing them seemed a wondrous first step, McKinley thought, but it hardly constituted a resolution to the problems they would face afterward.

Nolan and Jasmine had just finished supper when Obadiah returned to the house, his eyes swollen and his gaze filled with a painful sadness.

"Come sit down," Nolan offered. "Have you eaten?"

Obadiah nodded. "I fixed me some supper a while ago."

The boys came into the dining room, hand in hand, and Moses climbed into his father's lap and planted a kiss on his cheek. Obadiah squeezed his son and then put

Moses on the floor when he started twisting and squirming.

"Why don't you boys go play in the playroom while we adults talk in here," Jasmine suggested. They watched until the boys disappeared from sight.

"I spent all afternoon thinkin' 'bout Naomi and what I gotta do."

Nolan leaned over and patted Obadiah on the back. "Nothing has changed, Obadiah. We're going to continue searching for Naomi. She's bound to be found soon."

"Nossuh, I don' think so. I think Naomi's in da hands of slave traders who done took her back down South to sell her at auction or to any plantation owner who'd pay a good price. I gots to go after her. I don' know how or why any o' dis happened, but my insides are tellin' me she's gone. Spencer ain' said nothin', has he?"

"We haven't attempted to question him at all, and he's offered nothing," Nolan replied. "The doctor thought he was drugged to some extent the entire time they were gone. So even if he was awake, I doubt his thoughts would be clear."

"He's barely three years old, Obadiah. I don't think we could rely on anything he said," Jasmine added.

"Yo're right 'bout dat. 'Sides, I don'

wanna upset him none, and that's fer sure, but I gotta go and find Naomi."

Nolan sat down opposite Obadiah and leaned forward, resting his forearms across his thighs. "Surely you realize that if you go south, you put yourself in extreme danger. Even if you have your papers with you, there are those who would disrcgard them — even take them from you and declare you a runaway."

"I understand all 'bout what could happen ta me. But I know I can' live with myself if I don' go lookin' for Naomi. Tell ya da truth, I don' know if I can live without her. I come here ta ask if you would look after Moses fer me. I can't take him wib me, and I don' know if I'll ever make it back. I'd like to leave knowin' Moses ain' never gonna end up like me and Naomi."

"Won't you wait at least another week?" Jasmine asked. "Give the constables additional time to search the area and then make your decision. If they don't find her in a week, then you go and we'll keep Moses for you."

Obadiah shook his head. "Dem constables ain' gonna spend any time lookin' for Naomi. Only reason they kept lookin dis long is 'cause of Spencer. Don' nobody care 'bout findin' no colored woman. I done made up my mind, Miz Jasmine. I got to leave now. Will ya see after Moses fer me?"

Jasmine glanced at Nolan, who gave an affirmative nod. "Of course we will, Obadiah. We'll make certain he's well cared for."

"I lef' all his clothes and toys at da house. Figured you could get 'em tomorrow. If I don' make it back, ya tell him 'bout his mama and papa and how much dey loved him," he said as he rose from his chair.

"You know we will, but I believe you'll both be back." Her voice caught in her throat. She dared say nothing further for fear she would break down in front of him.

He gave her a weary smile. She knew what he was thinking, but neither of them spoke as they bid each other good-bye.

Two hours later, Jasmine helped the boys into their nightshirts and tucked them into bed side by side. She helped the boys say their bedtime prayers and then turned to her son. "Good night, Spencer. I love you," she said, placing a kiss on his forehead.

"I wuv you, Mama."

She kissed Moses and said, "Good night, Moses. I love you."

"I luff you, Mama," Moses parroted.

She didn't correct him.

CHAPTER 19

Late February 1851

Jasmine buttoned her wool coat and pulled on her black kid gloves. "Are you certain you want to watch after Moses and Spencer? I fear it's too much for you now that you have that sweet baby of your own."

"The boys will na be a problem, and ya can report anything of interest when ya return. Ta be honest, I find the meetin's a wee bit dry and borin'," Kiara said with a smile. "The only reason I attend is ta lend any help I can regardin' the runaways. The rest of the idle chatter and talkin' does na hold my attention. Besides, it's terrible cold ta be takin' the wee babe outdoors for so long."

"You're right on both accounts. I don't think little Nevan should be subjected to this merciless weather, and much of the time, the meetings do turn into visiting fests more than anything else. But I do want to remain abreast of what's being accomplished with the runaways. Since we've had no success finding Naomi, I feel this work is the least I can do."

"Do na give up hope. Obadiah is a strong, determined man. He'll find Naomi."

"Or die trying. That's my greatest fear — that we'll never hear from either of them again and poor little Moses will be left without both of his parents. I feel I should have done more to convince Obadiah to remain here with us."

"There woulda been no convincin' him. We both know that, so ya just as well quit blamin' yarself for somethin' ya could na control. Ya best be goin' on ta the meetin' or ya'll be late."

"The boys should be asleep for at least another half hour. Moses usually awakens from his nap first. . . ."

Kiara waved, as though shooing a fly away from the table. "Go on with ya. I been tendin' these boys often enough I do na need ya tellin' me when they might be wakin' up from a nap."

Jasmine laughed. "I know! By now you're as accustomed to caring for them as I am. And I'm truly thankful Rogan hasn't objected to the time you spend helping me — especially since Naomi's disappearance."

"Rogan does na feel neglected in the least. Now be off with ya."

Waving a quick good-bye, Jasmine hurried down the front steps. "Hello, Paddy," she greeted. "I'm sorry to keep you waiting."

"Do na worry yarself, ma'am. It's pleased I am ta be takin' ya to yar meetin'," he said as she stepped into the awaiting carriage.

As the carriage rumbled toward town, Jasmine settled back into the cushioned leather seat and pulled her fur collar high around her neck. Tucking a wool blanket across her lap, she mused, "I'll never become accustomed to these cold Massachusetts winters."

Her teeth were chattering when the carriage came to a halt in front of the Cheever home. A gust of wind entered the carriage as Paddy pulled the door open, and she shivered as he assisted her down.

"Thank you, Paddy," she said.

"If ya do na mind, I was thinkin' to go and visit with Mr. Kittredge for a wee bit. He's been wantin' to hear more about the Shagyas," he said with pride. "I told him ya would na be opposed if he was wantin' to come and 'ave a look at them."

Jasmine smiled warmly at him. "You go and visit. I'll be at least two hours, perhaps longer. And you tell Mr. Kittredge we're proud of our Arabians, particularly our new Shagyas, and to come have a look whenever he'd like."

A strong north wind caused Paddy to pull his cap farther down onto his head. "Thank ya, ma'am. I'll be back and waitin' fer ya within two hours."

Jasmine bowed her head against the persistent wind and hurried up the front steps of the Cheever house. Before she could knock, the front door opened and a smiling Violet Cheever greeted her. "I'm so glad you've joined us, Jasmine. We've missed you at the last several meetings."

Jasmine stiffened slightly. She was still feeling a bit uncomfortable from Violet's upbraiding regarding her love of Naomi. "I was otherwise preoccupied during those meetings. You'll recall Spencer and Naomi were still missing."

"Of course. I wasn't passing judgment. I merely wanted you to know you'd been missed," Violet replied.

Jasmine relaxed as she felt a wave of heat emanating from the parlor fireplace. "I know you weren't being critical, Violet, but I do feel a tinge of guilt when I miss a meeting."

Violet squeezed Jasmine's hand and smiled. "Well, you certainly need not feel one smidgen of remorse. If anyone had reason for being absent, it was you."

Jasmine glanced about the room, with her gaze settling on Elinor Brighton. "I see Elinor is here. I'm glad she's continued to attend," Jasmine said as she slipped out of her fur-trimmed coat and hat. "I think I'll go and visit with her before the meeting begins."

Elinor was sitting alone on the settee, while the assembling women seemed to cluster into small groups that excluded her. "Elinor! How good to see you. May I sit with you, or is this seat spoken for?"

"I'd be most pleased to have you sit with me." Her eyes appeared to glimmer with expectancy as she pulled her skirts aside to make additional room on the divan.

Jasmine smiled and nodded to several ladies as she sat down. "How have you been, Elinor?"

"Very well, thank you. I've not had an opportunity to tell you how pleased I am that your son was returned unharmed. I know you must have suffered terribly while he was missing. Has there been any word about the woman who disappeared with him?"

Jasmine felt a lump rise in her throat. Elinor was the only person to have inquired about Naomi since her disappearance.

There had been numerous questions and offers of assistance during Spencer's absence, but now it seemed as if Naomi had been forgotten. "How kind of you to ask. I wish I could report we've had some word. Unfortunately, that's not the case. In fact, her husband, Obadiah, has gone south in search of her. He believes her kidnapper has sold her into slavery. And as time goes on, I fear he is correct."

Elinor leaned closer. "We can pray he found her and they've attached themselves to the latest group of runaways scheduled to arrive in the next week."

"We also need to pray that things go more smoothly than with the last group coming through. How sad that after reaching Massachusetts, they would be apprehended and returned. With the passage of the Fugitive Slave Act, it appears there has been an increased interest in capturing the runaways. After all, with the local constables required now to assist in the detainment of escaped slaves, the lure of making money from the capture of fugitives has become appealing to a wider faction."

"I couldn't agree more," Violet said as she settled between them. "We must be particularly careful that there are no mishaps with this group of runaways while they're staying with Liam and Daughtie. Word has been received that they cannot be moved farther north for at least a week, perhaps longer."

"You mean they'll need to remain at the Donohues' for an extended period of time? That's very dangerous," Jasmine said.

Violet nodded vigorously, her carefully arranged curls wobbling back and forth. Jasmine stared in wonder, amazed the hairdo had remained intact. "Exactly! That's why there are only a limited number of people at our meeting today. The fewer people knowing details, the better — only those in charge of coordinating clothing, food, and shelter have been invited. We're certain those who are here can be trusted completely."

Elinor walked toward home, keeping a brisk pace. Mrs. Houston had offered her a carriage ride, but she'd declined. After all, the Houston home was in the opposite direction from the boardinghouse, and she didn't want to impose. That fact aside, she was accustomed to walking and, unlike most of her counterparts, found the cold air invigorating.

Her cheeks were ruddy and her fingers growing numb by the time she entered the boardinghouse. The sound of chattering girls wafted from the parlor into the hallway as Elinor untied her bonnet before removing her heavy wool cloak. Peeking into the vestibule mirror, she checked her hair and tucked a loose blond curl behind her ear before walking to the parlor door.

Luminous shadows of a man on one knee in front of several young ladies danced off the walls of the candlelit room. "Oliver! I didn't realize you were here."

Oliver swiveled, losing his balance and sprawling in a heap before the three girls seated on the divan. "Elinor! You startled me," he said while attempting to stand. By the time he had regained his composure, Oliver's complexion had turned nearly as ruddy as her own wind-stung cheeks.

The three girls continued to giggle, obviously enjoying the spectacle. Elinor bit her bottom lip and attempted to erase the picture of Oliver collapsed on the floor. Otherwise, she knew she would join the girls in their unmitigated amusement at the spectacle. "I apologize for surprising you. However, I didn't realize you were making deliveries this evening."

"I received my order earlier than expected and thought the girls would be pleased to receive their shoes," he said.

"And I'm certain they are."

"Oh yes," they said in unison. "Aren't mine lovely, Mrs. Brighton?" Abigail Morley lifted her skirt a few inches and revealed a pair of black calfskin slippers.

"Indeed, although they won't serve you well standing at the looms."

"They're not intended for work," Abigail replied. "I'll wear them when I attend the theater or a symposium."

"Or to church, when we can get her out of bed," Ardith Fordham added with a giggle.

"I go to church on the Sundays when I'm not feeling ill," Abigail defended.

Sarah giggled. "Strange how you feel fine every other day, but you always seem ill on Sunday mornings — and then have a rapid recovery when we arrive home."

Abigail glared at the other two girls. "I'm going up to my room."

"Aren't you coming to town with us? There's ample time before the shops close, and there was a sign at Whidden's Mercantile that a new shipment of gloves and lace arrived today."

Abigail hesitated on the stairway. "I'll change into my old shoes and be back down in a moment. Don't leave without me!"

Elinor watched as Oliver remained focused upon packing his wares, apparently ignoring the girls' repartee. Elinor neared his side. "Would you care for a cup of tea, or do you have other deliveries you must make?"

"A cup of tea would be very nice." He smiled broadly as he locked down the lid of his leather and wood case.

"The girls tell me you were gone to a meeting," Oliver commented as he followed her into the kitchen.

"Yes. The Ladies' Aid group was meeting at the Cheever home this evening."

Oliver watched quietly as she deftly prepared the tea and arranged a small plate of lemon cookies on a tray. "May I carry that into the parlor for you?"

She gave him a demure smile and nodded.

"I trust you had a fruitful meeting and there was a good attendance," he said while following her into the parlor with the tray.

"Oh yes. Thank you for inquiring. I was extremely pleased that Mrs. Houston was once again in attendance. What with the disappearance of Spencer and Naomi, she had been required to miss several of our meetings."

"You speak as though you know the family quite well," he mused.

"No, of course not, but the upheaval surrounding the disappearance of the woman and boy made most of us feel almost as if we knew them, don't you think?"

"Perhaps that's true. The entire issue was well discussed about town, and with so many people involved in searching for the boy, they likely developed a sense of association with the family."

"Precisely. At least I know that's how I was affected," Elinor said as she poured tea into his cup. "Mrs. Houston tells me her son appears to be doing quite well, although she worries somewhat over the boy having nightmares since he returned home."

"I suppose that's to be expected. Did she tell you about them?"

"His nightmares?"

"Yes. Does he remember anything about them?"

She gave him a quizzical look. "I don't know — she didn't say. Why do you ask?"

He hesitated. "I've heard it helps to talk about bad dreams and nightmares if you can recall them. Personally, I never remember my dreams."

The front door opened, and noisy chatter was followed by several girls calling out their good-nights as they ran up the steps. "I did inquire about the black woman, Naomi, and whether there had been any further word regarding her whereabouts. Poor Mrs.

Houston remains quite distraught over the woman's disappearance."

"Did she say if they had any new information?"

"No. Although Mrs. Houston now believes Naomi has been resold into slavery. Isn't that a sad thought? After suffering all those years as a slave and being set free — but then to be once again forced back into the misery of slavery! It seems more than a person ought to bear in one lifetime."

"Surely Mrs. Houston must have set aside talk of the woman and expressed joy over having her son returned. I would think she'd find her son's safety of greater importance than that of a colored woman."

Elinor felt compelled to defend Mrs. Houston — perhaps because of the harshness of Oliver's statement. "Well, of course, she is thrilled beyond words to have Spencer home, but the burden of such a loss lies heavy upon her heart. She tells me that Naomi's husband has gone in search of her. He left his son behind with Mr. and Mrs. Houston. I find the entire situation very sad."

"But having the Houston boy returned was of the greatest import," Oliver stressed.

"To Naomi's husband, I doubt that's correct, but I'm certain the Houstons would agree."

He sat up straighter and squared his shoulders. "Did Mrs. Houston happen to mention the important role I played in unearthing her son's whereabouts — the fact that I was the one who thought of the abandoned farm as a possible hiding place?"

Elinor stared at him for a moment. "No. At least she didn't mention it to me."

"I find it rather strange that with all her money, she didn't even offer me a pittance of a reward. After all, I doubt whether any of these locals would have ever thought of that old farmstead. The boy would still be missing if it weren't for me."

"Frankly I'm surprised you would expect a reward for doing a good deed. I believe the Houstons have continued to offer the reward for Naomi's safe return. I do hope she's able to be reunited with her child. That little boy must certainly be frightened and confused with both of his parents now gone from home."

"Seems they ought to be able to find her, what with her light color and beauty. She's one of the prettiest women, colored or white, I ever saw. She'd sure stand out in a crowd."

The hair bristled on the back of her neck.

"And how would *you* know about Naomi?"

Oliver shrugged his shoulders. "I measured her for shoes when I was at the Houston horse farm. Mrs. Houston had me measure everyone for new shoes. Hard to believe, but she was buying expensive shoes for everyone on the place — even the coloreds."

Elinor sipped her tea and stared across the brim of her cup into Oliver Maxwell's eyes. An increasing sense of suspicion and uncertainty had begun to settle in her heart.

CHAPTER 20

McKinley Wainwright stood at the bottom of the stairs awaiting his sister and her husband. "Do hurry, Jasmine, or we'll be late," he called up the stairs.

"We'll be down as soon as we tell the boys good-night," she replied. "Have Paddy bring the carriage around."

McKinley shook his head in exasperation. "Paddy brought the carriage around fifteen minutes ago. He, too, is waiting."

A short time later, Jasmine descended the steps in a pale green gown that trailed the steps in small billowing waves resembling the morning tide lapping at the shoreline.

"As usual, you look lovely," McKinley said.

"She's always worth the wait, isn't she?" Nolan agreed while following her down the stairway.

McKinley nodded. "However, it's Violet who is to be the center of attention tonight.

Let's hope your beauty this evening doesn't diminish her introduction into society."

Jasmine giggled. "Between the two of you, I could become quite vain. And I'm certain that if I were wearing jewels from head to toe, I couldn't surpass Violet's beauty in your eyes, McKinley."

Her brother winked and gave her a bright smile. "I do think she's quite captivating. Now that her parents are finally introducing her into society, I plan to ask Mr. Cheever's permission to court her."

Nolan gave his brother-in-law a fond slap on the back. "And what do you call these occasional rides in the country and visits to her home, if not courting?"

"Our outings have been simply as friends. I now wish to seek proper permission to come calling. My hope is that there won't be others standing in line to vie for her attention. I do worry that Mr. Cheever may have preconceived ideas about whom he would like his daughter to marry."

Jasmine worked her fingers into a pair of lace gloves before moving toward the door. "Arranged marriages seem to be considered rather old-fashioned here in the North. Although I have heard of one or two, most families do not seem to be inclined to marry their children off in such a fashion as we did in the South."

"I see nothing wrong in arranging marriages for the benefit of the family," McKinley admitted, then quickly added, "but only if true love can be found at the same time."

"Well, Mr. and Mrs. Cheever seem to be of an open mind — less than traditional I would think. I'd be surprised if he forced his daughter into a loveless marriage. After all, he married a woman for whom he had deep affection. Certainly he should understand the value of that concept."

"Let's hope you're correct," McKinley replied.

"And let's hope Spencer and Moses go to sleep and don't give Kiara a difficult time," Jasmine remarked. "I worry she may have her hands full with both of them as well as little Nevan." She looked back up the stairs and hesitated.

Nolan reached out and touched her arm. "I know you're still nervous about leaving the house and the boys, but Rogan will soon be here, and the other servants won't allow a soul to cross the threshold unless they are friend or family."

McKinley nodded. " 'Twould be unlikely for such an episode to happen more than once in a person's lifetime. I believe your troubles are behind you, sister."

"I pray you are right."

Nolan assisted his wife into the carriage and then sat down beside her. "Now stop fretting. Kiara won't be alone for long. Rogan was to be done with his work early today and told me he'd promised to come over to the house and lend her a hand with the children. To be honest, I doubt she needs any help. The boys both follow her instructions more quickly than they do ours."

"Unfortunately, I believe you may be right on that account."

McKinley laughed. "But then didn't we always obey Mammy better than Mother or Father?"

Jasmine looked at him oddly. "I never thought of it, actually. It's true that Kiara has been instrumental in helping me to raise Spencer, and she's spent a good deal of time with Moses. But certainly she hasn't been with them as closely as Mammy was with us. Especially with me."

"I was telling Violet about our childhood a time back. She finds it all fascinating."

"She no doubt struggles to understand our ways. Or perhaps I should say, our parents' ways," Jasmine admitted. "She was none too keen on my friendship and love for Naomi."

"But why?" Nolan asked.

"She thought it inappropriate. She said she could firmly get behind the cause of freeing the slaves, but not of associating with them," Jasmine recalled.

"I have to admit, sister, such thoughts reflect my own. Not because I think the black man or woman to be less than valuable. But what would we have in common? People in social classes come together as such because they value the same things, they work or live in similar fashion. Can you possibly see a former field hand wearing tails and sipping champagne?"

"But we were taught how to conduct ourselves in such situations. In the nursery, I was shown the proper etiquette for holding teas. I learned to dance because someone took the time to teach me the steps," Jasmine said, her tone intense.

McKinley recognized something in her manner that suggested he move cautiously. "I'm uncertain whom you would find with a willing heart to teach such things. The Negro isn't going to be allowed in regular schools. Their mannerisms are frightening to most white people."

"It's fear born out of ignorance and nothing more," Jasmine protested. "If people would learn to look beyond their fears, they might find their views drastically changed."

Elinor hesitated before entering the walkway to the Cheever home. She felt strangely out of place attending Violet Cheever's coming-out party. Yet Lilly Cheever had insisted, citing the fact that she and Mr. Cheever did not stand upon social traditions — along with the fact that much of her husband's success in the mills had depended upon Elinor's uncle's and brother's abilities making calicos and implementing new technology and patterns for the mills. And so Elinor had diffidently agreed to attend, though now she wondered why she had done so. Had her brother Taylor and his wife, Bella, not been in Scotland, they would have accompanied her. But when word of the unexpected death of their eldest sister, Beatrice, had arrived, Taylor and Bella immediately sailed for Scotland in order to lend their assistance to the family.

The Houston carriage came to a halt a short distance beyond where Elinor stood outside the house. "Good evening, Elinor," Jasmine greeted as she stepped down from the carriage. "Won't you join us?"

Elinor issued a silent prayer of thanks. At least she'd not have to enter the party alone. "Yes, thank you. I feel a bit awkward without

Taylor and Bella. I usually attend social functions with them."

"I understand they're visiting in Scotland," Jasmine said.

"Yes, with my sister's family. I don't expect them back for another six weeks."

"Then you must permit us the pleasure of escorting you this evening," Nolan said.

"Thank you. The party promises to be quite an event, don't you think?"

McKinley's lips turned up in a wide grin. "I heartily agree."

Jasmine took Elinor by the arm and leaned close. "He's hoping Miss Cheever will grant him exclusive courting privileges."

Elinor smiled at McKinley as they walked up the steps. "I wish you good fortune with Miss Cheever. She appears to be a fine young lady."

"Thank you, Mrs. Brighton," McKinley said while opening the door.

The music from the small orchestra floated into the entryway as Matthew and Lilly Cheever stood greeting their guests. Once properly introduced, Elinor made her way into the room and was planning to find a corner in which to quietly watch the festivities. Jasmine, however, remained close by her side, taking her by the hand as she and Nolan moved among the guests.

"I don't believe we've met these folks," Jasmine said to her husband as they approached a small cluster of men and women gathered near the double doors that led into the garden.

One of the gentlemen turned in their direction, and Nolan drew closer, extending his hand. "Nolan Houston and my wife, Jasmine, and Mrs. Elinor Brighton," he said.

"John and Jenny Riddell and my sons, Charles and Luther. Mr. Cheever graciously extended an invitation to our family. We're in Lowell planning several investment opportunities."

"Lowell is an excellent community in which to place your trust — and your money," Nolan said with a grin.

"Are you planning to invest in the mills?" Jasmine inquired.

"Possibly. However, my sons are more interested in the patent medicine business. They believe they'll encounter fewer problems dealing in a smaller enterprise rather than working through the layers of organization developed by the Boston Associates in their conglomerate."

"I'm not certain I agree with your thinking," Nolan said. "I believe you'll find James Ayer rather unwilling to permit you entry into his growing pharmaceutical venture."

Luther moved to Nolan's side and tilted his head closer. "If he doesn't desire a partner, then we may be inclined to compete with him."

"I do hope you have a new and inventive product in mind, as I don't believe you'll be able to compete with his Cherry Pectoral or Cathartic Pills. I believe he has captured the market."

"If my research serves me, Ayer began an apprenticeship with a gentleman by the name of Robbins not so many years ago," Luther said. "I'm certain he didn't know much about the pharmaceutical business at the time he began his apprenticeship. Ayer had seen a need for specific medicinal products and then developed a product to fill that particular void. He is obviously an astute businessman, but so are we."

"Then why not discover another need within society and fill that void, rather than merely choosing to expand upon the pharmaceutical business?" Jasmine inquired.

Elinor glanced toward Nolan, who was giving his wife a look of obvious admiration.

"As you've possibly surmised, my wife is an astute businesswoman, as well as an astonishing wife and mother," Nolan praised.

"Truly? And what void did *you* fill in the business world, Mrs. Houston?" Luther asked with a smirk.

"Are you familiar with Arabian horses, Mr. Riddell?"

"I've seen one or two. They're fine-looking animals, but quite expensive."

"Indeed! However, there is an exclusive market for Arabians in this country. I fill that void with my Arabians, and now we've expanded and are raising Shagyas, an even more exclusive breed of Arabian."

Luther Riddell gave a hearty laugh. "Pray tell, what is a Shagya?"

"It's an Arabian breed that was developed at the military stud farms of the Austro-Hungarian monarchy. The Shagya combines the advantages of a Bedouin Arabian with the requirements of a modern riding or carriage horse. This breed has inborn friendliness toward humans. President Taylor was quite interested in the Shagyas and had planned to visit our horse farm. His untimely death prevented the visit, but he had a true love for Arabians and was very enthusiastic about the breed."

"I must say that if you had the interest of a horseman such as President Taylor, you most certainly must be raising some exceptional horseflesh," John said.

"Thank you, Mr. Riddell. If you'll excuse us, I believe my brother desires to speak with me."

As they made their way across the room, Jasmine waved at Daughtie and Liam Donohue, then turned toward Elinor. "You did receive word the group of runaways we'rc awaiting won't be arriving as expected, didn't you?"

"No, I wasn't notified. Are you certain?"

Jasmine nodded. "Violet said she'd send word to everyone, but I fear with all of the preparations for her party, she may have forgotten any number of people. Now that I realize she failed to send word to you, I believe I'll check with the others, but first I must talk to McKinley."

"If you'll excuse me, I believe I'll go out to the garden for some fresh air," Elinor said.

"Outdoors? I fear you may be a little chilly," Jasmine said.

"I'll be fine."

Being careful to avoid the couples moving toward the portion of the room designated for dancing, Elinor wended her way through the crowd. She walked out the doors into the cool night air and immediately began briskly rubbing her arms. The garden appeared eerily forsaken. Swiping dead leaves from a nearby bench, Elinor sat down and contemplated the information Jasmine had just divulged, wondering what had occurred to cause the runaways' delay. Likely there had been a fear their plans had been compromised.

"Probably some unsuspecting person making idle conversation. Someone exactly like me," Elinor whispered, thinking of Oliver Maxwell and his suspicious behavior. She fervently hoped he would disprove her growing concerns.

A breeze cut through the leafless branches. She shivered and rose to her feet, pacing back and forth in front of the bench, hoping that the movement would warm her. Oliver's recent remarks had given her pause, especially his harsh statements regarding Naomi and the description of her appearance. Oh yes, he'd given her an explanation, yet she increasingly doubted Oliver's word. Even if he'd spoken the truth about measuring Naomi for shoes, how had he known about the capture of the last group of runaways? Even though she'd felt an urging to be honest with the marshal, she'd instead given him ambiguous replies to his many questions. Now she needed to know exactly what role Oliver Maxwell may have played in all of these incidents.

"And there's only one way to be certain. Prepare yourself to be tested, Oliver," she murmured, hoping that he would soon return from New Hampshire.

The girls gathered around the dining table, their hunger evident as they forked thick slices of ham onto their plates and ladled creamy gravy over heaping mounds of boiled potatoes. "Pass the apple butter," Abigail requested.

Mary handed the apple butter to Sarah, who passed it down the line of girls until it reached Abigail. "I heard one of the girls say that McKinley Wainwright received permission to court Violet Cheever at her coming-out party last night. Looks like he's going to marry himself right into a permanent position with the mills."

"There are going to be a lot of girls sorry to hear your news," Sarah said. "More than a few had their hopes set upon winning the heart of Mr. Wainwright."

"Obviously he has his sights set upon someone who can ensure him a place within the hierarchy of the wondrous Boston Associates," Abigail said.

Elinor refilled a bowl of green beans and placed them on the table with a thud. "I believe you girls are being unfair. You're judging a person and a situation about which you have no personal knowledge."

"Mrs. Brighton is correct on that account: we really don't have reliable information. Perhaps you'd be willing to share *your* personal knowledge with us since you had the privilege of attending the party last evening," Abigail replied with a smug grin.

"I'll respond by saying only that McKinley Wainwright is an upstanding young man who doesn't need to rely upon anyone else in order to succeed in life. From all that I have observed, his interest in Violet Cheever is based upon genuine affection, nothing else. But I certainly do not consider myself an authority on the topic."

"But he has asked and received permission to court her, hasn't he?" Abigail insisted.

"Yes. And they do make a striking couple," Elinor replied before turning on her heel and returning to the kitchen.

Once she'd completed the supper dishes and satisfied herself the kitchen was in order, Elinor retrieved her needlework and joined several of the girls in the parlor. She knew they'd soon leave for an evening stroll into town or go up to their rooms to write letters and visit. She'd just begun her stitching when a knock sounded at the front door.

Moments later, Sarah escorted Oliver into the parlor.

"Since Mr. Maxwell isn't carrying his case, it appears as if he's come to call on you, Mrs. Brighton," Sarah announced.

Elinor felt the heat rise in her cheeks. "Do come in and join us, Oliver."

Olivcr sauntered into the room but remained standing. "I thought perhaps we could take a stroll, where we could be afforded a bit more privacy."

Several of the girls covered their mouths and snickered while they exchanged gleeful glances, as though they'd been privy to a valuable tidbit of gossip.

Tucking her needlework into the sewing basket beside her chair, Elinor smiled. "Yes, of course. A walk sounds delightful, but I need to speak to you in private before we leave."

Oliver dutifully followed her into the dining room. "Why all the secrecy?"

"I didn't want any of the girls to overhear, but I received word only a short time ago that the runaways we weren't expecting until next week will be arriving by midnight tonight. I was asked to gather additional supplies from town since we weren't entirely prepared for them just yet."

Grasping her arm, Oliver looked straight

into her eyes. “Are you saying they will be here tonight?”

“Yes! That’s why I was delighted when you mentioned going for a walk. I can use your help carrying my purchases. I was concerned about how I would get the items home and then, thankfully, you arrived.”

“But I won’t be able to assist you,” he said beginning to edge away from her.

“Why not? You asked me to go for a walk . . . I don’t understand.”

“I’ve just remembered something that requires my immediate attention.”

“Surely it can wait,” she said, taking hold of his arm.

He pulled away from her and turned toward the door. “I must go now.”

Elinor watched as he all but ran from the housc. Shc leaned against the dining room table, weak from the realization that Oliver Maxwell was her enemy. He stood for everything she despised, yet she had helped him succeed. Her loose tongue had given him enough information to capture the last group of escaped slaves. Cupping a trembling hand over her mouth, Elinor collapsed onto the wooden chair and sobbed.

Chapter 21

Without taking time to apologize for his rude behavior, Oliver pushed his way through the small groups of mill girls and evening shoppers that unwittingly blocked his path. He must get to the livery immediately. Gone were the days when he had his strawberry roan at his immediate disposal. Instead, he now relied upon the use of Mr. Kittredge's livery horses while he continued to maintain his horse had been stolen when Spencer Houston and Naomi were abducted.

He had hoped the Houstons would give him a reward or, at the very least, a fine horse to replace his roan. They'd done neither, but after selling the group of runaways Enoch and Joseph would capture this night, he promised himself the ownership of a well-bred horse.

"Since they didn't appreciate my information enough to give me one of their horses, perhaps I can convince them at least to give me a good deal on one of those fine Arabians," he mused.

"You talking to me? 'Cause if you are, I didn't hear what you were saying."

Jumping back a step, Oliver turned and saw Mr. Kittredge bent forward, examining the hoof of a fine-looking sorrel. "You startled me."

"Did I now? I'd think you'd be expecting to see me in this place since I own it," Kittredge said with a hearty laugh. "You needing a horse?"

"Yes. I won't be taking my wagon."

Kittredge nodded. "Want to take this sorrel out and give him some exercise? I'm boarding him for a few weeks. Thought I'd get him out earlier today, but I got too busy. Won't charge you for the use if you give him a good run."

"Be glad to help you out," Oliver replied. He smiled at his good fortune and waited as Kittredge deftly saddled the animal.

He mounted the horse and kept the animal at a trot until they reached the outskirts of town. With more force than he'd intended, Oliver dug his heels into the horse's flesh and sent the animal into a gallop. He didn't slow the horse until they neared the overgrown path leading to the abandoned farm, where he hoped Enoch and Joseph were merely doing as he said — remaining well hidden. However, if the two of them hadn't yet returned, all would be lost — at least with this group of runaways. The thought of such a monetary loss was something Oliver didn't want to consider.

To the untrained eye, the farmstead appeared deserted. Oliver squinted and gazed toward the barn. Stars twinkled, and a sliver of moonlight shone brightly from the cloudless sky to reveal an unhitched wagon alongside the barn. His horse neighed, and Oliver drew back on the reins as Joseph lifted himself from the wagon bed and aimed his weapon directly at Oliver.

"Put that thing down before you kill me, Joseph!" Oliver called. "What's that wagon doing outside the barn?"

Joseph jumped down from the wagon as Oliver approached on horseback. "I'm using it to keep watch. Appears it worked, 'cause I got the drop on you."

Annoyed by his smug attitude, Oliver ignored his comment and rode into the barn. "Where's Enoch?" he hollered.

"Behind you," Enoch replied. "Whadda'ya think of our setup to stop intruders?"

Oliver dismounted and handed the reins of the horse to Joseph. "I think you'd be much wiser to do as I told you — remain hidden, and if anyone approaches, stay out of sight until you're certain they're gone. Instead, you put that wagon out there in plain sight, and Joseph draws his weapon on anyone riding onto the property. Don't you two see how that might cause suspicion? Sometimes I wonder why I ever brought the two of you in on this deal."

Enoch lit the stub of a candle, which illuminated the small area of the barn where they stood. "You needed us, that's why," he said simply. "You can rant and rave at us all you want, but you know we've done a good job. We got all them darkies sold at a good price and got back up here in less time than you ever figured."

"Besides, *we're* the ones taking all the risk and doing the hard part of this job. Ain't no reason for *you* to be complaining about nothin'," Joseph remarked as he pulled a small knife from his pocket and began using the blade to clean his fingernails.

"You two had best remember that the information about the runaways comes from *me*. Without me, you've got nothing but an empty wagon. Speaking of the good price you got for that bunch, how about turning over my share right now."

Enoch walked across the barn while holding the stubby candle in one hand. Oliver watched as he entered one of the ramshackle stalls and pulled a leather pouch from his saddlebag.

"Your share," Enoch growled, tossing the bag at Oliver.

Oliver dumped the contents onto the dirt floor and began counting. "Doesn't appear you got such a good price if this is my half."

"Half?" Joseph yelled, jumping to his feet. "You're lucky we're giving you a third. What makes you think you're entitled to half?"

Oliver turned to Enoch. "We agreed I'd get half and the two of you would split the other half, didn't we, Enoch?"

Enoch nodded. "We did. But our agreement was unfair and you know it. I guess you can take what we're offering or nothing at all."

"And what if I turned the two of you in to the marshal?"

"You ain't gonna do that — we know it and so do you. Greed ain't a pretty thing, Oliver. You need to remember there's two of us, and we plan to stick together," Joseph said in a menacing tone.

Oliver gathered the money and shoved it back into the pouch. "Fine. We'll go with an equal split, but you two had best not cheat me. And remember, without my information, there's no more money for either of you. Now get the horses hitched. There's another group coming through tonight."

"Tonight? I thought they wasn't due for three more days," Joseph said.

"The plans changed. I got word they're coming through tonight."

"When and where?" Enoch asked.

"About five miles down the road. They should come through around midnight, but we need to get hidden well before they arrive."

"You shoulda told us when you first got here instead of wasting time talking and worrying about your money," Joseph said.

"Is that my roan you're using?" Oliver asked Enoch while ignoring Joseph's condemnation.

"Yep. Sure is."

Oliver bristled at his casual reply. "I told you to board him down south and purchase another horse. Plenty of folks around here recognize that horse."

"We ain't got time to argue about it now," Joseph snarled. "We best head out or them darkies are gonna be long gone 'fore we get there."

Once Oliver departed, Elinor donned her bonnet and woolen cape. She truly couldn't afford the expense of a carriage but walking to the Donohues' was out of the question. She hurried toward town. If good fortune was with her, she'd locate a carriage for hire near the train depot. She drew closer to the Merrimack House and watched as several passengers stepped out of a carriage and entered the hotel. Boldly, she approached the driver as he unloaded a satchel.

"I need to hire a carriage immediately," she said.

"Soon as I unload one more trunk, I can take ya."

Elinor watched, pacing back and forth as the driver wielded the trunk onto his shoulder and carried it inside the hotel.

"Where to?" he asked as he returned moments later.

"The Liam Donohue residence."

The driver scratched his head and gazed heavenward. "Donohue," he muttered.

"The property adjoining the Houston horse farm."

"Oh! Right you are. I'll have you there in no time." The driver slapped the reins and urged the horses into a gallop that jolted Elinor's head against the back of the seat.

The driver was good to his word. He drew the team to a halt in front of the Donohue residence. After handing her down from the buggy, she rushed up the steps and rapped on the door several times before banging the metal door knocker.

"I'm comin'! I'm comin'!" Liam shouted before pulling open the door.

"Mr. Donohue, I must talk to you!" Elinor exclaimed.

"Ya need na shout, lass. I'm right here in front of ya," he said with a grin. "Come on in and sit ya down in the parlor. I'll fetch me wife."

Daughtie was already midway down the hall. "What is it, Liam?" she asked while wiping her hands on a checked cotton dish-towel.

"Mrs. Brighton's needin' to have a word with us."

The couple sat down and gave her their full attention, Liam leaning forward like a cat ready to pounce.

"I've something terrible to tell you," Elinor said, her tears already beginning to flow.

"Ya do na need ta be weepin', lass. Hard it is to be understandin' a cryin' woman."

Daughtie poked him in the side and then offered Elinor a handkerchief. "Take your time, Elinor. Breathe deeply. I'm certain nothing has happened that can't be set aright."

Her tone was soft and kind, and Elinor responded with a feeble smile. "You're wrong on that account. You see, I'm responsible for the capture of the last group of escaped slaves coming through."

Liam gave her a patronizing smile. "I do na think a wee lass like yarself was able to accomplish that feat."

"No, but I gave information to the man who was responsible."

"Ya *what*?" Liam shouted. "Why would ya do such a thing?"

Elinor shrank back in her chair. "It wasn't intentional. I thought he could be trusted — that he was working for the cause, but I'm now certain he's the one responsible for their abduction. I, however, am equally at fault, for had I not told him, those poor runaways would now be free."

"Are ya willin' to tell us the name of this man?"

"Oliver Maxwell," she whispered.

"The shoe peddler?" Daughtie asked.

Elinor nodded and then explained how she had unwittingly taken Oliver into her confidence, watching Liam's and Daughtie's changing expressions as they listened intently. "Because I wasn't certain of his involvement, I set a trap for Oliver this evening," she said as she finished her sad confession.

"Wha' kind of trap?" Liam asked.

"I told him another group of runaways was expected tonight, that they would be passing through the same route as the first group. If he's guilty as I suspect, he's already out there waiting for them."

"Yet he may very well be at home snug in his bed," Daughtie remarked.

"Aye. I can see there's some coincidences tha' make ya wonder if the man is true, but we need ta be findin' out if he's the black heart ya believe him ta be," Liam said. "If this shoe peddler is the culprit, then 'tis true ya've made a terrible error in judgment."

Daughtie gave Elinor an encouraging smile. "Let's hope he's not the guilty party."

"But I'm certain he is! Can't you see the depth of my transgressions?"

" 'Tis true that if ya're right, many a person has suffered fer yar error — and will suffer for a long time ta come. But ya can na change things. Ya've done right by comin' ta me and tryin' to set things aright. Thar's no doubt we all make mistakes in judgment."

"But my mistake is greater than those made by others. All those slaves who were tasting freedom are now back in captivity, likely suffering from an overseer's whip —

all on my account," Elinor moaned.

"If we find that what ya've told us is true, it's the shoe peddler that's ta blame," Liam said. "I'm na discountin' the fact that ya had a loose tongue, but yar heart was right. Ya were tryin' ta get shoes for the runaways, and that was an admirable thing."

"I fear the depth of my transgression is as deep as Oliver's," Elinor said as she pulled a handkerchief from her pocket.

"Ya judge yarself too harshly, lass. Thar's nothing tha' can na be forgiven by God."

"Liam's right. There's no doubt you made a mistake, Elinor, but you didn't intentionally set out to harm the runaways or aid in their capture. Oliver preyed upon you, realizing you were a member of the antislavery movement who might divulge important information. Unfortunately, he was correct. But God will forgive you if you'll but ask."

"I don't know if I can forgive myself," Elinor said, tears beginning to once again roll down her cheeks.

Liam jumped to his feet. "I'm goin' for Rogan. We'll ride out to the narrows and see if thar's any sign of Oliver."

Daughtie stood and grasped her husband's arm. "Promise me you'll be careful. If there's anyone out there, I doubt they'll give in without a fight."

Elinor watched as Liam bid his wife good-bye, now wondering if coming to Liam with the information was prudent. If anything happened to Liam Donohue or Rogan Sheehan, she'd never be able to live with herself.

"I should go," Elinor said. "I paid the driver to wait, and I need to be back to the house before ten."

Daughtie walked with her to the carriage. "Pray, Elinor. Pray hard."

Elinor nodded. It seemed their only hope.

Liam saddled his horse and rode the short distance to the Houston farm, entering through the second set of gates leading directly to the house Jasmine Houston had had built as a wedding gift for Rogan and Kiara. Before he could dismount, the front door opened and Rogan stood in the doorway, holding a lamp in one hand and a shotgun in the other.

"Who's there?" he called out.

"It's Liam. I do na have time to explain. I need ya ta come with me. Bring your weapon and saddle your horse as quickly as ya can. Do na permit Paddy ta come along."

Kiara stepped forward and took the lamp from Rogan. "What is it, Liam?"

"Do na worry, lass. We should be back

afore mornin'. A few problems with some runaways. Keep Paddy with ya. I do na want him followin' after us like he's done afore."

"Ya're riding inta danger, are ya?"

"Nothin' we can na handle."

Kiara gave Liam a faint smile. "Do na let anything happen to me 'usband."

"Ya have me word, lass."

Rogan clearly trusted Liam's instincts and followed his friend's lead as they rode in earnest through the countryside. Liam slowed his horse as they drew closer to the narrows and then signaled for Rogan to dismount.

"We'll leave the horses here and walk the rest of the way," Liam said, keeping his voice low.

"Are ya goin' ta tell me what's goin' on?" Rogan asked as they settled in a clump of bushes near the narrow path that cut between two hills.

"I'm na certain it's going ta work, but Elinor Brighton has laid a trap. She thinks the shoe peddler and some others are involved in capturing the runaways. She told him thar's a group moving through tonight. She believes we'll find him out here waitin' on 'em," Liam whispered.

They sat waiting, hoping they'd hear something — anything. Liam's legs began to cramp, and Rogan suggested they leave.

Liam grasped Rogan's arm and strained forward. "Listen!"

The voices grew louder and the two men sat quietly, eavesdropping on the conversation taking place nearby.

"We've moved places three times now, Oliver. Looks to me like you got a bad piece of information."

"Keep your voice down," Oliver warned in a hoarse whisper.

"Ain't no need. If them runaways was coming, they'd already be through here by now," Joseph snarled. "The last ones was here by eleven o'clock. It's way after midnight by now. I'm cold and tired. Let's get outta here."

"I was right last time, wasn't I? And you ended up with plenty of money, didn't you? The two of you need to be patient. Maybe something happened along the way to slow them down."

"Yeah. And maybe they already been captured — if there were any headed this way to begin with. Just because you was right last time, that don't mean you got good information this time. Come on, Enoch. Let's go. You know they ain't coming tonight."

"He's right, Oliver. We're leaving. You wait if you want, but we're heading back to the barn."

Oliver refused to relent, remaining in place while Enoch and Joseph rode off. He didn't intend to wait long — there would be little he could do by himself to stop the group of runaways if they did happen along. However, he wasn't going to concede to Joseph's idea. They'd been gone only a short time when Oliver heard the brush rustling behind him.

"Who's there? You decide maybe I was right and come back, Enoch? Joseph?"

"Yar friends are gone, Mr. Maxwell. But Rogan and me, we been sittin' nearby, and we heard every word the three of ya was sayin'. Seems ya got yarself involved in capturin' runaways," Liam said.

"You can't prove a thing. Besides, *you're* the ones operating outside the law — helping runaways. What *I'm* doing is perfectly within the law. I even have the right to request the marshal's assistance if need be. Something called the Fugitive Slave Act. Surely you don't dispute I'm in the right."

"You're not returning those slaves to their rightful owners," Rogan countered. "You're selling them to the highest bidder, and that's not legal."

Oliver gave him a brash grin. "Again, you have no proof of your allegations. You overheard my conversation. Do you believe the word of two Irishmen is going to be taken over my word and that of my two men when we insist every attempt was made to find the rightful owners before offering the slaves at market?"

Liam hesitated. "You weren't operatin' under the Fugitive Slave Act when ya rode off with Spencer Houston and Naomi."

"Maybe I wasn't, but nothing that's been said here tonight frightens me, nor do the two of you. There's no way you can prove anything we've talked about."

"So I don't frighten ya?" Liam asked, grabbing Oliver by the collar and slamming him against a tree. "When ya're countin' off the things that can na be proved, ya might remember thar's no way ya can prove it was *me* that beat that smugness outta ya on this night, is thar?"

Oliver knew he must appear in control or all would be lost. "Put me down. You need to remember that if you ever want to see that darky again, you best not lay a hand on me."

"Yar word is worthless. We do na believe a thing ya say, and I figure I may as well have myself a little satisfaction. If takin' it out of yar hide is the only thing I can get, then so be it," Liam seethed, balling his fist.

"Wait!" Oliver shouted, attempting to stave off a blow by thrusting his arm forward. "If you'll let me leave and go about my business, I'll send word to have Naomi released and sent back home." He hurried on when Liam's arm cocked even higher. "I'll even pay to have her transported — and I'll leave Lowell and give you my word I'll not return. You know there's no choice — let's do what's best for all of us."

"Ya best remember the promises ya've made here this night. Be a man and keep yar word, or ya'll find out what fightin' Irishmen look like," Liam warned.

Without a moment's hesitation, Oliver mounted his horse and rode off. He glanced over his shoulder and breathed a sigh of relief. Apparently, he could now consider himself a capable actor, for those simple-minded Irishmen had actually believed he was going to return Naomi. The fools!

"I can na believe you let him ride off," Rogan said as Oliver disappeared into the darkness. "We should follow 'im. Naomi might still be hidden in these parts."

"We have a group of runaways comin' through in a few days, and they're going to need us. I think he was tellin' the truth — I figure she's down South, and we can na risk the lives of the group coming through in a few days by leavin' and followin' Maxwell."

Rogan leaned against the trunk of a large birch and shook his head. "I know what ya're saying is right, but I do na like it. What if that man knows where Naomi is and we let 'im walk away?"

"I do na like it either. Thar's one thing that's certain, Rogan. We can na tell the women what 'appened here tonight."

CHAPTER 22

The early spring mix of snow and rain subsided during the nighttime hours, and by ten o'clock the next morning, the sun shone brightly through the stained-glass windows of St. Anne's Episcopal Church. Colored prisms cast their hues across the devout worshipers awaiting the beginning of the morning service.

After escorting his grandmother to her seat, McKinley Wainwright stood beside the Cheever pew near the front of the church. "Good morning," he greeted in a hushed voice.

Violet looked upward and gave him a bright smile. "Good morning." She scooped aside her lavender and green striped skirt and shifted closer to her mother. "It's going to be a beautiful day after all," she whispered to McKinley as he sat down beside her.

He nodded, enjoying the floral scent of her perfume. "I'm looking forward to spending the day with you."

Her smile and the glimmer of delight in her sparkling blue eyes warmed his heart on this chilly March morning. He settled as comfortably as possible on the hard straight-backed pew and silently prayed the sermon would not be excessively long or uninspiring.

However, as the morning progressed, McKinley realized he would be disappointed on both accounts. The visiting pastor appeared to be enjoying his return to the pulpit following a year of retirement, and after a forty-five-minute sermon, the good man didn't seem to be winding down. McKinley watched Mr. Ross, the organist, who had returned to the keyboard, his hands perched in obvious anticipation.

"As I draw to a conclusion . . ."

The remaining words were drowned out by the chords of the pipe organ bleating out the beginning strains of the finale. Before the preacher could say another word, the members of the congregation had risen and were making their way out of the pews and down the aisles.

"I believe I owe the organist a word of thanks," Matthew Cheever said as they exited the church.

"Matthew!" Lilly chided.

"You must admit that he could have ended that sermon after fifteen minutes," Mr. Cheever said with a chuckle. "The remainder was pure repetition. You agree with me, don't you, McKinley?"

Violet's parents turned their scrutinizing gazes upon him. "Perhaps it would be best if I withheld my opinion."

Mrs. Cheever smiled at McKinley and nodded her agreement. "You obviously learned at an early age that it's wise to remain neutral in marital disagreements."

"I didn't realize we were having a marital disagreement," Mr. Cheever retorted. "I thought we merely had differing opinions."

"We're married and we disagree. Thus, we are having a marital disagreement, Matthew."

"I stand corrected," Mr. Cheever replied before turning toward McKinley. "I understand you and Violet are going to your sister's home for a visit."

"Yes. And I promise to have Violet safely home by eight o'clock, if that's acceptable," McKinley said.

"I see you haven't left for Jasmine's just yet," Alice Wainwright said as she bustled her way through the crowd and neared the small group. "I was thinking perhaps I should join the two of you."

McKinley gave her a feeble smile. "Of course. Although I don't think we'll be returning until eight o'clock."

"Your answer makes it sound as though you don't actually want me to come along," Alice said with a shrewd glint in her eyes.

Violet stepped closer to McKinley's grandmother. "We would be honored to have your company."

"Why, thank you, my dear," Grandmother Wainwright said while giving McKinley a smug grin.

"I'm certain you're eager to see Jasmine," Lilly Cheever commented. "I haven't seen her or Nolan in church for some time now. I hope there's not some problem keeping them away."

"No problem except keeping them all healthy enough to attend, I suppose," Alice replied.

"I do hope they'll soon be able to return. I miss seeing Jasmine," Lilly said.

"I miss seeing her also," Alice said, "which is why I asked to intrude today."

Mrs. Cheever smiled gently at Violet and McKinley. "I'm certain the children are delighted to have your company. And we best be getting along so the three of you may be on your way."

They bid their good-byes, and Violet

stopped to brush a kiss upon her mother's cheek. McKinley frowned as he watched his grandmother take her place next to the carriage. Obviously she planned on sitting between Violet and him. He had spent the entire week anticipating time alone with Violet as they journeyed to Jasmine and Nolan's home, but now his grandmother was determined to intrude. Well, she might accompany them, but she was *not* going to insert herself between them.

"If you'll excuse me, Grandmother, I'll help you into the carriage once Violet has been seated," he said with as much decorum as possible.

"I thought she'd have a better view of the scenery from the outer seat," his grandmother said.

McKinley smiled down at the older woman. "Oh, she's quite familiar with the scenery. We prefer to visit on the journey, which is a feat much more easily accomplished if she sits beside me."

"I suppose you're correct," his grandmother replied before taking several steps away from the carriage and waiting until Violet was seated. "I wanted to see how assertive you'd be about the young woman. I do believe you care for her, McKinley. On second thought, why don't you just drive me home? I believe I'm a bit overtired for a trip to Jasmine's today." She gave him a fond smile as she settled onto the seat.

McKinley returned her smile. Women! He would never understand their thinking.

Jasmine walked out the door, relieved to see McKinley's carriage moving up the driveway. She waved and smiled as they drew nearer, pulling her shawl a bit closer against the breeze. "I was beginning to fear you had forgotten my invitation," she said as her brother assisted Violet out of the carriage.

"Of course not. How could we forget something we've been anticipating all week? Unfortunately, the church service was longer than usual this morning."

"And then your grandmother couldn't decide if she was going to come along with us or remain in Lowell," Violet added.

Jasmine peeked down toward the carriage. "It appears as if she decided to remain behind."

McKinley held the front door for the two women, then followed them inside. "Only after deciding she was overly tired and we should instead take her home."

Jasmine giggled. "Sounds exactly like Grandmother's antics. I hope you won't be disappointed, but as the hour grew late for dinner, I went ahead and fed the boys. They've already gone upstairs for their naps. However, they should be full of vim and vigor by the time we finish our meal."

"It's good you had the foresight to give them their meal. I imagine they would be quite cross if they had been required to wait for our arrival," McKinley agreed.

Nolan stepped forward to shake hands with McKinley and grinned. "Glad to see you've arrived. Jasmine wouldn't permit me to eat with the boys, although I protested."

"Tell the *entire* story. You wanted to eat with the boys and then *again* when Violet and McKinley arrived. I told him he'd soon not fit through the door if he began that sort of behavior," she said while patting her husband's arm. "And it appears you've survived the extra hour's wait in fine order."

"So I have, yet I fear I may soon suffer severe repercussions if we don't eat now," Nolan said, pulling her close to his side.

"Then we best get you into the dining room," she said, enjoying her husband's banter. "Why don't you and McKinley sit across from each other? I had Nolan remove the extra boards from the dining table so we could have a more intimate visit."

"How thoughtful," Violet said as she sat down.

Nolan immediately signaled for a girl to begin serving. The young woman moved quickly to offer a platter of baked chicken. Nolan held up two fingers. Jasmine chuckled at his excessive indulgence.

"It's a good thing I asked Cook to fix extra," she murmured as McKinley also asked for two pieces.

Violet turned her attention to Jasmine as the serving girl continued making her rounds. "I haven't seen you since my coming-out party, but my father tells me that you have acquired some admirers."

"You must be referring to Mr. Riddell and his sons, Charles and Luther," Jasmine replied.

"Father said they'd made a visit to see your Arabians and couldn't say enough good things about the farm. You obviously charmed all three of them."

"She is quite a charmer," Nolan said, "but I think their admiration went well beyond Jasmine's alluring personality. The Riddells were astonished both by the horses and Jasmine's business acumen — and rightfully so," he boasted.

"The proud husband," McKinley said with a wink.

"Absolutely! I'm blessed to have a wife with so many virtues. If she continues in this manner, she'll soon be equal to the woman of Proverbs thirty-one."

"Oh, I think we can cease the accolades," Jasmine said. "The truth is, the gentlemen are looking for investment opportunities, and after touring the farm, asked if I might be interested in partnering with them."

McKinley leaned back in his chair. "Truly? They're interested in a partnership? What did you tell them?"

Jasmine wiped the corner of her mouth. "Neither Nolan nor I have any interest in taking on *investment* partners."

McKinley gave her a quizzical look. "You make it sound as though you're interested in some other type of partners."

"As a matter of fact, we currently have two partners," Nolan reported.

"What? Whom have you partnered with?" McKinley asked.

"Rogan and Paddy," Jasmine said simply.

"Truly? I'm amazed." McKinley stared at her and gnawed on his bottom lip.

"Of course, Padraig is not yet a man," Jasmine said. "However, both Rogan and Paddy are buying an interest in the business with a portion of their wages. There's no better employee than one who owns a portion of the business."

"I disagree. The best investor is the one

who has knowledge and money," McKinley said.

"I believe a person need be invested with more than their purse strings," Jasmine stated. "A worker who has reason to care what happens to his position and livelihood responds in a much more attentive and devoted manner than does one who does not."

"People can be given reason to care, beyond owning a part of the business," McKinley protested.

Nolan took a sip of water and cleared his throat. "I think this may be a topic on which we will not agree. Perhaps we best move on to another subject. How are you enjoying your work for the mills?"

"Father says that McKinley is a natural born leader," Violet answered before McKinley could offer a reply. "He has a great deal of business sense, and my father values that above most everything else."

"My brothers are all intelligent men and good hearted as well," Jasmine agreed. "Although they were rather given to pranks when we were growing up. I remember more than one good scaring."

Violet cast a side glance at McKinley. "You purposefully tried to frighten your sister?"

McKinley grinned. "Only in fun. She gave as good as she received. Don't let her innocent look fool you."

"I cannot imagine my wife ever causing you so much as a moment of discomfort."

McKinley laughed out loud. "You, sir, do not know your wife if you say such a thing. Why, she loved nothing more than seeing us in discomfort."

"Enough of such talk," Jasmine declared. "We simply had great fun growing up."

"I can't imagine what it must have been like to have slaves," Violet said, surprising them all.

"Little different than having servants, as you grew up with," McKinley told her. "They worked around the house and took their orders from the master and mistress. Is that not the same as even here in Jasmine and Nolan's home?"

"Yes, but our servants may cease their employment whenever they desire," Jasmine threw out.

"But your servants cannot go far without a letter of recommendation," McKinley pointed out. "And employment is not always that available. So in some ways, it is no better."

"Are you backing away from your desire to see the slaves freed?" Jasmine asked in surprise.

"No, but neither do I believe freedom resolves the issue. They may indeed be set free, but I believe what comes afterward will be difficult to contend with."

"So, McKinley, what are the Boston Associates' plans for Lowell?" Nolan asked as he waved off the serving girl as she offered him more bread.

Jasmine gave her husband an appreciative smile as McKinley launched into a discussion of the decision of the Boston Associates to open yet another mill. "I know Samuel will be pleased to hear the news. After all, another mill means an ever-increasing need for more cotton and —"

McKinley's statement was cut short as Spencer and Moses came running into the room, both of them rushing toward Jasmine and burying their faces in her lap.

"If you've all completed your meal, perhaps we should adjourn to the parlor," Jasmine said with a laugh.

McKinley and Violet led the way, situating themselves side by side on the settee. "I believe Spencer has grown a full two inches since I last saw him," McKinley commented. "Come see Uncle McKinley," he said, holding out his arms to the boy.

Jasmine watched as Spencer ran into his

uncle's arms. McKinley and Violet showered her son with attention while completely ignoring young Moses, who now appeared near the point of tears.

"Come here, Moses," Jasmine said with a bright smile.

He ran to her, his smile matching Jasmine's. "Mama," he said, crawling onto her lap. Jasmine embraced the boy in a giant hug and kissed his plump cheek. Her gaze settled on Violet, and she was surprised to note the girl's patent aversion to the sight of Moses on her lap.

"You need to put a stop to that," McKinley said.

"To stop *what*?" Jasmine asked.

"Letting that boy call you Mama. It's unseemly, Jasmine."

"He's a little boy who has lost both his parents — he needs compassion, not condemnation. He hears Spencer call me Mama. It's only natural Moses would follow suit. There's no need to make an issue over such normal behavior. It's obvious you're lacking in Christian love. Did you leave it in church this morning?"

"Don't give me platitudes about Christian love, Jasmine. As I said before, I'm happy to see the coloreds freed. However, you carry matters too far with your behavior. Can you imagine what your friends in Mississippi would think?"

"I have few friends in Mississippi and care little what Southerners think — which is one of the reasons I chose to live in Massachusetts," she retorted.

Violet moved to the edge of the settee. "But surely you realize you're doing the boy no favors by rearing him as though he's white. To continue such a charade will only hurt him in the future."

"Perhaps now you realize why we haven't been in church of late. It's because I feared this type of repercussion from some members of the congregation. However, I didn't expect this type of reaction from either of you. I thought you were both strong in your stand against slavery and for freedom for the Negroes. Obviously I was incorrect."

McKinley's jaw tightened. "I've already said I stand for abolition — and so does Violet. However, abolition is an entirely different issue from what's going on in your house, Jasmine. Continuing down this path of reckless behavior will only lead to disaster for both your family as well as Moses. Did you not hear anything I said earlier?"

"Indeed I did. I tried to ignore and forgive it," Jasmine replied angrily.

Nolan stood and moved to stand by Jasmine. "I think we should all calm ourselves a bit. Let's not permit our emotions to rule. I wouldn't want any of us to say something we'd later regret."

Stroking Moses' cheek, Jasmine continued to rock back and forth. "I believe McKinley and Violet have already spoken their true feelings — as have I. When I gave my word to Mammy to help Obadiah, my promise was unqualified."

"You're a fool, Jasmine. You know that even a single drop of Negro blood is enough to categorize a person as colored," McKinley argued. "That boy may appear as white as you or me, but by law, he's a Negro. The entire country is dividing itself over issues such as these."

Jasmine clenched her fists. "I believe the Southern ways are morally flawed. Moses shouldn't be penalized because of his heritage. Truth be told, there's more white blood running through his veins than Negro blood. And you, McKinley! I can't believe we're having this conversation. It's obvious I don't know you. You increasingly appear as much a bigot as the Southern plantation owners."

Violet clasped a hand to her chest. "I do believe you've become overwrought, Jasmine. You know McKinley and I both support the abolition movement. We both oppose slavery, but you go too far. Raising a colored child as though he's white goes beyond the pale. You may think you're doing an admirable thing, but Moses is the one who will suffer for it."

Jasmine stood with Moses in her arms. "Before another word is said against this child, I want both of you to leave our home."

CHAPTER 23

Basking in the adulation of the evening's festivities, Malcolm Wainwright leaned back in the padded dining chair and smiled as his eldest son stood to speak to the gathered members of the Boston Associates. All agreed Samuel Wainwright had proven to be a wise choice as Bradley Houston's replacement several years prior. Although some members of the Associates had initially voiced their misgivings regarding Samuel's abilities, they soon withdrew their criticism. Moreover, Samuel had far exceeded the expectations of even the most hardened opponents, securing prices and suppliers that pleased both the Associates and the cotton growers.

"I thank you for your vote of support and the fact that you've been accommodating when circumstances required. Such willingness to negotiate has won the confidence of the Southern growers with whom I deal.

Consequently, they have become our greatest champions when securing new growers. They are vocal in their praise, and I now have growers contacting me."

Nathan Appleton raised his glass of port. "You've become one of our greatest assets, young man."

"Thank you, Mr. Appleton. I consider it a privilege and an honor to work for the Associates. And you may rest assured there will be no shortage of cotton for the new mill you plan to open this year. In fact, I may be required to turn away growers in the future."

"Such an event is difficult to believe. However, I, too, applaud the great strides you've made," James Morgan said. "I wonder if it would be prudent to begin accumulating and storing the cotton while the prices are good. If abundant supplies are now available, I think we should take advantage of them. After all, who knows what the future holds."

"Good point. However, before we begin stockpiling, we need to assure ourselves there's adequate space and ability to maintain the quality of the cotton. Let's remember, we're now producing fifty thousand miles of cloth annually. Matthew, could you or McKinley assess the viability of such a feat?"

"Of course," Matthew said. "We'd be pleased to take on the project and report to you at our next meeting, unless you want an answer prior to then."

Nathan glanced around the room. "I think the next meeting would be acceptable. After all, you'll need some time to survey the possibilities and formulate your report. Don't you agree, gentlemen?"

Murmurs of assent circled the room, and after the men had discussed a few remaining routine issues, the meeting adjourned. Malcolm watched as McKinley spoke briefly to Matthew Cheever before crossing the room. "Good to see you, Father. I knew you'd been invited to the dinner meeting but didn't know if you'd make the journey north. I'm pleased you chose to attend."

Malcolm grasped his son's hand and pulled him forward into a brief embrace. "Good to see you also, my boy. Appears as if things are going well between you and Mr. Cheever."

"Yes, quite well. I was hoping to accompany you and Samuel on the train — if you're returning to Lowell in the morning. Mr. Cheever is required to remain in Boston for several more days."

"Of course we're returning to Lowell. Your grandmother would have my head on a plate if I failed to visit, and your sister would never forgive me if I didn't spend time with her and the family." Malcolm's brows furrowed, his brown eyes filled with curiosity. "I'm surprised Jasmine didn't mention my arrangements. I sent an updated schedule for my visit in my latest missive to your sister and asked that she share the information with you and your grandmother. Have you not seen Jasmine of late?"

"Not for nearly three weeks. I'd prefer to wait and explain the circumstances as we travel to Lowell. I have another meeting with Mr. Cheever before I return to the hotel," McKinley said as he glanced toward several of the Associates standing nearby.

The next morning the trio boarded the train and once they had settled into their seats, Malcolm turned his attention to McKinley. "Now do tell me why you haven't been to visit your sister. I can't believe your work keeps you so busy you can't spend an occasional Sunday afternoon with her. Although our family is now scattered about the country, those of us who are near one another should be mindful to maintain strong familial ties."

"You're lecturing the wrong person, Father. Jasmine expelled both Violet Cheever and me from her home."

His father and brother looked like they didn't believe him.

"What nonsense is this you're speaking?" Malcolm said. "Do you truly expect me to believe your sister would bar you from her house?"

McKinley raked his fingers through his disheveled hair. "Believe what you will, but when you visit her, she and Nolan will both confirm the truth of my statement."

Malcolm frowned while lowering his spectacles farther down on his nose. "And what did you say or do to cause such an edict?"

"You immediately assume it is *my* impropriety that caused the breach between us. But you have been away from Jasmine too long and forget her behavior can sometimes become unruly when she doesn't get her way. Believe me, even Violet Cheever was appalled by Jasmine's conduct."

Certain he now had both his father's and Samuel's attention, McKinley launched into an explicit reenactment of the Sunday afternoon debacle, leaving no detail to the imagination.

Malcolm's jaw went slack as he listened to

McKinley's words. "So she actually plans to rear that boy alongside Spencer as though they're equal — like brothers?" He choked on the last two words.

"Yes. She's gone completely daft over the notion that she promised Mammy she'd help Obadiah. Pure nonsense. Mammy would never have expected such inappropriate behavior. Quite frankly, I'm certain Mammy would have preferred her grandson to be raised as he is — a Negro," McKinley said.

Malcolm frowned. "What are you talking about? Mammy had no grandchild. She had no children."

McKinley froze. He'd been certain that Jasmine had told their father the truth about Obadiah, yet it was clear that Malcolm had no idea what hc was talking about. McKinley drew a deep breath. "I suppose I'd better explain."

"I suppose you'd better," his father agreed.

"Before Mammy died, she called Jasmine to her side and told her that she'd given birth to a son many years earlier. I can't remember what happened to her husband, but he was gone. Her master, Mr. Harshaw, threatened to kill the child if she ever said so much as a word to you about him, because Harshaw knew your desire to keep families together."

"But why not just sell the boy with his mother?" his father questioned.

"I don't know. I presume because he figured to raise the boy to be a strong field hand. Obadiah was his name, and he did indeed grow up to be a strong man. After Mammy told Jasmine about it, she asked Jasmine to try to set Obadiah free."

"That seems so unlike Mammy." Malcolm looked at Samuel. "Did you know anything about this?"

"Nothing."

"I am sorry," McKinley began again. "I presumed that by this time you knew."

"I knew there were former slaves living on Jasmine's land," Malcolm admitted. "I just didn't realize why they were living there or the connection to Mammy."

"Jasmine felt honor bound," McKinley stated. "As I suppose she feels now with Obadiah's son, Moses."

"This is the boy she's raising as an equal with my grandson?"

McKinley nodded. "She'll hear nothing of protest against this. That's why I've long been absent from her company."

Malcolm balled his fists against his thigh. "She's insane to believe such a thing will produce anything but grief. She knows about the slave laws."

"Indeed, but she cares little for that or what people think. She merely sees her treatment of Moses as an extension of her abolitionist work. But it's not, and this will no doubt lead to trouble in the future."

Samuel nodded his agreement. "It's all this freethinking that's led to Jasmine's irrational actions. First she came up here and got herself involved in the antislavery movement, then she became an outspoken advocate, willing to set aside her Southern roots, and now she's breaking ties with her own family. What else will she do?"

"She's already done more. I failed to tell you she's permitted those two Irish workers to purchase an interest in the horse farm — and the young one, Paddy, not even a man yet," McKinley added, his anger building as he told the tale.

"It appears there's much at stake here," Malcolm said, "but I think the issue of Jasmine raising that colored boy as her own flesh and blood is my first priority. I sincerely doubt that Nolan will overrule Jasmine concerning the child. Years ago he expressed a deep belief in the right to equality for all Negroes. Consequently, it will be difficult to persuade either of them that their decision regarding the colored boy is flawed. Especially given her promise to Mammy. I must think on this matter."

The train car swayed and gently rocked back and forth over the tracks as they continued on toward Lowell. Malcolm leaned back, his thoughts filled with the information McKinley had shared. Frightful news for a journey he had hoped would be filled with pleasure. The only positive aspect of the entire conversation had been McKinley's comments regarding coloreds. Perhaps his youngest son was finally realizing that abolition was not the answer to the country's unrest regarding the slavery issue.

Malcolm thought about Mammy and the baby she'd been forced to leave behind. It grieved him, as he had always prided himself on keeping slave families together. It had been one way that he told himself he had risen above the rest. Slavery was a necessary evil, but a master needn't be cruel.

But I was cruel and I didn't even know it, he thought, closing his eyes against the world.

With Spencer on one side and Moses on the other, Jasmine knocked on the front door of her grandmother's house. "Good morning, Martha."

"Good morning, Miss Jasmine. Come in. Your grandmother's upstairs, but I'll tell her you're here," the aging housekeeper replied.

Martha stepped aside and moved toward the stairs. Glancing briefly over her shoulder as she ascended the steps, Martha said, "I'm certain your grandmother will be pleased to see you. It's been too long since you've visited."

"Thank you, Martha," Jasmine replied before leading the boys into the parlor. "Now sit nicely," she instructed them, seating the boys on either side of her.

"Jasmine! What a wonderful surprise," Alice Wainwright said as she entered the room and gave her granddaughter a hug.

"I should have sent word I was going to call. However, I discovered only yesterday that McKinley was out of town, and I wanted to be certain and tell you I had a letter from Father. He said you were aware he was coming for a visit but to advise you he'd likely arrive tomorrow."

Alice pursed her lips and frowned. "I wish I would have had a bit more time for preparation."

"I apologize, but I didn't want an encounter with McKinley. He's likely told you I've banned him from our home. I have no interest in being around him."

"And since he lives with me, I'm forced into the middle of your dispute."

Jasmine frowned. "If you've been placed in an uncomfortable position, that's McKinley's doing. After all, I've not even seen you for over three weeks."

"Exactly my point. In the past, you would stop whenever you were in town, and I could always depend upon having some time with you and your family on Sundays. Now all of that has changed. And from what McKinley tells me, your decision to stay away is due only in part to your argument with him."

"Why? What did he say?"

"He mentioned your lack of attendance at church is due to your feared reaction from church members — regarding Moses."

Moses immediately pointed to himself. "Moses," he said.

Jasmine smiled at the child. "Yes, you're Moses. Grandmother, if we're to have this discussion, perhaps the boys could join Martha in the kitchen for cookies."

Alice rang a small bell that sat near her chair, and within moments, the housekeeper appeared at the parlor door. "Would you have some cookies or fruit that might keep the boys occupied in the kitchen for a time,

Martha?"

Martha smiled. "I have some gingerbread I'm certain they'll enjoy. Come along, boys. I have a treat for you in the kitchen."

Spencer and Moses wriggled down from the settee and trailed after the housekeeper like goslings following a mother goose.

"Thank you, Martha," Jasmine called after the older woman before turning back toward her grandmother. "I do have concerns about attending church with Moses. There are many judgmental and self-righteous members at St. Anne's."

"There are judgmental, self-righteous people everywhere, child. The church is filled with imperfection. After all, this world is populated with sinners. I would like to say that from the time I became a believer, I no longer sinned, but that would be a lie, and one more transgression," Alice said with a chuckle.

"However, it appears those who profess their belief in the Lord are sometimes the worst offenders — always looking for reasons to find fault with others," Jasmine said.

"I learned long ago I can't change others and the way they act, but I can attempt to live in a way that I hope is pleasing to God. If others see a glimmer of Christ in me, perhaps they will have changed hearts and attitudes. If you believe rearing Moses as your own is what you should do, then have the courage of your convictions. You can't hide at the farm for the remainder of his life. Besides, you'd be doing both Spencer and Moses an injustice."

"Then you believe people will eventually accept the boy?"

"Accept? No. Tolerate? Possibly. Oh, there will be some who will be cruel and never attempt to understand, and there will be a very few who will accept what you're doing. However, you cannot base your decisions on what others think. If you believe this is what God is leading you to do, then take heart and have courage."

Pulling a handkerchief from her pocket, Jasmine wiped away the tears that had begun to form in her glistening brown eyes. "I'm not certain what God would have me do, Grandmother. None of this was planned. Obadiah made his decision to go and find Naomi, and the situation simply evolved after that."

"So this is more a matter of happenstance than planned behavior?"

The muted sound of the boys' carefree laughter could be heard in the distance and a faint smile curved Jasmine's lips. "Yes. My hope is that Obadiah and Naomi will return, but I promised Obadiah I would make certain Moses knew about his parents if neither of them came back to Lowell. I intend to keep my word. However, the first night Moses stayed with us after Obadiah's departure, I was putting the boys to bed and Moses mimicked Spencer and referred to me as Mama. I didn't have the heart to tell him no. I still don't. Such behavior seems cruel and could cause him irreparable harm. I love Moses very much and I won't hurt him."

Alice rose from her chair and walked to the doors leading to the garden. "You should make this situation a matter of prayer, Jasmine. I will do the same. I am sympathetic to your decision and want what is best for all concerned. Please remember you are always welcome in my home — and this is *my* home, not McKinley's. I do hope you will give careful thought to what I've told you. I believe you must continue to live your life as you always have in spite of the criticism you will surely receive."

"Thank you, Grandmother. Knowing I can depend upon your support gives me courage."

The metal latch on the front door squeaked. Before either of the women could say anything further, the three Wainwright men stood in the parlor doorway.

"Father! Your missive said you'd be arriving *tomorrow,*" Jasmine said as she hurried toward him.

Malcolm gathered her into a warm embrace. "You must have misread my letter. I'm certain I said we'd be arriving in Lowell today. But no matter. We're here and all is well. Now let me give your grandmother a much-deserved hug."

Careful to avoid McKinley, Jasmine turned her attention to Samuel. "It's good to see you, Samuel. We don't see you often enough."

Samuel gave her a measured look. "I'm generally too busy for social visits when I'm in Lowell."

"I'm surprised to see you here," McKinley said to his sister.

Jasmine ignored his remark and turned toward the noise in the hallway. The boys were running into the room, obviously determined to investigate.

"Look at how you've grown," Samuel said while giving his nephew a brief hug. "You're quite a fine young man, Spencer Houston."

Spencer giggled as he escaped Samuel's hold, immediately running toward Jasmine with Moses following close behind. "I trust you had a pleasant voyage, Father," Jasmine said.

"A fine voyage — on one of the Houston ships. Come here, Spencer. I haven't had an opportunity to say hello to my grandson."

Jasmine tugged Spencer out from behind her skirt. "Spencer, don't pretend to be bashful. Go and give your grandpa a proper hello."

Her son's eyes grew large when his grandfather pulled a piece of candy from his pocket to entice him away from his mother. Jasmine gave the boy a gentle nudge.

Propelled by the lure, Spencer moved to his grandfather. "Hello, Grappa," Spencer said with a sweet smile.

Moses edged from behind Jasmine and then quickly darted toward the older man. Pointing to his tiny chest, Moses said, "Me candy, Grappa."

"He is *not* your grandpa," Samuel barked.

His eyes wide and filled with obvious fear, Moses rushed to Jasmine's arms. "You're fine — don't cry," she said, cradling the boy and rocking him back and forth.

"Disgusting!" Samuel said through clenched teeth.

"*You're* the one who is disgusting, Samuel. How *dare* you bring your prejudice to bear on a tiny child — especially one who has been welcomed into this home. I find your behavior abhorrent. I'm sorry to leave abruptly, Grandmother, but I fear that if I remain, I will be forced to tell my brothers exactly what I think of their behavior. Father, I trust you will come to the farm and spend several days with us."

Her father appeared perplexed and merely nodded before Jasmine escorted the boys from the house.

Malcolm remained silent, watching his daughter while she assisted the boys with their wraps and hastily exited the house. Jasmine's departure created a deafening silence that hung in the parlor for several minutes.

When Malcolm could no longer bear the quiet, he turned toward his mother. "What happened to my gentle-spirited daughter?"

Alice laughed. "Jasmine is the same compassionate girl she's always been, Malcolm. In this instance, her gentle spirit, as you so aptly refer to it, is directed toward Moses and not toward her brothers. Therein lies the difference. I believe she has chosen to protect the boy at all costs, including the loss of her family. Yet I do pray that none of us will permit *that* to occur."

Malcolm rubbed his throbbing neck, hoping to release the tension. "Why don't we go down to the mills? I understand our final cotton shipment of the season sailed for Boston two days before we left New Orleans. Surely it's been delivered to the mills by now. Right now I think I'd prefer a discussion of cotton and the manufacturing business."

"What about dinner?" Alice inquired.

"If we're hungry, we can find our way to the restaurant in the Merrimack House, Mother. Don't worry yourself on that account," Malcolm replied. "I'll be back by midafternoon, and we can have a peaceful visit."

The three men departed without further discussion. "If you don't object," McKinley said, "I'd prefer we stop first at the Appleton. With Mr. Cheever still out of town, I want to assure myself all is well. Besides, the major portion of the cotton shipment was destined for the Appleton."

With the agreement of Malcolm and Samuel, the three men disembarked the carriage at the Appleton Mill a short time later.

"I'll stop in the office and the two of you can go —"

"Mr. Wainwright! I'm relieved to see you," the accountant called out while rushing toward McKinley. "You need to go down to the unloading area. The shipment of cotton we've been waiting on has arrived, but all the bales are terribly flawed. There's total confusion what with you and Mr. Cheever both gone. Seems one of the men signed for the delivery and he's now fearful he'll be held accountable. No one wants to make a decision. The men are standing around arguing about whether to unload the remainder of the shipment or let it sit."

The Wainwright men hurried off to see for themselves, each one hoping the information they'd received would prove incorrect. However, it took only one glance to see the words of the accountant were true.

Chaos reigned.

Chapter 24

Elinor heaped the fried potatoes into a large china bowl, thrust a large serving spoon deep into the dish, and carried it to the sideboard. After filling her plate, she took her place at the end of the table and joined the girls, who were already eating their supper. While in the kitchen, she had managed to hear bits and pieces of the girls' excited conversation but hoped she'd misconstrued their discussion. After offering a silent prayer for her supper, Elinor speared a forkful of the savory bread-and-butter pickles she'd preserved and momentarily enjoyed the results of her accomplishment.

"I fear this incident is going to have far-reaching effects upon all of us, at least temporarily," Cecilia said.

"There's little doubt there will be girls who will lose their positions for a time," Sarah agreed.

"Excuse me for interrupting your conversation, but exactly what is the problem at the mills?" Elinor inquired.

"There was a vast shipment of cotton delivered to the Appleton today," Janet Wilson explained. "It appears the entire shipment is of such inferior quality and full of debris the management has declared it unsuitable for use by any of the Lowell mills. The cotton was intended for use by several of the mills, but the Appleton will be most deeply affected since our supply of cotton is nearly depleted."

"Mr. Cheever came out to the mill yard and spoke to us at quitting time this evening," Sarah added. "He said they are still hopeful they'll find some resolution for the problem, but he didn't appear convinced. He said some of us should be prepared for layoffs, as the work force may need to be reduced if there is insufficient cotton to operate the mills."

Elinor listened carefully to the explanation. "Did they indicate how many workers may be laid off?"

"No, but I fear they may close down the Appleton until they receive new shipments," Sarah said, "which would likely mean waiting for the delivery of the first crop next year before they'd reopen. Mr. Cheever talked as though this had been the last shipment expected until the next harvest. In fact, this cotton had been held in storage in New Orleans awaiting shipment to Lowell until it was needed."

"Oh, surely they wouldn't need to close down until next year," Elinor objected.

"From what Mr. Cheever said, if they must wait for the next picking, they'll supply all the other mills with cotton before proceeding to reopen the Appleton," Janet said. "It's a terrible situation."

"And the layoffs will be determined by length of employment, which means some of us will likely be going home," Mary commented.

Elinor winced at Mary's statement. She had a full house and didn't want to lose any of her boarders. Although the mills closed from time to time duc to accidents, an unexpected repair, or a spring freshet, those closings were seldom and brief. In contrast, this sudden depletion of cotton would affect many more employees and for a longer period of time.

Sarah glanced down the table at Elinor. "Do you think they'll close any of the boardinghouses?"

Elinor's fork slipped from her fingers and clanked on the white china plate before sliding off the table, to her lap, and down to the floor. Why hadn't she immediately thought of the consequences the mill closing might have upon her boardinghouse? Her thoughts began to race wildly. She couldn't remember if the contract she had signed included a clause regarding the closure of a house. And even if it did, where had she placed her contract?

"Do any of you know if the Corporation has ever closed a boardinghouse?" Elinor asked.

"I've never known of them to close one," Sarah replied. "But they've never closed down a mill for any length of time either."

"They'll likely close a number of houses if they close the Appleton mill," Elinor mused.

"Oh, I hope they don't close this house. I don't want to move to another house. I'd have to get accustomed to new roommates and take whatever bed is left," Janet said, her voice growing shrill and whiney. "We'd be the new girls all over again with no choice, forced to accept any open space."

"Don't be selfish, Janet. There are girls who will lose their positions, and perhaps even Mrs. Brighton will be without her position as a keeper." Cecilia's face was filled with compassion.

"Please don't worry overmuch, Mrs. Brighton," she continued. "My mother says we fret most about those things that never actually happen."

Elinor tried to smile, but her attempt was in vain. With each passing year, it seemed as if her life became even more catastrophic than the last — a vicious, unending whirlpool of misery sucking her downward and now threatening to dissolve her very livelihood. The chatter of the girls grew faint as a parade of dismal events marched through her mind: memories of the husbands she had buried; the towheaded, laughing children she had never conceived; the house and worldly possessions she had been required to sell in order to pay off encumbrances; and a life of drudgery in this boardinghouse that scantily supported her. And now it appeared even that meager crumb would be taken from her. Was she destined to remain in penury for the remainder of her life?

Why her? What had she done to deserve losing even this pitiable existence?

Retribution! The thought crystallized like the thin layer of ice on a freezing winter morn. Losing her position at the boardinghouse was surely God's reckoning for the part she'd played in the recapture of the slaves. It had been her loose tongue to blame, and now she must suffer, just as those poor enslaved Negroes were surely suffering.

"Mrs. Brighton! Mrs. Brighton!"

Somewhere in the distance, Elinor heard the faint sound of her name. She startled at the touch of a hand upon her own. "What? Oh, I'm sorry, Cecilia. I was caught up in my thoughts. Is there something you needed?"

"No, but I wanted to be certain you were all right before I went upstairs."

Elinor glanced around the room. She and Cecilia were the only ones remaining in the dining room. "The girls finished their supper?" she asked.

"Yes," Cecilia whispered.

Cecilia was staring at her as though she'd taken leave of her senses. "I'm quite fine, Cecilia, but thank you for your concern. Please feel free to go to your room. I'll get busy with these dishes."

"If you're certain," Cecilia replied hesitantly.

Hoping to reassure the girl, Elinor stood and began removing the supper dishes. She exhaled deeply when Cecilia finally departed the room, relieved to be alone with her work. Reminding herself that busy hands and a tiresome routine would surely prove advantageous, Elinor returned to the kitchen and began washing the dishes. Perhaps the mundane task would help clear her mind. The idea, however, proved futile. A myriad of thoughts continued to skitter through her mind like the mice rushing to and fro behind the plastered walls.

Lowering a stack of plates into the steaming water, Elinor shuddered as she remembered Oliver's deception and her own foolishness. She had permitted him to exploit her! The dishcloth dripped over the basin as she relived the humiliation of confessing to Liam and Daughtie she had been responsible for disclosing information regarding the runaways. The Donohues had been kind and supportive, declaring Oliver the true villain. Daughtie had even come to visit with her, praying and directing her to the story of Joseph and his brothers in the Old Testament. But Elinor had turned a deaf ear, unwilling to be assuaged. She hadn't wanted to be reminded of Bible stories that showed how God used evil for good. For there was no way the evil she'd done could become right with the Lord — or with those poor slaves. Throughout the entire ordeal Daughtie remained kind and compassionate, asking only that she go back and read the account of Joseph and meditate over the Scriptures. However, Elinor had never done so.

She had confessed her offense to both God and man; she had asked forgiveness as the Bible instructed. Yet obviously her compliant behavior was not enough. For if God had actually forgiven her transgression, her position with the Corporation would not now be in jeopardy.

Since hearing the news of the possible mill closing, the girls had been in a constant state of unrest, their behavior rapidly changing from giddy laughter to overflowing tears. Elinor had neither laughed nor cried — she was too angry and fearful to do either. A loud knock sounded at the front door, and she ceased clearing the table and wiped her hands on the frayed apron that covered her faded blue calico dress.

With a heavy step, she trudged down the hallway and pulled open the front door. "Mr. Cheever!"

Matthew Cheever stood in the doorway, his gray felt hat in his hands and a hesitant look on his face. "Good morning, Mrs. Brighton. May I have a word with you?"

"Yes, of course. Do come in, Mr. Cheever." Her fingers trembled on the doorknob as she permitted him entry and then closed the heavy wooden door. She hung his hat and coat in the hallway before leading him into the parlor as though she'd expected his visit.

Mr. Cheever sat down in one of the overstuffed chairs, his gaze finally settling upon her. "I've come as the bearer of news that will likely result in difficult circumstances for you, Mrs. Brighton. Because of my close business association and friendship with your brother Taylor, I wanted to bring this news to you personally, especially since Taylor and Bella are currently so far from home. As I'm sure you're aware, we've been required to lay off a number of workers at the Appleton."

Elinor nodded. The cottony taste in her mouth made speech impossible. She clutched the arms of the wooden rocking chair, her eyes fixed upon Matthew as she waited for the completion of his discourse.

"There is a very strong possibility we will be forced to close one of the boardinghouses. Should that occur, you would be the keeper who would lose her position — the other keepers have been with the Corporation much longer," he quickly added.

"I expected it would come to this," she replied.

"Then you've already begun to make plans? For that is why I've come in advance

— to encourage you to formulate some ideas for your future."

Elinor's lips formed a wry smile. "I've made no plans, Mr. Cheever. I've never wished to decide to whom I shall be obliged. I'd rather delay my decision until I know it's a certainty."

"I do wish your Uncle John were still alive," he mused.

"Or that he'd left me a portion of his inheritance — but neither fact is a reality. I have but one living relative in this country, Mr. Cheever, and he is currently in Scotland."

"Do you know when Taylor and Bella will return?"

"At the time of their departure, they were hoping to return by April, but Taylor did not book their return passage. He was uncertain of the situation in Scotland and said they would make their decision after he had an opportunity to assess the situation. I'm surmising he may bring some of Beatrice's family back to America."

"There's little doubt Taylor will want you to come and live with him. I'll do everything in my power to keep you in your current position until his return," Matthew said. He stood, obviously convinced there was nothing more to be discussed.

"I'll retrieve your coat," Elinor said. She jumped to her feet and hurried into the hallway, remaining silent while he donned his coat and hat.

"I'm sure you are most grateful to have a brother in this time of need," Matthew said as he departed the house.

Elinor closed the door and then leaned the full weight of her body against the hard wood. "Glad to have a brother in this time of need? Is that what Mr. Cheever really thinks? That I should be thankful because I must now grovel and beg my brother for a pittance of charity?"

She balled her hands into tight fists and banged them hard against the door — once, twice, and then repeatedly until her hands ached with pain. "How dare he treat me like some pitiable creature? And how dare God place me in this wretched circumstance? I held myself accountable for what I did, asked for forgiveness — yet that is not enough, is it? What is it you want from me? Have I not suffered enough? Is my sin so much more than others' that you cannot forgive me?" she screamed toward heaven.

Elinor dropped to the floor, her body wracked by uncontrollable sobbing until she was totally spent. When she finally stood up, a swollen red face surrounded by unkempt hair greeted her in the hallway mirror. She held both hands to her temples, hoping somehow to diminish the searing pain that threatened to incapacitate her.

"Tell me what I am to do, God," she whispered, dropping to sit upon the hallway stairs.

In the distance, she heard a whisper in return. *Trust me.*

Startled, she turned to look up the stairway, but no one was with her. No one . . . but God.

Chapter 25

Malcolm propped his feet upon the footstool in his mother's parlor and swallowed a gulp of hot tea. His eyes watered, and he covered his mouth for a moment. "I wish you would have warned me the tea was hot."

Alice glanced at her son and chuckled. "The tea is *supposed* to be hot, Malcolm. That's why I place a cozy on the pot — to keep the contents hot."

Hc grinned and nodded. "Yes, Mother. I had forgotten your penchant for scalding beverages."

Before Alice could rebut Malcolm's comment, Samuel entered the front hallway and, with a loud whack, slammed the front door. Without taking time to clean his boots, he strode into the parlor and thrust a folded missive into his father's hand. "Look at this," he said in a commanding tone.

"And you look at *that,*" Alice ordered while pointing her index finger at the mud her grandson had tracked across the floor and onto her carpet.

Samuel scanned the damage and then lifted his boot to check for mud. "I'm sorry, Grandmother, but this is urgent business."

Her lips tightened into a pucker. "I doubt taking a moment to wipe your feet would cause insufferable damage to your existing problems, although it *does* damage my new carpet."

Samuel gave his grandmother an exasperated sigh. "If Martha is unable to remedy the destruction I've caused, I'll purchase you a new rug."

"So they're summoning us to a meeting!" Malcolm slapped the piece of paper onto the marble-topped table, his hand hitting the saucer and causing his teacup and its contents to fly helter-skelter across the carpet, the cup shattering into several pieces.

Alice grabbed her small brass bell and began to violently shake it back and forth. The ringing didn't cease until Martha's footsteps could be heard skittering down the hallway. The housekeeper came to a screeching halt as she entered the room, her unsettled gaze flitting from one catastrophic sight to the next.

"Oh, madam!" she gasped with one hand

clasping the bodice of her dress.

"I fear we've created quite a mess for you, Martha. My apologies," Malcolm said. "Samuel and I must be off to this meeting, Mother. I don't know when we shall return."

Alice flicked her wrist, shooing the men from the room as if they were two naughty puppies. "Off with you both. I fear I'd be unable to pay for the damages should the two of you remain in the house much longer."

"Do you have your grandmother's carriage?" Malcolm asked as he strode to the hallway and donned his hat and coat.

"Yes, and I asked Martin to wait for us."

"Good. I'm in hopes we'll have at least a short time to confer with McKinley before the meeting begins. Hopefully, he can give us somc insight as to the best way to approach these men. From the tone of their note, they're going to be completely unreasonable. What if I hadn't been available at their beck and call? Since several of the Boston Associates are in town for the discussion, it's obvious they planned this meeting in advance."

"I couldn't agree with you more fully," Samuel said as their carriage rolled toward the mill.

Malcolm stared out the carriage window,

his brow furrowed. "McKinley acted completely normal at supper last night. In fact, when I asked if there had been any further developments regarding the shipment, he said there had been none. Do you suppose he was aware of this meeting yet withheld the information from us?"

"I doubt he would be privy to much information. The Corporation wouldn't want him forced to compromise his loyalty. And even if he did know, his first obligation is to his employer, not the cotton growers in Mississippi," Samuel replied.

"His first loyalty is to his family — or at least it should be," Malcolm contradicted.

"Father, let's not get caught up in a discussion regarding McKinley's obligations to the family. We need to remain focused upon the meeting."

Malcolm nodded. "You're right. Do let me take the lead if they become antagonistic."

"Thank you for your concern, but you're not the one responsible for resolving this problem. I'm the one who was selected as the buyer for the Lowell mills."

"I am, however, the one who recommended you for the position, and the end result of this issue will affect the entire family as well as our friends and neighbors in

Mississippi. However, I will acquiesce if that's what you prefer."

"It is," Samuel stated with a decisive nod.

They disembarked the carriage outside the Appleton Mill. After a brief glance toward the interior of the mill yard, Malcolm followed Samuel inside. On their previous visit, they had been confronted with the defective bales of cotton; today's meeting would likely prove every bit as taxing. Samuel led them directly into Matthew Cheever's office, where Wilson Harper, Nathan Appleton, and Leonard Montrose had already gathered. McKinley was seated behind a table piled with ledgers, directly to Matthew's left.

"Gentlemen," Samuel greeted. "Good to see all of you."

"I wish I could say the same," Leonard muttered.

Matthew glowered at Leonard. "Please take a seat and we'll get started. I know all of you are busy, and we want to make this meeting as productive as possible."

"Don't see how that can be done," Leonard murmured.

"Leonard, would you please cease your comments. They're distracting and unnecessary," Nathan said before turning his bespectacled gaze upon Samuel. "On behalf of the Boston Associates, I am requesting a full report of what has occurred regarding the latest shipment of cotton, Mr. Wainwright. We will expect your explanation, remedy, and plan for guaranteeing we will not undergo a repetition of this ruinous episode *if* we decide to continue using you as our buyer. For now, I would at least appreciate some form of oral explanation I can share with the other members. Needless to say, they are more than a little unhappy."

Malcolm's gaze had shifted back and forth between his two sons during the course of Nathan's reproach. Samuel had turned pale. Behind the pile of books and ledgers, McKinley's complexion shone bright red. Malcolm wanted to rescue his sons — the eldest obviously overwrought with fear, the youngest appearing completely embarrassed or angry, he wasn't certain which.

Samuel sat with his hands tightly wrapped around the arms of his chair, his fingers turning the whitish-purple hue of a corpse. "You may assure all of the Associates I will be filing a detailed written report," he said. "However, it is impossible to give you information until I've had time to investigate. After a cursory examination several days ago, I've been unable to probe into this matter any further. May I have freedom to examine the entire shipment? Depending upon what I find, I'll know the next step that must be taken."

"What do you need to examine? The product is unacceptable, and we're left to develop a plan for the operation of the mills without adequate cotton," Leonard snarled.

Nathan signaled Leonard to silence himself. "As I'm sure you surmised before arriving here today, tempers are short and nerves are stretched taut. We've been placed in the precarious position of closing down at least one mill. That means telling employees they no longer have positions with the Corporation. Obviously the Associates want answers, and they are looking to you, Samuel. We will give you freedom to examine the shipment, but I'd appreciate something to report back as soon as possible."

Samuel massaged his forehead for a moment. "I want to more closely examine the markings on the bales to assure myself they all carry the stamp designated for the shipments to Lowell and satisfy myself that the entire shipment is flawed."

"Even so, we remain without the necessary cotton to continue production," Nathan reiterated.

"Is there no way we can use the cotton we

received?" Leonard asked while scratching his beard.

Nathan slapped his palm on the desk. "Absolutely not! Doing so would be worse than closing down the mill. We've worked for years to build our reputation. I'll not jeopardize it by using inferior product."

Wilson Harper, who had been unusually silent, addressed Samuel. "Does anybody use cotton of that substandard quality?"

"A few of the smaller mills here and the mills in England will take whatever they can get from us," he replied.

Nathan cleared his throat. "I'm sorry to say that the majority of the Associates have lost their trust in your ability to act as buyer, Samuel. It brings me no pleasure to tell you that your position with us is tenuous at best."

McKinley gasped at Mr. Appleton's statement and Malcolm jumped to his feet, no longer able to remain silent. "Tenuous? Perhaps you need to explain to the remainder of your Boston Associates that they have benefited greatly by Samuel's representation among the Southern cotton growers. Do you so quickly forget the plaudits all of you heaped upon Samuel at your dinner meeting in Boston? Should Samuel lose his position, your Corporation will lose all of the Wainwright cotton as well as every other grower we've brought to you. It is the Wainwright power that has caused you to significantly prosper these last few years, and that influence can be withdrawn at any moment."

"Is that a threat?" Nathan asked.

"That, sir, is a promise," Malcolm replied, his voice low and menacing.

"Father . . ." Samuel started.

Malcolm shook his head. "I'll not be silenced. If these men want to intimidate you by saying your position is *tenuous,* after one mistake — a mistake that most likely was not of your doing, then let them know the truth: their cotton supply depends upon the Wainwrights. When you return to Boston," he said, setting his eyes on each man in turn, "do take a moment or two and tell your Associates that I can produce a myriad of letters from mills all over England that are willing to go to any length in order to have our cotton. It is not the Wainwrights or the cotton producers who will suffer by your actions; it is your own corporation. You will close more than one mill if you continue down this path."

Matthew motioned Malcolm to take his seat. "No need to become overwrought. We must all work together to resolve this situation. There are, after all, many who are going to be laid off and possibly lose their jobs. I heartily believe that Samuel did not intentionally send us a bad shipment of cotton. However, the fact remains, a bad shipment is what we received. Neither side will accomplish anything with idle threats. We need to work toward finding a resolution."

"Then if we're agreed to that fact, may I go and examine the bales?" Samuel asked.

"Absolutely," Matthew replied. "I believe everything has been said for now. We'll look forward to your report."

Malcolm donned his hat and fell in step with Samuel as they departed, both equally determined to uncover what had gone amiss with this latest shipment. Not only was Samuel's position at stake, but the Wainwright family name also hung in the balance. And Malcolm would not see their reputation tarnished — particularly by a group of Northern businessmen.

"Father, wait!"

The sound of clattering footsteps and McKinley's urgent plea caused Malcolm to stop and turn. His brows arched in surprise. "Yes?"

"I told Mr. Cheever I could not sit idly by while Samuel was taken to task for an error over which he'd had no control. You've performed exceptionally for the Corporation, Samuel, and I'm appalled by their ability to forget your record of accomplishments when one error occurs. Mr. Cheever needs to realize that my family is important to me also."

"Thank you, McKinley. I appreciate your loyalty," Samuel said. "However, if this issue cannot be quickly resolved, you may decide your loyalty has been misplaced. The Associates may decide they want neither of us."

Malcolm tugged at his collar. "And what difference? We were doing well with the English before Bradley Houston convinced us to change our loyalties to the American mills. My statement to those men was no idle threat — they'll go begging for cotton if they continue down this arbitrary path of intimidation." His words shot through the air like tiny darts bearing lethal venom.

With a wry grin upon his lips, Samuel said, "But aren't you behaving in the same manner, Father? That's why I asked you to let me speak at the meeting."

"Too late now. We've placed our cards on the table. At least they know we're not frightened."

McKinley nodded. "Of that fact, there's

little doubt."

Malcolm clapped Samuel on the back. "Aha! You see? A strong offense is exactly what was needed."

"No, Father," Samuel said. "What is needed is a truthful explanation of exactly what occurred. If I don't find the answer, neither the Associates nor I will ever again feel comfortable in our working relationship."

"You may not feel comfortable, but you'll be their buyer until *you* decide to terminate your position. And therein lies the difference," Malcolm retorted in an austere tone he seldom used with his family.

"McKinley, I want you to return to work," Samuel directed. "You've expressed your feelings to both Mr. Cheever and to me, and I appreciate that fact. However, there's nothing more you can do, and I would prefer you went back to your office."

McKinley looked back and forth between Samuel and his father, his gaze finally settling upon Malcolm. "Do as your brother has requested. Who knows? You may garner information that will be helpful to us," Malcolm instructed.

"If you believe that's what's best, I'll do so, but know that if you need my assistance, I will make myself available to you," McKinley promised.

Malcolm settled beside Samuel as the train departed the Lowell station. "I'm certain your grandmother is going to be unhappy when Martin delivers the message we've departed for Boston without so much as a good-bye."

Samuel grinned. "While the Boston Associates cause you little fear and trembling, it appears Grandmother has maintained her touch."

Malcolm laughed aloud for the first time in several days. "Your grandmother is a woman to be reckoned with, and it's best none of us forgets it!"

"I believe Jasmine's the only one who of us who has developed the ability to influence Grandmother, rather than the other way around."

"You may be correct on that account. Curiously, they do seem to get on rather well — perhaps because they have much the same temperament."

They fell silent, and Malcolm stared out the window, his thoughts flitting about like pebbles skipping across a vast expanse of water. What if they couldn't resolve this issue with the cotton? He'd blustered about the English and their desire for his cotton, yet he had little desire to realign with the overseas market. Not that he wouldn't do so, but he much preferred the current arrangement. And Jasmine! What was he to do in order to heal the widening breach among his children? He wanted to die knowing they could always rely upon each other. They were family, and family needed to remain intact, even if disagreements occurred.

"Father. . . . Father!"

Malcolm startled to attention and gave Samuel a sheepish grin when he realized the train was pulling into the Boston station. "Sorry. I wasn't very good company. I'm afraid I became absorbed in my own thoughts. What is it?"

"I assume we'll go straight to the docks?"

"Yes. I'll talk to the agent and examine the company's ledgers. If the *Americus* has not yet set sail, see if you can locate the captain and gather any information from him."

The docks were teeming with passengers wielding their cumbersome baggage and surrounded by families who had come to bid them farewell. The beefy dock workers paid the intruders little heed while loading goods onto the ships lining the harbor. Malcolm grasped Samuel by the arm as they neared the Eastern America Shipping Company's office. "I'm sure the agent can tell us if the ship has already sailed."

Samuel hurried into the shipping office and leaned across the counter. "Has the *Americus* set sail for New Orleans?" he called to the agent.

The agent strode toward them and glanced at the clock. "Not due to cast off for at least another hour."

Malcolm shook hands with the agent. "Malcolm Wainwright and my son Samuel."

"Pleased to make your acquaintance. Jacob Hodde," the agent replied, pointing to the inscription of his name above the counter.

"Any chance they'd depart ahead of schedule?" Malcolm inquired.

The agent gave a hearty laugh. "Unless the captain chained his crew on board the ship last night, I doubt they'll cast off for at least another three hours. They'll all be nursing the effects of too much rum and ale — probably take the better part of that time for the crew to stagger on board."

"You see if you can locate the captain, and I'll remain and visit with Mr. Hodde," Malcolm said.

"It's Captain Whitlow," the agent called after Samuel.

Samuel waved and continued moving toward the door.

The agent shook his head. "Young folks — they're always in a hurry."

"Indeed," Malcolm agreed, giving the agent a friendly smile. "I wonder if you might allow me to examine the records you maintain for the *Americus* — only those concerning our shipment, of course."

"Is there a problem?" he inquired.

"Yes. However, we're not yet certain who's responsible. The cotton destined for Lowell did not arrive."

The agent traced his finger down the open page and began running it alongside the entries. "What? You didn't receive your shipment? But my ledger reflects it arrived and was shipped to Lowell." The agent peered over the top of his spectacles at Malcolm while tapping his finger alongside an entry.

"I misspoke, Mr. Hodde. A shipment arrived in Lowell — a shipment of cotton, defective cotton. Certainly not the cotton purchased and baled for shipment to Lowell."

"Take a look," the agent said as he turned the ledger toward Malcolm.

Samuel thanked the captain and disembarked the *Americus.* With his head bowed against the ocean breeze, he began to slowly wend his way through the crowds.

"Samuel! Samuel Wainwright!"

Shading his eyes against the sun with his hand, Samuel turned toward the sound. A short distance away, Taylor and Bella Manning were smiling broadly and waving him forward. John, the youngest of the Manning children, stood on tiptoe while brandishing his hat high in the air. Samuel hastened his step and smiled in return.

"What a surprise. I didn't realize you were due back from Scotland," Samuel greeted while shaking hands with Taylor.

"I would have preferred to remain a few more weeks. However, Bella was growing homesick, and we'd accomplished everything we set out to complete on the journey. I believe my sister's family is well in hand for the present. I take it things are going well in Lowell or you wouldn't be down here on the docks. Shipment due in?" Taylor inquired.

"No. I was checking on my last shipment. There are problems."

Taylor's forehead creased beneath the wave of dark blond hair that crossed his brow. "At the mills or with the shipment?"

"Both," Samuel said. "I'm on my way back to the agent's office to meet my father, and then we'll be returning to Lowell."

"We're hoping to board the last train," Taylor said. "We'll meet you at the station. You can explain everything during our return to Lowell."

Chapter 26

Elinor gave one final pat to the dough before setting it to rise in a large crock. With a swipe of her hand, she gave the dough a light coating of lard and then covered the bowl with a clean linen cloth before checking the beans with pork she had begun cooking earlier in the morning. Her decision to serve half of the baked beans at supper that evening and the remainder with corn bread for dinner the next day had stretched her food budget for the week. And she had been able to purchase enough plums for two of the moist, fruity cakes the girls had requested for supper. Dipping a cup into the flour sack, she began to measure the required six cups as a knock sounded at the front door. "Who could that be?"

Before she could reach the door, a voice called out, "It's me, Elinor. We've arrived home from Scotland, and I couldn't wait any longer before coming to call."

"Taylor! What a fine surprise."

He took in her flour-smudged apron. "It appears I've come at an inconvenient time. Shall I return later?"

"If you don't mind joining me in the kitchen, I'd be pleased to have you remain and keep me company. I'm most anxious to hear about your journey to Scotland. How did you find Beatrice's family? I thought you might bring several of her children home with you," she said as they walked down the hallway and into the kitchen. "Pull up a chair and sit down. I'll fix you a cup of tea. When did you and Bella return?"

"Thank you," he said, tugging a chair from under the wooden table. "We arrived on the final train from Boston last night. Had it not been so late and both of us weary from our travels, I would have stopped to see you then. I must say I'm surprised by your demeanor. I rather expected to be greeted with anger rather than hospitality."

Elinor placed the teacup in front of him. "Why is that?"

"I understand the boardinghouse may soon be closed."

"Word does travel quickly in Lowell. How did you receive the information so soon?"

Taylor took a swallow of his tea and placed

the cup on its saucer. "We happened upon Samuel and Malcolm Wainwright at the docks in Boston. The five of us traveled from Boston to Lowell."

"I see. Then it's likely you know more than I. Mr. Cheever paid me a visit and explained my boardinghouse would close if they didn't receive the anticipated cotton shipment. A few of my girls will be sent home — others will move to another boardinghouse if they're needed in any of the other mills. I'll miss this place and I'll miss them if the boardinghouse closes."

Her brother was staring at her as though she were a stranger. "You'll *miss* the girls?"

"Strange, isn't it? After all my complaints about their selfish behavior and my station in life, I find myself longing to remain in my position."

"You've changed, Elinor. You appear to have lost your . . ."

"Anger? Not completely. But I have come to the realization I hold no sway over the situation at the mills. And there is nothing I can do to alter my circumstances here at the boardinghouse. However, I *can* control my attitude. So I've decided to trust God and see what He has in mind for me."

"May I say I heartily approve of the change?"

"Thank you," she whispered, her cheeks growing warm at his praise.

"I came to tell you that Bella and I talked after we arrived home last night. Should the boardinghouse close down, we want you to come and live with us. I know it's not ideal, but we would truly like to have you join our family."

"Two women under the same roof is never a good thing, Taylor," she said.

He met her gaze. "You find Bella difficult to abide?"

"Oh, no, not at all. I love Bella and I appreciate your kindness. I worry having me about would make your lives more complicated. I could help with the house and young John, but I would worry for fear I'd overstep my boundaries."

"Don't be silly. You're creating problems where none exists. Say you'll agree," he insisted.

Elinor poured the cake batter into two large pans and set the bowl on the table. "If the boardinghouse closes and there is no other position available for me, I will come and live with you. However, I want you to know that I would leave as soon as I could find other work to support myself," she added.

"Agreed." Taylor stood and kissed her

cheek. "Now I must be off to attend to a few matters or Bella will be unhappy with me."

McKinley entered the office of the Appleton Mill and situated himself behind his small desk. There were accounts and ledgers that required updating, but he'd found concentration difficult of late.

"Glad to see you've come in early," Matthew Cheever said as he entered the front door. "I was looking at the ledgers last night. I don't want you falling any further behind on those accounts — makes calculations much too difficult. Have I assigned you too much work?"

"No," he replied while watching Matthew hang his coat and hat on the ornately carved coatrack that had been a birthday gift from Mrs. Cheever the preceding year.

"Then enlighten me, my boy. What's the difficulty?"

"My level of concentration isn't what it should be, I suppose," McKinley said, "what with the problems regarding the cotton shipment."

Matthew nodded. "Ah — so it's your family's troubles with the cotton shipment that's to blame for your inability to maintain the ledgers."

McKinley's grip tightened on his pen. "You're putting words in my mouth, Mr. Cheever. The ledgers will be brought to date."

"From all appearances, those ledgers won't soon be reflecting any payments to your family for cotton," Matthew said, his comment followed by an exasperated sigh. "I understand your father talked briefly to Nathan after examining the shipment, but he has yet to give me any explanation. Consequently, I'm assuming the entire debacle remains unresolved. I don't believe the Corporation has ever experienced a blunder that has the probability of causing so much damage. As you know, we stand to suffer significantly due to this mismanagement."

The hair along McKinley's collar bristled. "I believe you are unjustly blaming my family members, Mr. Cheever. Human error is something one must expect from time to time. The cotton had been properly stored awaiting shipment, and Samuel's paper work is faultless. He did everything possible to ensure your shipment would arrive in a timely fashion."

"And it did. Time is not the concern, McKinley. Unsuitability of the product we received is the problem. As buyer for the

Corporation, Samuel is responsible for guaranteeing our product is received on time and as specified. You say he did everything possible to ensure the shipment arrived properly. But did he? If so, it seems we would not be faced with this problem. Obviously he didn't watch as the shipment was loaded, or he would have known of the problem, don't you agree? What has occurred affects many lives. If he's not accountable, then who?"

McKinley combed his fingers through his hair. "Samuel can't be expected to oversee loading every bale of cotton placed on a ship. This error is not his doing. It appears that although Samuel has performed his duties with excellence in the past, that fact is now forgotten. Gone are thoughts of those beautiful shipments of perfect cotton; gone are the memories of those new suppliers he signed on one after another; gone is the praise Samuel received for bartering reduced cotton prices on behalf of the Corporation. The Associates forget too quickly what they have gained from the Wainwright family — particularly Samuel. He has been a good and loyal employee who is now being treated as a leper."

Matthew rested his palms on McKinley's desk and leaned forward until their faces nearly touched. "I must remind you that you, too, are an employee of the Corporation. If you wish to work as my assistant, your loyalty must remain with me and with the Corporation, McKinley. If I do not believe I can trust you, then I do not want you as an employee of the Corporation."

"As I've told you in the past, Mr. Cheever, my family is of great importance to me. I do not always agree with them, but in this instance I know they are correct. Would you respect a man who did not remain loyal to his family?"

"I've told you what I expect, and if you plan to continue in my employ, you'll think long and hard about where you place your loyalty. Be a man and think for yourself, especially if you have intentions of ever becoming a part of *my* family."

Matthew grabbed his coat and hat from the rack, slamming the door behind him on his way out.

McKinley rubbed his forehead. "So much for bringing the ledgers up to date," he muttered.

Strolling down Dutton Street, Violet breathed deeply, enjoying the feel of springtime in the air. She stopped to view the merchandise displayed in several store windows along the way but came to an abrupt halt in front of Hatch and Taisey, surprised to see McKinley inside the shop. She entered the door and quietly approached him. "Whatever are you doing in here? Purchasing some tripe or pigs' feet? Perhaps placing an order for a butchered hog?" she asked with a grin.

His gaze was clouded, almost as though he didn't recognize her. "What?" he asked, suddenly coming to his senses and looking about. "I believe I entered the wrong door," he finally said.

"You don't seem yourself, McKinley. Is something wrong?"

"Yes. I promised Grandmother I would stop at Paxton's on my way home and purchase some soap — 'fancy soap,' as she so fondly calls it. I dare not forget or she'll send me back to retrieve it."

"You're just now leaving the mill?" Violet asked as McKinley guided her out the door and into the neighboring establishment.

He nodded. "The ledgers required updating. My work had fallen behind. All this upheaval over the cotton shipment makes it difficult to concentrate."

"No doubt. How terrible this entire ordeal has been for your brother and father, but I'm confident it will soon be resolved. I'm certain Father and the Associates will aid them in remedying the situation. After all, there surely is some credible explanation," Violet said while leading him toward a section of shelving containing the toilet and fancy soaps.

McKinley gave a sardonic laugh. "Your father and the Associates have expressed nothing but disparagement and anger throughout this ordeal. Only this morning I attempted to explain that Samuel and my father had gone to Boston and talked with the shipping agent and captain in an effort to determine what happened."

"Father wouldn't listen to you?" she asked with a hint of incredulity in her voice.

McKinley picked up several pieces of soap. "Oh, he listened, but he doesn't believe there is any acceptable excuse for what occurred. He says only that Samuel is to blame, no matter what the cause."

Violet placed her hand atop McKinley's. "Truly? Father generally listens to reason. It's difficult for me to hear that he would be so callous."

"Indeed. He further said that if I intended to continue in his employ or ever become a part of his family, I should determine exactly where I place my loyalties. His warning was clear. If I side with my family, my position with the Corporation will be jeopardized and, more importantly, he may withdraw his approval of our relationship."

Violet's knees buckled and she grasped McKinley's arm, feeling as though she might actually faint. "How could he behave in such a manner? I've never known my father to be so ruthless."

"I must admit his behavior has seemed out of character ever since this mishap. I realize he's in charge of daily operations, but it's the Associates who hired Samuel, not your father. When Samuel and Father went to Boston they discovered there may have been an error in the shipment. Although they hold no evidence, they believe the stamps were wrongly affixed to the bales, causing the error in shipment. But your father and the Associates aren't willing to listen."

"Why not?"

He shrugged. "Your father said he doesn't want excuses. The delivery of high-quality cotton is what he requires, and nothing else will suffice."

Violet accompanied him to the counter and waited while McKinley paid Mrs. Paxton for the soap. "Any word on the cotton shipment?" the store owner inquired while wrapping McKinley's purchase in brown paper.

"Nothing that I care to speak of," he replied.

"This is going to mean a loss of business for all of us if they close down the Appleton," she remarked.

"Yes, so I've been told — numerous times," McKinley said as he and Violet exited the store.

"I would enjoy nothing more than to keep company with you, but I fear any further tardiness will cause Grandmother distress. She tends to forget I am a grown man."

The apologetic tone of his voice made McKinley even more endearing, and Violet smiled at him as she released her gentle grasp on his arm. "I understand."

He brushed her fingertips with a kiss, whispered a soft good-bye, and departed. Violet watched until he was no longer in sight and then turned on her heel and marched toward home. Gone was her tender emotion. In its place, her anger began to simmer slowly, like a kettle of water with tiny bubbles circling the edge, waiting for the heat to escalate before bursting into a churning boil.

She lifted her skirts, ran up the front steps of the house, and burst through the front door. Her father sat reading in the parlor while her mother stitched a piece of decorative needlepoint.

Her father glanced up from his book. "Back so soon?"

Without taking time to remove her cape, she firmly planted herself directly in front of her father. "What has come over you?"

"I beg your pardon? Whatever are you talking about?"

"McKinley! How dare you say he must choose between his family and me? Your attitude is appalling. What were you thinking? Or were you?"

Her father rose from his chair, a tinge of scarlet inching upward from beneath his white-collared shirt. "Whom do you think you are speaking to, young lady? Have *you* forgotten proper behavior?"

Tears threatened and Violet bit her lower lip, hoping she could maintain control of her emotions. "I'm no longer an impudent child. Nor am I a chattel you can withhold as a bartering tool in order to maintain control over McKinley's actions."

"Although you're no longer a child, your actions *are* impudent. You cannot begin to fathom what is at stake in this matter."

"So you're telling me manipulation is acceptable if the stakes are high? That is not a principle you taught me when I was growing up. You told me I should live my life in a manner that would be pleasing to God — and I listened. Although I haven't always been successful, I do attempt to mend my mistakes when I realize I'm incorrect. Will you not do likewise, Father?"

Moving in front of the fireplace, her father crossed his arms. His eyes grew dark and somber. "My responsibilities reach far beyond this family. I'm forced to make decisions at work that impact *many* lives. Jobs are being jeopardized, and much money will be lost because of Samuel Wainwright's inattention. I cannot condone such behavior, nor can I tolerate people working for me who do not properly place their priorities."

"I pray you will rethink your decision, Father. You're forcing me to choose between the two men whom I love the most in this world. Please realize there is much at stake here at home also."

Chapter 27

With Spencer and Moses at her side, Jasmine read from the Brothers Grimm volume of fairy tales while the three of them enjoyed the warm springtime weather. "Grappa!" Spencer shouted, pointing toward the horse-drawn buggy that had turned toward the house and now drew near.

Jasmine shaded her eyes against the bright sun and looked toward the carriage. Surely Spencer was mistaken. "It's Grandmother I'm expecting," she murmured, but it was her father who was now stepping down from the buggy. Shifting forward, Jasmine returned his wave before rising. Grasping the boys' hands, she walked to meet him.

Her father's steps grew hesitant as they neared one another. "Father," she said, opening her arms to embrace him.

"Jasmine — how I've longed to visit with you."

She heard the tremble in his voice. "No

need to be nervous, Father. I'm surprised by your visit but pleased beyond belief that you have come. I must admit it was Grandmother I was expecting, but Spencer spied you in the carriage as you came up the driveway."

He winked at his grandson. "I'm pleased to see you're happy to see Grandpa." He stooped down and pulled the boy into the crook of his arm. "And you come here for a hug too." He extended his other arm toward Moses, and the child rushed forward giving a delightful giggle.

"Thank you," she whispered.

"No need for thanks, my dear. Come along, boys. Let's see if we can find some cake and lemonade in the house."

"You'll spoil their dinner," Jasmine cautioned.

"That's what childhood is for — special treats to spoil our dinners as well as the pleasure of enjoying each day," he said with a chuckle.

"I don't believe that was your attitude when *your* children were growing up," she said, giving him a broad smile as they walked arm in arm toward the house.

He nodded. "But that is the special pleasure of being a grandparent. Besides, if the boys are busy with their cake, we can have some time to ourselves for a visit."

For the first time since his arrival, Jasmine became uneasy. "I hope that doesn't mean we are going to argue. I want this rift between us to heal."

"As do I. However, my hope is that we will arrive at a solution that will heal our family while doing what is best for Moses — not necessarily what is most agreeable to *you,* but what will best serve the child. Do you have someone helping with the boys since Naomi's . . ." He hesitated, obviously unsure how to broach the topic of Naomi's disappearance.

"We are rather short on help. We had a young girl who helped in the kitchen and another who helped with the upstairs. Both have quit to move to Boston. Kiara comes each day, but as her baby grows older, I'm certain she'll be unable to help as much as she has in the past. With Rogan working here at the farm and also assisting Liam with his business, they have become self-sufficient. And Kiara continues to receive more orders for her lace than she can fill. I know she would never refuse to assist me, but my hope has always been they would become independent. She's here today, however, so perhaps she wouldn't mind caring for the boys while we work on your *solution.*"

"Oh and fer sure here are a couple of hungry boys," Kiara said as she looked up from peeling potatoes. She smiled at Jasmine and then gave a brief nod toward her father.

"We thought perhaps some treat would occupy them so that I might have a talk with my father."

"But of course. Just be sittin' 'em down. I'll fetch some milk and a wee bit of cake."

After settling Spencer and Moses at the small kitchen table, Jasmine smoothed the folds from her skirt. "You're certain they won't disturb you?" she asked Kiara.

A bright smile curved Kiara's lips as she sliced pieces of cake for the boys. "O' course na'. Nevan's sleepin' sound as can be," she said, nodding toward the baby's cradle in one corner of the kitchen. "Besides, Cook will be back shortly. She had Paddy take her to town for a few supplies. I'm expectin' her any time."

"You boys be good while I visit with Grandpa, and we'll go back outdoors this afternoon," she promised as she turned to leave the room.

Her father appeared weary — or was age to blame for the new lines creasing his face and the additional gray hair fringing his balding pate? With each visit to Lowell, he appeared more fatigued and a little older. His mortality entered her thoughts more frequently than she would like nowadays. "Have you been resting well, Father?"

His smile was warm and familiar as he patted the seat cushion next to him. "As well as one can expect when away from home. Come sit beside me."

She leaned close and embraced his arm. "You're anxious to return home?"

"Only because I'm weary of the many trials and tribulations that have occurred during my visit. The difficulty with the cotton shipment has been extremely distressing, coupled with the rift that's occurred within our family."

Jasmine sighed. "In some measure, *that* portion of your concern was brought about by my quick temper, and I apologize for the part I've played in causing strife. I know your visit has been fraught with turmoil. However, I must add that I believe Samuel, McKinley, and Violet overstepped the boundaries of suitable behavior. Their condemnation of me and lack of sympathy for Moses and his plight are quite distressing — and you didn't come to my defense either. I want resolution for our family's disagreement, but my primary concern is Moses. I made a promise to rear him as if he were my own. I won't go back on my word."

"Not even if it's in the boy's best interests?"

Jasmine scooted on the cushion, quickly distancing herself from her father. "I know what you're thinking! You believe I should send him to The Willows. Are you so attuned to Southern ways that you can't see the harm he would suffer? Not only would he be living in an unfamiliar home, he would also be surrounded by strangers. I won't send him to become a slave on the family plantation. Out of the question!"

"Do settle yourself, Jasmine. You've rushed to incorrect conclusions. Taking Moses to the plantation never entered my mind. I agree such a decision would be harmful to the child."

Her rigid shoulders relaxed at his words. "Then you're on my side in this matter?"

"I'm on the boy's side," Malcolm hastened to reply.

Her forehead crinkled and she tilted her head to the side. "What does that mean? I'm also on his side."

Patting her hand, her father leaned toward her with a judicious look in his eyes. "Let's see if that's true. I have a proposal to make. And I believe the plan I've developed is best for Moses. Will you listen?"

Jasmine gave him a begrudging nod.

"First, let me tell you what I see for Moses if he remains a member of your household," he began.

She leaned farther into the deep cushions of the settee, not wanting to hear his predictions for Moses' life. She had her own thoughts about the boy's future should Obadiah and Naomi not return. However, she had agreed to hear her father out. "I'm listening," she said.

"Your compassion is admirable, Jasmine. I know you want only the best for Moses, but think about what you will do if you raise him to know only what it is to live as a white child. You're denying the boy his own roots. What if Obadiah and Naomi return in two or three years? I know you doubt they will ever be able to come back. But what if they should? Their son will believe he is white and that you and Nolan are his parents. How would you correct that damage? And it's not as though people in this area don't know the boy is colored. One day someone will take great pleasure in telling him the truth. He'll be devastated and possibly turn against you for withholding that information."

"I *do* plan to tell him about Obadiah and Naomi — when he's old enough to understand," she defended.

"Don't you see, Jasmine? You'll put off telling him for one reason or another until you've buried the past deep inside and begin to believe he *is* your child. You'll cause him great pain if you continue down this path."

She wilted, nodding her head. "Late at night, I'm plagued with these thoughts. I don't want to do anything to hurt Moses, yet I cannot send him away from here."

"I have a young slave couple at the plantation. . . ."

Immediately Jasmine came upright, her eyes flashing. "I've already told you, I will *not* send Moses to The Willows or anyplace else, for that matter."

"Please! Let me finish."

"I'm sorry. Continue."

"I have a young slave couple I would be willing to set free and send to you. Nolan could make arrangements for them to sail into Boston on one of your ships. They could remain here on the farm and raise Moses. The boy would return to the house where he lived with his mother and father, and you would be keeping your promise."

She was silent for several minutes, allowing the idea to take hold in her mind. "Such a plan would likely return our lives to a semblance of what they had once been. But what if this couple doesn't want to come — or if Naomi and Obadiah should return?"

"Why wouldn't they want to come, Jasmine? I'd be offering them their freedom, an opportunity to live in the North with a place to live and receive wages — a new life. If Obadiah and Naomi return, they would be reunited with Moses. Simon and Maisie could stay on if you had sufficient work for them, or they could seek employment somewhere else. I'll explain the possibility that Obadiah and Naomi might return, if that makes you feel easier."

"It's only fair they know the complete circumstances under which they'd be coming. Do they have children of their own — Maisie and Simon?" she asked.

"No — not yet. If memory serves me right, she lost a baby in childbirth a year ago."

"But she likes children?"

Malcolm shrugged and gave his daughter a grin. "I have no idea — I thought *all* women loved children. I think you'd find her very acceptable, and Simon puts me in mind of Obadiah. Strong, hardworking, big smile. I know this isn't what you planned, but I believe it truly is the best for Moses. He'll still have your family close at hand, and you can aid him financially in the future, if you desire. Send him to school, do whatever you like in that regard, but don't raisc him believing he's your son or Spencer's brother. In the end, you'll harm Moses as well as your own son."

As tears began to trickle down Jasmine's face, her father quickly retrieved a folded cotton square from his pocket and wiped her cheeks. With a gentle motion, he pulled her into a warm embrace.

"No need for tears, my dear. I know that together we're going to do what is truly best for Moses."

Taking a deep breath, Jasmine attempted to contain her sobbing. "In my heart, I know this is the right thing to do, but I truly don't want to give him up."

"But you're *not* giving him up. You're merely returning him to his own home. He'll still be here playing with Spencer, enjoying the very life he would have had with his own parents. Don't you see how attached you've already become?"

"Yes, and it seems inequitable that things cannot continue as they were."

"But God has a plan even in this, is that not right, daughter?"

She nodded. "I'm afraid I've not been speaking regularly with the Lord. I . . . well . . . I suppose without the fellowship of other people, it's been easy to let myself slide away."

"And you've not been going to church because of Moses?"

"I've been afraid of how they might receive him."

Her father rubbed his chin. "That hardly seems like something the Lord would approve of, now does it?"

She sighed. "No. Even Nolan said as much."

"We want to do right by the boy. He deserves that much."

Jasmine looked at her father. "Please do not think me harsh, but why do you care what happens to him? Why do you care when you own slaves and treat them as property?"

Malcolm lowered his gaze. "Mammy." He blew out a heavy sigh and looked up. "I care because he's Mammy's grandson."

Jasmine realized then that someone had told her father the entire story. She reached out to pat his hand. Tears poured down her cheeks.

Kiara walked into the parlor with Nevan in her arms. "The lads are near done with their cake and are wantin' ta go outdoors. I'm going to take Nevan and join . . . Forevermore, why are ya cryin'? Yar eyes are puffed as big as hen's eggs."

The comment brought a tiny smile to Jasmine's lips. "We've been discussing Moses," she whispered.

Lifting Nevan to her shoulder, Kiara turned to glare at the older man. "I see ya've been a success in causin' her more heartache."

"No, not at all, Kiara. I believe Father has helped me to resolve Moses' future," Jasmine said.

Kiara bobbed her head up and down. "And I see his plan has made ya mighty happy too."

"Sit down and let me explain. The boys will be fine in the kitchen for a few moments."

Kiara sat down with the baby cradled on her lap and appeared to listen attentively while Jasmine explained her father's plan. "Well, what do you think?"

"Is it the truth ya're wantin' ta hear?"

"Of course," she replied.

Kiara glanced back and forth between the Wainwrights and gave a brief nod of her head. "Then I'll tell ya. No offense, but under the same set of circumstances, I'd be wantin' Nevan raised by someone that was Irish. I'd want him growin' up knowin' about Ireland and who we were. Even though Nevan is white, I'd still want 'im raised by his own people. Have I insulted ya?"

"No. You've been honest, and your answer affirms what Father has been attempting to tell me. I'd like to believe that one day people will be more accepting and issues of race and color won't need to be the determining factor in matters such as this. But for now we can only continue to work toward that end."

McKinley looked up from his desk as Matthew Cheever rushed into the office at the Appleton and excitedly grasped McKinley by the arm. "Put the ledgers aside and come with me, McKinley."

"Has there been an accident in the mill?" he asked, immediately jumping up from his desk and hurrying to keep pace with Mr. Cheever.

"No accident — this is good news. Come see what's in the mill yard," he hollered over his shoulder, by now nearly running.

McKinley increased his speed as a group

of boxcars entered his line of vision. Men had already unloaded several bales of cotton. "What's this?" McKinley panted, doubling over from the waist until his breathing slowed.

"Cotton — the excellent grade we've come to expect from Samuel," Matthew said.

"How can that be?"

"I don't know — I sent word for your father and Samuel to meet us here before I fetched you. They should be arriving soon."

McKinley watched in amazement as the cotton was unloaded. "Have you spot-checked it to assure yourself it's of good quality?"

"Yes. That's the first thing we did. I've told the men to hold up before unloading any more of the shipment until I talk to Samuel. I must make certain this cotton was destined for Lowell. He didn't tell me he was expecting another shipment. Did he mention anything to you?"

"No, of course not. I would have promptly told you — as would Samuel. I know Samuel apprised you of his plan to return to New Orleans on the next Houston ship leaving Boston. He is determined to further investigate what occurred there," McKinley said before moving closer to check a few bales of cotton. "These bales appear to carry the proper stamp."

"As did the others," the older man mentioned.

Mr. Cheever pointed toward the front gate of the mill. "That may be your grandmother's carriage arriving now."

McKinley shaded his eyes against the sun and stared toward the front gates. He waited until the men disembarked the carriage. "Yes, it is Samuel — and Father has accompanied him. Shall I go and escort them?"

"Why don't we both go?" There was obvious excitement in Mr. Cheever's voice and a noticeable spring in his step as he accompanied McKinley up the sloping grade toward the carriage.

McKinley waved them onward. When they drew near, he clasped his father's hand as Samuel shook hands with Mr. Cheever. "Come down to the mill yard."

"I realize it has taken longer than expected to remove the unusable bales, but I have now made final arrangements for their return to New Orleans," Samuel said.

"That's fine, but this is another matter entirely," Matthew told him as they made their way to the boxcars.

Samuel stopped and stared, obviously

overwhelmed by the sight. Hurrying forward, he checked one of the opened bales and then rushed forward to inspect the stamps. "These bales also contain the special stamp we developed for the Lowell shipments. I don't understand what has occurred. Both the last shipment as well as this one bear our stamp."

"The overseer brought this letter," Matthew said. "He said it accompanied the shipment and is addressed to you."

Samuel tore open the missive and began to scan the contents of the letter. McKinley and the others stood silently waiting, all of them obviously anxious to know what information the letter contained. After several restless minutes, Samuel folded the letter and tucked it into his jacket. "It seems our mysterious shipment has been explained," he told them.

"Is this cotton ours? May I let the men continue unloading?" Matthew inquired jubilantly.

"Absolutely!" Samuel exclaimed.

Resounding yelps of enthusiasm filled the mill yard as the men began calling out the good news. Quickly, they scattered throughout the area, calling the rest of the men to assist them in the yard.

"I'd like to know what the contents of

your letter revealed," Matthew said, raising his voice so that he could be heard over the clamoring noise.

"Why don't we go back to the office and I'll tell you," Samuel suggested.

Once the men had departed the mill yard and settled themselves in Matthew's office, Samuel withdrew the letter from his pocket. "This letter is from my good friend and associate, Walter Rochester. He sends his deepest apologies. His letter states that the shipment we first received was one destined for England. It was instead routed to Boston. When Walter realized the error, he immediately set out to correct the problem by shipping the original bales to Boston. He has agreed to waive all fees for our shipment and pay any damages caused by his carelessness."

"Does he give further explanation?"

Samuel nodded. "It seems he sent a new employee, a young fellow with no prior experience, to stamp the bales with our Lowell imprint. The boy misunderstood and stamped all of the bales in the warehouse with the imprint. When it came time to load the ship, the dock workers had a bill of lading in their possession detailing only the number of pounds they were to load and that the bales should bear the Lowell imprint. Unfortunately, the bales near the front of the warehouse were the ones of poor quality but they bore our imprint."

"And of course the dock workers wouldn't know the difference," Malcolm said. "They'd merely look for our imprint and load the weight listed on their paper work."

"Exactly," Samuel said. "The next day Walter went into the warehouse and discovered what had occurred. He immediately placed our bales on the next ship departing for Boston."

"And what of the first shipment? Did Walter say what's to be done with it?" Malcolm inquired.

"He's asked that I reroute it to Manchester, England — at his expense, of course."

"Quite a mistake," Matthew said as he leaned back in his leather-upholstered desk chair.

"Yes," Samuel agreed, "but Walter is a good man, and I don't intend to push aside the years of excellent service he's rendered to my family for one mistake. He tells me in his letter that he has put safeguards in place to prevent another such occurrence in the future. If the Associates decide I should remain on their payroll, it could be only with the understanding I'd continue to use

Walter's services."

"There's little doubt the Associates will want you to continue as their buyer. That said, I believe I owe several apologies. Samuel, I hope you'll forgive me. Given your excellent performance in the past, I should have come to your defense instead of going along with whatever the Associates decided. I'm sorry for my behavior." Matthew paused and inhaled very slowly. "I was blinded by the worry and concern for so many lives. I should have trusted God to have an answer, but I did not seek Him. I pray for His forgiveness as well as yours." He looked to Malcolm Wainwright. "I know my lack of support for you and Samuel came as a painful blow to you. Please accept my apology."

Samuel and Malcolm alternately shook hands with Matthew. "Apology accepted," Malcolm said.

"But please remember to caution the Associates," Samuel said. "I will not continue to work for them if they insist I contract work with anyone other than Walter."

"Point taken. I don't believe there will be a problem," Matthew replied.

"Then I think we had best be on our way." Malcolm stood and Samuel followed suit. "I'll want to share the good news with Mother, and Samuel needs to modify the arrangements for shipping the original load of cotton to Manchester. We'll see you at supper, McKinley?"

Before he could answer, Matthew interceded. "Once I've had a chat with McKinley, I'm hoping he'll join *our* family for supper tonight. If that won't interfere with your plans."

Malcolm tilted his head and smiled. "Not at all. Samuel will be boarding the train for Boston. Perhaps Mother will agree to supper at the Merrimack House. If not, I think the two of us can enjoy a quiet supper at home."

McKinley bid Samuel and his father good-bye and then turned a questioning look toward his employer.

"A moment of your time, please," Mr. Cheever requested.

"Of course," McKinley replied.

"I also owe *you* an apology, McKinley. I am ashamed of my behavior and ask your forgiveness. Ordering you to choose between your family and your employment as well as my comment in regard to becoming a member of our family constituted shameful behavior on my part. I fear I acted in haste and desperation, more concerned about my position than my own family. In short, I'm ashamed of myself. If it helps at all, please know that Violet or Lilly would have forced me to my senses before permitting me to stand in the way of love. That aside, I was wrong and hope we can begin afresh."

The sun suddenly appeared more radiant as it shone through the office window. "I believe I would like that very much," McKinley said with a broad smile.

The sound of the girls' enthusiastic chatter drifted toward the kitchen, where Elinor was ladling boiled corned beef, potatoes, and turnips into several large serving bowls. She heard the scraping of chairs in the dining room and quickly checked the bread pudding. It would need another few minutes in the oven.

"You have time to wash up before supper," she called to the girls.

"Do hurry! We have exciting news," Lucinda told her.

The comment was almost enough for Elinor to break her rule and permit the girls in the kitchen during meal preparation. Almost as quickly, one of her grandmother's old adages rang in her ears. *Once permission is given to break a rule, it's never again taken seriously.*

"I can wait to hear the news," Elinor muttered aloud as she gave the pan of bread pudding a firm shake. Done enough, she decided, placing it on the cabinet to cool before filling small china bowls with the horseradish sauce the girls enjoyed with their corned beef. With an agility that surprised even her, she deftly sliced two loaves of rye bread and carried them to the table.

"Please tell the others supper is ready," she asked Lucinda, who was sitting at the table with her hands folded, obviously anxious to be there when the important news was announced.

Lucinda nodded. "But please let me tell you," she whispered.

"I will," Elinor replied, giving the girl a pleasant smile.

By the time they had all gathered around the table, filled their plates, and offered the blessing, Lucinda was wiggling like a vigorous newborn babe.

Elinor carefully tucked a frayed napkin onto her lap. "I believe you had some news you wanted to share with me, Lucinda."

The girl immediately perked to attention. "None of us is going to have to leave, and you're not going to lose your position as our keeper. The house will remain open," she spurted, her cheeks aglow with excitement.

Elinor sat back in her chair and gazed around the table. All of the girls appeared to be nodding affirmation of what Lucinda had told her. "How can that be?" she asked. Her heart pounded intensely beneath the bodice of her calico dress.

"A new shipment of cotton arrived at the mill. There was a mix-up of some kind in the shipments, and now that the mill has received the proper cotton, none of us will lose her job or be required to move! Mr. Cheever made the announcement as we left work this evening. Isn't that marvelous news?"

"Answered prayer," Elinor whispered.

"What?" Lucinda asked.

"I said this is an answer to my prayers," she said aloud. "Even though my brother and his family generously offered me a home, it has never been my desire to be an added member of another family. I've come to think of you girls as my family. And now we'll be able to remain together," she said with a bright smile.

Steam spiraled upward and hovered over the pan of hot dishwater awaiting the supper dishes. Elinor gingerly dipped her hands into the heated water and enjoyed the relaxing warmth before beginning the dreary chore. But unlike evenings in the past, she issued a silent prayer of thanksgiving for the soiled dinner plates and grimy cooking pots that needed her attention. And tonight she thanked God that her position as a boardinghouse keeper was once again secure.

A hesitant smile made its way across her face. "Once I turncd loose my anger and believed you would keep me safe, you wrapped me in your arms and protected me. Now I pray I will remember always to place my trust in you," she murmured.

That night when the house was quiet and the girls were asleep, Elinor took up her Bible and opened it. Without looking upon the pages, she began to pray. "I know I'm a terrible sinner, Lord. My faith has been so weak that it was hardly in existence. Thin threads that barely held together. It's not been easy, but then, I suppose you already know that, because you know everything."

She paused and leaned back against her simple headboard. "I'm lonely, Father. Lonely for the company of my family. Lonely for friends. Lonely for the lost love of my husbands. I want to believe that you will fill that lonely place — that emptiness. You've asked me to trust you, and I am trying. But I know too that I'm weak. I know I will fail you. But it is my heart's desire that my faith should grow strong. That the strands of faith would thicken into cords bound by your love. Please help me, Father."

She sat in the silence a moment longer, then read the words of Isaiah fifty-four. *"Fear not; for thou shalt not be ashamed: neither be thou confounded; for thou shalt not be put to shame: for thou shalt forget the shame of thy youth, and shalt not remember the reproach of thy widowhood any more. For thy Maker is thine husband; the Lord of hosts is his name; and thy Redeemer the Holy One of Israel; The God of the whole earth shall he be called."*

Elinor wiped her tears with the cuff of her dress and continued. *"For the Lord hath called thee as a woman forsaken and grieved in spirit, and a wife of youth, when thou wast refused, saith thy God. For a small moment have I forsaken thee; but with great mercies will I gather thee. In a little wrath I hid my face from thee for a moment; but with everlasting kindness will I have mercy on thee, saith the Lord thy Redeemer."*

Elinor let the Bible fall to her lap, sobbing freely into her hands. The Lord had spoken to her heart as though He sat by her side. The words of this declaration felt as if they'd been penned just for her.

"I am redeemed," she declared. "I am not forsaken."

CHAPTER 28

August

Violet looked across the elegantly dressed table and smiled at McKinley. She knew he was nervous, anxious about something. He wouldn't tell her what it was, but Violet had ideas of her own. For weeks McKinley had hinted at asking for her hand, but so far as she knew, he'd failed to move forward on this.

She toyed with her half-filled goblet as her father droned on about warehousing cotton and shortening the length of time by ship. She hated to say she was bored, but the business of the mills had always put her to sleep. Perhaps it was wrong to feel this way; after all, the mills were responsible for her fine social standing and wealth. Still, it was the business of men, and she could hardly be expected to care about profits and losses and schedules.

Violet knew it was expected she would

marry and produce a family, and to her that was quite acceptable. However, it was the wait that wearied her mind. Men would take forever to resolve such matters if not prodded by women.

"I disagree with your approach," Violet heard her mother exclaim.

"But you're a woman, and you would no doubt have the entire mill designed with lovely cushioned French furnishings and a tea stand in every corner," Violet's father teased. She had no idea what the conversation was about, but she took the opportunity to lean toward McKinley just as her brother, Michael, boisterously entered the conversation and took the attention of both of her parents.

"McKinley, I just want to know something," Violet began softly.

He looked up from his plum pudding with a questioning expression.

Michael had raised his voice to what was generally an unacceptable level as he protested his mother's comments. Violet smiled and leaned closer.

"Do you plan to marry me or not?"

The entire table went silent as everyone turned. Violet hadn't meant for the words to come out so loud. She felt her cheeks grow hot as she caught the stunned expressions. Then without warning, everyone, McKinley included, burst into laughter.

Violet shrank into her chair, wishing the earth would simply open up and swallow her whole.

"I think you'd better answer the girl," her father declared.

McKinley recovered and straightened his shoulders. "I had intended to ask you properly, later tonight. Of course, now that you've clearly made the room our audience, perhaps I should simply proceed." He got up from his chair and came around the table to where Violet sat. Pulling her to her feet, he gazed tenderly into her eyes.

Violet thought she might well swoon, although she had never been given to such things. She forced her knees together to keep her legs from trembling.

"I have fallen in love with the most beautiful woman in all of Lowell," McKinley began. "A Northern girl with a heart of gold. It is my desire that you would accept me as your husband — that we might marry and live here for the rest of our lives. To answer your question, I do plan to marry you, Miss Cheever . . . if you'll have me."

Violet grinned, no longer caring about the embarrassment she'd caused herself. "I will happily take you as my husband, Mr. Wainwright."

Violet's family began to applaud, but she only had eyes for McKinley. Her dreams had all just come true. What did a little embarrassment matter?

The sound of an approaching carriage drifting through the open parlor window captured Jasmine's attention. She moved to the front door, fanning herself against the onslaught of yet another warm spell. Clouds of dust plumed from under the horses' hooves as the carriage neared the house. Pushing open the door, she walked onto the porch and immediately gained an improved view of the conveyance. Violet Cheever waved from the window of the carriage, her face illuminated by a bright smile.

"This is a surprise," Jasmine said as Violet made her way up the front steps.

The two women briefly embraced. "Mother chided me for calling on you without proper notice. In fact, she followed me to the carriage in order to upbraid me for my rude behavior. Obviously she was distraught that I failed to heed her warnings over breakfast this morning." Violet cleared her throat. "But I couldn't let matters remain unresolved between us. I acted in a poor fashion . . . making an undue judgment against you. I have come to seek your forgiveness."

Jasmine smiled. "It is my harsh words that need to be forgiven. You sought only to share your concerns. I pray you might forgive me as well."

They embraced again, only this time there was much more feeling. It was as if a dam had burst open to free a flood of emotion.

"I'm so sorry," Violet said, tears forming in her eyes. "I never meant to hurt you or Moses."

"And I am sorry for my sharp tongue," Jasmine said as they pulled away. She wiped her tears with the tips of her fingers. "Please know how much I love you. You are as dear to me as a sister. Indeed, soon to be my sister."

"Yes, sisters. I've always wanted a sister."

"Come," Jasmine instructed. "Come and sit. Tell me all about my brother's proposal."

Violet laughed. "You mean you haven't heard the embarrassing truth of that day?"

Jasmine shook her head. "No, I suppose I had no idea of there being any reason for embarrassment. Pray tell, what did my brother do?"

"It wasn't him at all," Violet protested. " 'Twas I. I'm afraid I grew weary of waiting for his proposal. As my family argued at the dinner table, I leaned to ask him . . . quite boldly . . . if he intended to marry me or not."

Jasmine grinned, then put her hand to her mouth as a giggle escaped.

Violet shrugged. "I'm afraid McKinley will always tell our children of their mother's bossy nature and how she pressed him to propose."

"Oh, it will be a dear story," Jasmine assured. "Now come and tell me all about the wedding plans." She pulled Violet into the house.

Violet removed her pink silk bonnet that had been fashionably trimmed with an ivory feather and matching ribbons. "That's one of the reasons I've come. I've been busy making plans for the wedding, and I'm hoping you'll agree to aid me with your insight."

"I would be delighted. Kiara made a fresh pitcher of lemonade only a short time ago. Why don't you sit down while I fetch a glass for each of us?"

"A cool drink would be most enjoyable. I'll come along and help you. The heat this summer has been most agonizing. I don't recall an August quite this warm."

"Yes, it almost makes me think I've returned to Mississippi," Jasmine said as they walked to the kitchen. "One must feel sympathy for all those Southerners who have come north to escape the scourge of summer's unbearable temperatures, only to be greeted by much the same discomfort when they arrive."

"Yes, indeed. Although McKinley mentioned that many of them come here not only to escape the heat, but also to escape the possibility of contracting malaria or yellow fever."

"True. Many a planter's family has been stricken by one of those dreadful diseases, and God alone knows how many slaves have succumbed to one of those maladies. My own mother and beloved mammy might be alive had they not taken the fever," Jasmine said, sorrow thick in her voice. She sighed and reached for the pitcher. "There are always griefs to bear." She poured lemonade into two glasses, each one etched with a beautifully scripted *H.* "Let us speak of happier things."

Violet nodded and picked up one of the glasses and ran her finger over the engraving. "Wedding gift?" she inquired.

"Yes — received when Bradley and I married." She put the sorrow behind her and smiled.

Violet giggled. "Works out nicely that you may continue to use them."

Memories of her marriage to Bradley momentarily clouded Jasmine's visage. These thoughts weren't the happier things she would have pondered, but her marriage had been an important part of her young life. The experience had taught her many things, but best of all, it had given her Spencer. She smiled. "Yes, it worked out quite nicely. Especially since I'm now able to use them in much happier circumstances."

"I do hope my marriage to McKinley will prove joyous," Violet said softly.

Jasmine forced her thoughts back to the present. "Why, of *course* it will. McKinley is a wonderful man, and I know he loves you very much. I wish you the happiness Nolan and I have enjoyed since our union. Treat him with respect and he will love you beyond your expectations. Now come sit and tell me of your plans. McKinley mentioned the two of you have set a September date. I must admit that will put a rush to things. I cannot imagine you bringing such a large wedding together in less than a month's time."

"Mother has been planning my wedding since I was twelve," Violet said with a laugh. "Fear not. She has more things already arranged than either of us could imagine. However, she cannot arrange my witness in the ceremony. I came today particularly to ask if you would be willing to stand with me. McKinley has asked Samuel, but since I have no sister, I would be most pleased if you would agree."

"I'm honored you would ask. I would be delighted. Now, do tell me what plans you've made thus far."

"Several months ago, Mother purchased the finest bolt of satin, and unbeknownst to me, has had Kiara fashioning the lace since last December. Naturally, Mrs. Hepple will be making the gown. Mother says her work far surpasses that of any Boston seamstress, although I'm not certain that's true."

Jasmine took a sip of her lemonade and wiped the sweating glass with a napkin before placing it on the table. "I believe your mother is correct. Mrs. Hepple does fine work, and I'm pleased to hear Kiara will be making your lace — a treasure for certain. Your mother was prudent to put her to work so long ago. Making lace is tedious work."

Violet nodded. "Mrs. Hepple has been working on a sample of the pattern using my measurements. I'm having a fitting this afternoon."

"And what of the wedding location?"

"We'll be married at St. Anne's, of course, and Mother insists upon a gathering at the house afterward. I believe McKinley would prefer to leave immediately on our wedding journey."

"Yes, I'm certain his preference would be to have you to himself as quickly as possible, but I know your mother to be a woman of great determination."

"Indeed," Violet said, taking another sip of the lemonade. "Mother has plans for an orchestra to serenade us as we receive our friends and family. She's reserved every flower in Lowell, and probably those in Boston as well. I think it will be a great ordeal. The more I hear of her plans, the more overwhelmed I become."

"With all of that, there seems little I can add." Jasmine smiled and offered to pour Violet another glass of refreshment.

The girl shook her head. "You can help me with the invitations. Mother says I must tend to them, but I have no idea what to say, and my penmanship is quite bad. I've seen your script and it is so very lovely."

"I'd be happy to help."

"I think men get the better part of the arrangement in marriage. They have nothing to do but show up for the wedding."

"Is my brother not planning a lovely wedding trip?"

"I suppose, but that hardly seems as taxing."

"Have you determined where you'll be going? Please say you're not taking an extended voyage. You'd be gone much too long for my liking if you did that."

"I suggested we travel to The Willows since I've never visited there, but McKinley said there was time for us to make that journey at a later date. He would like to show me Washington. He enjoyed his time there with your father — particularly his tour of the president's house. Most of all, he insists we visit White Sulphur Springs in Virginia. He mentioned having fond memories of going there when you were young."

"Indeed, we did visit and had a lovely time — back when Mother could be coaxed into occasionally leaving the house. I'm certain you'll have a most enjoyable time at the Springs and Washington. And what of your other plans? Housekeeping and such?"

"Did McKinley tell you Father and Mother purchased us a house as our wedding gift?"

Jasmine nodded enthusiastically. "He did, and I know he was exceedingly astonished by their generosity. I understand the house is quite lovely and not overly far from the mill, which certainly pleased him."

"I believe that was Father's doing. He doesn't admit to it, but I think he's come to rely more and more upon McKinley and has begun to enjoy having extra time to spend at home with Mother. They've even begun talking of a voyage to England next year."

"Well, the house sounds lovely."

"That's the other thing I have to ask of you," Violet admitted. "I do not care for Mother's ideas on decorating, but I'm enchanted by the way you've arranged things here. I'm hoping you will help me with my house."

"I'm flattered." And truly she was. Jasmine had never honestly considered that her home was anything special in a physical sense. Rather it was her family's enjoyment of it that made it valuable to her.

The chattering sounds of Moses and Spencer drifted into the parlor, and Jasmine turned her attention toward the doors leading to the small flower garden. She spied one of the boys running toward the rosebushes and quickly jumped to her feet and rushed toward the door.

"Spencer! Don't run near the bushes or you'll scratch yourself on the thorns," she warned as Kiara rounded the corner with

Nevan on her hip and Moses following close behind.

"It appears they've become a bit unruly. Why don't we go outdoors and lend Kiara a hand. Do you mind, Violet?"

"No, of course not."

Jasmine moved toward a small bench situated under a cluster of trees as Violet walked along beside her. "Come over here, boys," Jasmine called.

The two boys immediately did as she ordered. "I'm going to make a large circle around this bench, and if either of you goes outside the circle, you must go inside and take a nap. Is that understood?"

Spencer eyed her for a moment. "Where's the circle?"

"In just a moment, I'm going to show you. Wait here."

A few minutes later, Jasmine returned with a large ball of twine. She began unraveling the numerous pieces and tying them together. "Pieces I've accumulated from my purchases in town," she explained to Violet.

Once she'd tied the bits of twine together, Jasmine circled the bench in a wide loop, dropping the string as she walked. "You must remain inside the twine," she cautioned.

The boys smiled, obviously entranced by

this new constraint. There was little doubt they immediately considered it a game, going as close to the twine as they dared without stepping over. Jasmine smiled and shook her head. "I hope one of them doesn't err in judgment, for I dare not go back on my word."

Kiara smiled as she shifted Nevan to her other hip. "Aye, but fer the time, they seem to think it great fun."

"I'll watch after them, Kiara. I understand you have a new order for Violet's lace, and I'm certain you have many chores of your own to accomplish."

"Aye, that I do. If ya're certain ya won't be needin' me. It's fer sure Nevan could stand to be put down for a nap."

"Then off with you," Jasmine said. "The boys will be fine. Besides, I'm expecting Nolan within the hour."

"Things are ready at the cottage, and I'm sure the new folks will be pleased as punch ta see what all ya've done ta make them feel welcome. Will ya send someone ta fetch me when they arrive? I'd like ta welcome them."

"Of course," Jasmine replied.

"You have guests arriving?" Violet inquired.

"Not guests. The slave couple Father agreed to free and send north to care for

Moses. Nolan went to Boston to meet their ship and accompany them to Lowell. He thought they might feel more welcomed if someone met the ship and escorted them for the remainder of their journey. I'm certain that they're frightened and unsure about what awaits them."

"I do admire your willingness to heed your father's lead in this matter. I know you thought McKinley and I had turned on you and were unduly harsh when we sided with your father and Samuel. And, in retrospect, perhaps we were. But I believe what you are now doing is best for all concerned."

Jasmine gazed toward the two boys, who were busily playing with the small hand-carved wagons Obadiah had whittled for them. "So do I. However, I must admit that when you and McKinley took your stand against me, I wondered if either of you were truly dedicated to the antislavery movement. For a time I thought perhaps you were merely paying lip service to the cause. However, through Father's counseling, I've come to realize we all spoke in the heat of the moment. Although we all felt justified in our stand, none of us was completely correct."

"You're right. I fear that when you moved too far in one direction, the rest of us immediately attempted to pull you back into alignment. However, we yanked a bit too hard in the process. I can now see how you would question our integrity."

"In any case, there's no doubt that God has been faithful throughout. He has given us the wisdom to find a path that will restore our family as well as provide a good and loving home for Moses. I cling to the thought that Obadiah and Naomi may one day return and their family be completely restored again. But if not, I'm trusting these new parents God has provided will supply a supportive and loving home."

Violet smiled as Moses dumped a pile of dirt into Spencer's wagon. "And the boys will continue to have the company of one another."

"Yes. And of this new babe I now am carrying."

"What? You're expecting another child? Jasmine, how simply wonderful! You and Nolan must be delighted beyond compare."

"Indeed. Of course, I'm hoping for a healthy little girl, but we'll also be most pleased to have a little brother for Spencer."

"Oh, but when will the baby come? The wedding is next month. Will that be too taxing on you?"

"Not at all," Jasmine assured. "I am told

the baby will come in spring."

"What a wonder. I'm so happy for you." Clicking open the small watch pinned to her bodice, Violet's face lined with disappointment. "Oh, I fear I must be returning home. Mrs. Hepple is due shortly for my fitting. I wish I could stay and visit with Nolan upon his return."

"You mustn't be late or your mother will be concerned. Come back tomorrow if you like, and you can meet our new arrivals — Simon and Maisie."

"I'll plan to do just that. You remain with the boys. I can see myself to my carriage."

"No, we'll accompany you. Come along, boys," Jasmine instructed, extending her arms to take them by the hand.

The three of them stood on the front porch and watched until Violet's carriage pulled away from the house. "All right, my little men," Jasmine said as she turned them toward the front door. They'd not yet entered the house when Spencer tugged his hand free and pointed at the driveway.

"Daddy! Daddy!"

Jasmine glanced over her shoulder. "You're right; it is. No need to go inside," she said as they stood waiting on the front steps.

"What's this? A welcoming committee come to meet us?" Nolan asked as he jumped down from the buggy. He kissed Jasmine and then swooped the boys into his arms. "And how are my fine fellows?"

Moses immediately began to wiggle in his arms, apparently anxious to get back on the ground. Jasmine watched as the child's eyes filled with recognition of someone from his past as Simon heaved his large-framed body from inside the buggy. Hesitating for only a moment, Moses ran to Simon and held open his arms, appearing to sense a connection to his own father.

Simon leaned down and raised the boy high in the air. "You's a nice big boy. Is you Moses?"

Moses bobbed his head up and down and gave Simon a toothy smile. "You knowed me. I be Moses."

"Well, so you is. We's gonna have us some good times," he said, giving a hearty chuckle.

"Mama?" Moses looked beyond Simon to the woman behind him. The look on his face told Jasmine he was confused. She wondered if she should intercede, but Simon had it all under control.

"I be Papa Simon, and this here be Mama Maisie. We be heppin' you mama and papa."

"Papa Simon," Moses said, slapping his hands twice on the big man's shoulders.

Simon laughed and tossed him in the air.

"That be right. Now come see Mama Maisie."

"Let me help you down," Nolan said, extending a hand to Maisie.

The woman was obviously stunned by Nolan's kindness but accepted his hand nonetheless. "Thank you," she whispered.

Maisie came to her husband and smiled up at Moses. "Moses, I be Mama Maisie."

"Mama May-see," Moses repeated. He looked hesitant, as if he were trying to understand the situation. "You help me — help my mama. My mama went away."

Maisie gently stroked the boy's cheek. "You be a right fine boy."

Moses reached up and touched Simon's face and then leaned down to touch Maisie's face in turn. "You be like me."

Jasmine felt her breath catch in the back of her throat. The boy clearly saw unity in Simon and Maisie because they were black. Black like him. Only his skin was so pale that Jasmine could hardly believe he understood they were the same race. Could everyone have been right in believing that even at this tender age, Moses knew that he was not white?

Nolan seemed to understand the discomfort of the moment. He cleared his throat.

"This is my wife and my son, Jasmine and Spencer Houston. Why don't we go and see your new home," he offered. "We can see to your belongings in a bit." He motioned them toward the path that led to the house.

Moses wiggled in Simon's arms. "Come on. Come wif me. I show you my house."

"That'd be mighty fine," Simon said, putting the boy down. Moses reached for his hand and then Maisie's. The two exchanged a smile with the boy and allowed themselves to be led.

"You've done a good thing here, my love," Nolan said as he lifted Spencer. They followed behind the trio in slow steps to give them time together.

"Do you think they'll be happy?" Jasmine whispered as Moses led them into the house. He hadn't stopped talking since pulling the couple along with him.

"They are a wonderful young couple, and I think Moses will be most content with them. Did you see how he rushed to Simon?"

"There's such a striking resemblance to Obadiah that it nearly took my breath away when Simon stepped out of the buggy."

"I thought the same thing when I met them in Boston. For the briefest of moments, I thought Obadiah had returned."

"It's as if God's hand has guided them to us and He's restoring us to bearable circumstances. Surely the future will hold good tidings for all of us."

"I wanna go too," Spencer said, growing weary of being held back by Nolan.

Putting his son to the ground, Nolan gave his permission. "Go ahead then. Join your friend."

Spencer laughed. "Moses is my friend. I love him." He ran off to the house, leaving Jasmine and Nolan to stare after him.

Jasmine breathed in deeply. "It's so hard to let Moses go with Simon and Maisie, even though I know it's for the best. You see, I love him too."

Nolan lifted her face to meet his. He tenderly stroked her jaw. "As do I. The boy will no doubt need all of our love as the future plays itself out. Perhaps in time, Maisie and Simon will give him a brother or sister to play with."

Jasmine smiled, knowing the time had come to share her secret. "As we will give Spencer . . . come spring."

His eyes widened in surprise. "A baby?"

She laughed, feeling freer and happier than she'd ever been before. "Yes. A baby."

Nolan lifted her in the air and twirled her around until Jasmine was quite dizzy. The strands of faith that had once threatened to break under the strains of an unhappy union, the kidnapping of her son, and the threat of her family ties dissolving had thickened into a solid cord of hope. Grandmother had once said that faith had to grow, just like a fine tapestry being woven line after line. It didn't look like much when there were only a few rows, but with time and effort . . . and love, the beauty and strength of the piece was soon discovered in the whole.

Jasmine nuzzled the neck of her husband and sighed. *And that is what I am,* she thought. *I am whole.*

ABOUT THE AUTHORS

Tracie Peterson is a popular speaker and bestselling author who has written over sixty books, both historical and contemporary fiction. Tracie and her family make their home in Montana.

Visit Tracie's Web site at: *www.traciepeterson.com*.

Judith Miller is an award-winning author whose avid research and love for history are reflected in her novels, many of which have appeared on the CBA bestseller lists. Judy and her husband make their home in Topeka, Kansas.

Visit Judy's Web site at: *www.judithmccoymiller.com*.

The employees of Thorndike Press hope you have enjoyed this Large Print book. All our Thorndike, Wheeler, and Kennebec Large Print titles are designed for easy reading, and all our books are made to last. Other Thorndike Press Large Print books are available at your library, through selected bookstores, or directly from us.

For information about titles, please call:
(800) 223-1244

or visit our Web site at:
http://gale.cengage.com/thorndike

To share your comments, please write:
Publisher
Thorndike Press
10 Water St., Suite 310
Waterville, ME 04901